W9-BYH-118

STEAL THE SKY

"Blend two lovable rogues, a magical doppelganger, and a nasty empire, and you have O'Keefe's *Steal the Sky*. It's like an epic steampunk *Firefly*."

Beth Cato, author of The Clockwork Dagger

"Megan O'Keefe's stories are always vivid and compelling."

Tim Powers, author of Declare *and* Three Days to Never

"Megan E O'Keefe's prose is so full of fascinating twists and delights, you won't want to put it down. Go ahead, open it up: I dare you!"

David Farland, author of the bestselling Runelords series

"Holy **** this was good. The storyline and world building were impeccable, as were the depth of the characters that inhabited it."

Koeur's Book Reviews

MEGAN E O'KEEFE

Steal the Sky

A SCORCHED CONTINENT NOVEL

ANGRY
ROBOT

ANGRY ROBOT
An imprint of Watkins Media Ltd

Lace Market House,
54-56 High Pavement,
Nottingham,
NG1 1HW
UK

angryrobotbooks.com
twitter.com/angryrobotbooks
From the sands of Aransa

An Angry Robot paperback original 2016

Copyright © Megan E O'Keefe 2016

Cover by Kim Sokol
Set in Meridien by Epub Services.

Distributed in the United States by Random House, Inc., New York.

All rights reserved.

Angry Robot and the Angry Robot icon are registered trademarks of
Watkins Media Ltd.

This is a work of fiction. Names, characters, places, and incidents are
the products of the author's imagination or are used fictitiously. Any
resemblance to actual events, locales, organizations or persons, living or
dead, is entirely coincidental.

Sales of this book without a front cover may be unauthorized. If this book
is coverless, it may have been reported to the publisher as "unsold and
destroyed" and neither the author nor the publisher may have received
payment for it.

ISBN 978 0 85766 490 7
Ebook ISBN 978 0 85766 491 4

Printed in the United States of America

9 8 7 6 5 4 3 2 1

For Mom.
More.

CHAPTER 1

It was a pretty nice burlap sack. Not the best he'd had the pleasure of inhabiting, not by a long shot, but it wasn't bad either. The jute was smooth and woven tight, not letting in an inkling of light or location. It didn't chafe his cheeks either, which was a small comfort.

The chair he was tied to was of considerably lesser quality. Each time Detan shifted his weight to keep the ropes from cutting off his circulation little splinters worked their way into his exposed arms and itched something fierce. Despite the unfinished wood, the chair's joints were solid, and the knots on his ropes well tied, which was a shame.

Detan strained his ears, imagining that if he tried hard enough he could work out just where he was. No use, that. Walls muted the bustle of Aransa's streets, and the bitter-char aromas of local delicacies were blotted by the tight weave of the sack over his head. At least the burlap didn't stink of the fear sweat of those who'd worn it before him.

Someone yanked the bag off and that was surprising, because he hadn't heard anyone in the room for the last half-mark. Truth be told, he was starting to think they'd forgotten about him, which was a mighty blow to his pride.

As he blinked in the light, the blurry face of his visitor resolved into an assemblage of hard, almond-brown planes with sandy hair scraped back into a tight, professional plait. Ripka. Funny, she looked taller than the last time he'd seen her. He gave her a stupid grin, because he knew she hated it.

"Detan Honding." He liked the way she said his name, dropping each syllable in place as if she were discarding rotten fruit. "Thought I told you to stay well clear of Aransa."

"I think you'll find I've been doing my very best to honor your request, watch captain. I am a paragon of lawfulness, a beacon for the truthful, a—"

"Really? Then why did my men find you card-sharking in Blasted Rock Inn?"

"Card sharking?" he asked in the most incredulous voice he could muster. "I don't even know what that *is*. What's a sha-ark? Sounds dangerous!"

Ripka shook her head like a disappointed proctor and took a step back, tossing the bag to the ground. Detan was sorry to see such a fine sack abused so, but he took the chance to take in his surroundings. The room was simple, not a stick of furniture in it aside from his own chair and the corner of a desk peeking out from around the eclipsing curve of the watch captain.

By the color of the warm light, he guessed there weren't any windows hiding behind him, just clean oil lamps. The floor was hard-packed dirt, the walls unyielding yellowstone. It was construction he recognized all too well, though he'd never had the pleasure of seeing this particular room before. He was in the Watch's station house, halfway up the levels of the stepped city of Aransa. Could be worse. Could have been a cell.

Ripka sat behind what he supposed must be her desk. No books, no trinkets. Not the slightest hint of personality. Just a neat stack of papers with a polished pen laid beside it. Definitely Ripka's.

Keeping one stern eye on him, she pulled a folder from the stack of papers and splayed it open against the desk. Before it flipped open, Detan saw his family crest scribbled on the front in basic, hasty lines. He'd seen that folder only once before, the first time he'd blown through Aransa, and it hadn't had anything nice to say about him then. He fought down a grimace, waiting while her eyes skimmed over all the details she'd collected of his life. She sighed, drumming her fingers on the desk as she spoke.

"Let's see now. Last time you were here, Honding, you and your little friend Tibal unlawfully imprisoned Watcher Banch, distributed false payment, stole personal property from the family Erst, and disrupted the peace of the entire fourth level."

"All a terrible misunderstanding, I assure–"

She held up a fist to silence him.

"I can't hold you on any of this. Banch and the Ersts have withdrawn their complaints and your fake grains have long since disappeared. But none of that means I can't kick your sorry hide out of my city, understand? You're the last person I need around here right now. I don't know why you washed up on my sands, but I'll give you until the night to shove off again."

"I'd be happy to oblige, captain, but my flier's busted and it'll be a good few turns before she's airworthy

again. But don't you worry, Tibs's working on getting it
fixed up right."

"Still dragging around Tibal? Should have known,
you've got that poor sod worshipping your shadow, and
it's going to get him killed someday. What's wrong with
the flier? And stop trying to work your ropes loose."

He froze and mustered up what he thought was a
contrite grin. Judging by the way Ripka glowered at him
he was pretty sure she didn't take it right. No fault of his
if she didn't have a sense of humor.

"Punctured a buoyancy sack somewhere over the
Fireline Ridge, lucky for us I'm a mighty fine captain
myself, otherwise we'd be tits-up in the Black Wash right
about now."

Her fingers stopped drumming. "Really. Fireline.
Nothing but a bunch of uppercrusts taking tours of the
selium mines and dipping in at the Salt Baths over there.
So just what in the sweet skies were *you* doing up there?"

A chill worked its way into his spine at her pointed
glare, her pursed lips. Old instincts to flee burbled up
in him, and for just a moment his senses reached out.
There was a small source of selium – the gas that elevated
airships – just behind Ripka's desk.

A tempting amount. Just small enough to cause a
distraction, if he chose to use it. He gritted his teeth and
pushed the urge aside. If he were caught out for being a
sel-sensitive, it'd be back to the selium mines with him –
or worse, into the hands of the whitecoats.

He forced a cheery grin. "Certainly not impersonating
a steward and selling false excursion tickets to the baths.
That would be beneath me."

She groaned and dragged her fingers through her hair,
mussing her plait. "I want you out of my city, Honding,
and a busted buoyancy sack shouldn't take more'n a day

to patch up. Can you do that?"

"That would be no trouble at all."

"Wonderful."

"If it were *just* the buoyancy sack."

Her fingers gripped the edge of her desk, knuckles going white. "I could throw you in the Smokestack and no one in the whole of the Scorched would lift a finger to find out why."

"But you wouldn't. You're a good woman, Ripka Leshe. It's your biggest flaw."

"Could be I make you my first step on a downward spiral."

"Who put sand in your trousers, anyway? Everyone's wound up around here like the Smokestack is rearing to blow. Pits below, Ripka, your thugs didn't even take my bribe."

"Watch Captain Leshe," she corrected, but it was an automatic answer, lacking any real snap. "You remember Warden Faud?"

"'Course I do, that fellow is straight as a mast post. Told me if he ever saw my sorry hide here again he'd tan it and use the leather for a new sail. Reminds me of you, come to think on it."

"Well, he's dead. Found him ballooned up on selium gas floating around the ceiling of his sitting room. Good thing the shutters were pulled, otherwise I think he would have blown halfway to the Darkling Sea by now."

Detan snorted. He bit his lip and closed his eyes, struggling to hold down a rising tide of laughter. Even Ripka had a bit of a curl to her mouth as she told the story. But still, she had admired the crazy old warden, and Detan suspected she might just consider carrying out the man's wish of turning him into leather if he let loose with the laugh he was swallowing.

He risked opening his eyes. "How in the pits did it all stay in there?"

Her face was a mask of professional decorum. "The late warden had been sealed with guar sap. On all ends."

"Still got him? ... I could use a new buoyancy sack."

Detan was too busy laughing until the tears flowed to see her coming. She swept the leg of his chair away and he went down with a grunt, but he didn't care. It was just too much for him to let go. When he had subsided into burbling chuckles, Ripka cleared her throat. He felt a little triumphant to see a bit of wet shining at the corner of her eye.

"Are you quite finished?" she asked.

"For now."

She produced a short blade of bone-blacked Valathean steel. It probably had a poncy name, but all Detan cared about was the fresh glint along the cutting edge. It was a good knife, and that was usually bad news for him. Good women with good knives had a habit of making use of them in his general direction. He swallowed, tried to scoot away and only dug his splinters deeper.

"Now, there's no need for–"

"Oh, shut up."

She knelt beside him and cut the ropes around his wrists and ankles. He knew better than to pop right up. Irritable people were prone to making rash decisions, and he'd discovered there were a surprisingly large number of irritable people in the world. When she stepped away he wormed himself to his feet and made a show of rubbing his wrists.

"Some higher quality rope wouldn't be too much to ask for, I think."

"No one cares what you think, Honding." She jerked

the chair back to its feet and pointed with the blade. "Now sit."

He eyed the rickety structure and shuffled his feet toward the door. "Wouldn't want to take up any more of your time, watch captain…"

"Did I say you could leave?" Her knuckles went bloodless on the handle of the blade, her already thin lips squeezed together in a hard line. Detan glanced at the chair, then back at Ripka. A few traitorous beads of sweat crested his brow. He thought about the selium, looming somewhere behind her desk, but shunted the idea aside. She pointed again.

He obliged. He had a life philosophy of never saying no to a lady with a knife if he could help it. And anyway, something had her wound up crankier than a rockcat in a cold bath. She needed something, and needful people often played loose with their gold.

"Thought you wanted me gone yesterday," he ventured.

"Then it's too bad you're here today. I want a timeline from you, understand?"

"Oh, well. Let's see. In the beginning, the firemounts broke free from the sea–"

"Stop. Just. Stop."

He shut up. He didn't often know when he was pushing it, but he knew it now.

"Thratia is making a grab for the warden's seat, understand? I can't have you in my hair when I've got her in my shadow."

"Oh."

"Yeah, *oh.*"

He grimaced. Detan had been all over the Scorched Continent a half dozen times easy and he had yet to run into a woman more ruthless than ex-Commodore

Thratia Ganal. Sure, she was Valathean bred and all
sweetness and light to anyone with gold in their pockets.
But it had to be the right amount of gold, backed by the
right intentions.

Poor as a smokefish? Better work for her. Enough
gold to buy a proper uppercrust house? Best pay your
fire taxes, Aransa was a dangerous place, after all. More
gold than her? Better invest in whatever she wants and
then sod right off to wherever you came from.

A pleasant conversationalist, though, so that was
something.

Rumor had it Thratia didn't appreciate the spidery
arm of Valathean law meddling with the Scorched
settlements, which meant Ripka was in the shit if
Thratia took over. Even with the whole of the Darkling
Sea between Valathea's island empire and the Scorched,
the empire's control over its frontier cities was absolute
through its selium-lifted airships and its watchers. The
watchers held to imperial law, and kept the Scorched's
selium mines producing to fill Valathean needs and
Valathean coffers.

And Thratia didn't much care for Valathean needs,
now that they'd kicked her loose.

He stifled another *oh*, watching the honorable watch
captain through enlightened eyes. The way she kept
glancing at the door, as if she were worried someone
would barge in. The way she held her knife, point-out
and ready to dance. She was scared senseless.

And scared people were easy to play. Detan leaned
forward, hands clasped with interest, brow drawn in
grave understanding.

"You think she was behind the warden's death?"
he asked, just to keep Ripka talking while he worked
through the possibilities.

"That crow? I doubt it. It's not her style, wasting something as valuable as selium to make a point. The favorite theory going around right now is it was a doppel." She snorted. "Caught one a few days back, impersonating some dead mercer. City's been seeing them in every shadow ever since. Might as well be a ghost or a bogeyman, but I can't ignore the possibility. Your mouth is open, Honding."

He shut it. "Are you serious? A *doppel*?"

He'd heard of the creatures – every little Scorched lad grew up with stories of scary doppels replacing your loved ones – but he'd never seen one before. The amount of skill and strength it'd take to use a thin layer of prismatic selium to cover your own face, changing hues and sculpting features, was so far beyond his ken the thought left him speechless. He was all brute strength when it came to his sel-sensitivity. He even had trouble shaping a simple ball out of the lighter-than-air gas.

"They're not pets, rockbrain," Ripka said. "They're extremely dangerous and if they're geared up to attack the settlements then we're going to have to send word to Valathea."

Detan's mouth felt coated in ash. Valathea liked its sel-sensitives just fine, but as Detan had found out to his own personal horror it liked them weak, fit for little more than moving the gas out of mines and into the buoyant bellies of ships. Anytime the sensitives got too strong, or their abilities deviated from the accepted standard, Valathean steel came out ringing.

"That'd mean a purge," he said.

She tipped her chin down, and her gaze snagged on the knife in her hand as if seeing it for the first time. For just a moment, her mask slipped. Detan squinted, trying to read the fine lines of her face. Was that sadness? Or indigestion? Ripka rolled her shoulders to loosen them and retightened her grip.

"I can't have half this city's sel-sensitives wiped out because they might be breeding too strongly. The Smokestack is an active mine, we need the sensitives to keep it moving. I'll find the murderer before Valathea needs to get involved."

He shook off the thought of a purge and focused on what mattered: Thratia was filthy rich. And, even as an ex-commodore, the owner of a rather fine airship.

Even trolling around the smaller, ramshackle steadings of the Scorched, Detan had heard of Thratia's latest prize. The *Larkspur*, she was called, and rumor had it she was as sleek as an oiled rockcat. Being both fast and large, that ship was making Thratia mighty rich as mercers across the empire paid a premium to have her ferry their goods to the most lucrative ports long before slower, competing vessels could catch up. Detan had no need for the *Larkspur*'s goods-delivery services, but he rather fancied the idea of ripping the rug out from under Thratia's quickly growing mercer collective. And anyway, he thought he'd probably cut a pretty handsome figure standing on the deck of a ship like that. Although he'd have to upgrade to a nicer hat.

"Well, watch captain, maybe we can help each other out."

She looked like she'd drunk sour milk. "You're kidding. Only way you can help me is by getting gone, Honding. You understand?" Ripka turned away from him and sat behind her desk once more, her thigh bumping the side with a light clunk as she did so. Detan allowed himself a little smile; so the brave watch captain wore body armor while in his presence.

"Oh, pah. You and I both know that if Thratia wants

the wardenship she's going to take it. People fear her too damned much to risk not voting her in. And you'll be too busy chasing your boogeyman to do anything about it."

"Fear? You got it wrong. They respect her, and that's the trouble of it. She'll get voted in, nice and legal. No need for a coup," she said.

"So what if I could... undermine that respect? Make a public fool of her?"

"The only public fool around here is you."

"Well, you want me gone, don't you?"

"Yes."

"And I don't have a flier to get gone with, do I?"

She just frowned at him.

"And you want Thratia undermined, right?"

"I suppose..."

"So I'll steal her airship!"

"You're out of your sandbagged mind, Honding."

"No, no – listen up, captain." He leaned forward and held his hand out, ticking off the fingers with each point he made. "Thratia's got power here because she's got respect, right?"

"And money."

"Right, and money. So we can get rid of her respect, and a substantial chunk of her money, in one big blow." He made a fist and raised it up.

"You only made one point there, and you've got five fingers."

"Er, well. That doesn't matter. It makes sense, Ripka."

"Watch captain."

"Watch captain." He gave her a smile bright as the midday sun and leaned back in his chair with his fingers laced behind his head. "It's brilliant. She'll look like a doddering fool and you can swoop in and save the day.

Then let me go, of course."

She snorted. "Why in the blue skies would I want to do that?"

"Because I'd tell Thratia it was your idea if you didn't, obviously."

"And then I look the fool for letting you escape."

"No, we let it sit for a while. I'll slip away after you've got the wardenship secured. Tell everyone you shipped me off to serve hard labor on the Remnant Isles."

She started, eyes narrowing. "You think I want to be warden?"

Had he misjudged? Detan held his hands up to either side, palms facing the sweet skies to indicate he would defer to her better judgment. "Well, you must. Or you've got someone in mind, surely?"

She pressed her fingers together above the desk, the arc of her hands outlining the mouth of a cave, and leaned forward as she thought. It was odd she seemed to be thinking so hard about this. He'd thought she'd have someone in mind worth the promotion, but he still couldn't help but grin. Her body language was open, interested. There was a little furrow between her brows, deep and contemplative. He'd got her.

"Mine Master Galtro would be a good candidate," she said, and he chose to ignore the hesitance in her voice. Didn't matter to him who she picked. He planned on being long gone by the time that particular seat was being warmed.

He leapt to his feet and clapped once. "Good! Marvelous! Hurrah! We have a warden! Now you just need to let me do my–"

"Whoa now. What's in this for you?"

"The thrill of adventure!"

"Try again."

"Fine." He huffed. "Say, perhaps, the ship has a little accident in all that excitement. Say, just for example, that some convincing wreckage is found made of the right materials, with the right name emblazoned on the heap. Say *that* to all the citizens, and let me keep the blasted thing."

She drummed her fingers on the desk. "Thratia's compound is the most secure in the whole city. Just how do you think you're going to get anywhere near her ship?"

"That's my worry, partner."

"I am not–"

"Watch captain."

She scowled at him, but quieted.

"Look, don't worry over it all too much and don't count on it yet either, understand? I'm going to have a look around, see if it's even doable, and then I'll contact you again with our options."

"You get snagged, and I'll swear I sent you packing this day."

"Wouldn't expect it any other way."

"And if you can't find a way to work it?"

"Tibal will have the flier fixed up by then, nice and smooth."

Ripka eyed him, hard and heavy, and he thanked the stable sands that he had a whole lot of practice at keeping his face open and charming. She grunted and dragged open the top drawer of her desk.

"Here." She tossed him a thin cloth pouch and he rolled it over in his hands, guessing at the weight of the grains of precious metal within. "You'll need to stay upcrust if you want any chance of getting eyes on Thratia, and I'm guessing ole Auntie Honding hasn't provided you with an allowance fit for something like that."

Detan winced at the mention of his auntie, the stern-faced warden of Hond Steading, a mental tally of guilt piling up for every day of the calendar he hadn't bothered to visit her. Forcing a smile back into place, he vanished the pouch into his pocket and half-bowed over upraised palms. "You are as wise as you are generous."

"Get gone, Honding, and don't contact me again until you've got a plan situated."

Detan Honding prided himself on being a man who knew not to overstay his welcome. He made himself scarce in a hurry.

CHAPTER 2

"Fresh up from the southern coast," Sergeant Banch said as he passed her an amber bottle, its contents labeled by a stamped blob of wax so cracked and chipped she couldn't make it out. Like it mattered. Ripka tipped her head back and drank.

The mud wall of the guardhouse was cool against her back, the bottle warm in her hand, and the memory of the rising sun still rosy on her cheeks. So what if the bench was stiff beneath her? So what if the stench of fresh blood clung to her nostrils still? She drank deep, ignoring the murmur of the crowd dispersing just outside the guardhouse door.

It'd been one sand-blighted morning. Executing a man was never her favorite service to perform on behalf of the city, but with rumors flying wild about a killer on the loose, and Warden Faud not two days in the dirt, the city was wound up tight. She'd never seen such a turnout before. She only wished she could have given them the blood of Faud's murderer, instead of some sandbagged thief. Doppel or no, she had no taste for executing nonviolent criminals.

Ripka glanced toward the ceiling, squinting as if she could see through the rafters to the freshly minted corpse of the doppel who'd stolen Mercer Agert's ship. Brave son of a bitch, he hadn't blinked when she'd asked if he wanted to meet the axe or walk the Black. He'd opted for the axe, which always surprised her. But then, walking the Black was one pits-cursed way to go.

The Black Wash spread out between the city's lowest wall and the rugged slopes of the Smokestack – the great, looming firemount from which the city mined its selium. Composed of glittering shards of firemount glass, the path between the city and the Smokestack was blisteringly hot during the day. Merely standing on the black sands could leave your face burned within a quarter-mark.

As long as Ripka'd been in Aransa, she'd never heard of a soul making it across the sands alive. First your face burned, crisped up under the glare of the sun, and any stretch of skin not covered in cloth was quick to follow. If your shoes weren't sturdy enough – and most condemned were forced to walk in prison garb: thin boots, linen jumpsuits, no hat – then the unweathered shards of black glass would work their way through to your feet before you'd reached the quarter waypoint. By halfway, you were leaving bloodied smears in your wake. By three-quarters, most lay down to die.

With no water, and no shade, the heat of the air dried out your lungs, made every breath a pink-tinged rasp. Dried out your eyes, too, and many were weeping blood while they were still close enough to the city walls for people to see what should have been the whites of their eyes turned angry red. Most were jerky before they made it within throwing distance of the Smokestack.

It was miserable, and it was deadly. But it was a whole lot less final than a beheading. At least you had a chance out there. Under the axeman's swing, your chances were used up in one swoop.

She took another draw on the bottle. It did little to wash away the memories of this morning's execution, the phantom heat of the black sands at her back.

"Think the vultures are gone yet?" she asked.

"'Nother half-mark, I bet. The undertaker's not done dicing him up, and there's some that will want a memento. Bit o' hair, a real knuckle bone to throw. Shit like that."

Ripka cringed and took another swallow. "Damn savages."

"Says the Brown Wash girl."

She laughed, alcohol burning in her throat, and fell into a coughing fit. Oh well. At least the guardhouse was nice and cool. "Don't see why they have to chop the poor bastards up anyway."

"You know how Valatheans get about graves. Put the whole body in one place and people will make a shrine of it. Then we've got a martyr on our hands."

"Pah, no one's going to make a martyr of a doppel. They're piss-scared of them."

"You'd be surprised," a woman said.

Ripka glanced up from the bench and squinted at the backlit figure. Tall, strong, womanly in a way that rankled Ripka with jealousy. Thratia. She wore a simple bloodstone-hued tunic, martial leggings and tall leather boots. No fancy attire for Thratia – she liked to keep her appearance akin to the common folk of Aransa, never mind her massive compound sprawling across half the city's second level. Sad thing was, most of the locals fell for her of-the-people charm.

Ripka snapped her a half-hearted salute and nearly clanged the bottle against her head in the process.

"Morning, Thratia. You do know this is a guardhouse? Not usually open for visitors, if you take my meaning."

Thratia brushed the long warbraid from her shoulder and shut the door behind her, dipping them all back into the dim light of dusty lamps. Ripka made a note to have the men who usually manned this place scrub it down.

"I do not mean to interrupt your–" she let her eyes roam over the bottle in Ripka's hand and the blue coats of their uniforms slumped over the backs of chairs, "–work. But, after observing today's execution I wanted to commend the forces of the Watch for your fine administration of justice here in Aransa."

"Really. That's all?"

"Well…"

Ripka chuckled and waved the bottle in her direction. "Go on then."

"I had expected you to encourage the condemned to walk the Black."

"Encouraged? That's not our place. It's been the condemned's choice since the day Aransa was settled, and it'll stay that way."

"I understand there is a certain level of patriotism involved in the display of choice, and that is valuable. However, walking the Black is a unique feature of Aransa, and I believe it would do the people good to see the condemned die not only by the will of the city, but a feature of the city itself. In the case of doppels, it would also enhance the message that they are not wanted here, as they would be cast out. Forced to walk away from the city to die."

Ripka frowned, wondering just how much Thratia had

rehearsed that little speech. "And how do you suggest we encourage them to make that choice?"

"Oh, I don't know." Thratia waved a dismissive hand through the air. "You could always get rid of the option of the axemen. Make it hanging or walking."

"Hanging's a sorry way to die."

"Exactly."

Ripka leaned forward, sat the bottle on the bench beside her, and rested her forearms across her knees. Thratia stayed where she was, a single step in from the door, her charcoal arms crossed over her chest and a little smile on her face so small and warm Ripka half expected her to offer up a sweetcake to share. Ripka cleared her throat.

"I'll take that under advisement, Thratia. Thank you for your visit."

"I hope to share many more visits with you, watch captain. Best of luck in apprehending the doppel who murdered Warden Faud." She bowed at the waist, nothing mocking about it, and stepped back out into the bright of day.

Banch and Ripka sat for a while, letting the rum they'd drunk warm up the chill Thratia had left behind. She ground her teeth, then plucked a wax-wrapped nub of barksap from her pocket and popped it into her mouth to chew over.

"There goes our new boss," Banch said.

Ripka chucked him in the arm, nearly missed and had to put a hand on the bench to keep from sprawling to the ground. "Resigned to it already? Mine Master Galtro could win it. Thratia's a skies-cursed murderer. Even *Valathea* thought she was too brutal to keep around. You think Aransa will vote in the woman they call General Throatslitter behind her back?"

"Please, they call her that to her *front*. It's practically a rally cry. They love that she stuck it to the empire."

"She refused to relinquish power after her conquest at the behest of Valathea of the Saldive Isles. Nothing heroic about that."

Banch rolled his shoulders and snagged the bottle back, tested its weight with a disappointed scowl. "Tell it to the folk in the lower levels she's been sending food to. Tell it to the mercers who've been promised they can use that fancy new ship of hers for faster trade."

"I just don't trust her, Banch. She's up to something."

"O' course she is. Everyone on this sunblasted continent is."

Ripka rolled her eyes and dropped her head back against the wall, letting the chill of it seep through her hair and soothe the itch of her sun-kissed scalp while she thought.

Just why was Thratia so keen to send people to walk the sands? Walking the Black meant that if you were very, very lucky you just might survive. If Ripka was sure about anything, it was that Thratia felt no mercy for those who stood for judgment on the guardhouse roof. Why would she want a doppel, of all things, to have a chance at life?

So she could use them.

Ripka shot up from the bench and heaved herself up the ladder to the roof where the execution had taken place. The undertaker was still busy at his work and gave her a cheery, gore-smeared wave when she glanced his way.

Clenching her jaw, she strode to the back edge of the roof and leaned out just as far as she dared. The Black Wash splayed below her, glittering so bright she had to squint and bring a hand up to shade her eyes. She stared straight on at the sharp crest of the Smokestack and the Fireline Ridge spread out around it, waiting for her vision to get used to the blinding light. Banch hauled himself up beside her.

"Just what in the pits are you doing, captain?"

"There, look." She pointed at two glints of light, figures moving across the rugged side of the Fireline up toward the ferries that shuttled people back and forth from the city to the selium mines and Salt Baths. The mines were shut down for the day due to an infestation in one of the pipelines, and the baths were clear on the other side of the Fireline – too far by half for a leisurely stroll.

"Aw shit. Do you think we'll have to send a rescue?"

"Those aren't lost bathers."

The figures sped up, moving with expert ease over the rough terrain. The glints she had noticed came from low about their waists, about the right place for a sword handle to rest.

Banch's voice was very, very quiet. "Thratia's?"

"Who else? I suppose now we know why she wants us to make the doppels walk."

She turned away from the vista and forced herself to look at what was left of the nameless doppel. He was a brave man, and now she suspected she understood why he'd been so sure of the axe. She'd heard horror stories of Valatheans enslaving the doppels, using their desire to be close to selium to secure their loyalty. It was illegal, of course, even the imperials saw using the doppels as cruel and unsavory. But Thratia hadn't been exiled to the Scorched Continent for being kind and cuddly.

"Come on, Banch. We've got to find our killer."

Before Thratia does.

CHAPTER 3

The downcrust levels of Aransa were hotter than a draw on a jug of spicewine. Ripka had set Detan free just a mark or so after sunrise, and already the streets were baking. He tugged his shirt-ties loose as he wandered down the cramped streets to where he'd left Tibs with the flier, winking at ladies as he passed.

Not that there were many ladies with a capital "L" this far down in the city. The real desert flowers liked it up top where parasols and shade trees were plentiful. He figured the women down here were more fun, anyway. At least they weren't shy with their hand gestures.

He found Tibs lying under the fronds of a reedpalm, his hat pulled down over his eyes and his back propped up against the carcass of their six-man flier. Tibs was a scrawny bastard, long of limb even when he was slouched. Last night's clothes clung to him in disturbing pleats of grime and sweat, and his boots were beginning to separate from their soles. Hair that Detan suspected had once been a pale brown stuck up in strange angles from under his hat.

Detan crept up on him, squinting down into the shadow that hid his sun-weathered face. Tibs was breathing, slow and even, so he turned his attention to the flier.

It was long and flat, maybe a dozen and a half long paces from end to end, crafted in the style of old riverbarges. Its sel sacks, which would normally be ballooned up above it under thick rope netting, lay crumpled on the deck. Though rectangular of body, Tibs had worked up a neat little pyramidal bowsprit to make it a tad more aerodynamic, and Detan had made blasted sure that the pulley-and-fan contrivance of its navigational system was made of the best stuff he could afford. Or steal. Even its accordion-like stabilizing wings, folded in now, were webbed with leather supple and strong enough to make a fine lady's gloves feel coarse and cheap.

Midship, right behind the helm, rose a plain-walled cabin just wide and long enough to house two curtain-partitioned sleeping quarters. It was a good show for guests, but the real living space was hidden in the flat hold between deck and keel. Though the space was not quite tall enough for Detan to stand straight within, it ran the length of the ship – a sturdy little secret placed there by the smugglers who had originally built the thing. To Detan's eyes, it was the most beautiful thing in the whole of the world.

Unfortunately, the buoyancy sacks lay flaccid and punctured and the right rudder-prop was cracked clean off, rather ruining the effect

Detan glowered and kicked Tibs in the leg. He squawked like a dunkeet and flailed awake, knocking his hat to the black-tinged dirt.

"The pits you doing, Tibs? You haven't even touched the old bird."

Tibs reached for his hat and picked off a spiny leaf. "Oh I touched it all right, just couldn't do a damn thing for it. What you think I am, a magician? The buoyancy sacks are as airtight as pumice stone and the mast is as stable as mica on edge, lemme tell you."

"Please *do* tell me, old chum, because I sure as shit don't understand your miner-man rock babble."

The lanky man rolled his eyes as he hoisted himself to his feet, and to Detan's never-ending consternation took his time about brushing the dust from his trouser legs. Damned funny thing, a mechanic with a fastidious streak.

"Simple-said, there's no repairing either of the buoyancy sacks. They were half-patches long before they took this latest damage and that mast is about as stable as a– well, uh, it's just fragile, all right?"

"Was that so hard?"

Tibs grunted and wandered over to the flier. He gave one of the sacks a nudge with his toe and shook his head, tsking. "Got no imagination, do you?"

"I got enough imagination to figure out what to do with a lippy miner."

"I'm your mechanic."

"Mechanic miner then."

Detan snatched Tibs's hat off his head and put it squarely on his own. Tibs plucked it back with a disappointed cluck of the tongue. "Tole you to bring a spare."

"Well, I didn't think I'd be doing barrel rolls over the Black Wash last night. Sweet sands, Tibs, what were you thinking?"

"I was thinking I'd like very much to get away from the ship shooting spears at us. Sirra."

Detan ignored his smirk and took over his old chum's

spot under the reedpalm. He sank down onto the black dirt and tipped his head back against the tree's rough trunk. In the shade, the breeze didn't feel like it was trying to steal his breath away. His eyes drifted shut, his muscles unknotted.

Tibs kicked his foot.

"What?" Detan grumbled.

"You win us enough to fix her up?"

"Better." He wrestled with his belt pouch and tossed it up to his companion. Tibs poured the contents out in his wide, flat hand, barely able to contain all the fingernail-sized grains of copper and silver. He whistled low. "Mighty fine haul, but may I ask who's going to be hunting us down to get it back?"

"You lack faith, old friend. That there is a genuine upfront payment from Watch Captain Ripka Leshe herself."

Tibs did not look as impressed as Detan would have liked. "Payment for what?"

"She's hired us to steal Thratia's lovely new airship, the *Larkspur*, of course. Seems the ex-commodore is getting a mite too comfortable here in Aransa, and needs to be shown her place."

He beamed up at Tibs, relishing the slow shock that widened his eyes and parted his lips. It was good to surprise the shriveled smokeweed of a man, but it didn't last. Tibs's eyes narrowed and his shoulders tensed. "That doesn't sound much like the watch captain."

Detan frowned. "No, it doesn't, does it? But that's the way it's been played to us. We just have to get a step ahead."

Tibs sighed and cast a longing look at their downed bird. "Sounds like a mess. Maybe we should just take the money and move along. Thratia isn't known for her forgiving nature, you know, and monsoon season's coming. Wouldn't want to get stuck in a sel-mining city come the rains, would we?"

Detan flinched at the thought of being stranded here, so very close to the Smokestack. All that tempting selium being pumped out from the bowels of the world no more than a ferry ride away. It was hard enough keeping his sensitivity to himself when they were in the sel-less reaches of the Scorched. Stuck in a city full of it? He'd give himself away in a single turn of the moon.

For the barest of moments he considered writing to Auntie Honding for enough grain to get the flier airworthy again. But any response from his dear old auntie would come with strict instructions to return home at once for a lengthy stay, complete with brow-beating. And he knew damned well that lingering at Hond Steading, with its five selium-producing firemounts, would make hiding his sel-sensitivity from the proper authorities a sight more difficult than managing Aransa's single mine.

Detan squared his shoulders, forcing his body to display the confidence he wished his mind held. They had time before the rains came. He was sure of it. "Make off with Ripka's money? She'd have us hanged if we ever showed up here again!"

"More like have our heads lopped off." Tibs grimaced and spat into the dust.

"What's that supposed to mean?"

"City's all worked up over it. Seems a doppel got caught impersonating some puffed-up mercer. Our new benefactor took his head clear off at sunrise. Not a friendly town for sel-sensitives of deviant abilities, you understand."

At sunrise. He glanced up the city toward the station house, and though he couldn't see it from this vantage he imagined all the little watchers returning to it after a good morning's work.

Takes some time, to lop a man's head off and clean up the mess. Enough time for Ripka to make it back to the station, little more than a mark after sunrise, to question him then kick him loose? And what of those who had arrested him – they'd said they were acting on the captain's orders. Where had she been, to see him and order his arrest at the Blasted Rock in the wee hours of the night while preparing to execute a man? He'd never seen her at the inn, true, but...

Detan cleared a sudden hitch in his throat, and Tibs narrowed his little lizardy eyes down at him. Stranger yet, in all her talk of doppels Ripka had failed to mention that she'd done one in just that morning.

He decided not to mention the watch captain's lapse of memory to Tibs. It was usually best not to worry the man with silly things like that. Ole Tibs liked straight paths, and dithered at forks. Tibs would spend his life wasting away at a crossroads if Detan wasn't there to push him along. He smiled at what a good friend he was.

"Don't worry yourself overmuch, Tibs, it'll give you wrinkles. Now, the watch captain has asked for our help and on my honor I won't be leaving the poor woman without assistance. Could you do that? Just leave her here with Thratia itching to take power?"

Tibs gave him a rather ungentlemanly look, but Detan fancied himself too well bred to be given a rise by that sort of thing.

"I suppose we must help the watch captain," he grated.

"Splendid!" Detan clapped his hands as he sprang up and strode over to the downed flier. "Now we have to get this old bird airworthy again."

"I thought we were soon to acquire a much finer vessel?"

"Have you no sentimentality? We can't just leave it!"

A little smile quirked up the corners of Tibs's dry, craggy face. "I suppose not."

"Brilliant! One step ahead already!"

They hired a cart to help them move the flier up a few levels to the inn Detan had scouted on his way through the city. It wasn't upcrust by any stretch of the imagination, and he figured that made it the perfect place to lay low. Thratia never came down this way herself, and Ripka only when there was something that needed cleaning up. It was a nice bonus that the innkeeper didn't know him, and that he was less likely to run into any of the uppercrusts he'd swindled in the past.

Their room had a half-door in the back that swung open into an old goat pen, just big enough to stash the flier in. Wasn't likely anyone would steal it, but he felt better about having it close. From the edge of the pen they could see the sweep of Aransa, or at least all those levels that tumbled out below their room.

The downcrust levels were a hodgepodge of daub and stone construction with a few brave souls throwing up the occasional scrap-wood wall. The houses huddled up the side of the mountain, clinging to the good stable rock beneath, and the city was a mess of switchbacking streets. Glittering black sands reached across the distance between Aransa and the Fireline Ridge, the firemount they called Smokestack spearing straight up through the center of the ridge, belching soot and ash. The winds were in their favor today, and so the greasy plume drifted off to the desolate south instead of laying a film of grime over all Aransa.

Blasted dangerous place to stick a city.

From this far away, the glint of metal holding leather-skinned pipes to the Smokestack's back was the only evidence of the firemount's rich selium production. Dangerous or not, there'd be folk settled here until the sel was gone. Or until the whole damned place blew.

"Enjoying the view?" Tibs slunk up beside him and wiped his hands on the filthiest rag Detan had ever seen.

"Hasn't changed much, has it?"

"Don't suppose it has a need of change. Anyway, bags are stored and the flier's tarp-tied. Smells like goat piss in there so don't come whining to me when the whole blasted contraption stinks of it later."

"I'd never blame the odor of goat on you, old chum. Your bouquet is entirely different, it's..." He waved a hand to waft up the right word. "It's *distinct*."

Tibs ignored the slight and kept his eyes on a brown paper notebook clutched in one hand. Somehow he'd rummaged up a bit of pointed charcoal and was using it to sketch broad strokes that eventually came together to form their flier. Or, what would have been their flier, if it were in one piece. New formulae appeared around their cabin, and Detan went cross-eyed.

"You can't possibly know what you're doing there."

"Just 'cause you're an idiot doesn't mean everyone else is. Sirra."

"We're gonna need something to wreck," he said, anxious to be of some use, "a decoy."

Tibs just grunted.

Detan grinned. Couldn't help himself. Some sense was emerging from the mist of numbers and angles, familiar shapes made bigger, stronger. Their tiny little cabin adapted for an entirely larger vessel altogether. Adapted further to be modular, easy to piece apart and slap back together again. Easier still to wrap around their current cabin until the time it would be needed.

It was perfect, really. This way they didn't need to know what Thratia's ship looked like ahead of time – all ships had cabins on their decks of some kind or another. Once the ship was in hand, he and Tibs could break off a chunk of Thratia's original and leave it as a wreck somewhere in the scrub beyond the city. Work up a good fire around it and no one would go looking for the rest of the ship; they'd assume it'd all burned up and give up the trail.

Then he and Tibs could shift the knock-down cabin from their flier onto the deck of Thratia's ship to cover any holes their hasty carpentry might leave behind. Nothing more suspicious than a big ole ship trundling around the skies without a cabin.

"Oh, that's clever!" he blurted as Tibs's plan crystallized in his mind.

"One of us has to be. I'll need to get a look at the real bird to make sure it all connects, but it should work well enough for a quick switch."

He gave Tibs time to work out the finer details, then watched in admiration as the crusty man ran his charcoal bit back over all the salient points, thickening the lines as he committed them to memory. When he was finished, Tibs tore the page out, crumpled it, and shoved it in his pocket.

Detan threw an arm around his shoulder. "Come along, now. Let's go spend some of Ripka's grains."

CHAPTER 4

The market bazaar of Aransa was precisely how Detan remembered it. Unfortunately.

Shops were scattered all over the middle level of the city, as if some drunken god of mercers had waved a full bottle about while staggering his way home and wherever the droplets landed a filthy stall had sprung up. Some trades attempted a clumped confederation, but the edges of all of these were loose and fraying.

Produce vendors clustered along the rail that marked the edge of the level, protruding slightly over the level below. When the day was done they hucked the worst of their wares over the edge. Rumor was, some pretty choice mushrooms could be plucked from the shadow of that overhang. Mushrooms which were then resold by the very same purveyors of the fertilizer. Detan shuddered at the thought, or the smell, or really just the whole cursed experience.

Tibs glided through the press of cloth-hawkers and fruit gropers, somehow managing not to bump so much as an elbow with another soul. For his trouble, Detan was jostled and stymied, his feet trampled and his coat wrenched all askew. With a curse, he slapped away the third set of little fingers to go dipping about his pockets, and finally broke through the crowd to the more sedate stalls of the metalmen and woodworkers.

Here, at least, order had been imposed. It seemed even choice real estate wasn't worth the risk of getting an errant ember in your stall's awning, and so the hodgepodge of transient sellers stayed far away. Tibs's sizable head swiveled, seeking the right shop, and Detan left him to it.

He liked to think he had a silver tongue, but these were folk close to the work, real crafters of wood and metal. They didn't much care for Detan's style of dealings. Tibs claimed they could smell the Honding blood in him.

Detan doubted they could smell much of anything over Tibs's own unwashed trousers.

The shop Tibs picked was a good one by the standard of the others. Its paint was fresh and its sign had actual words on it in place of the myriad pictographs its neighbors used. The door hinges didn't even squeak when Tibs swung them inward. Detan shuffled along behind, hanging back as he let his eyes adjust to the smoky lamplight.

It was smaller than it'd looked from the outside, but then Detan realized that there was a big desk cutting the room in half with a curtain behind it. Workshop adjacent, then. Possibly even a sleeping space. The burly old man behind the counter certainly looked like he might sleep here, he practically had wood shavings for hair.

"Morning, sirs." The shopkeep adjusted a rather fine looking pair of spectacles and shut the cover on the sketches he'd been muddling through. Nice sketchbook, that. Smooth, pale paper with a creamy hide cover.

Detan prepared himself to pay more than the supplies were worth.

"Got a flier needs fixin'," Tibs said, cutting straight to the quick of it so fast Detan thought the shopkeep would blanch with offense. But no, if anything he looked a mite relieved to get the pleasantries over with.

"Let's see it then." He brushed his journal aside, making room for Tibs to place his own sketch on the desk. Tibs set it down and smoothed it out, not too careful, then let it sit there curling back in on itself like a smashed bug.

"Hrm," the shopkeep said.

"Got the stuff I need?" Tibs prompted.

"Sure, sure. Well, the stuff you need, I got. The stuff you're asking for won't be easy."

Detan blinked at the shopkeeper's audacity, and Tibs shot a hand back, palm out, telling him to hold still, which was right insulting, because he hadn't been planning on... oh. He'd taken a half step forward without realizing it.

"The stuff I'm asking for is the stuff I need."

"This, here, I understand." The shopkeep traced something on the paper with a finger. "Your flier looks in bad shape, and I can see how you want to patch her up. Looks good, too. Anyway, that's fine, okay, but your materials take a shift here. You got reinforced leather for the sacks, proper stuff but nothing too fancy, and local wood for the supports and the rails, but all your cabin stuff is just too blasted big. And you've designed the whole mess to be removable. I can't even imagine why you'd want that.

"I'm sorry, sirs, but I can't recommend this at all. You're asking for imported materials. They'll be worth more than the whole thing. And anyway, you don't need it, yeah? Outfit like this would work well on just a handful of vessels. I can only think of one in the whole city big enough not to be thrown off balance by... ah. I see."

He stopped, blinked over his glasses at them, screwed his face up tight as he looked at Tibs. Detan couldn't see Tibs's expression, but he knew well enough the coot wasn't good at feigning calm when he'd been had.

Time for Honding blood to stink things up, then.

"You told me these market men were discreet!" He stormed up to Tibs and shook a finger at him. "What will our mistress say, hm? Every mog in Aransa is wagging their lips over the tiniest bit of gossip surrounding her, and you bungle this? By the pits!"

Tibs ducked his head down, looking proper contrite, then dragged his hat off and set to fussing with the brim. Detan spared a sideways glance at the shopkeep and found him pale as a desert bone. Good.

"Now, there's no need for upset, sirs. I'm happy to work quietly. I just needed to be sure you weren't overreaching yourselves, you understand. Don't want to be sticking my nose in anyone's business, just want to make sure I offer a fair deal to all."

"Well." Detan cleared his throat, cracked his neck, and smoothed the front of his shirt. "I suppose that will have to do. When can you have these materials?"

"Day or two, sirs. Last shipment of Valathean wood came across on Mercer Agert's vessel and, well... It's in escrow, but should be out soon. I'll put pressure on it."

"See that you do." Detan leaned over and flipped the man's sketchbook open, then scribbled the name of their inn on a blank sheet. "Have it all sent there when it's ready."

"That's not the most, ah, pleasant of addresses."

"No." He slammed the sketchbook shut. "It isn't."

"Right. Right. Happy to oblige, sirs. Now, ah, about payment..."

The shopkeep glanced to his book, scrawled upon so carelessly, and Detan had to bite back a grin. Just like that, the shopkeep knew they had grains to spare. And people with grains to spare were often the cheapest of bastards.

"Here." Detan pulled open Ripka's pouch and tossed a pinch of silver grains down – worth maybe a quarter of the total. "You'll get the rest on delivery."

"Yes, sirs, very good, sirs." He swept up the bits of metal, and by the time he looked up again Detan and Tibs were gone.

Standing in the dusty street, Detan threw a companionable arm about Tibs's shoulders and slipped his hand up toward the back of his hat. "Almost fouled the whole thing up, rockbrain."

Tibs shrugged. "Didn't see another clean angle. We needed that stuff, just like it was. No hiding it."

Detan narrowed his eyes, realization dawning bright as the desert sun. "You sly son of a–"

"There are women and children present in this market. Sirra."

Dean jerked his arm back and rolled his eyes, but didn't needle him further. Tibs could be a pricklebush about that sort of thing.

"Now." He rubbed his hands together. "For some paint."

Picking a direction at random, he strode off in search of a sign that might give him a clue. He felt flush with success, the sun warm on his shoulders, a slight breeze alleviating the greasy texture of his hair. If they could just get this one point settled, then they'd be well on

their way to calling Thratia's airship their own. For
Ripka, of course. Or whoever she was.

"Not that way." Tibs's hand closed over his shoulder,
drawing him to a sharp stop. Up ahead, he could just
make out the corner of the telltale dyer's sign, a pot with
a brush crossed over it.

"You blind oaf, it's right down there–"

A door opened beside him, spilling familiar aromas
into the sun-warmed air. Hints of pine and sweet, golden
cactus needle sparked old memories. Sharp memories.

Memories of blood and pain and straps, of his skin
sloughing off and his eyes stitched open. Sweat broke
across his brow, sticky and cold.

The woman exiting the shop was slight, stern. The
simple sight of her long, white skirt set him trembling.
With the dye of her shirt faded by the bright glare of the
sun she struck him, so clearly and for just a moment,
as a whitecoat. One of Valathea's dread experimenters,
torturers. One of his own jail keepers, not so long ago.
Awareness crowded his senses, sharp and frenzied. An
animal need to destroy the thing which tormented him
welled bright and hot and desperate within his chest.
He lifted a trembling hand, outstretched toward the
oblivious woman. There was selium in the woman's
bracelets – a Valathean fashion – and a dinghy of an
airship passing close above, its buoyancy sacks half-full
but tempting.

Tibs squeezed his shoulder, cutting off his sense of the
sel. "Just a plain apothik. No whitecoats here."

"Right." Detan's voice was rough and clotted. He
cleared it. "Right."

"Whitecoats don't come to the Scorched, they stay in
their tower," Tibs said.

"Yes... Of course."

"Seems to me." Tibs removed his hand and drifted a step back, away from that accursed building. "That the paint can wait until we get the equipment, eh? And anyway, I'm ravenous as a silk-widow that's spent all day making a new web."

Detan followed, snared by the need to be close to a friend. To safety. Glad for air that smelled of nothing but dust and wood and vegetal rot. He rubbed his palms against his thighs, leaving sweaty smears. Took a breath. *Steady, Honding.*

"Food? But Tibs! You only just ate lunch yesterday. Are you really so insatiable?"

"Like a wild beast. I know it's not very genteel of me, but I reckon I make up for it with my table manners."

"Well." He clapped Tibs on the back. "Two gentlemen such as ourselves certainly cannot go out to dine in this state." He gestured to his ragged clothes, stained with the black dust that permeated all of Aransa. "It would not be proper, I'm sure of it."

"I believe we're adequately attired for that meatstick cart." Tibs gestured toward a market cart tucked amongst the other foodmongers. The enterprising street chef had jars marked with a variety of symbols crowded on the top of his cart, each filled with a sauce of a different color. As patrons handed over their smallest grains, the proprietor produced a spitted piece of meat from somewhere below the cart's top and dipped it into a sauce of the purchaser's choosing.

The smell of it made his stomach rumble. Detan half-turned, edging toward the cart, when he caught another aroma – bitter, tannic. A tea cauldron simmered at the elbow of the meatstick-maker, its cutting aroma reminiscent of the medicinal brews the whitecoats had pressed upon him. He shivered and turned away.

With a hand on his companion's shoulder Detan clucked his tongue, forcing himself to light-heartedness, and steered Tibs firmly back down the street. "But how will I enjoy a proper display of your table manners at a *cart*, old friend? No, no. No slumming it for us."

With a flourish he produced a droop-brim hat from within his coat and thunked it on his head. It was a much nicer fit than the burlap sack had been. Tibs looked at him like he'd stepped on a fire ant mound while pantless.

"Hey, that's my hat. I just had it–"

"I believe you'll find it's on *my* head. Now, let us away to the Salt Baths so that we may present a proper image when we go for supper later."

"Oh? And that proper supper wouldn't happen to be at Thratia's fete tonight, eh?"

"I can't imagine what would make you think such a thing, Tibs. I, for one, was not even cognizant of the–"

"I saw you nick the handbill off the fence by the inn on our way out."

Blast! Detan was beginning to think that Tibs could be halfway across the Scorched from him and still know whenever Detan helped himself to something useful. Or pretty. Or nifty. He adjusted the hat and smiled. At least the old rockbrain still missed some things.

"Oh. Well." He cleared his throat and ushered Tibs onto the main road. "I may have procured a certain advertisement to that effect, yes. What better opportunity to survey her ship?"

"You do realize that there are baths at our inn, which is considerably closer – and already paid for."

"Baths? Pah. If you count a lukewarm bucket as a bath." He swept a pointed gaze over Tibs. "Which you obviously do. And, regardless, do *you* have attire worthy of one of Thratia's fetes? Because I certainly don't."

Tibs jingled Ripka's grain pouch. "I don't mean to shock you, but we can buy those things. With *money*."

Detan rolled his eyes. "And do you think she'll just hand over a ticket to us? Or are you going to buy a ticket, too? Sweet skies, Tibs, I thought you were the cheap one!"

Tibs gave him that sour, you-just-can't-help-yourself look which never failed to wind his gears. This time, he resolved to rise above. Ignoring his companion's dour disposition he took the stairs up to the next level two at a time, drawing an annoyed glare from the guards stationed at either end on the top of the steps. Too bad for them, it was still open-market hours, and upperpasses weren't required to move from one level to the next until well after moonrise. Not that he had a pass.

Not that that tiny little fact would have stopped him.

It'd been awhile since he'd perused Aransa, and though his extended absence had clearly eased Ripka's heart he found he was a bit sick with the missing of it. It was a good city, laid out nice and clear, and was free with water due to its proximity to a network of flush aquifers. The ladies here didn't fuss about with modesty, either. It was blasted hot, and even the uppercrust bared their shoulders and trusted in wide, shadowy hats and parasol bearers to keep the burn off.

Yes, Aransa was a good city indeed.

"Tibs, my good man, can't you keep up?"

Tibs was staring overlong at what was advertised to be a rack of lamb roasting in a shop window, but Detan rather suspected it was a gussied up sandrat. Detan snagged Tibs's arm and dragged him off to many a weak protestation.

"If we bent the winds at every rumbling of your gullet, old friend, we'd still be in shanty towns picking sand from our teeth."

"As you say," he muttered.

The line for the ferry to the Salt Baths was long, but not so long they couldn't all be crammed onto the floating conveyance. Detan, tugging Tibs along beside him, sidled up to the end of the line and freed his friend's arm. He worried Tibs would go wandering off at the merest sniff of scallion, but Detan was too busy working at blending in with the uppercrust to keep an eye on him. When you're with the high-tossers, it's all hands-in-pockets and slouching like a loose grain slide. He couldn't be seen *caring* about anything, that would give the game away.

And these were definitely the uppercrust. Seemed no one wanted to arrive at Thratia's with sand in their hair or dust on their trousers. All the better for him – he liked a variety of marks to choose from.

As he tipped the brim of his hat down over his eyes to add that roguish mystique the upcrust ladies were all aflutter over, Detan reflected that all the posturing in the world wouldn't make up for the holes in the knees of his britches. Which left the gentleman's last resort – good, hard grains.

It didn't help matters much that Tibs was trying to blend in the same way. Detan leaned over to hiss a whisper at the man, which was a funny thing to do when you were both slouching like your spines were made of rotwood.

"You're supposed to be my manservant, remember? Don't look so blasted confident."

Tibs rolled his eyes. "Why can't you play the manservant for once?"

"Because I actually know the plan. And besides–" he waved an arm down his torso, "–no one would believe it."

"You're right, you'd make a terrible manservant."

"You dustswallower! I'd be a marvelous–"

"Excuse me, sirs." The ticket seller reached their spot in line, his little pad of yellowed passes ruffling in the breeze. "It's two silver grains each to the baths."

Detan wasn't much surprised to see Tibs's jaw drop open at the price. Tibs wasn't a man to go about wasting his grains, and during normal circumstances Detan was right glad for his persnickety friend's tight-pocket affectations. Now, however, required a different sort of dealing. The kind of dealing that got filthy men past top-button gatekeepers. In Detan's experience, such a thing required the liberal and unfettered lubrication of gold. It was just a crying shame he didn't have any.

"Only two? By sel! Such a bargain. Certainly fair enough to leave a little left over for yourself, eh my good chap?" Detan leaned in as he spoke, plunking the requisite grains into the official looking pouch as he plunked another silver in the man's personal pocket. While the ticket seller had been looking at them like something unpleasant scraped off his shoe, he now seemed inclined to their favor. Or, at least, he wasn't scowling.

The ticket seller tapped his pocket with the edge of his hand, feeling the weight, and shrugged. He took their names on a slip of paper, his brow raising slightly at Detan's, but the silver weighed enough to stifle any comments.

"Enjoy the baths," was all he said.

After he shuffled off, Tibs hissed in Detan's ear. "Moonturn's worth of rent, that was."

"And a lifetime's worth of goodwill!"

"If by a lifetime you mean until we find ourselves in this line again."

"Do you ever plan on seeing the baths again?"

"Well, no…"

Detan beamed and threw his arm around Tibs's shoulder. "What did I tell you? A lifetime's worth of goodwill!"

CHAPTER 5

Pelkaia sat before her vanity mirror and squinted at the unfamiliar face staring back at her. Somewhere along the way she'd gotten wrinkles. Common enough in the desert, where the air was dry and one was prone to spend most of one's days squinting under the sun, but she'd missed the transition. Too long spent beneath other people's faces. She was beginning to forget herself.

She dipped her fingers into a jar and spread beeswax ointment around the corners of her eyes, the creased side of her lips. Fat lot of good it would do her now, but at least it was something. Replacing the lid, she glanced down and realized her hands were still smooth – too smooth. With a sigh she attuned her mind to the fine second skin of selium over them and peeled it away. Once freed of her shaping, the substance lost its warm skin tone and shifted back to the strange, multifaceted pearlescence that was its natural state. She gathered up the modicum of it, forming a ball, and danced it through the air before her eyes.

Child's play, such a simple shaping, but it had always

amused her. Had. With an unneeded wave of her hand she guided the hovering ball toward a vellum sack sewn within the mattress of her bed. She knelt beside it and concentrated for a moment, making sure all the selium already within would stay put, then whisked the mouth open and bundled the little sphere in with the rest. Pelkaia sat back on her heels, letting wrinkled hands rest over her kneecaps.

She was running out of time for play.

She made quick work of checking the weights hidden in the hollows of her bedposts – it wouldn't do her any good to have the thing floating off – and then stood and gathered her hair into a matronly bun. Slipping her fingers into her pocket she touched the little note card that warned her that the Watch would soon knock on her door. It paid to be known as the lady who handed out sweets to the young scoundrels of the neighborhood. Never a strange occurrence passed her by, never an odd event was missed. The coming visit wasn't a direct inquiry, of course, just a general checking-up on those sel-sensitives who claimed aged or injured retirement.

The very thought still tied her stomach in knots.

If the knock had come a day ago, she would have gladly turned herself in. Pelkaia held no illusions that her crimes would remain undetected much longer, that she would be able to escape the net tightening around her. She had done what she meant to do, and then sat back and waited for the axemen to catch up. Now... Now she realized her work was not yet done. And she had found a way out. A hole in the net.

She smiled when she recalled spying the Honding lad in the Blasted Rock Inn, savored every whisper she'd ever heard about his strange abilities. His simple presence had reminded her that she was not alone. That the Scorched was not comprised of only those who could find and move selium, and those who couldn't. There were others like her – many, perhaps – whose abilities deviated from what Valathea accepted. Others, maybe, who might rally to her cause. If only she could find them.

When she'd had him taken to the station house, she'd intended only to needle him to discover what he knew about the state Aransa was in, to see if she could push him into assisting her crusade against the empire in some way or another. When he'd mentioned stealing Thratia's ship, well, it had been all she could do to keep from squealing with delight. She shivered as she recalled how close she'd come to blowing the whole thing when he'd asked who Ripka would support as warden. How the thought of failing then had turned her stomach to ice.

Funny, that, how quickly one's mind can change.

She felt the watch captain's presence moments before the knock sounded, one-two, firm and insistent. It was nice to know that the coat she'd traded for Ripka's original had gone unremarked. It'd taken her ages to sew tiny bladders of selium into the hems of it so that she could feel when the real article was near. Getting the amount just right so that the whole thing didn't float away had given her quite the headache at the time.

Pelkaia gathered herself, faked a smile, and kissed the locket which held her dead son's face. When she opened the door, she found herself staring into the face of the watch captain, a shrewd young woman with serious eyes. Pelkaia noted that she had a freckle on the underside of her chin, and a tilt to the nose that she'd missed. She made a mental note to include those disparities in her next iteration of her.

"Good afternoon, Miss…" Ripka glanced down at a

list of names. "Miss Pelkaia Teria. I am Watch Captain
Ripka Leshe, and this is Sergeant Banch Thent. May we
come in?"

"Yes, of course." She stepped to the side and opened
the door wide for her new guests. "I'm afraid the place
is not very big, but you are welcome to it. Can I make
you tea?"

The watchers spilled into her little sitting room, their
brilliant blue uniforms gaudy against the drab simplicity
of her few possessions. They stood, critical eyes sweeping
the place from top to bottom, and Pelkaia was certain
they saw nothing of interest. Just the small pieces of a
lonely woman's life. Ripka shook her head.

"Thank you, ma'am, but no. We are quite busy today.
Have you heard of the death of Warden Faud?"

"Who hasn't? I don't get out much anymore, you
understand." She eased herself into a chair and rubbed
her knees with an embarrassed smile. "But I do get to
the market one level down twice a week. Why, I was just
there yesterday. It's all anyone can talk about. Did you
say your name was Ripka?"

The watch captain blinked. "I did. Is that significant?"

"Ah, well, it's just that it's a Brown Wash name, like
my own. I bet you have an Uncle Rel or Rip, eh? Silly
unimaginative lot, our folk. Slap an 'a' or 'aia' on the end
and, ta-da, you have a beautiful baby girl."

That got a genuine smile, eyes crinkling at the corners.
"I do indeed, but I have been gone from that village a
long time."

"Me too, me too." She rubbed her knees some more,
letting them see a bit of pain in her face. They didn't
hurt, but no one ever feared a viper with broken fangs.
"What can I do for you?"

"There has been some speculation that the late warden

was murdered by a doppel."

Pelkaia rankled at that, but kept her face as smooth as she could make it without sel. Being called a doppel was deeply disrespectful, but she doubted this girl knew any better. Illusionists could do so much more than hide beneath another's face. Fires above, the girl didn't even realize Pelkaia *was* a proper illusionist.

"You don't say? Well, I'm just an old sel mover, not even a shaper. I can shuttle the stuff along all right, but I'm no illusionist. I don't know any, either. Most of us don't chat much once the contract with the mine is up, you understand."

Ripka's brows went up at the term illusionist, but she let it hang. Many of Aransa's older citizenry refused the new terms for the strongest of the sel-sensitives. The elderly carried more of the indigenous Catari blood, from the time when Valathea suspected interbreeding was the only way to raise sensitives. The words of their great-grandparents filtered down the generations to their lips. Ripka couldn't rightly suspect her for such a small thing. Still, it felt like a little rebellion. A tiny triumph.

"I'm sure that's true, ma'am, but in the interest of protecting the city I'm afraid we're going to have to search your residence. Do you consent?"

"Certainly."

Pelkaia was proud at the breeziness of her voice, the unconcerned wave of her hand inviting them to have a look-see. Inside she was furious. The question of consent was moot, and the theater of Ripka even bothering to ask insulting. Pelkaia was damned sure that if she'd refused she'd find herself in the clink while the Watch tore her home apart.

The man, Banch, strode forward and began opening cupboards, rooting around her plain stone mugs and lifting up pictures to see if there were any hidden cubbies lurking behind. Pelkaia watched the watch captain's face as she observed her partner's proceedings.

Captain Leshe was thin of lip and kept them pressed tight, her small pupils following each of Banch's intrusions. There was distaste in her posture, a certain rigid formality that was an attempt to separate what she knew was wrong from the job she had to do. Ripka seemed to be a good woman. It was too bad Pelkaia's plans might eventually require her disposal.

"How long have you been living here?" Ripka asked, as if her little piece of paper didn't say.

"Oh, ten years now. I was able to buy the place outright when my boy Kel died at the mines. The bereavement stipend, you understand."

The captain's gaze flicked back to Pelkaia, leaving Banch unwatched as he poked around her bookshelf. Apparently, that little piece of paper didn't have all the facts after all.

"You had a son, Miss Teria?"

"Oh yes, fine boy he was." Pelkaia licked her lips and looked away. To make herself vulnerable to this woman, this authority figure, was asking too much. And yet, she had a duty to Kel, didn't she? He'd died a working man, the victim of unsafe conditions allowed to fester in the mines. It might rustle the captain's suspicions, but Pelkaia reasoned that if she let her voice waver and her eyes mist Ripka would view her as sunk deep in grief, too tired and worn to do any kind of damage. Pelkaia found it too easy by far to dredge up the required quaver to her voice, the moisture to her eye.

"He had a real talent for sel-sensing. Might have become a shaper, with practice, maybe even an airship captain. But he died in that rockslide on the Smokestack's third pipeline. His whole line went with him."

"I am sorry for your loss, ma'am, and I thank both you and your son for your service." Her words were automatic, rote. Pelkaia wondered just how many times she'd spoken them.

Service? More like servitude. "Thank you kindly, captain."

"What's through here?" Banch had given up his search of the bookshelf and stood pointing to the thin curtain that separated her sleeping room from the common. Pelkaia's skin went cold, her palms clammy. She had to resist an urge to clear a knot of fear from her throat.

"Just my bedroom."

Banch exchanged a look with Ripka, who gave him a curt nod.

"I am sorry," she said when Banch pushed the curtain aside and went within. "But the protocols are very precise."

"Don't worry, dear. I understand the shackle of protocol. I worked a line myself, you know, before I became too infirm for it."

Ripka frowned at her chart. "Forgive my prying, ma'am, but it says here you're only forty-eight."

"Yes, but I took some damage to my knees and haven't been right since. The bonewither caught up fast with me, you understand. I hope you'll forgive me sitting down through this interview of ours. Please do help yourself to a seat if you'd like."

The watch captain waved away her offer, shifting her position so that she could better keep an eye on her sergeant. Pelkaia turned to watch as well, and had to suppress a flinch as he dipped his head under her bed. The sel sack was well hidden, but if he were to touch the underside of the mattress he would surely feel the seams. She forced herself to breathe easy.

"Captain, you best look at this," Banch said.

Pelkaia's heart raced, sticky sweat beading on her brow. With an apologetic shrug Ripka stepped half into the bedroom, head cocked to one side to see whatever it was Banch had found. "What is it?" Ripka asked.

Pelkaia knew. Slowing her breath, she slipped her hand down the side of her chair and nudged aside the flap of quilt draped over the back of it. Cold steel met her fingertips, and she coiled a fist around the grip of a hidden blade. Tensing her core muscles so that she would be braced to strike, Pelkaia leaned forward, sliding her feet back, bending her knees like springs.

She could stash the bodies somewhere. Pretend to be Ripka in truth for a while.

Banch thumped her bed on its post. "Let the record show that this is some fine construction."

"Ah, well." Pelkaia played off the nervous tremor in her voice with a contrite chuckle. "My Kel made it for me. Saved up his wood allowance for a year to get the materials and make it. That was after my accident, mind you. The mattress is no sel cloud but it's llama-stuffed and just fine for me."

The sergeant pressed his hand into the mattress top and nodded appreciatively. "Fine mattress. Your son did good work, ma'am."

"You'll have to excuse Banch," Ripka said while suppressing a smile. "He's a connoisseur of naps."

He snorted and rolled his eyes. "Nothing worse than an uncomfortable rest, I stand by that." He brushed his hands together, the search forgotten. "Might sweeten up your disposition, getting a good rest, captain."

"But I'd still have to see you every morning. It would spoil the whole effect."

Despite her distaste of what these people represented,

Pelkaia caught herself chuckling at their camaraderie. It would be a shame indeed if the watch captain became too much in her way. Maybe… Pelkaia chewed her lip, thinking. Maybe she could scare her off.

"Thank you for your time, ma'am," Ripka said as Banch caught her eye and shrugged, a pre-arranged signal which must have meant he'd found nothing of import. "We'll be in touch if we have any other questions."

"Happy to oblige, watch captain."

The official pair bowed their official thanks and crisp-stepped from her little living room into the street. They shut the door behind them, firm but without banging, leaving Pelkaia alone with her sel and her memories. She sighed and rubbed her temples. Unlike her knees, those did ache.

Pelkaia sprang to her feet and hurried back to her bedchamber. Opened the bag, pulled a little sel out. She perched on the low bench before her vanity, staring into the pearlescent ball hovering a hand's width from her nose. Every possible shade, hue, and texture lay within that undulating prism of lighter-than-air fluid. Gas. No one had ever been certain just what it was, only that it worked.

She dipped her fingers into the little ball and smoothed some of it against her chin and cheek, recalling the fading freckle on the bottom of the watch captain's chin. All the fine folk of Aransa would be at the Salt Baths by now, primping and scrubbing for the night ahead.

If only preparing herself were as simple as a soak and a brush. She needed to start now, if she were to arrive at Thratia's fete in time.

Just a day ago, she would have turned herself in. So much can change in a day.

CHAPTER 6

The ferry was a narrow contraption with an open-air deck for the passengers and a closed cabin for the captain to escape his clientele within. He was a fine, proper looking captain in the sharp maroon uniform of the Imperial Fleet, with little tin and brass bars arranged up and down his broad lapels. The insignia were all nonsense, of course, but it made the gentry feel like they were getting the real airship experience.

The captain gave the ferry's airhorn a toot and it slithered out above the abyss, sliding along two thick guy wires attached to the underside of the ship's deck by large eyelets. The ferry itself had a middling buoyancy sack, just enough to keep its weight from bearing too much on the wires. Aransa wasn't about to waste a full airship or its selium supply on simple civic transportation. As it toddled along, Detan spared a worried glance at the breadth of his fellow passengers. A little more sel in the sacks probably wouldn't have gone amiss. It'd ease his nerves, at any rate.

Despite the lackluster arrangement, Detan enjoyed

the opportunity to take in the view. Every landscape of the Scorched Continent was a mishmash of rock and scrag-brush, but they were all still beautiful to him. The geography of the area maintained hints of the lush tropic it had once been, before the firemounts opened their mouths and blanketed the place in death. He couldn't imagine the verdant wonder of the past, but he could appreciate the rugged charm of the present.

The closer they drew to the firemount and its adjacent baths, the easier it was to make out the bent backs of the line-workers. Selium-sensitives, born with the ability to feel out and move small amounts of the stuff, were arranged in lines along the great pipeways that ran from the mouth of the Smokestack to the Hub. They urged raw selium gas they couldn't even see out of the firemount and through the pipes to the Hub's refinery.

Some of them – the shapers – could do it without moving a muscle, but most had to lean from side to side, channeling their ability through the motion of their arms. Back and forth, back and forth. A rhythmic dance of servitude all down the line. Didn't matter who you were, if you were born sel-sensitive you worked the lines. If you were very lucky, you got to be a diviner or a ship's pilot instead.

Detan turned away from the scene. As a young man, he had never been very lucky.

As the ferry bobbed along toward the baths, Detan put a hand on Tibs's shoulder and turned him about to look back the way they'd come. Aransa was half shadow in the light of the sinking sun, its terraced streets winding down the face of Maron Mountain to the inky sands of the Black Wash below.

For a Scorched settlement, it was a city of impressive size. Maybe fifty thousand souls packed those streets, nothing like the sprawling island cities of Valathea, but substantial all the same. Most of the denizens were born to it now, but a few generations ago it was filled only with those who came to mine the sel, and those who came to profit off their backs. The population boom was perfect for Detan's purposes – a man like him could pop in and out without being remembered by too many sets of eyes.

"See there?" Detan pointed to the easterly edge of the second level from the top, at a rock-built compound which spread down into the next two levels below. At its highest point a great airship was moored, sails tucked in and massive ropes reaching like spider's legs from it to the u-shaped dock which cradled it. No buoyancy sacks were visible, though it floated calm and neutral. Just a long, sleek hull, like the sea ships of old. Stabilizing wings protruded from the sides, folded in for now. He had no doubt that airship was the *Larkspur*. "Looks like Thratia is going to be giving tours tonight."

"I doubt we'll find ourselves on that guest list."

"Pah. Just you wait and see, old friend. Thratia's no dunce, she'll be wanting the company and support of such fine upstanding gentlemen as ourselves."

"As you say."

The ferry thunked to a stop against the Salt Baths' port, a jetty of mud-and-stone construction sticking out like a twisted branch from the rock face. A tasteful sign hung above the entrance into the basalt cavern, claiming peace and relaxation for all who entered. From the outside, it looked like the type of crummy dive bar people like Detan were likely to turn up in.

"Thought this place was more cream than water," he muttered.

A gentleman in a coat just wide enough to encircle his

impressive orbit sniffed and looked down a long nose at him. "Well it certainly shouldn't look it from the outside, young man. This is the Scorched, after all." He waved an expressive hand. "Ruffians abound in these troubled skies. Wouldn't want to advertise the place. Could you imagine? Thieves in the baths! What a terror."

The girthy man shuddered and clasped his waif of a woman closer. Arm-in-arm they disembarked, and as the man stepped onto the dock Detan felt the ship lift just a touch.

Detan shared a look with Tibs. "Thieves in the baths?"

"A terror indeed."

Grinning, Detan sauntered under the basalt arch with its plain sign. Once within, he found himself blinded by an expansive field of white, brilliant light. As he squinted, bringing a hand up to shade his eyes, he heard a soft chuckle beside him. He could just make out the shadow of a steward shaking his head. "My apologies, sir, but it does take a moment for the eyes to adjust. Blink slowly and keep your head down, it helps."

Detan thought it was a damned stupid thing to do, blinding your guests, but he kept his head down and his lids pressed shut all the same. It didn't take long for his pupils to settle down and, as he lifted his head again, his mouth opened just as wide as his eyes.

The cavern was a labyrinthine mishmash of glimmering white stone. Must have been quartz, though Detan'd be the first to admit he didn't know sandstone from shale. Sel-supported pathways hung through the air, connecting spacious meeting areas which were suspended from a combination of sel bags and guy wires. The cavern was open to the sun up top, which was what had made it so blasted bright. Light bounced off the smooth planes of quartz – no, he squinted at the wall nearest him, that wasn't right. He stepped closer and brushed a finger against it. The surface was slick, as if it were hungry for the wee bit of moisture in the desert air. He gave it a dubious sniff.

"I'll be blasted. Is that all… salt?"

The steward was a hard slab of a young man in a crisp black suit, his brass buttons polished to perfection and his mud-brown hair oiled into non-negotiable stillness. He was giving old Tibs a once-over, and it was clear to Detan that the fellow didn't know what to make of a patron bringing along his manservant. To clear the air a bit, he gave Tibs a companionable thwack on the shoulder and gestured to all of what surrounded them.

"Can you imagine, Tibs? All this must have been drug up from the flats, that's halfway to the Darkling Sea from here."

Tibs gave an appreciative whistle, and the steward rallied to his profession, sensing his rank was indeed somewhere below the manservant.

"Indeed, sirs, the salt bricks you see here in the Grand Cavern were quarried to the specifications of Aransa's Founder, Lord Tasay, who missed the luxurious bathing houses of his home in Valathea and sought to make Aransa a destination of luxury as well as commerce."

"Well, aren't you just the font of history."

The steward bowed. "It is my duty to guide and inform, sirs. Is this your first visit to the Salt Baths?"

Detan stepped out of the way of a few of the folk they'd ferried in with. Now that everyone's eyes were adjusted the regulars went about their business like they owned the place, and Detan considered the possibility that at least some of them must have a staked interest. After all, someone had to pay for the upkeep.

"That obvious, eh?"

His smile was dutifully abashed. "I mean no disrespect. It is my duty to assist, sirs."

"Lead on then, my good man."

The steward bowed again, something Detan wasn't quite sure if he liked. Sure, the respect it afforded him was nice, but all that bobbing about was starting to make his head spin.

Tibs eyed the grandeur all around them with deep-rooted suspicion, his wrinkled face pinched up tight. "Don't suppose this is what Ripka had in mind when she paid us," he whispered.

Detan waved a dismissive hand. "I doubt the dear watch captain would complain about the improvement to our…" he wrinkled his nose, "auras."

They followed the steward out onto one of the sel-lifted walkways, milling along behind the group of uppercrust who'd come over with them. The pack of well-to-dos were making a sweet time of it, putting their heads together and whispering between giggles.

He tried to ignore it, he really did. But when he heard them make a smart remark about Tibs's hat he couldn't help himself. Opening his senses, he felt for the sel in the walkway and gave it a little nudge.

Ahead of them, the walkway lurched. If anyone had thought to look Detan's way at that moment they would have seen him put a steadying hand on Tibs's shoulder just before the thing went wonky. The upcrusters cried out, toppling and tangling in a tumbleweed heap, and Detan got his other hand out just in time to grab the steward's jacket to keep him from going full over.

The steward's jacket twisted, skewing around his neck, and for the barest of moments Detan caught a glimpse of tattoo snaking across the strident young man's skin. Scales, yellow and red ink with a slash of black through it, the hint of a serpentine body. He thought he recognized the mark, but couldn't quite place it.

When the swaying came to a stop the steward rushed forward, leaving Detan alone to suffer a sharp elbow in the ribs from a surly Tibs.

"Oof!"

"You deserved that, sirra."

Realizing that there was no point in arguing just who, exactly, deserved what while Tibs was in such an uncharitable mood, Detan decided to take advantage of the situation. He swaggered forward and offered helping hands to the felled noblebones, hefting them to their feet while his fingers helped themselves to their pockets. Not one of them noticed. They were all too busy working out where to place the blame.

"Just what sort of hovel are you running here?" The man who had expressed terror at the presence of thieves jabbed a stubby finger at the steward as he was hauled back to his feet.

"I assure you, sir, that the Salt Baths have your safety as our top priority–"

"Hogwash! I will see this place–"

"Well, now," Detan drawled as he helped a lady to her feet and dipped his fingers in her one unbuttoned pocket. "I daresay this isn't the fault of this fine establishment."

"Oh? You do, do you?" The man rounded on Detan, the steward all but forgotten in the face of a juicier target. "And what would a dustswallower like yourself know about *fine* establishments? Why, the very idea that they even let you in here–"

"I reckon it's not the establishment's fault." He stomped a foot down on the path. "Because these selium-supported walkways *do* have a weight limit."

The noblebone's mouth opened and worked around,

his cheeks going firemount red as he choked on anger. Detan just stood there, fists on his hips, giving the wide man a wider smile, all full of teeth. He waited, letting the silence drag on, letting people come to their own knowledge that the man had nothing more to say.

With a confounded grunt the noblebone threw his arms in the air and stormed off, the meeker members of his party drifting along in his wake. When they were well out of earshot, Detan turned to the steward and clapped his hands together. He was not surprised to find a tight smile on the man's otherwise professionally placid face.

"Well! There's that. Now why don't you show us the baths, New Chum?"

He bowed. "This way, sirs."

The baths were set aside from the salt-brick cavern, and the bemused steward explained that it was to keep the steam from melting the walls, which made sense, now that it was brought to his attention. Salt and water got on a little too well to be expected to keep themselves presentable in close company. Detan and Tibs found themselves alone in the western wing of the bath halls, a coincidence no doubt engineered by the sharp-eyed steward.

These were the *nice* baths, no mistake about it. The tub they occupied was a massive affair of green-veined soapstone, or so Tibal insisted. It stuck out from the walkway on a narrow spur of matching rock, its weight supported by virtue of its walls being hollowed out and filled with sel.

They were higher up than the other bathers, and if Detan glanced down he could see similar arrangements sticking out all along the cavern walls. Tubs burdened with a mingle of male and female uppercrusts were arranged in such a way as to grant each group a semblance of privacy, and the venting ground below which kept the tub water warm sent up wafts of nearly-scorching steam.

The steward had assured them it was perfectly safe, that their particular bath had been in operation since the place's very founding and had never faltered. That didn't reassure Detan much. Things that had lasted since time immemorial had a way of going to the pits whenever he stuck a toe in them.

"Can I get you anything, sirs?"

Tibs poked at the slab of pink-veined salt floating on the surface of their tub. "What's this for?"

"That's the salt part of the bath, sir. It is good for softening the skin and detoxifying the humors."

"If you detox ole Tibs, he might come apart at the seams," Detan said.

Tibs shot him a sour look that he felt rather proved the point.

"I assure you it is perfectly safe, sirs."

"Welp, tallyho then."

Detan dropped his towel and eased down the slick steps into the warm water. He'd experienced a lot of nice things in his days, mostly having to do with whiskey and women and the occasional warm rainfall, but this was pure bliss. He murmured his appreciation, feeling his joints give up their stiffness, and closed his eyes. For a moment, he almost forgot this wasn't at all why he'd come here.

Tibs followed him in, looking rather like a drowned sandrat. The steward placed a couple of glasses of cactus flower liqueur on the salt slab, delicate red buds perched on the rims of the glasses. Presumably, the idea was to drink them before the salt ran out, and that seemed like a grand old time to Detan.

"I'll return to check on you in a mark, sirs. Please do ring the bell if you require anything."

"Will do, New Chum."

The steward beamed at them, lingering a moment to see if he were needed further, then hurried back down the steps. Detan watched him go and let loose with a low whistle as soon as he was out of earshot. "Poor sod, I don't think he has a chum in the world."

"Sorry luck he's found one in us then, eh?"

"If by sorry you mean marvelous, then yes. Did you see the ink? Methinks our stalwart steward is hiding a less than reputable past."

"Something you'd be familiar with."

"Oh, come off it. Ever seen anything like it?"

"You think the kid's got a crew?"

"He might have, *some* people are capable of making more than one friend. Didn't seem much impressed with the noblebones, come to think on it. Might be he's casing the place."

Tibs let out a low and weary sigh. "Leave the lad be, not everyone's neck deep in conspiracies just because you are."

"As you like. We really gonna sit round in this stew all day?"

"Long as they'll let me."

Detan drained his glass and hiccupped. "Pah. You've no imagination. Did you see the cubbies where we put our things? No locks!"

"This is a respectable place. Things don't go missing."

He slapped the water with his open palm. It was a meaty, satisfying slap. Then he snagged up Tibs's glass and downed that, too. The old fool was likely to get drunk and careless if Detan didn't get the good stuff out of the way for him.

"You heard the man, he's giving us a mark to have a look-see."

"He's giving us a mark for the soak."

"Nonsense. Let's go!"

Detan moved to the steps, but Tibs grabbed his arm so hard and fast he slipped and flopped face-first into the water. He came up sputtering, and gave Tibs a shove. "What was that for?"

"Just wanted to remind you, real clear, that the young Lord Honding is said to have lost his sel-sense in a *tragic* mining accident back in Hond Steading. Your freedom depends on that neat little rumor."

He flushed. "Oh, come off it. That overinflated sack deserved it."

"Might be, but Aransa isn't a friendly town for your type. Watch yourself. Sirra."

Detan rolled his eyes and pulled himself out of the tub, sloshing water over the edge. An angry hiss issued from the vent far below, and he shuddered. It was one thing to work the firemounts for selium, there was just no other way to get it, but surely there were safer methods of taking a bath. He wrapped his towel round his hips and waited for Tibs to do likewise.

He did not.

"What's the problem now, Tibs?"

"I'm going to soak."

"Huh. Well. I suppose it will improve your aroma. Carry on, good man, and look for me to return before the mark burns down."

"Try not to get killed."

Detan sniffed and set off, wet feet slap-slapping on the warm rock walkway. The amenable steward had done him the favor of showing him the most direct route between the lush baths and the men's cubby room, where the gentle guests left their outer shells for the duration of their luxury. Trusting lot, these bathgoers.

The way was clear as far as the cubby room, and there Detan hovered at the entrance for a good long while with his ear pressed up against the door to make sure there wasn't so much as a mouse-shuffle inside. Gauging the room empty, he slipped through the narrow door and shut it with a soft click behind him. He winced. The steward had been flapping his lips so much that Detan had missed that particular noise the first time through. Nothing for it, he decided. And anyway, there wasn't a soul around to hear it so far as he could tell.

He tiptoed down the row, peeking into the stuffed cubbies until he came across one that appeared more stuffed than most. Marking the spot, he doubled back to his own accoutrements and slipped his leather money pouch from the folds. It was his favorite pouch, it'd been the first thing he'd stolen when he returned to the Scorched, and he'd be sorry to lose it. But then, he was pretty sure he'd be seeing it again quite soon. He kissed the goatskin and tucked it in amongst the robust man's vestments. Then he shoved Tibs's into the cubby of the big man's friend for good measure.

If he was going to stick his neck out, he'd be fried if he wasn't going to invite ole Tibs along for the ride. It wasn't right, leaving your friend out of things just because he was a mechanic. And anyway, Tibs's clothes were reeking just as much as his own were.

Doubling back to his cubby, he scooped up both his and Tibs's clothes, then fled the scene.

CHAPTER 7

The warehouse district had always been dark, but now that Thratia's compound loomed above the wide mudbrick buildings, the once familiar streets seemed to grow seedier in her shadow. Somewhere from within the compound the thready whisper of music struck up. Soft, but growing. Thratia's entertainment getting ready for her guests tonight.

Ripka bit her lip, forcing herself to ignore the swathe of excess shade laid over the building she was reconnoitering now. She could not let her prejudices against the ex-commodore cloud her judgment; make her rash. Not tonight.

She crouched alongside Banch and their newest recruit, Taellen, relying upon a hip-high stack of ruined crates to obscure their presence. On the opposite side of the targeted warehouse five other watchers lurked, awaiting her signal.

The cold of the desert night bit into her flexed knees, stiffened her tensed back. She shifted her weight, pretending to adjust the angle she held her crossbow at, but found no relief. They had been a half-mark lurking behind that pile of detritus, and the sour stench of alley garbage was growing disturbingly less noticeable. Ripka resolved to give herself a full, hot bath just as soon as she got home.

"That's the place, I'm sure of it," Taellen murmured and gestured with his charcoal-blackened crossbow.

"So you've said," she whispered, nudging his weapon back below the line of the broken crates. "Now hush."

He grunted, sullen, and she bit her tongue to keep from reprimanding him further. This had been his find, and she was grateful for it, but the lad was too eager to lay claim. Too eager, she suspected, to prove he served Aransa. He'd only moved to the Scorched a single moonturn ago and still carried a Valathean accent – and a Valathean name, despite her urging to change it. Aransa may be governed by Valathea, but the people of the Scorched liked their names harsh as the landscape that housed them.

Banch lifted a hand in the air, his finger extended, circled it, then pointed. Setting aside her annoyance, she squinted through the dark at the window he indicated. The curtain flicked aside, the edge of a man's face peering out into the dark. Ripka held her breath as he scanned the area beyond, then let the curtain fall back into place. Had he seen them? Heard them? She cursed her inability to communicate with her other team.

A rumbling echoed down the street. She tensed, straining to make out the details. The sound was a dull, rhythmic clunk punctuated by two soft thumps. *Clunk-thump-thump-clunk.* Ripka raised her brows at Banch, a silent question, but he only shrugged.

Something dark moved down the street, the finer details of it erased by the shadow of Thratia's compound.

Ripka made a note to later insist that these streets were kept bright by the lamplighter children. It was well past time to chase the shadows out of Aransan commerce and she, quite frankly, would be delighted to light some fires under the hides of those mucking about with shady dealings.

A wide cargo door slid open on the face of the warehouse, its hinges so well greased she would have missed it if she weren't looking right at it in that moment.

Faint light spilled from the door, illuminating a small section of the road. Plodding toward the opened door was a cart pulled by the slow trod of a hump-backed donkey. Ripka squinted, and saw that both the creature's hooves and the wheels of the cart had been wrapped in thick cloth. Shady dealings, indeed. Enough to reasonably demand the right to search them. She smothered a hungry grin and put on a smooth, professional expression.

"You see?" Taellen hissed, his voice high and eager.

Ripka cringed and grabbed the lad's arm, dragging him back down as his head popped up. "Quiet," she whispered. "Wait until we have a better idea of what it is they mean to do." *And to see if they do anything obviously incriminating*, she thought, but Taellen was too young for that train of thought just yet. Too green.

Green things did not last long on the Scorched.

Taellen grunted but ducked his head, annoyance simmering in the set of his shoulders. Banch caught her eye over the lad's bowed head, one brow arched in amusement. To keep from grinding her teeth she pulled a pinch of barksap from her pocket and popped it into her mouth, rolling the sticky, resinous heap around until it was narrow enough to fit down one row of molars. The sharp flavor calmed her, the viscous lump gave her tongue something to worry over, something to do while she waited for an opening.

A man in a tight-fitted, slate-grey coat drove the cart, his narrow back slumped over the slack reins. He leapt from his perch as a man and a woman in matching grey coats stepped into the light from within the warehouse. Their hands hovered at their hips, though Ripka could see no weapons on them. She bit her lip, thought better of it and shifted the sap so that she could chew it instead. The three peeked beneath the mottled cloth covering the cart's contents, nodded to themselves and waved the donkey-driver in.

"What do you think?" Banch whispered.

"I think a few questions wouldn't go amiss." She pursed her lips, stroking the forward curve of her crossbow. "But let's keep the others in reserve, for now."

Ripka stood, straight as an arrow, the blue coat of the Watch comfortably snug about her waist and shoulders. The weight of the cudgel at her hip brought her confidence, the shadows of her colleagues rising beside her strength. Chin up, crossbow leveled, she strode through the dark toward the warehouse, trying to smooth the eager thumping of her heart, the heady twitch of her fingers toward the bolt trigger.

The scene felt sharper, brighter. Her past as a prizefighter raised its head, calculating how fast she could close on the big man, judging the reach of the woman's legs. She licked her lips and twisted a manic grin into something like an affable smile. It was a relief to be effectual, to put the shade of the doppel out of her mind for a while. Even if she couldn't, ethically, come in swinging.

The two leading the cart stopped cold upon sighting them, hands disappearing beneath their coats to seek weapons until the color of the Watch blues took root in their minds. A thrum of excitement tingled over Ripka's skin as recognition settled, their eyes narrowing and their lips thinning with irritation. The cart driver disappeared within the wide cargo door, so she tipped her chin to Taellen, motioning him to circle them at a wider berth and keep an eye on the door.

"Evening, watch captain," the woman drawled as she raised her hands into the air. The man followed her lead, taking a half-step back. "Come to help us unload this delivery?"

"I'd sure like to have a look at it," Ripka said, keeping her bow trained on the woman while Banch and Taellen fanned out around her. She drew up within five paces of the woman, close enough to see the wrinkles like cracked mud around her eyes. The woman's face twitched, her lips fighting down a scowl.

"We're not doing anything illegal, now, we got our paperwork in order."

"Then you wouldn't mind Sergeant Banch here having a look at it."

Banch stepped forward, one hand held out expectantly while the other propped the butt of his crossbow against his shoulder. The woman pulled a sheaf of papers from a leather satchel strapped to the donkey's side, each movement orchestrated with such precision that Ripka wondered if she'd rehearsed the motions. If she'd been anticipating the Watch's interference all along.

A tickle of worry scratched at the back of Ripka's mind, and she flicked her gaze to the side just as Taellen loped further inward, drawing in towards the warehouse door. What was that fresh-blooded idiot thinking? He was meant to watch the door, not enter it. There could be a dozen or more of the thugs lurking beyond, and though they would be wary of attacking a watcher, Ripka had made it a habit not to rely on someone else's fear to keep her skin intact.

"Distribution approval here says for honey liqueur, though the house importing isn't noted." Banch handed the papers back to the woman.

"Difficult to get distribution in Aransa without a mercer house to back you." Ripka raised her brows in innocent question at the woman. "How'd you manage it?"

The woman took back the papers and spread her arms wide as she shrugged. "The Mercer Collective has become amenable to independent enterprise as of late."

"Lucky for you." Ripka motioned toward the cloth-covered cart. "I'm sure you won't mind if we check the goods against the manifest, then."

The woman's expression rippled, a subtle disturbance, but enough to put Ripka on sharper guard. She swallowed her barksap and stepped toward the cart, sparing a glance to make sure Banch had her covered. With one hand she peeled back the cover to reveal a mound of stacked crates, each one no bigger than the length of her forearm on each side. She tipped her head to the man. "Open it."

He glanced at the woman, got a nod of approval and shrugged. From somewhere on the cart he grabbed a pry bar and heaved the crate's lid open, wood and metal groaning with each tug. The man tossed the levered top to the ground and nudged aside a fistful of straw packing. Between the dried grasses Ripka could just make out the deep amber of liqueur bottles, their tops sealed by red wax stamped with the shape of a bee.

"Remove one," Ripka ordered.

"Here to levy a tax, watch captain?" the woman said, this time not bothering to hide her smirk.

Ripka ignored her, instead keeping her gaze on the bottle the man removed. It was in the round-bottomed style currently fashionable, made possible by funneling sel into the glass during the manufacturing process. She frowned, something not quite right about the shape of it twisting through her mind.

"You see?" the woman said. "Nothing strange about a bottle."

Except that it was too short to fill the crate. Ripka returned the woman's smirk. "True, but I'm more interested in what's in the crate's false bottom."

The woman's grin lost its mirth, her eyes went hard as flint. "I don't know what you mean, captain. Perhaps you'd like to take a bottle to try? To make sure the quality is up to the standards you expect for Aransa."

"Bribes?" Ripka clucked her tongue. "You must think you're talking to someone else." She caught the man's gaze and flicked her eyes to the crate. "Break that open completely. Now."

The man shifted his weight, fingers going white around the neck of the bottle he'd presented to her. The woman chewed her lip, and Ripka allowed herself a small smile at the recognition of nervousness, of distress.

"Scatter!" the woman yelled loud as her lungs would let her.

Before Ripka could get a shot off, the man threw the bottle at her feet, a foamy explosion of alcohol-drenched honey sweetening the air. She swore and fired at the woman, swore again when she saw the bolt skim off the woman's cheek without causing more damage than a rockcat scratch.

Banch loosed his shot, missed, then leap-tackled the man who had thrown the bottle as he bolted right by him. Ripka jumped over the tangled pair, reloading her bow with practiced ease as she ducked into the warehouse after the woman.

Mountains of identical crates dotted the warehouse, great stepped pyramids of them rising up on all sides. Ripka spared them only the briefest of glances. Some part of her couldn't help but register the expense involved in such an operation. Her steps were silent, the dirt-packed floor smoothed by the passing of many feet. Half of the wall sconces had been lit in anticipation of the night's work, the flickering flames throwing strange shadows in her path.

"Turn yourselves over, and we won't use force," Ripka called, though the words felt pointless, perfunctory. These people, whoever they were, had been ordered to run. Which meant that they more than likely had orders to keep themselves out of official hands at all costs.

"Captain!" Taellen yelped from around a pile of crates to her right, his voice high with surprise.

Before she could move two steps in his direction a crash broke through the night, the splintering of wood and shattering of glass louder to her overstrained senses than any crack of thunder.

Rounding the crate-pile, her foot went out from under her. The world skewed as she crashed down hard on one knee, bright spikes of pain lancing up her leg. Ripka got a hand down to steady herself, old instincts overriding momentary terror. The floor was sticky mush, sugared mud. She peeled her hand free and glared down at the syrupy muck coating her palm. Tried to ignore the needles of pain radiating from the knee she had fallen on.

"Look out!" Taellen barreled into her from the side just as a crate went flying through the air where her head would have been. Ripka grunted and gasped once, quick to recapture the air that had been driven from her lungs. Taellen rolled away from her and sprang up, the easy agility of youth driving his knees. He dragged his cudgel free and brandished it, the crossbow lost.

Ripka heaved herself upright with, she supposed, far less grace but just as much effectiveness. The cart driver was opposite them, his scrawny arms flailing like a broken windmill as he clambered up the stepped mountain of crates. Where in the pits did he think he was going? The ceiling?

"Easy now," she called, reining in her anger. "That's not the most stable of locations."

"To the pits with you!" he screeched and whirled around. Ripka blinked, slow as honey rolling downhill, as the driver grabbed a crate from the pile he was climbing and flung it one-handed straight at her. She skittered away and the cheap wood crashed into dozens of pieces, throwing its delicate cargo high into the air.

The crate's bottom broke, spilling weapons onto the liqueur-drenched ground. They gleamed in the flickering light, wicked expanses of steel winking at her out of the dark. She took a half-step back and scanned the mountains of crates all around her once more.

There were thousands. Did they each carry a deadly gift?

And how had he managed such a ferocious throw? The crates weren't big – they barely came up to her knee – but they were laden with thick glass bottles, liqueur, and steel. Too heavy by far to pitch around like toys.

Another crate burst upon the ground, just before her feet, and she flinched back into reality.

"Cease this immediately!" she demanded, keeping the man in her line of sight as she skirted the detritus, looking for her crossbow. Where were Banch and the others?

"Blasted skies he's strong!" Taellen called out as the man flung yet another crate one-handed without so much as a grunt. The heavy wooden box sailed through the air as if it were as light as a paper airship. Ripka froze, squinted down at the thick puddles, their surfaces pockmarked with tiny bubbles, and realized just why the man found the crates so light.

"Surrender!" Banch's voice echoed all around, the heavy tromp of the other five watchers hard on his heels.

The cart driver's eyes went wild – mad.

"He's sensitive! There's sel in the booze! 'Ware the crates!" Ripka yelled.

Too late. The man's hand shot out toward a pile opposite him, his fist clenched around empty air, and yanked. The crates groaned, shifted, wood cracking as the heavy contents pushed against the friction of being stacked one atop the other.

Ripka spun around, saw her watchers running her way, faces red with exertion and boots slamming the ground so hard they could scarcely hear the complaint of the wooden heap beside them. It twitched, leaned.

The face of the cart driver went red, sweat sluicing down his cheeks. Ripka made her decision, and sprinted.

Her knee complained, her shoulders burned, but still she flung herself at the pyramid the man had climbed and heaved herself upward. He saw her, his expression of intense concentration flickering only a moment as he catalogued this new threat. In that moment he lost his tug on the crates threatening her people. It was enough.

With a roar of effort she leapt upward and threw one arm out, cudgel raised high, and brought it down in a punishing arc against the side of the sweating cart driver's head. He slumped, a leaf cut free of its branch, and began to slide down the stacks. Ripka scrambled, gathering the fabric of his coat in one numb fist, and leaned her weight against the mountain, breath coming in sharp gasps.

"Captain!" Banch called from the ground below, his expression a mix of bewilderment and fear.

"Get ready to catch this sonuvabitch, because I can't hold him much longer," she called back.

The five scrambled to get into position, and she tossed the cart driver so that he wouldn't bounce all the way down the sharp corners of the crates. When he was safely in hand, she let herself down with care. By the time her feet touched the ground they had bound the blasted man.

Taellen offered her an arm of support. She was grateful to take it.

"The others?" she asked Banch.

"Our rear guard detained the woman, but the man made it out." Banch glanced away as he spoke, a flush of embarrassment mingling with the fresh bruise on his cheek.

"That will have to do." Ripka ran her hand through her hair, then immediately regretted it as her hair stuck up in a mass of sticky spikes. She sighed. "I need a bath."

Banch chuckled and clapped her on the shoulder. "I'll secure the area, don't you worry captain."

Shrugging off Taellen's support, she directed the loading of the prisoners into the donkey cart, making sure to offload all the selium-enriched bottles of liqueur just in case the sensitive were to awaken. The last thing she needed was another avalanche of overly sweet booze coming her way.

Taellen grabbed the reins to the cart and she took up guard in the back with another of the Watch. Her sticky crossbow she kept close to hand, but it was one of the smuggled blades she held, turning it over in the slim light as Taellen drove the donkey back to the station house.

The metal was smooth, the forging done well enough to keep any pits from marring the surface of the blade. It had been oiled recently, an unctuous film coating her finger as she stroked the length of steel. Ripka sniffed the smear on her finger and frowned when she did not recognize the scent. Where had these weapons come from? And why so many? Importing weapons was not illegal in Aransa, but clearly someone wanted to avoid raising suspicions.

Someone. Hah. She knew full well who had done this, even if she couldn't prove it.

"Captain." Taellen's voice drifted back, soft and uncertain.

"Yes, watcher?"

"How'd you know?"

"Know what?"

"That he was a sensitive... That there was even sel in the liquor."

She smiled to herself. "Simple observation. As you commented yourself, the man was unusually strong."

The watcher keeping guard alongside her snorted, shifted his weight. Ripka raised her brows at that, but the man didn't look at her, just kept his gaze tight on the prisoners. As he should. And yet... Something in the stance of his shoulders, in the purse of his lips, set her ill at ease. What was his name, Jetk? She shook her head. The Watch was getting too big – too fragmented.

"Oh. Thought you might be sensitive yourself," Taellen said.

A cold knot formed in Ripka's belly. "No. Not even a little bit. Don't forget it."

Taellen grunted apology, but Ripka couldn't shake the

serpents of dread worming their way into her thoughts. The last time someone had accused her of being sensitive she hadn't been able to prove otherwise. It was so obvious to her, the way sensitives worked. Illusions broke down under hard scrutiny, subtle movements gave away attempted mirror manipulations.

She never could understand how anyone else didn't see it. But after rumors began to spread through the Brown Wash that she was hiding sensitivity her fights had grown more violent, the crowd's taunts more pointed. No one had a kind word for the woman they thought was shirking the duty that bound their own loved ones.

The second night she'd left the ring to find some flea-bitten bastard waiting for her in the alley with a broken bottle and lungful of curses, she'd taken her prize purse and left the Brown Wash behind, joining Faud's mercenaries on the long caravan to Aransa.

She clenched her fist on the blade's grip, watching her knuckles grow so pale the scars didn't show. In Aransa, she was watch captain, not some cracked-toothed fighter living from purse to purse. She had sway here. Allies. And it was true, anyway – she was no sel-sensitive. They'd believe her.

CHAPTER 8

By the time he returned to the bath their salt brick was halfway gone. Detan eased himself into the hot water and tipped his head back with a hearty sigh.

"You look right pleased with yourself."

"I am right pleased, old chum. This is a lovely establishment Lord Tasay has left us. Shame his line died out, or Thratia wouldn't be able to muss it all up by angling to get herself elected warden."

"Right," Tibs drawled, "because the rule of heirship has worked out so well for the other landed families and their cities."

Detan scowled and scratched the Honding brand seared into the flesh of the back of his neck, deciding to ignore Tibs's dig.

"Now," he scooped up the little bell and gave it a good, bold ring, "where is that New Chum? Somebody drank all our booze and I've worked up quite a thirst."

The steward came loping down the hallway, a bottle in one hand and a cheese plate in the other. Detan gave Tibs a triumphant grin, but the codger just rolled his eyes. Not a fan of subtlety, his wiry old mechanic.

"Would sirs care for another drink?"

"You're a wonder, New Chum, a wonder!"

The steward poured out the drams and, while Detan watched, the young man's nose began to wrinkle. "Do either of you sirs smell something burning?"

Tibs gave him a glare that could cut glass, but Detan ignored it and leaned forward over the edge of the tub, sniffing the air. "I do! Is that normal?"

With a face like an undercooked fish, the steward set the bottle and cheese down and scrambled to the end of the walkway. He stuck his head over the edge and peered about while Detan downed a few of the cheese bits. Tibs followed his lead. He'd never been the type to turn down a free plate.

"There's something burning on one of the vents!" The steward pointed and Detan dragged his gaze along the man's finger as if he hadn't known where he'd be pointing. He let loose with what he hoped was a heart-broken screech and leapt to his feet, sending bath water flying in all directions.

"My hat!"

Tibs got the picture then, and lurched to his feet. "*My* hat!" But his mouth was full of cheese, which rather ruined the effect.

Regardless, Detan thought they both looked positively dashing as they leapt from the bath and snatched up their towels. With a hasty wrap for modesty, they charged down the perilous steps, the steward nipping at their heels, and spilled out into the dangerous terrain of the venting ground. Detan hesitated, drawing back an anxious step and chewing on his lip.

"Follow me, sirs, the way is treacherous."

The steward strode ahead, and Detan forced himself

to check his pace as he scurried along behind. His legs were longer than the young man's, and he'd scouted the area ahead of time, but being first on the scene would let the sel out of the sack and bring the whole thing crashing down in a hurry.

When they finally made it to the vent in question, Detan pushed ahead of the steward and grabbed up his hat. Tibs's hat. Detan was rather fond of the old thing, so he'd left it sitting on the edge just close enough to give it a character-building singe.

"Someone has burned our clothes!"

"It must have been a mistake, sirs, I can't imagine that anyone here would do something like that."

Detan floundered a little, but good old Tibs had caught up now and gotten all the gears of his mind grinding away.

"Whose vent is this?" Tibs demanded.

"Oh, well…" The steward flicked out the guest list folded in one pocket. Detan grinned, recognizing it from the pad the ticket-taker had written their names on. Perfect.

New Chum's face went fishy again. "This would be the vent below the bath of Renold Grandon and his party, sirs. The man with whom you had the small confrontation on the sel bridge."

Detan pumped his fists in the air in victory, but he hoped it looked more like anger to the young steward. Either way, it was energetic enough to set the man reeling. "That mounded ass! Come, Tibal, let us go claim our compensation. Quickly, to the cubbies, before that demon can make off with any more of our personals!"

Allowing the steward to presume he had learned the way from their walk to the vent, Detan shoved the singed hat on his head and charged off through the craggy ground after the culprits.

The timing was sweet as sel wine. Just as Grandon and his group arrived and began to attire themselves, Detan and his entourage of two burst in upon them.

"You!" He pointed a quavering finger at the man, making his eyes wild and wide.

Grandon looked up, yawned, and began toweling off his feet. Detan rather wished he'd left the towel where it was, but he was on a roll now and not about to stop for modesty's sake.

"You bulbous, petty thief!"

That got his attention. The granite-fleshed man secured his towel and crossed his arms under what, Detan was disturbed to realize, were the male equivalent of bosoms.

"Are you accusing me of something, little man?"

"You and your foul aficionados stole my and my man's clothes and tossed them to the vents!" He pointed at the singed edge of his hat. "This dear old thing barely escaped your brutality."

Grandon grunted. "If your clothes were burned it was probably because the cleaning staff thought they were rags. You have no proof."

"Proof! I have all I need!" He took the hat off and waggled it at Grandon. "No one would be stupid enough to go to the vents without a guide."

"A terribly stupid thing to do indeed, sirra."

"Yes. As I was saying, no one would *brave* the danger of the vents alone, and therefore you and your gaggle are the only ones who had access to the thing! A simple task, to tip them over the edge from your tub."

"He does have a point, sir," the steward said, and Detan jumped a bit because he'd damned near forgotten New Chum was standing right smack beside him.

"A point? That rat? Do you have any idea who I am?" Grandon hauled himself up to his full height and pinched his face in a way that might have looked hawkish on a narrower man, but in truth just ended up looking constipated.

"I reckon you're Renold Grandon." Detan tapped the guest list poking out of the steward's breast pocket. "Like the paper says."

"You're blasted straight I am! Got a ten percent ownership in Aransa's selium mine, and I will not be treated like this by some withered example of wormwood."

Detan re-adjusted his slipping towel. He was not about to back down on account of an accurate insult.

"And do you have any idea who I am, Grandon?"

"Oh, sirra, I don't think that's really nec–"

He shushed Tibs with a wave of his hand. His heat was up again, something about this fellow just didn't sit right in Detan's mind, and some things were worth sticking your neck out over. Things like his own sorry pride.

"Yes, I do." Grandon smirked.

He swallowed. Had he miscalculated? Had he swindled this overinflated sack in the past? Is that why he got his goat up so easily?

"Oh yes." Grandon trudged forward and stabbed a finger at Detan's chest. "I know your type, boy. You spend your time slithering about the downcrust scraping together coin from sap to sap until you've got enough in your filthy fist to think you can make it up here with the Right Sort. Well, you've pushed the buttons on the wrong man, you swine. I will have you run out on the Black Wash with the morning sun for the mild inconvenience you've caused me and mine. You understand? I will see you *burn* for wasting my time."

Detan put his hand out and laid it flat on the big man's chest. He quirked a smile, saw Grandon's confusion, and gave him a light shove. Grandon had to either take a step back, or topple.

He stepped back.

"So. You don't know who I am."

Grandon opened his mouth, but Detan stepped toward him and Grandon gulped air as he took another step back to avoid coming chest-to-chest with him. Rage colored his cheeks and chest like an allergic reaction. Detan pressed on before he could recover his momentum.

"My name is Detan Honding." He shoved a hand out. "And the pleasure's all mine, Grandon."

The big man narrowed his eyes at the extended hand. His friends went quiet. "You're not a Honding."

"Check the guest list."

"You lied on it."

Detan sighed and turned around. He caught Tibs's eye as he turned, and he had his lips pressed together like it was the only thing keeping him from using some mighty cruel words. Oh well. He was in it now.

He reached back and lifted the hair that hung above the nape of his neck. There, burned in white scar flesh with puckered pink edges, was his family crest. A pickaxe and sword, crossed over the full sail of an old sea ship with the three stars of the landed below. A bit redundant, those landed stars, as the Honding family had been the first of them all to claim land rights on the Scorched. They'd earned it, the whole damned continent, by finding the secret veins of selium gas with sensitives they didn't even know they had.

"Thought all but Dame Honding died off. Thought her nephew died in a mining accident," Grandon croaked. It was a lame protest. There were people who would fake a crest, sure, but not a Honding one. There were easier things in the world to pretend to be.

"Sorry to disappoint you then, Grandon, but here I am."

Grandon wasn't a landed man, but he knew his manners. He backed off with a grumbled apology.

"Now, the steward here is going to have a look around your cubbies. If you're clean, then we'll forget about all this. If not, well, we'll work that out when we come to it."

The steward glided forward as if shaking down one of the wealthiest men in all Aransa was just another daily toil, and gave a good and thorough search of Grandon's cubbies and all his accomplices. Out came Detan's fine leather money pouch, and then Tibs's cloth pouch stuffed with Ripka's.

Tibs gave him a hard look as he took his pouch back, no doubt wondering just what in the fiery pits Detan's plan had been if they'd ended up losing all their money and the stall tab for their flier. It seemed to Detan he couldn't rightly complain. They'd gotten it back, after all.

"We have robes you can borrow," the steward said. "Until the watch captain gets here to take your statements. I will order some new clothes for you right away, sirs."

"No need to get the Watch involved, but I won't be the one wearing the loaner robe." He grinned over at the steward. "You handy with a needle and thread, New Chum?"

"Yes, sir."

The steward sent Grandon and his companions on their merry way with nothing more than a thin robe each to their names. At least they smelled fresh, and Detan figured they might think twice before messing with a dirty sod next chance they got. He sighed. More than likely they'd go whining to their friends about those bully Hondings. He clenched his jaw. It's not like his aunt would ever hear about it, and people probably wouldn't believe them anyway. They'd think he'd just gone and got himself swindled by an imposter.

Which was half right.

"Hold still, sir."

Detan grumbled as he forced himself to stand still. It wasn't easy with Tibs glaring at him like that, but even old Tibs had to admit he looked good in his new ensemble. Grandon's friends had sported some pretty refined taste, and one had been remarkably close to Tibs's measurements. Only Detan needed the adjusting – he'd always been weirdly narrow in the shoulders compared to other men his size. He figured it made him better at getting out of tight spots. Or into them.

"You know we can take your measurements and send for a whole new set of clothes, sir," the steward mumbled around the pins held between his lips.

"It's the principle of the thing, New Chum. I want Grandon and his pals to see me strutting about in their own suits. Serves 'em right. And anyway, these seem fresh made."

And their inner pockets were stuffed with tickets to Thratia's fete. Tickets Grandon and his chums had gone and forgotten all about when they'd realized they'd be marching home in loaner robes.

"I suppose they were made for the party tonight, sir. We've been busy all day with people coming in to get cleaned up for it."

"It's a fete, New Chum. Parties are for toddlers and drunk academy kids."

"I'm afraid I don't see the difference, sir."

"Fancier booze."

The steward's smile was dangerously wide, pins drooping from the corners. "Will you be going, sir?"

"The thought had crossed my mind."

Tibs crossed his arms and snorted. As the steward leaned downward to pull a stitch tight on the cuff of Detan's new trousers, his shirt slipped, once more revealing the hint of a snake's back wending its way over the steward's shoulder. He bit his tongue, recalling Tibs's admonishment to let the poor lad be, then said anyway, "What's with the pet viper, New Chum?"

The poor steward jerked upright, sticking his thumb with the needle, and scurried back a step. Eyes darting, he shoved his thumb in his mouth to suck the blood – or, no, Detan realized. The man wasn't licking his wounds, he was using the prick as an excuse to stall for time while he thought through what to say. Detan grinned.

"Come now, what's a reptile between friends?"

New Chum straightened his collar and regained his composure so quickly it made Detan dizzy. "It is the mark of poor decisions in my past," the steward said as he floated forward to take up the hem once more, studiously avoiding all eye contact.

"That's a Glasseater's mark," Tibs drawled, and Detan watched in amazement as the steward's shoulders drew in with shame. Detan scowled across the steward's bent back at Tibs. Curse him and his leave-the-lad-be nonsense, he'd been holding out on Detan – had known all along the lad was sporting criminal ink.

"It's crossed," the steward blurted, shifting his shirt aside so they could see the thick black line running through the snake's body. "I'm not associated with them anymore."

"Not a friendly bunch, Glasseaters," Detan spoke with

care, watching the muscles of the steward's back bunch with growing tension. "What do they control nowadays?" He looked at Tibs, brows raised. "Selling mudleaf?"

"And a handful of cardhouses," Tibs amended.

"Not a lot of work there for a nice young man such as yourself."

With a heady sigh the steward pulled the last stitch taut and rose, once more straightening his shirt and jacket. "My family–" He cleared his throat. "My family has long been in service as valets to bosses of a particular nature. I declined to continue that tradition."

"I see. Delicate information, that. Why share it with yours truly?"

The steward shifted his gaze pointedly to Detan's new pockets – pockets he'd been attempting to pick when he'd tipped the walkway with the noblebones on board. "It had occurred to me that you might be sympathetic to certain aspects of my past occupation. Sir."

Detan grinned and clapped once. "I knew I liked you! What's your name, New Chum?"

The lad actually flushed. "Enard Harwit, sir."

"Oh. Ah. I see. Shall we stick with New Chum, then?"

"That would be acceptable."

"Marvelous." Detan jumped down from the dais and clapped him on the back. "You've been a treasure! Here you are." He pressed some gold into his hand from the stash he'd taken out of Grandon's lady's pockets on the walkway. "Treat yourself, eh? And thank you for taking care of an old Honding."

"It's been an honor, sirs."

Detan could tell by the gleam in his eye the poor sod really meant that. He felt a twinge of guilt, then turned on his heel and hurried out.

•••

When he and Tibs were back on the solid rock of Aransa, the old rat gave him a sturdy punch in the arm.

"You're a mad bastard, Honding."

"Pits below!" He jumped and rubbed at the ache. "I was perfectly safe navigating the vents. I got a good look at them from above."

"It's not the vents I'm on about," Tibs said as he marched ahead, taking the lead back into the winding ways of the city. Detan reached up to ruff his hair in frustration, then shook himself and scurried to catch up. Dusk was descending over Aransa, the purple-mottled sky making Tibs little more than a silhouette before him. He stomped with every step he took, wiry fingers curled into knobby fists at his side. Detan slowed his steps and shoved his hands in his pockets, ducking his head down like a whipped dog.

"Is it the clothes?" Detan ventured, "Because, well, I figured that–"

"Nope, that ain't it either."

"Er. Well…"

Tibs stopped cold, pinning Detan down with his gaze as easily as he'd drive a nail through a board. "Dame Honding is going to hang you from your toenails, using your name with just anyone like that."

"Oh! That. Well, it is *my* name, Tibs."

"You had better write her a letter, sirra, before the rumors get back."

Detan sighed and sat down hard on the top of a low, stone fence, heedless of the dust that undoubtedly coated his backside now. "I suppose. Wouldn't want the old badger to worry, eh?"

"I suggest you do not address it to 'the old badger'."

"She'd laugh!"

"She'd fly right out here and beat you with her parasol."

Detan broke a small rock from the fence and hucked it half-heartedly at Tibs, who stepped nimbly around it. There was still a bit of stiff anger in his posture, a crease of annoyance around his eyes. Detan took a slow breath, and probed.

"Isn't just the name, is it?"

Tibs stared at some distant point over his shoulder. "Grandon needled your temper, and your first instinct was to reach for *it*. You losing control?"

It. His sel-scnse. Didn't need to say the words out loud – not on the street, anyway, not where they ran the risk of being overheard. Tibs's head tilted, his gaze skewing toward the edge of the city, toward the Smokestack, that great firemount from which Aransa mined all its selium gas. Whole lotta' sel in the city, and not just in ships. Walkways and jewelry, booze and fairycakes. All were laced with the stuff. He could feel its ubiquitous presence, if he let himself open his senses. A grey buzz in the back of his mind, like a swarming of locusts.

It'd be one thing, if he were just hiding his sensitivity to avoid working the mines or the ships. But his own flavor of sensitivity – deviant, as the empire and its whitecoats called it – could be just as destructive as that locust swarm, if he let his temper slip.

He slammed his senses shut, forcing mental barriers into place even as he plastered a goofy smirk onto his chapped lips and laid a hand against his collarbone as if deeply taken aback. "Me? Lose control over that worthless dune slide? Perish the thought!"

There was a smile back in the corner of Tibs's mouth, little more than a shriveled curl, but that was the best Detan could hope for.

"Now, let's go make use of these tickets, eh?" Detan ventured a grin.

"Tickets?"

"Check your interior breast pocket, my good man."

Tibs poked one finger into the fine linen, then hit him with another surly glare. They were fine tickets, he'd snuck a peek while changing. Thick paper with Thratia's name in big, embossed letters. There was no way Tibs could miss it.

"You expect me to believe you did all that for tickets?"

"Well, and the clothes. I did promise you a feast tonight."

Tibs scowled. "And is there a reason you couldn't have just filched them when you were busy rummaging through their pockets on the walkway?"

Detan pulled open the breast of his jacket to display the inner pocket where the ticket was stowed and gestured to the oversized bone button holding it shut.

"They were kept behind buttons, Tibs. Buttons! Sweet sands, but I hate buttons."

Tibs sighed as he turned to go. "You really are terrible at this," he muttered under his breath. Detan smiled to himself as he followed his old friend out into the deepening dark.

CHAPTER 9

Even from their narrow vantage, hunkered down under the shadow of a recessed doorway across the street, Detan could tell that Thratia was a woman of fine taste in parties and in guards. The whole of her compound was alight with oil lanterns slung from the eaves, hired hands keeping a careful eye on the flames as they wavered in the dry breeze. The great stone wall that encircled her abode had one side of its black iron gate propped open, three guards with seven facial scars between them keeping an eye on the ticket checkers and guests alike. It all would have been simple as sand in their new suits with their official tickets, if those rats weren't checking for family crests.

"Chances of admittance do not look good," Tibs said. "There's no way Thratia put the Honding family on the nice list."

"I'm aware of my familial peculiarity, old chum, but thanks for the chin-up."

"My job's to keep the ship buoyant, not your spirits."

"Oh? And where is this buoyant ship you speak of?"

Tibs went quiet, and that was all right by Detan's thinking. He was, after all, trying to concentrate, and the prattle of his erstwhile companion was most distracting. On the other side of the great wall, Detan's extended senses could just pick up hints of selium.

Thratia was a grand host, and she had provided floating dining tables for the favorites of her guests to dine upon. There appeared to be a few of the platforms meandering the garden, not yet burdened with the bustles and bootstraps of the noblebones, and he was having a pit of a time finagling one nearer. They remained stubbornly just beyond his natural reach. He could strain himself, but not without risking the fine edge of his control. He hissed through his teeth in frustration.

"Come on then, let us have a closer look at the festivities." Detan tried to keep his voice light, but he knew Tibs would see through to the strain of his annoyance.

Tibs's face soured, but he fell in step and slunk along beside him. Thratia hadn't made any effort at all to blend in with the local residents. Her compound was bigger than any normal house had a right to be, and as such she'd had to stick it in amongst the warehouses, claiming their superior infrastructure better suited her needs. Clever little witch. It also put her stronghold right in the heart of the city's commerce, and Detan would bet his own shorthairs there wasn't a deal that went down in the whole of Aransa she didn't have her spidery eyes on.

Clever or not, the neighborhood was a right peach to sneak around in. Great shadows extended from the eaves of overlarge buildings, and as the sun was long since set the only establishments with any life and light in them were those who served cheap, hard brews. And what would you care about a couple of men slinking around in the dark if you had a pitcher of liquid fire to yourself?

Detan allowed his senses to guide him, homing in on the one dining platform that was set further off from the others. He only stepped in a foul puddle once.

Twice.

"Here's the place," Detan said as he shook out a disturbingly damp pant leg.

It was a good spot, generally speaking, in that it was well shadowed and smelled of piss in the way only a secretive alley can. It was particularly good for him, because hovering on the other side of that thick stone wall was the object of his sensory affection. It occurred to him then, that even if he could get the thing to come up to them, they had no way of getting up to the top of the wall to meet it. He could bring it back down the other side to meet them, but that may just push his luck a tad too far.

"Huh." He scowled at the wall, willing a solution to present itself.

Tibs cleared his throat. "Is sirra, perhaps, thinking we would have better luck if we were to climb the ladder there and join those few revelers on the roof of this establishment?"

Detan was more than a little abashed to find the roof Tibs indicated was just behind them. Its top was aglow with wavering beeswax light – the cheapest candles to be had on the Scorched – and a dozen or so malformed shadows danced and sang at the night. Not *to* the night. No, they were definitely singing *at* it. The aroma of cheap beer wafted down, along with another sickeningly familiar bouquet.

He then realized why the alley smelled of piss.

Detan grabbed Tibs's arm and hauled him out of the way just before they would have been anointed, and heard wild laughter from above.

"Hey, you two!"

Detan tipped his head up for a look, fearing another downpour, but it was only a face stuck over the edge. "Hullo!" Detan called.

"Got any beer?"

"We've got money!"

"That buys beer! Come on up!"

Detan scrambled up the ladder, Tibs quick on his heels. The rooftop party was stuffed with the type of folk Thratia might have hired to guard her doors or watch the lamps, but clearly their services had not been needed this night. The young man who'd called them up staggered over and shoved out a hand, snapping his fingers. "We don't take paper tickets here, you hear?"

"Splendid!" Detan dropped a full silver grain into the man's hand.

He squinted at it.

"This real?"

"Yup."

"Whoo! Hey, guys! We're going to Milky's tonight!"

A cheer went up, but it wasn't for Detan, it was for Milky's. Which he supposed was well deserved, as he had yet to meet a harder working bunch of girls. With the revelers' time committed for their immediate future, Detan grabbed Tibs's arm and dragged him to the edge of the roof nearest the wall.

From this new perch, he could make out the extravagant garden Thratia kept with the extra water rations she no doubt paid an exorbitant sum for, and he cursed her for having the forethought to plant a variety of thick-canopied trees just on the other side of her long wall.

"It seems Thratia was aware of this fortuitous proximity, old chum."

"It does indeed."

"No matter. Allow me to concentrate."

He closed his eyes, ignoring the reek wafting up from the alley and the jeering of the revelers. He expanded his senses just to the selium in the immediate area, and found his floating dining station with ease. He nudged it, just a touch, to see if anyone had already come aboard, and found it delightfully without passengers.

"Uh, sirra…"

"Let me concentrate."

Emboldened, he tipped the platform so that anything not anchored would slide off, and was rewarded with the platform's sudden but invigorating lift. He subdued it, listening for a cry of alarm, but heard none.

Tibs tugged on his sleeve, and he swore as he nearly lost control of the platform. He shook the old lizard off and scowled into the dark, "Keep your pants on, old fool."

Guessing the area to be empty for the time being, he allowed the platform to drift upward until it rested just beneath the treetops and then leveled it with care. He opened his eyes and squinted into the brush.

There, he could see it. A bit of yellow-painted wood peeking between the branches.

He could also feel something rather sharp pressed against the small of his back.

"Seems to us." Beer-laden breath wafted over Detan's shoulder. "That men in such fancy clothes would have more than one silver grain. Eh lads?"

A grumble of consent was raised behind him, a few hoots thrown in for good measure. With his hands up to show they were empty, Detan turned around very, very slowly. It was no less unsettling to have a knife pointed at your front than to have it sneak up behind you. He tried an affable grin. The young man appeared rather unimpressed.

"Hand it over."

Detan edged back a step, sweat dampening his back while he strained to hold the platform and keep his guts in his belly. "Now, now, we're all reasonable gentlemen here, and I've got it ready, Tibs."

"Don't you fucking talk to him! Hand it over!"

"'Bout time," Tibs said.

He grabbed the front of Detan's shirt and shoved.

For a moment, he thought this was the best idea Tibs'd ever had. He arced backward, huffing in fresh air while his body floated free in the endless sky. To be without tether, even without a selium craft, was beyond his imagination.

He was quickly reminded why he didn't do this kind of thing very often.

The treetops rushed up to meet him, slapping his cheeks and twisting his limbs. He wanted to cry out, but all the air whooshed from his lungs as he thunked into the selium-floated platform. In the moment of impact he almost released his hold on the craft, but pain kept him sharp and he held on.

Tibs landed beside him with a grunt, looking quite a bit better for having suffered the same experience. Detan rolled to his back with a groan and glared up at him.

"How'd you avoid the branches, Tibs?"

"I let you go first."

Tibs gave him a hand up, and Detan grinned as he gave him a playful slug in the shoulder. Crafty bastard.

Refocusing his sel-sense, he forced the platform down, drifting lazily toward ground. As they drew closer, he could make out patterns in the rocks below, different colors of stones raked with care. Well, except for the spot where he'd dumped the platform's table and other accoutrements. Broken wood marred the design, twisting what he thought might have been a fish into some sort of nightmare creature.

When he heard guards start to raise the alarm nearby, he let his control drop and nearly let his stomach slip his lips as the whole thing clattered to the ground faster than he'd expected. Must have damaged one of the buoyancy sacks in the process, he thought, as very angry men with very long swords came rushing up.

Still better than being knifed in the gut by a petty thief.

"I say!" He leapt to his feet and shook leaves from his hair, hiding a grimace as pain lanced through his growing collection of bruises. "What sort of deathtrap is this? Can't a man have a drink with his friend without fearing mutilation? By the pits!" He swung around and hauled Tibs to his feet. "Get these blasted things fixed, you swine, or I'll report this!"

The guards exchanged uneasy glances. Detan finished brushing off his stolen suit and strode right through their line as if they bothered him not a whit in all the world. In truth, his skin was crawling with the proximity of so much fine, sharp steel, but they responded to his confidence with rushed apology.

Once safely away from the guards and the wrecked platform they paused, breathed deep, then shook themselves and stood up a little straighter.

"That was a might close, sirra."

"I felt the press myself. Shall we?"

He gestured toward the wide open doors to Thratia's compound, and they sauntered inside.

CHAPTER 10

Detan found himself stuck in a herd of uppercrust, all clumped up toward the entrance and goggling at the decorations. He didn't mind a bit. Thratia had really put her back into it, and he wondered just how much this was about raising support and how much it was about flaunting her wealth and connections. Probably the two motives were so finely intertwined the distinction was irrelevant.

The lanterns inside were covered with thick paper, cut-outs in the shapes of those family crests which supported her throwing shadows over the partygoers. The hard stone floor thrummed with the pounding of hundreds of dancing feet and deep-throated drums. His skin prickled with the nearness of so much human energy. Somehow, she'd managed to import great ropes of green vines with crisp white blossoms and had strung them all around the railing of the second-story balcony which looked over the dance floor below.

Tibs whistled low. "Thistle blossom, those are." He gestured to the vines. "Damn brave of her to trot those

out, tastiest treat in the world to selium-addicted insects.
Heard a rumor there was a hive of sel bees round here,
dangerous to tempt 'em."

"Thank you for your entomological insight, but I'm
rather more interested in the disposition of the crowd
than the native vermin."

"There's a difference?" Tibs said as the band struck
up a song Detan'd never heard of. He rose to his toes
and glanced about, looking for the musicians. He found
them on a sel-supported stage, drifting over the dancers'
heads. Every time they passed above, the partygoers
threw their arms into the air and cheered. Detan's mouth
hung open.

He hadn't even realized there were this many
noblebones in Aransa. He swept his gaze over the crowd,
estimating, and decided he was right. There was no way
every last body here tonight was from the privileged lot.
That meant a good chunk of them were the top dogs of
the downcrust. Thratia was *not* messing about here. She
wanted every soul she could get on her side.

"Where to?" Tibs called over the thump of drums.

"Er." He tried to get a better look at the crowd, but
the band was frenzied enough to keep them moving
in constant flux. Who was he looking for, anyway? He
wanted to get eyes on Thratia's flagship, not her bosom
companions. What he needed now was a solid lay of the
land, something he could get his teeth into.

"Let's go up," he yelled.

They hurried up the steps, squeezing past people
who were pressed together in the dark, near-privacy
of the stairwell. By the time they reached the balcony,
the band had transitioned into a slower tune and the
dancers swirled at a less nauseating pace. They crowded
up against the balcony rail and Detan scanned the press,

looking for the lady of the hour, but couldn't spot her amongst the revelry.

"Has it occurred to you, Tibs, that this is all a bit overkill for the wooing of one city?"

"Seems the ex-commodore wants to prove she can take a city through legal channels."

Detan frowned at that, something about it not quite sitting right in his mind. "Think she's courting the empire? Angling to get back into their good graces?"

"Can't imagine a woman like her would be satisfied with exile." Tibs waved a hand through the air as he spoke as if outlining a celebratory banner. "Commodore Ganal's Triumphant Return."

"Charming," Detan drawled and turned back toward the interior of the balcony, and nearly jumped out of his skin at a tap on his shoulder.

"Detan Honding."

He spun around at the familiar voice, laced with honey-venom, and beamed into the watch captain's scowling face.

"Hullo, Ripka."

"Captain," she corrected. "Where's your better half?"

"Tibs is right–" The little devil had slunk off somewhere, leaving him alone with the law. "That rat."

"I only see one rat here." She snorted her derision, and Detan drew his head back at the sharp bite of wine that laced her breath. He waved the cloud away and scowled, scarcely resisting the urge to chastise her for getting drunk while they were working together.

"I thought you said I was a snake," he muttered.

Her brows creased in mild annoyance, or confusion, he couldn't really tell the difference when it came to her. "What? Don't be stupid, Honding, if you can at all help it."

He leaned forward and dropped his voice down to a sand-whisper. "Is it wise for us to be seen chatting in public like this?"

"I'd rather not chat with you at all. Just what are you doing back in Aransa?"

That was... odd. Detan frowned, squinting at Ripka's face. With timid care he extended his senses, feeling for the presence of selium about her. It was there, but faint, hardly worth remarking on, and his abilities were so unreliable that he could just as easily be picking up on the phantom of Thratia's ship – or any other source of selium nearby. Pinpointing tiny caches of the stuff had never been his specialty.

He tried to conjure up the memory of the way he'd seen her in the morning. Sandy hair pulled back? Yep. Grey eyes looking mighty pissed? Still got 'em. Forehead good for headbutting? Flat and affirmative. Had she had those freckles this morning?

Nope.

He poked her in the face. Nothing changed, save her expression getting darker.

"Have you lost your mind, Honding?"

Detan choked on a laugh. "No more than usual. Fancy a drink?"

"Just stay out of trouble. I have enough worries without you getting tangled up in things."

"So I've heard."

She stepped close enough for him to scent the cactus-flower extract she wore, mingled with the greasy tinge of her blade oil, and narrowed her eyes. "What have you heard?"

"Oh, nothing. Nothing at all." He gave her his winning smile, and even this Ripka seemed to hate it, which was something of a relief. "Just old nanny-gossip, you know the type. Oh, look, there's Tibal! Tibs! Tibs old chum!"

He waved at him, but Tibs was busy chatting with a rather lovely woman in a low-backed dress. She had her back to Detan's view, and Tibs shot him a glower over her shoulder. He didn't seem too pleased with the lady's company, but Detan figured anything would be a sight more pleasant than getting pinned down by Ripka Leshe. The real one, at any rate.

"Pleasure to see you again, watch captain. Have a good evening! Enjoy the party!"

He wiggled away from under her stern eye, feeling it bore a hole through him as he sauntered with affected nonchalance toward Tibs. He felt those eyes peel away and slumped with relief. He needed more time to work out an angle before he could let the real Ripka know that they were plotting to steal Thratia's ship together. Doppels really knew how to throw a spanner in the works.

A few steps away from Tibs, and that's when it hit him. The tall woman who was wagging in Tibs's ear was the Lady Halva Erst. Detan recalled, with mounting horror, the iron straight edge of her back and worse, the cutting barbs that often left her lips. No wonder poor Tibs looked so sour-faced.

Three years. He couldn't believe it'd already been three years since he last saw the stern side of her jaw, lifted in hatred as he skimped out at their engagement party. It had been regretful that matters were forced to progress to that point, but Detan had needed a foot-in at the Erst estate to pinch old Daddy Erst's atlas. A singular work, that atlas.

Finest he'd ever used, and his aunt couldn't have been cheerier when he gave it to her for her birthday. She did, after all, loathe the Ersts and all they stood for. Which he found odd, considering they were just a family of sel diviners, but he wasn't fool enough to ever question his auntie's taste.

Tibs seemed to be doing a good job of extricating himself from the lady. He had made it damned near to the drink table, and Detan well knew the fair lady couldn't stomach being in the presence of a drunk. Realizing he was not at this party to socialize, he tipped his hat in apology to Tibs and slunk off toward the back of the balcony in search of the airship's moorings. He was, after all, a professional. And there was work to be done.

CHAPTER 11

Ripka went in search of another drink. She was not technically on duty tonight, this was a personal appearance, and yet she still felt strange pouring herself out a deep red draught while wearing her blues. Oh, to the pits with it.

She let the mulled almond flavor wash down her throat until the glass was empty. Maybe, if she were drunk enough, then she could do as Banch suggested and force some answers out of the woman they'd captured at the warehouse. That damned smuggler had proven taciturn at best, not even giving up her name.

Without the information rattling around in that woman's walled-off mind, there was no way to say for certain who those weapons were for, or where they were coming from. The papers had been empty of house seals, signatures carefully obscured, and the honey liqueur could only be traced back to the stone wall of the Mercer's Collective. None of them were willing to throw their fellows to the Watch, lest it start a chain reaction, and Ripka couldn't even be sure that the owner of those bottles knew of the deadly cargo hidden beneath them.

Ripka snorted to herself. She'd done her fair share of damage in a fighting ring, but if she ever got drunk enough to be party to torture, she'd more likely fall flat on her face the moment she stepped in the woman's cell. At least they still had the sensitive man. He was holding out, but he sweated so much every time Ripka interrogated him they had to supply him with a change of clothes after each encounter. It was, she hoped, only a matter of time.

At least she'd managed to scour that honey-crap out of her hair.

With a sigh, she reached for the bottle again, and found Tibal handing it to her. "Looks like you be needin' this, captain."

She set her glass down a touch too fast and had to grab at it to keep it from tipping over. "I'm quite finished Tibal, thank you."

"Suit yourself."

Her nose wrinkled with distaste as he took a draw straight from the bottle. At least he looked cleaner than the last time she had seen him, though whatever ablutions he'd attempted for the party had failed to pry the axle grease from his fingernails. "Neither of you should be here, you know."

"Got nowhere else to be at the present. What about yourself? You don't strike me as the fete-going type, and Thratia's got enough muscle here that she doesn't need the Watch. Surely you've got your own business to be about."

Her jaw clenched, clamping down words too sharp and raw to let loose. Phantoms of her own little apartment rose in her mind, the too-clean living room and the spotless hearth, its cookstone as fresh as the day she'd bought it. The only foodstuff she owned was a bottle of wine, as dark as the one Tibal drew from now.

"Just why do you hang around with that lout, anyway?" she said, forcing her voice to aloofness, though that proved difficult when her lips felt thick and numb. Damn Thratia and her unwatered wine. Or just damn Thratia all together. "He's a liar and a thief, a bad man any way you look at him. You have talent, Tibal, you're a damn fine mechanic and a dutiful soul. I remember offering you a job, once–"

"Answer's no, captain. I got a job."

"What you do is not a job, it's survival."

"All jobs are about surviving, just on different levels. Like the city here." He shrugged and drank deep. "Look now, I owe a great deal to that man and I won't have you poison my mind against him. You're better than that."

She crossed her arms and tried to look stern, but the flush of wine was in her cheeks and she knew she just looked surly. "And just what is it that you owe him? Did he lock you into some sort of commitment?"

Tibal took another draw and then set the bottle down with care. He wiped his mouth on the back of his hand and his hand on his trouser leg, his eyes narrowed and sharp as flint. She was too tired to deal with any of this tonight. The doppel was out there still. Or worse, in here. She didn't need Detan and his partner... manservant... mechanic? What *was* he? No matter, she didn't need them demanding her attention.

"You fight in the war, captain? I did."

She stiffened, not liking the direction this was headed. "No. Too young. I didn't know you served," she said, affecting politeness. She itched to abandon Thratia's showboating and get back to the streets. Even digging through mounds of files in search of a clue about the warehouse, or the doppel, would be more relaxing than this farce.

"I'm a grown man of Valathea, captain, 'course I served. Damned continent didn't stay Valathean property by the grace of the blue skies, now did it? I didn't have the favor of youth at the time. Joined with Valathea, as I was descended from them. Strange, don't you think? My family hasn't used Valathean names for the last three generations and still I think myself a part of them. I'm light as a Catari." He held out an arm to the shadow-splintered light, and Ripka bit her tongue. He looked dark as wet sand to her, dark as most Valatheans. Dark as her. "Got a name like a Catari. But I don't think of myself as such.

"Anyway. We cleaned them out, pushed 'em back into the sel-barren reaches of the Scorched. I worked on the ships, then, didn't see any real fighting myself. Wouldn't know what to do with the sharp end of a saber, but I could keep the killing machines going. Keep 'em raining fire from above, turning good sand to glass." He cleared his throat, glanced around and lowered his voice.

"You know what I brought back from all that?"

Ripka licked her lips, tasting the specter of wine there, wishing her pride would let her grab for the bottle again. Valathea's war against the native uprising had happened on the fringe of her life. She'd seen Catari refugees filtering through the Brown Wash as a girl. Wretched, beige-skinned exiles who covered themselves head to toe in brown cloth to keep the glare of the sun off. They'd never stayed long, always moving on, deeper into the desert, retreating from the resources that had once been their birthright. Rolled under the advance of Valathea.

Without the Scorched's selium mines to keep airships moving, the empire's commerce would grind to a halt, stymied by the unsteady seas that surrounded the imperial archipelago. It was just too bad for the Catari they happened to be here first.

"I can't imagine," she said, not able to help the softening of her voice. Her father had served. He hadn't come back the same, either. Hadn't stayed home long, once he got back, though she'd been too young to understand it at the time.

"I got a temper like a lit forge, when I'm struck just right. A vicious streak dark as the sea. You ever meet someone like that?"

"Of course, I'm a watcher. I see uncontrollable tempers all the time. I haven't known you long, Tibal, but that's not you. Those rabid souls are completely out of control, while you're one of the calmest folk I've ever met."

"You can thank Detan for that."

Her face must have given her away, because he laughed. "Look," he said, "I know it doesn't seem right, but it's the truth. Fact is, Detan came 'round my steading near on six years ago now looking for a light tune-up for his flier. Got it done all right, but in the meantime the old man who owned the shop I was working at said something I didn't like and I lost it – I just... I lost it. Felt like I was back in the Catari war, and everything was fire, so it didn't matter what burned. I think I *woulda'* killed him, had Detan not come back when he did. He pulled us apart and sat me down. Tole me he knew what it was like, to walk that line of fire, that he could help. So I went with him. And he was right, captain, it has helped. Just so long as we keep moving, it helps."

He looked up then, and she followed his gaze to see Detan staring right at them from across the room. No, it wasn't them he was staring at, it was just Tibal. As she observed, they locked eyes and Detan raised his brows.

Tibal gave a little nod and the other man grinned, going back to whatever mischief he was up to.

"You see?" he said. "We check in on each other like that. If one of us is starting to lose it we scramble, no matter what we're into at the time."

"You're telling me that bumbling idiot has a fearful temper too? Sweet sands, he really should be locked up."

"Naw, not like mine. He got a handle on his own self, but I needed his help to get a handle on mine. If I'm a lit forge, he's the slow burn of the desert, and if either of us is a bad man, captain, it's me."

Something foul clicked into place in Ripka's mind, sharp and insistent even through the fog of alcohol. "You met him after the accident on his line, the one that burned half the sel pipes at Hond Steading, didn't you? His temper have something to do with that accident?"

Tibal's nostrils flared. "No." The word was snapped off, defensive, and she filed that reaction away to ruminate upon later. He refilled her drink without asking, and she downed it in one.

"You two are into something, aren't you?" she asked to cover how unsettled she felt.

"Don't pay a man to stay still, captain."

He winked and shuffled off before she could press him, leaving her alone with the bottle and her thoughts. No one bothered to come up to her. Not here. Not in her blue coat with its polished brass buttons.

She sat her glass down, and picked up the bottle.

CHAPTER 12

Tibs, that old devil, had worked his way clear of the Lady Erst just in time to occupy Ripka. With all the malignant eyes of the house off him for the time being, Detan slunk along the balcony, scouting the entrance to the airship's dock. When he found it, he wondered why he'd bothered with any semblance of stealth at all.

Thratia had the great double doors to her airdock thrown wide open. A couple of rough looking lads, veneered for the evening in butler's black, lingered near the entrance, checking the tickets of everyone who passed through. Detan slipped Grandon's ticket from Grandon's pocket and squinted down at the elaborate script. It had the round bastard's name on it.

He shoved it under his shirt, rubbed it against the sweat of his back, then crumpled it and stuffed it back in his pocket. Affecting a drunken stagger, he sauntered forward.

"Your ticket, sir."

"Oh!" He swayed and patted his breast pockets, then down to his hips. Fumbling, searching, his cheeks flushed as he offered the guard an apologetic smile. "So sorry, I know it's here somewhere... Ah!" He produced the wadded ticket, the fine paper crumpled tight enough to fit into his fist.

The guard took it and gingerly unfolded it, smoothing the battered mess against his thigh to work out some of the wrinkles. It didn't do any good. While the tickets themselves were block-pressed, the names had been scribed in by hand. Cheap ink, and the guard squinted down at a smudge where Grandon's name had been.

The guard glared at it, as if he could threaten the letters into making sense. Eventually, he just sighed. "Go ahead."

Detan took his ticket back and bowed his thanks before shuffling through the door on wobbly feet. He made sure he was well out of eyesight before straightening up again.

The dance floor was the central attraction for the time being, so he found the airship's mooring bay thin on visitors. This side of the compound opened up to the night air, and what he had glimpsed from the ferry to the Salt Baths resolved itself into grandeur. He stood on a u-shaped balcony, hanging out over the empty air high above the city. The balcony wrapped itself around the airship, the great behemoth held steady by thick ropes reaching from its deck to tie-points all along the edge of the dock.

A long gangway extended from the ship's deck to the dock, lamp-lit and inviting. He ascended, unable to help a little tremble of excitement rippling over his skin.

It was unlike any ship he'd ever had the pleasure of setting his boots on before. Sure, he'd seen some mighty fine vessels pass through nearby airspace. Vessels bigger, vessels more ornately adorned. But this craft, this ship Thratia had named *Larkspur* was, to his mind, the perfect ship. She was streamlined, her body the shape and size of the old sailing ships that had first brought the Hondings across the seas to the Scorched. The only mars to its clean lines were the subtle, accordion protrusions of stabilizing wings. Folded in for now, they were easy to overlook.

He brushed a hand along the fine-grained wood of the railing, marveling at the simple fact that he couldn't place the species of tree. Detan knelt, gathered up a length from a coil of silk-soft rope, tugged on it and found it stronger than any normal rope had a right to be. This was new. This ship was something special.

"It's funny, but I don't recall placing any Hondings on my guest list."

Detan startled from his contemplation of the fine materials and jerked upright. He turned to find Thratia at his side, close enough to gut him if she felt inclined. Detan swallowed. One never knew just where Thratia's inclinations lay.

She was a dangerous woman, this exiled commodore of Valathea, yet she looked positively delicate in the long linen skirts of her fellow desert creatures, her hair tied up with ornamental jewels. But Detan saw the sharpened points of her jewel pins, the long slit of her skirt under which she wore martial tights and leather boots in place of silken slippers. Thratia stood with her hands clasped behind her back, shoulders straight and squared. Though Valathean stock ran dark by nature, Thratia's flesh was deep as the night. She was all muscle and teeth, a fiercely beautiful creature, and Detan admired her in the same way he'd admire a rockcat getting ready to tear his face off.

"Commodore Throatslitter," he said and snapped a salute.

She grinned. It was not a pleasant experience. "I stopped being a commodore the moment I set sail for the Scorched."

"And the Throatslitter?"

She shrugged. "We all do what we must to thrive."

"And what makes you thrive, Thratia?"

Her smile was coy as she took a step toward him. He held his ground, though he felt he'd be considerably more comfortable if he were to leap from the edge of the ship.

"You digress and distract, Honding. You will tell me why you are here, and how."

He sighed. There was just no dissembling with a woman like that. "My flier's sacks tore on my way over the Fireline, then I heard about your lovely ship and decided to have a look-see." He patted the handrail. "I'm glad I did, she's beautiful."

"Yes, she is." Thratia cast a loving eye over the whole of her craft. "But you did not tell me the how of it."

"Oh, well." He cleared his throat. "I fell over your garden wall."

She laughed, and it was worse than her grinning. "You're an entertaining man, but you come with your own reputation. If I find you near my ship again I will regretfully decide that your continued existence is no longer conducive to my ability to thrive. Understood?"

"Funny, you still talk like a commodore."

She waved a dismissive hand. "You are but a small distraction, Lord Honding, and I use small things as stepping stones to greater glories. No matter if they are crushed beneath my heel in the process."

Detan was starting to wish he was better at keeping his mouth shut when a commotion at the entrance drew Thratia's attention away. There was Ripka, pits bless her, striding across the walkway with two young lads in their official blues flanking her. Thratia's lip curled and she spat over the railing of the ship. Somehow, she managed to make even spitting look delicate and controlled.

While Thratia and Ripka locked eyes and lifted chins, Detan gave a surreptitious kick to the coil of rope tied to the railing. It slithered off without drawing notice. Another option for him to draw upon later.

"Watch Captain Leshe, this is a surprise." Thratia's tone made it clear it wasn't a pleasant one. Detan was just working out how best to drift back and escape the notice of either of those two dirt devils when damned Ripka pointed a finger straight at him.

"Pardon the interruption, Thratia, but I am obliged to take that man into custody."

"So soon?" The commodore smirked. "He's only been in town a day."

A chill prickled Detan's back – how did Thratia know that?

"Apparently that was all the time he needed to get into trouble. Come with me please, Honding."

Detan glanced between Ripka, Thratia, and back again. Thratia seemed amused, and Ripka just a touch bored, which was really insulting. "Hey, now, hold on a tick, what is it I've done?"

"We'll discuss your charges at the station."

The watchers strode up the gangplank. He had half a mind to make a run for it, to leap into the abyss and trust to his luck, or just bolt straight through them. Neither option was likely to result in him coming through with all his bits intact. So he acquiesced, allowing his wrists to be bound behind his back. No burlap sack over the head this time, which he took as a good sign.

"Take him through the servant's exit, please. I'd

rather not have him paraded through the celebration."
Thratia waved her hand toward the opposite side of the
dock where a narrow door stood without a single lantern
nearby to light it.

"Not wasting oil on the servants, eh?" Detan said.

"They function fine without it. I trust you won't trip."
She smiled, patted him on the cheek with one chilled
palm, and sauntered back across the deck to entertain
her guests.

"Easy now," one of the watchers said as he grabbed
Detan's shoulder and steered him back down the
gangplank.

"I'm always easy," he quipped, but his heart wasn't
in it.

The way Ripka moved wasn't right. Sure, she carried
herself with the sort of self-assured confidence only a
uniform could muster, but there was something relaxed
about it. Something swaying. Ripka normally had the
body language of a cave bear: guarded, wary, but still
certain she was the biggest bad in the room. A sort of
lock-step manner.

This Ripka, who strolled along beside him with her
freckled chin tipped up and a smile plastered on her face
as if she knew a joke no one else did, was too smooth.
Too sure. Entirely too likable. This Ripka, he decided,
was not Ripka. He kept his trap shut until they had made
their way down the narrow stairs, past a half-drunk set
of guards playing ten tiles, and out into the anonymizing
bustle of the city.

He leaned close, catching the scent of spiced vanilla
oil in her hair, and grinned to himself. The real Ripka,
who'd cornered him on the balcony, had been wearing
cactus flower. "So, what's your name?" he whispered.

She startled, just a touch, drawing her head back in

surprise as she looked down her borrowed nose at him. "I am Watch Captain Leshe. Please try to remember it."

"Really?"

She smiled with all her teeth. "Really."

The so-called watch captain drifted to the back of the group, leaving behind nothing but the memory of her scent, and let her clueless companions in blue haul him along to the station house. They found him a nice cell, with mud-daub walls and a big wooden door that made a satisfying clang when they shut it on him. There wasn't a light in his room, or a window to the outdoors, just a little portal cut in the door with iron bars shot through it. He leaned against it, pressing his face to the bars to get a better look at his surroundings. It was all in darkness, only a smudge of light from the guard's lamp breaking up the shadows.

"Do you need anything, captain?" a watcher asked.

"No, thank you," not-Ripka said to the men he could no longer see. "I will take matters from here."

There was some shuffling, an exchange of paperwork, and then the hall door shut and they were alone. A pair of old oil lamps kept the room beyond his cell lit, and though his view was limited he could make out the thick wooden desk both lamps rested on. Not-Ripka crossed to it and sat on the edge to face him, her arms folded.

"So," he drawled as he let his hands hang out between the bars, "what's your name?"

She smiled. "What gave it away?"

"Your legs are too long."

"Are you a connoisseur of the watch captain's legs?"

"I'm a connoisseur of all ladies' legs. But I wonder – you took a mighty risk traipsing into Thratia's fete like that. Ripka could've been just around any corner at any moment. What if her watchers catch you two in the same room? The same building?"

A sly smile graced the doppel's lips as she ran her fingers along the lapel of her blue uniform. "I've made arrangements that allow me to know where she is at any given moment. I'm shocked you haven't noticed. Your lack of diligence does not invest me with confidence, but I suppose some things can't be helped."

"Oh, it's my diligence you're worried about? Miss, you should spend some more time worrying about Ripka's. That's a thornbrush you're trifling with."

"Miss?" She allowed her voice to shift, to grow tired and aged. Showing off, no doubt. Detan wondered how long it'd been since she'd an audience for her talents. In her new gruff voice, she shifted the tones down to be distinctly masculine. "You assume too much. I could be male for all you know, or old and withered."

"Sel can't hide the way you move, lady, or the way you smile. I've spent a long time watching people. The way they tip their heads when they're curious, or flatten their lips when they're frustrated. I know every eye twinkle and every lip curl. You're good, but now that I know what I'm looking for, well, you can never be that good. The real question I have for you, doppel, is when am I going to get some food in here?"

"Illusionist," she snapped the word off, bringing Detan's eyebrows up. Touchy girl, when it came to her talents. He could work with that.

"Fine, fine, you keep the old traditions, eh? One of the last holdouts, I would think. Most of the old sel workers are dead to bonewither or in diaspora in the south. But here you are, trotting out Catari words like they're the common vernacular. Now why is that?"

"Just because the words are old doesn't mean they're wrong. It was your people who insisted on learning them, after all, and I do mean *your* people."

He grimaced and tipped his head down to study all the little cracks in his door. "Wasn't me on that expedition, I can't be blamed for what's passed."

"But you can be for perpetuating it."

"Illusionist, then. Fine. Makes no difference to me."

"It should."

"Well, it doesn't. And what do you want with me, anyway? I'm a Honding, remember, and you've made it clear as a calm sky you're not a fan of us founders."

"Founders?" She snorted. "I don't have the time to correct what's wrong with that notion. And what I want, Honding, is assurance that you're going to do what I paid you for."

"Paid for with stolen silver."

"You're the last person I'd think would quibble about a bit of pinched grain."

"True." He picked his head up. "But why do you want me for it? You can't even fly the thing yourself, and there have to be easier ways out of the city if it's the law you're running from."

She laughed a little, shaking her head. "I'm not running from anything. And that ship is perfectly suited for single-pilot flight, if that pilot is an illusionist."

That startled him. He frowned at her, extending his senses. His knowledge of the way the doppels worked their illusions was rough at best. He knew any color could be pulled out of selium with careful manipulation, that furrows could be filled in and bulbous bits sculpted, but he was shocked to feel the impossibly thin layer of sel the doppel had coating her skin.

In his mind's eye, he could just see the topography of her real features beneath the veneer, an indistinct muddling under the fine manipulations of the sel. He came back to himself, panting.

"My control is complete, as you can see for yourself."

"How..."

She shrugged. "It is natural for me. Manipulating the sel bladders of a ship is not such a difficult thing in comparison."

"Fine, you can fly it. Marvelous for you, I'm sure, but that still doesn't mean I'm willing to get my head lopped off for your trouble."

"Here's the deal, Honding. I'm not going to threaten you, I just want you to watch. Carefully."

She stepped away from the desk and pulled a slender hand mirror from her pocket. She peered at herself, then her eyes looked a touch glassy and her face began to change. Detan scowled, struggling to see past the obscuring bars on his window and the eclipsing mirror.

Giving up on regular sight, he extended his sel-sense and focused on her minute movements, manipulations on a scale so small he was certain he could not see the effect with the naked eye.

Curious, he extended his own control of the substance and tried to pry a piece of it loose. She made a small grunting noise, annoyance, but nothing budged. She had mastered the selium she commanded, it was not for him to manipulate.

Her face seemed to lift off, the mask floating just before her real skin. He could not see her through it, and he gritted his teeth in frustration. As he watched, the elements rearranged themselves. Stretching, compressing, separating and joining at different angles. The hues changed. Now deeper, now bright, and when she pulled the mask taut against her skin he found himself looking straight into the eyes of Tibal.

"Now that's... That's just not right."

Tibal's face, Ripka's body. The stuff of nightmares. He shuddered.

"You understand? I will see him walk the Black, just to spite you, if you do not do this thing for me."

"Fine, yes, all right. Just please put the pretty face back on. Pits, woman, you have no idea what you've just done to my dreamscape."

Tibal-Ripka rolled its eyes and the sel mask pushed away from it again. Hovering, reshaping, coming to settle back in an arrangement he was perversely glad to see.

"Better."

"I will hear your plan now."

He blinked, and laughed. "Plan? I don't make plans. I allow for options."

"Fine, what are your options?"

"Not likely, lady. You got me on the leash to steal the *Larkspur*, fine. But how I go about doing it is my own business. If I need your assistance, I'll need a way to contact you."

"Not going to happen. You do this without my hand in it, or not at all. I have other things worth doing for the moment. This is why I hired you, Honding. I suggest you live up to your name."

She turned and snuffed one of the lamps, picked up the other one.

"You're going to leave me here?"

"Oh yes. The watch captain needs a reminder of my reach. Enjoy your night."

She strode from the room, taking the lamp with her, and when the door clinked behind her Detan dropped his forehead against the metal bars. He did it again, harder, just for good measure. He really wished he'd eaten at Thratia's.

CHAPTER 13

The doors to the station house were opened as the sun climbed over Aransa, inviting the citizens inside to file their complaints and concerns. A long line had already formed, and many of them Ripka picked out as sympathizers of Thratia come to put in a good word for the would-be warden in an official manner.

Ripka grimaced and slowed her pace. She was in no mood to plaster on fake smiles for the sake of diplomacy. "Let's go around back."

Banch heaved a relieved sigh and they skirted the sprawling building, coming up to the locked door through which prisoners cleared of their wrongdoings were spewed back into the city. Ripka produced the key and led Banch into a dark hallway. It was cool within, the yellowstone still holding onto the chill of night, and the cooking aromas of early morning Aransa had yet to penetrate. Ripka took a deep breath, felt some of the tension ease out of her temples.

They slogged past dozens of wood and iron doors, ignoring the plaintive voices behind them. Banch peeled away from her at the end of the hall, going to check his new notices, while Ripka followed the same weary path she did every morning to check on the late-night intakes. Drunks and domestic disturbers, mostly. The average scum of any city, skimmed from the top for the evening and dispersed back into the system the next morning.

She found Taellen on a stool beside the drunks' communal cell, his head lolling and his eyes forced wide as he fought off sleep.

"Morning, watcher," she said, hiding her smile as he jerked upright and nearly kicked over his stool.

"Captain! I, uh, didn't hear you come in." Taellen straightened his skewed seat and pulled the loose flaps of his coat tight.

"That's all right," she said, and resisted the urge to tell him not to worry – that all of them had dozed off watching the night holds at least once. She'd leave that information for his colleagues to share when they were ready to accept him fully as one of their number. "Any standouts?"

He handed her a stack of files with far more care than was necessary and gave her a tight, albeit belated, salute. "Nothing too out of the ordinary. More than usual, due to Commodore Ganal's party. The guards down at Milky's had a rough night, seemed the clients were more interested in fighting than fucking." A sunset spectrum of embarrassment painted Taellen's cheeks. "I mean, uh, they were a rowdy lot. Ma'am. Uh. Sir."

Ripka hid her grin behind an opened folder. "Sir is appropriate, watcher. And as for Thratia, remember she carries no title here. She is no longer a commodore."

While Taellen stammered an apology she took the intake sheets to a nearby desk, dipped a pen, and began the wrist-aching process of signing off on each morning release. If

she got them all out before the eighth mark of the morning,
the Watch wouldn't be obliged to supply their breakfast.

Rabble released, she abandoned Taellen to the task of
ushering them back to the street and turned toward the
station's meager break room. There she found a cup of
thick black tea fresh from Mercer Agert's purloined ship
awaiting her, curls of steam wafting from the anise-dark
surface. *Thank you, Banch.* She scooped it up and stole
into the interrogation room to drink it in silence before
anyone else had need of her.

A single lamp was left from the night before, the
second missing. Sighing at the negligence of her staff, she
struck it to life with her flint and then settled back into
one of the two thick chairs. The one with considerably
less bloodstains.

Ripka eyed the other, her thoughts drifting to the
woman they'd arrested at the warehouse. Banch seemed
convinced they would have to make her questioning
hard to extract anything of value.

The rusty stains on the back of that chair turned
her stomach. Ripka glanced away, pushing such
unpleasantness from her mind. Those stains were old,
from a time well before her tenure as watch captain. She
would not add to them. It would not come to that. They
had the sensitive, and he had already proven anxious to
be free. It wouldn't be long before he talked. She tipped
her head back, closed her eyes, and sighed.

"Hullo, Rip old girl."

She bolted upright, upending her tea, and whirled on
the holding chamber door. There, framed in iron and
oak, was a face familiar enough to make her whole body
tense with tightly reined-in rage.

"What in the sweet skies are you doing in my holding
cell, Honding?"

"Why, you put me here last night. Funny, you never did tell me what I was charged with. Mind giving me a recap?"

She scowled and righted the still dribbling teacup, gave the wood a perfunctory swipe with her sleeve, then abandoned the effort. Another stain on the desk wouldn't matter. "I did no such thing. How did you get in here? If one of my watchers brought you in they'd throw you in with the rest of the night intakes."

"Special treatment just for me? Oh Rip, you shouldn't have."

"I *didn't*."

A heavy knock sounded on the door, followed by an equally heavyset watcher. Ripka clenched her teeth. It took her a moment to realize what she was seeing – Belit was heavy with child, the sharp edges of her coat pushed wide by the swell of new life. How long had Belit been working like that? Ripka had known the woman was pregnant, but things had clearly progressed faster than she'd anticipated. Or had she simply forgotten? Blue skies, she really was losing her connection with the Watch as a whole. Ripka forced herself to calm.

"What is it, Belit?"

"Pardon, captain, I didn't know you had a man in the box."

"Neither did I."

Belit frowned at that, confusion wrinkling her forehead. Ripka sighed and snapped her fingers twice to move her along. "What do you need?"

"Banch sent me to warn you that Mine Master Galtro demands you speak with him right away."

"Yes, fine, thank you."

"Do you need anything, captain?"

She scowled at Detan. "Yes. The intake records for *this room* from last night."

"Yes, sir."

"And Belit?"

"Yes, sir?"

"Talk to Banch and arrange for someone else to take over your patrols until well after the child is born – whatever you need."

"Yes, sir. Thank you." A real smile flitted across the woman's face as she saluted and stepped back into the hallway.

"Nice lass. Bit big for the ole uniform though, don't you think? I bet it costs the city extra, all the fabric."

"None of your business, Honding. Now tell me what happened last night."

"Why? You know it! You picked me up on Thratia's airship and marched me in here like a common crook."

"You are a common crook."

"I am not *common*."

She was considering the merits of throwing her teacup at him when Belit returned with the files. She shooed Belit away and flipped through, looking for the number of Detan's current cell. Sure enough, there was his name neat and clear, and on the appropriate line a signature that looked very much like her own, but most certainly wasn't. Her jaw clenched. She snapped the folder shut and strode closer to the cell door.

"I'm afraid you were detained by an imposter."

His brows furrowed. "Are you sure? She looked an awful lot like you. Well, she smiled more, but I just figured you were drunk."

"That. Was. Not. Me." She slammed her palm against the door, the impact startling her back into calm. Detan just blinked at her.

"Oh!" He slumped forward and let his forehead rest against the bars, then lowered his voice to a conspiratorial whisper. "Was it the doppel?"

"Quite possi– wait. Who told you about a doppel?"

Detan poked her in the face.

She jumped back a step and brought her hand up to her cheek, feeling the spot, and found nothing at all changed. "What in the pits was that for?"

He shrugged. "Just making sure. And rumors are wild about a doppel loose in the city, haven't you heard them?"

"More than rumors, I'm afraid."

"It *is* true then! Marvelous! I can't believe I met one and never knew it. She was *just* like you Ripka, all pissy and… er, nevermind."

Tapping the folder against her thigh, she crossed back to the desk and sat on the edge, facing him. He smirked a little, privately amused by some trivial nonsense, and she ignored it. What did the doppel hope to accomplish, putting this rat in her nest? Was it just out to prove it could do what it liked, or was it a personal threat? She frowned while she thought, wondering if she'd rustled the creature with her interviews the previous morning.

"Did she say anything at all to you?" Ripka asked.

"Not much, just the usual niceties of being arrested. Speaking of, can I get some breakfast?"

"Not now."

He looked positively defeated by that, and she wondered at the depth of the stomachs of men.

"She's the suspect in the warden's murder, isn't she?"

"It's possible. It's a she? Are you sure of that?"

Detan deliberated for an infuriating moment. "Yes. Well, she looked very womanly… It's possible otherwise, but I would lean toward it being a woman. Why? Have you interviewed anyone?"

"Too many. The whole seventh level is filled with

retired sel workers and none of them have seen
anything at all. Not that they'd tell me about it if they
did." She caught herself before she could divulge more
information. Detan may sport a charming demeanor,
but he was a scoundrel of the highest order. For all she
knew, he was working in league with the doppel and
his presence in her cell was a plant to squeeze Ripka's
knowledge level from her. The thought rankled.

She stood, squaring her shoulders. The early hour
and comfort of the station house had made her sloppy,
it wouldn't happen again. She flicked the folder to the
desk and stalked forward, shutting down her expression,
drawing her thin brows into a sharp angle. The knot of
his throat bobbed as she approached.

"Tell me," she said, pressing her palms against either
side of the window that framed Detan's face. She leaned
forward, giving him no room in which to hide his
expression, his tells. A small muscle at the corner of his
lips twitched in surprise. She suppressed a smile. "When
did my impersonator first make contact with you?"

She kept her voice stern, leaving no room for
argument.

He glanced sideways and down, searching for the right
answer. She slid a hand over to clutch one of the bars in
his tiny window, let him see her knuckles go white from
the strength of her grip. Let him believe she was just
barely keeping a handle on her anger and liable to take
her frustrations out on him at any moment.

"Er," he stammered, flicking his gaze to her hold on
the bar. "I was speaking to Thratia on the deck of the
Larkspur when you – I mean she – so rudely interrupted.
Had a coupla' your blues with her, too. Were a bit rough
with the old ties."

This time she did smile. "Describe them."

"They, uh, weren't Banch? Pits below, Ripka, all you blue coats look the same to me – no offense. The one who had my lead was a bit shorter, slender, male. Younger lad was trailing him, pimples about the lips. We didn't exactly exchange family histories, you take my meaning."

"The imposter," she pressed before he could gather his wits. "Tell me what she said. Leave nothing out."

His face scrunched in genuine thought. "Went on about the weather–"

"No she didn't," she cut him off, recognizing the slight rambling lilt his tone adopted when he meant to distract. "Try again."

A flush crested his cheeks. She allowed herself a moment to savor having flustered him. "I confess to being in a state where my memory was somewhat lacking. Thratia was not cheap with the booze. I might, have, ah, made a comment or two about your – that is to say *her* – legs. Though I hardly see how you can hold that against me."

"That is what *you* said. What did the imposter say? Stall once more and I'll lock you up until the next new moon."

He blanched, then pursed his lips, as if tasting what he were about to say next. "She said some people needed a reminder of her reach. I didn't understand it at the time, but I'm starting to see the reason now. That is all I can recall, captain, I swear it."

That, at the very least, had the ring of truth about it. "Very well. If anything else comes to that selium-filled head of yours, report to me immediately."

He looked thoughtful, and for one mad, desperate moment she considered asking him what he thought of the whole mess. Luckily for her pride, Banch interrupted and poked his head into the room.

"Someone to see you, sir."

"Galtro can wait."

"It's not Galtro. I've got a man here who says you have his friend locked up somewhere, but I can't find him in the files."

She crossed back to the desk with an exasperated sigh. "That's because I have them. Send him in."

Banch stepped aside, and Tibal shuffled into the room, looking scruffier than ever now that he was out of his fete attire. "Begging your pardon, Captain, but I think you have my friend somewhere in your holdings."

"Tibs!"

Detan stretched his arms out between the bars and waved them about. "Save me, Tibs, they're starving me!"

"I rather think you should be familiar with that notion, sirra."

Ripka plunked down in the clean chair and flipped the file open. She sought out the appropriate release paper and signed it with a flourish. "Take this and get him out of my sight."

Tibal took the paper and bowed as Banch came over to unlock the cell.

"Honding," she said.

He froze in the open cell door, eking his foot forward so that it couldn't be closed again without trouble. "Yes, watch captain?"

"You see any sign of the doppel, you come to me. *Immediately.*"

He snapped an overly formal salute. "Yes sir, happy to serve, sir."

"I mean it, Honding. No delays. Now get gone."

He blinked, startled, then shook himself and disappeared out the door with Tibal. Banch hovered a moment, concern on his overly broad face, while she drummed her fingers against the desk with undue force. "Want me to get you more tea, Captain?"

"Too late for that, Galtro is waiting."

She left the interrogation room behind with the distinct feeling she was missing something.

As Ripka stepped out of the interrogation room, Galtro stormed down the hall, his eyes bloodshot and his fists clenched. She drew a deep breath and took the opportunity to fortify herself. She squared her shoulders, clasped her hands behind her back, and tipped her chin up. At her side, Banch did the same, and she found the effect much more intimidating when hung on his expansive frame.

"Watch Captain Leshe, I must speak with you immediately." His voice sounded like an over-tightened string, wound with anxiety, not anger.

"Of course, mine master. Please come this way."

She led them through the catacomb twists of the station to the cool, quiet confines of her personal office. The captain before her had kept his office toward the front of the station on the second floor, overlooking the central hall so that he could keep a sharp eye on all the comings and goings of the place. Ripka had found the noise too distracting, the stern watchfulness damaging to her team's morale. Complaints had gone down since she'd moved to the back of the first floor. Maybe she was just too far away for anyone to bother bringing them to her. Either way, it suited her just the same.

"Would you care to sit?" She gestured toward the fresh chair she'd had brought in after the old one had collapsed beneath poor Banch without warning.

"Not at the present, captain. I am too distressed by far."

Ripka walked behind her desk and opened her drawer to take out a small pad of paper. She sat, dipping her pen, and poised it over the blank sheet, presenting him with the perfect picture of professional calm. Despite the fact she felt like thwacking him on the back of the head and telling him to get on with spilling his worries. "May I make a note of this conversation?"

"Yes, yes." He waved a hand and opted for the chair after all, throwing himself down with a thud. "Certain suspicious people have been seen wandering around the Hub, and some young devils have been busy darting about the place spreading unrest. I saw no less than three posters in support of Thratia on my way out of the station this morning, three! If Thratia's thugs can enter the Hub at any time they like then I fear for my well-being. I'm sure you can understand that."

"I do, but surely you have your own people to handle this?"

"Hah! Hardly. They are too worried about upsetting the younger lads by intervening. They fear a strike if they crack down, and I fear my head on a spike if they don't. Most of all, captain, I worry about the distraction. If the sensitives are busy thinking about this nonsense then they aren't moving the selium safely and efficiently. Accidents could happen. I would rather have my head on a spike than an accident."

She twisted her pen between her fingers, thinking, shunting aside the urge to throw everything she had at this mess to protect Galtro, and to the pits with professionalism. She couldn't lose him too, not so soon after Faud.

"I am short-staffed as it is, but I can spare you three personal guards, no more. To keep excitement down, I can explain them as a standard thing for those in the running for the wardenship. But, to do that, I will have to offer the same concession to Thratia."

"Fine, very well." He shrugged. "I doubt she will accept them anyway. And if she does then we will have ears and eyes by her side, eh Leshe?"

She smiled. "My thoughts exactly. Now, Banch here will assign you your people."

Galtro's eyes flicked to her sergeant, a little crease between his brows. "There's something else I'd like to speak with you about."

Ripka frowned, her mind marching ahead through all the tasks she had yet to complete today. "Will it take long?"

"It might…" His stern face fell, bushy brows turning inward in disappointment. The expression wrenched at her heart, but she couldn't comfort him here, even if it meant making him feel as if she were blowing him off. Not now, not with Banch nearby. She trusted her sergeant, of course, but she must seem to be impartial in all things. Especially now that the rule of the city hung in the balance.

"I am very busy at the moment…" she attempted, willing him to see between her words.

He leaned forward, placing his palms flat on her desk. "One of my sensitives has gone missing. Good lad. Worked the fourth line. None of his line mates have seen hide nor hair of him in two days. I have no proof of anything, he could just be drunk in a brothel somewhere, but it's possible…"

Ripka felt her face twist in a grimace despite her attempt to remain impassive. Galtro sat back, brows raised. "You know of this?"

"Scrawny lad, pale hair, doorknobs for elbows?"

Galtro leapt to his feet and slapped a hand upon her

desk with enough vigor to rattle her ink well. "That's him! That must be Feter! Is he injured?"

With care she laid her pen aside, forced herself to forget that this man who was her friend was about to become very, very angry with her. "It is good to know his name, he hasn't told it to us. He's well, if indignant. We arrested him smuggling weapons into Aransa with a known associate of Thratia."

The color bled from Galtro's face, his fingers curled and uncurled at his sides as if he were grasping for something solid to hold onto. Despite her resolve, guilt wormed its way into Ripka's heart and made her queasy. She leaned forward, trying to look open, understanding. Deliberately she spread her palms out to either side and patted the air. "He's young, and Thratia's people can be very persuasive."

"I want him released." Galtro's words fell like lead, one after the other, offering no room to argue.

"He was caught in a smuggling operation, mine master, I cannot release him until we discover what he knows." She flicked her gaze to Banch, who was doing everything he could to look like a blank wall. The boy was on the verge of talking, if they lost him now… It would be hard questions for the woman. Ripka hoped Galtro couldn't hear the soft waver constricting her throat.

"I'll front money against his release, for the good of the city. He *is* young, watch captain, and if he has anything to say I'll wring it out of him. But Aransa needs him back on the line. Now. Our production is down as it is, what with one pipe suffering a clog we can't get clear and the pipe's so-called investor, Grandon, dragging his feet to get it fixed. We need all hands." He leaned forward, and this time it was fists he pressed against the desk. "You should have come to me immediately."

"There was no way to be certain he was yours," she said, but the protest was weak and she knew it. Any able-bodied sensitive without a pilot's imperial contract not working at the Hub was a rogue who should be hauled in and immediately disclosed to the mine master so that they could be put to work. She should have told him. But then, she had known what he would do.

"Very well. Go with Banch and he will release the young man into your custody. If he tells you anything, Galtro…"

He waved a hand through the air. "You have to eat sometime. Come by my apartment later tonight, where we can be assured of privacy and better wine. I'll have everything I can for you by then."

"I'll come by after I'm off duty."

Galtro nodded, and Banch ushered the man out. When the door was closed she pressed her palms against her forehead and groaned, not so loud as to be overheard. Without the boy… Banch was right. They needed answers, and the woman had proved taciturn at best. Still, there were other ways. There must be. She would find them.

Ripka reopened the drawer she had pulled the notepad from and grimaced. Her emergency money pouch was missing.

CHAPTER 14

The absolute first thing Detan did was find a food cart. He stuffed his face with half-burned grit roots and old, unidentifiable meat while Tibs watched, chewing around something wrapped in what looked suspiciously like a leaf. When the rumble in his stomach had settled, Detan slumped back against the wall of a building in the shade of a reedpalm and sighed.

"May I ask why you were arrested, sirra?"

He grimaced, dragged back from his contemplation of the gentle breeze and the warm, contented feeling only a full belly can bring. "To make a point, I'm afraid. It was the doppel who dragged me in and the real thing who found me. Those two are dancing round each other like territorial scorpions."

"Dancing around *you*?"

He winked and waved his arms to take in his whole body. "I am quite the prize, as you can no doubt see."

"Did it occur to you they might be interested in me?"

"Aren't you married, Tibs?"

Tibs scuffed a shoe in the dust. "Only a little."

"I'm afraid that's an all or nothing sort of situation for most women."

"Well, it's only on paper. And I haven't seen Silka in a year, you really think she isn't taking care of her needs without me?"

Detan recalled the stern-faced woman who had nearly gotten him arrested by planting stolen property on him and shuddered. "I try not to think on it…" He trailed off as Tibs's expression soured.

"You know, because the very idea of her betraying you is too terrible."

Tibs's brows lifted, two fuzzy worms threatening battle to one another. "Really?"

"Sure."

"You expect me to believe that?"

"I'm hoping you'll do me the kindness of pretending you do."

Tibs kicked a gnawed animal bone into a trash heap and shrugged. "What now? You get any good eyes on the ship?"

Detan sucked air between his teeth and nodded. "You'd wet yourself if you saw it, the thing is beauty wrought of plank and sail. The hull is formed like an old trader vessel, with the sel sacks inside of it. Made of half a dozen woods I can't even identify. Even the tie-ropes are soft as silk, the stabilizing wings made of the supplest leather I've ever seen. Softer than the commodore's hands, that's for sure. It's gorgeous, Tibs. Gorgeous."

"Well now that we know you've proper appreciation for the aesthetics, can we move on to the part where we steal it?"

"Oh." He shrugged and pushed away from the wall, wandering down the packed road toward the level-stairs. "When I was arrested we went out the servant's entrance. Guarded, but not astutely, and before that I kicked one of those delightful little ropes over the edge, so we can get the flier under it and climb on up. I feel you're rather missing the salient point, however. What was really interesting about last night, Tibs, was the freckles."

"The freckles?" Tibs drawled, and Detan got the distinct impression the old goat was humoring him.

"Indeed. Yesterday morning's Ripka had none, and yet the real deal at the party was quite spattered with them. And the second Ripka, the one who threw me in the clink, had sprouted freckles as well."

Tibs chewed empty air a moment while he thought. "So the doppel must have revised her appearance."

"Indeed, and that means she'd seen Ripka in the personal after our encounter and before the party. And guess who was rustling up all of the seventh level poking around for disaffected sensitives of unusual strength?"

"The watch captain." Tibs came to a rather annoying halt at the bottom of the level's steps. "Our rooms are in quite the other direction. Unless you fancy an upgrade?"

"Oh, come on, Tibs, we're going to go find that doppel." He bowed before the steps up to the city and gestured Tibs forward, drawing an irksome glance from the slate-grey uniformed guard posted nearby. Detan frowned. Weren't all the city guard meant to wear a blue uniform one shade lighter than the Watch?

"Are you sure about this?" Tibs said, drawing Detan's thoughts away from the odd guard.

"Pah, calm down. Ripka intimated that she interviewed every retired sel-sensitive on the seventh. There can't be that many."

"Certainly. But how do you propose we find them?"

"You can't have forgotten how this works so quickly. Now hush."

"You seem mighty desperate to find this doppel," Tibs said.

Detan cringed, remembering the creature's little trick the night before. As he glanced at his old friend, he imagined his face as if it were a mask, the body belonging to something altogether different. Steal the ship for the doppel, or Tibs gets framed for whatever she has coming. He shivered.

If he could catch her unawares, then maybe he could change her mind. Maybe he could force her to let him and Tibs just go.

"You look sick," Tibs said. "What happened?"

"Try not to think so hard, old chum, you'll get more wrinkles."

"Sirra." Tibs stopped cold, hands shoved in his pockets, wiry eyebrows pushed down in annoyance. "Tell me."

"We can't keep the ship," he blurted.

"Why?" His voice was almost calm enough to sooth Detan's frayed nerves. Almost.

With a muted growl of frustration he dragged his fingers through his hair and tugged. "Listen, Tibs, about last night…"

While he explained the doppel's threat, Tibs's expression soured, his relaxed demeanor giving way to tightened, bunched shoulders and fists clenched so hard Detan could see the bulge in his pockets. When he finished the sordid little tale, Tibs let out a heavy breath and shook his head.

"We should scamper. We stay much longer, we'll both lose our tempers."

Detan grimaced. "She'll chase us. I've no doubt of that."

"Then what?"

"We find her, and try to make a deal."

Tibs grunted, but held whatever retort was coming. They sped up and crossed straight to the seventh level. The locals ignored them as they went about their business, buying bland fruits and leaf-flat breads from the few stalls set up to capture those unwilling to brave the market level below. Detan felt strange in last night's finery, but then there were a great many people milling about with rumpled hair and twisted collars much like his own. Thratia's fete, it seemed, had carried on well after he'd been hauled off.

Detan spotted a slender alley and ducked inside, thinking it a good enough place to keep an eye on the comings and goings. Didn't hurt that the shade of the high, canted walls was a balm to his sun-tired skin.

Tibs leaned his back against the dusty alley wall, and Detan was quite surprised to see just how well he blended into the mud brick and black grit. Out in the street, urchin children scrambled back and forth, nimble hands weaving a familiar pattern around the more savory looking denizens. Detan chuckled as one particularly enterprising youth slipped the rings off an older woman's fingers and skittered off.

When one drew near, Detan eased himself out of the shadows just enough to be seen and the kid stopped short, his dust-coated face hard and impassive. "Wha' you want, mister? I don't do nothin' perverted."

"Nothing like that, young chap." He knelt down to get a better look at the bony creature and proffered a crust of bread stuffed with the mystery meat and veg. The kid snapped it up and dug in, little jaw working around a cancerous looking bulge. "Just need some information."

"What kind?"

"Residences."

"What?"

"Who lives where, kiddo."

His small eyes narrowed. "You looking to bunk a place? That's Skelta's territory, I don' wan' nothin' to do with it."

Detan shook his head. "We just want to visit someone, no bunking of any kind involved."

"I don' know everyone."

"You know the old sel workers? They've got more than most, probably good pickings there."

He nodded, unwilling to confess outright.

"Right. So, point their places out to me and it'll be a silver grain for you."

The kid's eyes bulged. "I'd be beaten to tar, walkin' round with silver."

"I'll break it into coppers then, so you can hide half."

He shrugged. "Okay. Money first."

The kid slunk into the alley and Detan handed it over, counting by twos. The kid's lips worked as he followed along the count, then he stuffed half in one pocket and half in a bag around his neck.

"Got paper?"

Detan produced the only paper he had, his filched party ticket, and handed it to the kid who smoothed it flat on the ground. The urchin crouched over the paper, a little nub of charcoal from a fire clutched in his knobby fist, and licked the charcoal tip so that it would draw a darker, finer point. With care he sketched out the street and its primary crossroads, drawing right to the edges of the ticket. Then he began to mark little stars in certain spots, putting numbers beside them. When he was done, he jumped up and secreted the charcoal away before dusting his hands on his trouser leg.

"There you are, mister. Number is the count of doors down from the right, then up."

The kid ran off while Detan was still staring open-mouthed at the makeshift map. It was a genius system, the counting pattern, and he was certain it was code amongst the urchin's fellows. For once, he didn't feel like he'd overpaid.

"Clever kid."

"You got that right."

Detan picked up the map, careful not to smudge the lines. "Well, let's start with 6-3 here."

"Lead the way."

Detan gave the first door a rapid one-two-three thump, and it opened almost before he could take his hand back. Bushy brows peered out at him, granite-grey ridges over black-brown eyes.

"What?" the man grunted, pipe smoke heavy on his breath.

"Hullo, good sir! We're visiting with the honored sensitives of the city to inquire about their—"

"Are you from the Watch?"

"Er, well, no."

"The Hub?"

"I'm afraid we're not acquainted with the specifics of—"

The man spat at Detan's feet and slammed the door shut. A little wuff of dust wafted onto his face, shaken from the lintel by the man's over-exuberant use of his portal. Detan coughed.

"Well, couldn't have been him anyway." He brushed dust from his shirt, found it already mingling with his sweat and well on its way transforming into mud.

"Really? You convinced he doesn't dress up as the lady watch captain in his off hours?"

"Mightin' be that he does, old friend, but he's still not our creature. I remain convinced that the doppel is a woman. And taller."

"As you say."

He scratched out 6-3, and they moved on to the next.

The second door wouldn't even open for them despite the light in the window and the alluring scent of cooking spices seeping from within. The third produced a perfectly pleasant woman who offered them a rather terrifying mug of hot tea, her hands trembling so that the clay cup clanked against its saucer. Detan sensed sel in that woman's house, but he was beginning to realize such secret caches were far from unusual in this neighborhood. Sensitives felt comfort in being close to a source of sel. It wasn't a compulsion, but he certainly understood the appeal.

At the fourth door, a hunched woman with grey-green eyes and a slump to her shoulders opened the door a crack, her gaze narrowed in suspicion. Sweet spices drifted on the air, they must have interrupted her baking. His stomach gave a hopeful rumble.

"May I help you?"

"I hope so." He beamed and thrust out a hand. She just looked at it. "We're here conducting a small review of the retired sel workers in the area, ma'am. I was wondering how being retired is treating you?"

"It was rather quiet and pleasant until a few moments ago."

"Oh... ah. Do you mind if we come in?"

"Yes."

She closed the door, leaving Tibs and Detan locked out of yet another home of Aransa.

"This is going great, sirra."

"Oh, shut up. That woman had a sel supply somewhere in her house. She's a candidate."

"So? The last one did too. You said yourself almost all of them have. And this one had a limp, anyway."

"Could have been an act."

Tibs sighed and looked down at the map. "Come on then, six more houses we have yet to get banned from."

They dragged themselves back that night exhausted, with stubbed toes and an annoyingly persistent lack of leads. Detan threw himself down on the bed and groaned as the tired muscles of his back stretched.

"Happy with yourself, sirra?"

Tibs was, he noted with no small amount of irritation, looking quite vibrant. Detan chalked it up to him having had the luxury of their rented room to himself the night before.

"Shove it, Tibs. You just don't understand what it's like to spend the night in jail and find your plans all thwarted in the morning."

"Thought you didn't make plans." There was bitterness to Tibs's voice, a sharp edge that raked thorns over Detan's consciousness. They'd failed to find the doppel. Now they had a choice to make, and the unspoken weight of it hung between them, heavier than any sel ship's ballast. Leave town and risk pursuit, or dance on the doppel's strings. Neither option was appealing.

He grimaced and flopped over onto his side, staring out into the little goat pen that housed their flier.

It was gone.

"Tibs, did you take the flier somewhere last night?"

"No. I spent the evening fixing it up. Why? Oh."

Detan sprang to his feet, but wiry old Tibs still beat him to the door. There was a fierce ache in his legs, but he didn't let that stop him from pounding down the dusty hallway with Tibs at his side. They reached the rickety desk their proprietor sat behind at the same time, both whoomping as their stomachs and hands smacked into the edge of it.

A little puff of dust wafted up. The proprietor didn't seem to notice.

"Excuse me." Detan cleared his throat and the proprietor looked up from his accounts. He was a man of middling years with hair gone all to ash and his cheeks gaunt from a steady diet of spicewine and more spicewine, judging by the smell of him. He peered up at them from his little alcove, squinting against the low lamplight so that his brow and cheeks wrinkled right up and covered his eyes.

"What?" he said.

"Upon careful purview my companion and I have discovered that the contents of our acquired place of rest have gone missing."

"*What*?"

"Our flier's gone." Detan sighed and slapped the ticket stub for the pen on the desk. "And our account is paid in full, I assure you."

The proprietor squinted over the desk at the stub and smacked his lips. "Number eight-six, eh. Yeah, your man came and picked that wreck up earlier today, round lunch hour. Said to thank you kindly fer it and give you this."

Gnarled and smoke-stained fingers passed a folded slip of paper across the desk. Detan snatched it up and danced away from the proprietor, turning the paper over to make out the droopy wax seal. Despite an overabundance of wax muddying the details, the family crest was clear enough in the crimson globule. It was just too bad he hadn't a clue what it meant. Despite the intense education of his youth, Detan found all the iconography of the sigil a mystery to his eyes. He suspected Auntie Honding would turn her nose up at it as a gaudy example of the peacocky nature of the new-rich.

"Go on," Tibs urged.

Detan broke the seal and flipped the thick, cream-hued paper open. Tibs crowded him, peering over his shoulder to get a better look.

Dear idiots,

I have taken your heap of a flier in trade for the clothes you wrongfully acquired this evening. The thing is such a wreck that I hardly think the trade fair, but I suspect you possess nothing of equal or greater value in all the world. I suppose after some much needed repair it will make a suitable gift for my daughter's birthday.

Regards,

Renold Grandon

A cold shiver of rage added a tremble to Detan's fingers, and he was annoyed to see the paper shake with it. As his anger mounted, his senses widened. Awareness of all local sources of sel bled into his mind. A little stash behind the proprietor's counter – probably infused in alcohol – a great pool of it in a nearby buoyancy sack, no doubt a part of a neighbor's flier. Their presence called to him, cloying and hot, an inviting outlet for his fury. Detan closed his eyes, willed cool sense into the blood pounding through his body.

Beside him, Tibs chuckled.

"What's so funny?" Detan snapped, though at the sound of Tibs's amusement the rising tide of his anger crested and broke.

"Well, it's a pretty good move, don't you think? I reckon you'd do the same, if you were him."

"Pits below, Tibs, don't encourage the man."

"Not like he's here to hear it."

Detan scowled, but the raw edge of rage had gone out of him. His sense of sel closed, his heart slowed its frantic pace. It was, in fact, a tidy little move. Put in the same position, he probably would have pulled something similar.

He was going to enjoy ripping it all apart.

"I say." He whirled back upon the proprietor. "Try not to let any more strangers walk off with our things while we're out, if it's not too much trouble."

The wiry old bastard snorted and flipped a page on his ledger. "No promises, boys. No one in Aransa who's got all their sand between their ears is going to help you against Grandon. That man keeps a grudge closer than a lover and has the grains to back up anything he wants to do. He comes back asking for your shitshorts and I'll hand 'em over with a smile."

"Charming," Detan muttered.

Then brightened.

"There *is* one brave soul in all Aransa willing to stand with us against Grandon."

"Oh," Tibs groaned. "We're going back on the ferry again, aren't we?"

Detan threw an arm around Tibs's shoulders and ushered him back out into the street. "Didn't I tell you? A lifetime's worth of goodwill!"

CHAPTER 15

Ripka sat in a creaking chair by Galtro's low fire, watching the man bumble about the place like he was the visitor. Between them was spread a selection of Aransan street-cart delicacies. As far as Ripka could tell, the mine master's hearth didn't even have a cooking pot.

But the mug in her hands was warm with thornbrush tea and, if she were being honest with herself, her own dinner would have been comprised of street-cart foods. In fact, she knew the morsels arrayed before her well. It was nice to know that Sala on the next level up was making his pulpleaf pastries again, sticky with agave syrup. Ripka picked up a spitted wing of shaleowl, breathing deep of the peppery spices rubbed into the crisp skin.

"Who needs a wife, eh?" Ripka said around a mouthful of crunchy meat, and suppressed a grin as she watched Galtro flush. The full saying was, *who needs a wife when you've got street-carts and whores.* Language like that was forbidden to Galtro's sel-sensitives, at least while they were Hubside. She'd heard a fair share of crude things leave the miners' lips once they were back in the city, and deep in their cups; usually directed at her, after she'd herded them into a cell for the night so they wouldn't be a danger to themselves or others.

"A wife's the last thing on my mind, captain."

"Ripka," she corrected.

"Names matter, lass."

She wiped grease from her fingers on a small cloth napkin. "I know it well."

A real smile flickered across his craggy features, but only for a moment. His eyes turned down to his folded hands, his own selection of foods left to go cold.

"Feter told me nothing of worth," he said, and the words fell like cage bars over any pleasure she had fostered.

"I see. Thank you for trying." She swallowed hard, working the meat down a throat gone dry as the Black Wash. By the way he spoke – no preamble, straight to the point – she surmised that Feter's lack of professed knowledge was the last thing weighing down his mind. But it was, at the moment, the greatest weight upon hers.

Her whole tenure as watch captain had passed without the need of torture. Maybe the answers the woman held weren't that important. Maybe she could be left to stew in boredom on a poor bed. Maybe she'd eventually talk just to have something to do.

And maybe that would take months, and they'd all be ground under Thratia's boot by then.

After a moment's pause, Galtro rose and paced to the window. Ripka did not bother to look at the view, she knew he'd stare straight across the Black to the faint lights of the Hub clinging to the Smokestack beyond. Even at night, watchfires were left lit and guards lingered against the slim possibility of a selium thief.

No, the view wasn't what was interesting. Galtro kept his shoulder blades angled inward, his hands clasped tight at the small of his back. His chin was downcast, his gaze flitting erratically. He could not be still. His fingers fidgeted, twisting a ring on his right hand around and around. If he were in her interrogation room, she would expect a full confession any moment. And so, she did what every good investigator does. She chewed her food, and waited for someone else to fill the silence.

"Do you know why I decided to run for the wardenship?"

She had thought she did, but the reedy tone of his voice told her the answer would not be what she expected. "No."

"I know I won't win, of course."

"There's always a chance."

"No, my dear. Even if the people were to vote for me en masse, it would only be a matter of time before an accident befell me. It is safer, for me, to be the clear loser, I think. That way Thratia will not fear reprisal from my supporters, because there won't be enough to pack a ferry."

"Then why bother?" The words came out bitter and clipped. He *should* want to win. If Thratia took power, there was no telling which path Aransa would march down. Ripka was certain Thratia would be quick to dissolve the Watch and fill it with her own people. Or worse, threaten those already wearing the blues into marching to her beat. She'd already made it clear she'd raise the Hub's production quotas, putting the line workers at risk for the sake of surplus. Galtro's lack of care needled Ripka, pushed the fine edge of her temper.

Fearing what she might say next, she pressed her mug to her lips and sipped slowly, carefully, breathing deep of the steam. Giving Galtro a chance to make himself heard while she settled her irritation.

"So that the sensitives will understand that they have an advocate, a voice. Someone willing to stand up and speak for them, even if they won't be heard."

She sat the mug down with as much care as she had used when sipping from it, and allowed her hands to curl into fists against her thighs. "The miners are the most cared-for people of any Scorched city. Food, housing, it's all seen to. Why would they need an advocate beyond what they already have?"

"They have those things because they are press-ganged."

She opened her mouth to protest, but he turned from the window and cut a hand through the air to silence her before she could begin. She sat, dumbfounded, strangely relieved. She hadn't even known what she was going to say.

"Sel-sensitives are born with a gift, yes, but due to the nature of their inheritance they are stripped of their futures. Yes, they will be cared for. Only the finest of apothiks, and the best pick of food for them. But that is a small prize in exchange for the possibilities lost. The sensitives spend their lives moving selium around, or scouting for it in the deep caves, or else traveling as diviners, rarely pilots. And that is all they will do.

"Those who spent childhoods dreaming of following in their mother's or father's stead? Forget it – it's the mines, or the ships, nothing else. Whole mercer houses have collapsed, dissolved and been divided, because all the heirs were sensitives. Pits below, Ripka, some of the more influential houses vacation back in Valathea now, to conceive their children, lest they risk birthing sensitives.

"And so they are prized, yes, but also oppressed. What do you think will happen, when Commodore Throatslitter takes control of Aransa? She has no connection to the miners herself, and she will demand higher production to help secure her position. Her blade at our throats is inevitable."

Ripka leaned forward, dragged her fingers through her hair.

"What do you expect me to do about it? We've outlawed private militias, but some allowance must be made for personal guards. And so she keeps them, dozens of groups of armed men and women. All with different colors on their vests, sure, but all holding out their hands to the same boss. That is why I wanted... I wanted you to try. To show the city that it has other options; that it doesn't have to bow to brute power. Everyone here respects the miners, there'd be no Aransa without them and so, as the mine master–"

"Hush, girl."

She clamped her mouth shut with a click, breaking off the rambling flow of words midstream. When had she become so needy? If Galtro didn't want this, if he feared it would bring him harm, it was not her place to thrust him forward.

"Forgive me." She stood, back stiff despite the warmth of the hearth beside her. "I did not mean to invalidate your concerns."

"The safety of the miners is my primary duty."

And the safety of the entire city is mine. She forced herself to smile, the same tight little expression she used on whining uppercrusts, and held her hand out to him. Galtro eyed it, clearly unsure of the meaning. Ripka remained still as a boulder, arm unwavering, until his cold fingers curled around hers. Cold, like hers. Some chills even the warmest of fires couldn't shake loose.

"I will see to it that the Hub receives a fresh batch of watchers in the morning. The city has been quiet, we can spare them until this is over."

"Ripka…" He frowned at her, her transition into stiff formality placing him ill at ease. So be it.

"I will oversee the selection of personnel myself. Now, it is late, and I must see to other matters. Thank you for your hospitality."

Before he could protest, she dropped his hand and crossed the small sitting room, out into the harsh desert night. The door snicked shut behind her, old hinges moaning their complaints. They hadn't been oiled in years, she was sure of it. She was also sure Galtro rarely slept in his state-issued home. No surprise, that. He was obviously bonded more deeply to the Hub than she had ever imagined.

Ripka glanced to the sky, trying to estimate the angle of the red face of the moon. How long had she been behind those little-used doors? The red moon's fatter, silvery sister would not rise until the monsoon season began, but that was creeping ever closer now. She had never been good at guessing the mark with only one moon to go by.

With a sigh she set off down the narrow road, residential windows black all around her. This was the level on which the miners themselves lived, their provided homes rolled into neat little lanes with uniform boxes stuffed with flowering succulents set outside each door.

But theirs were not the only state-issued homes on this level.

Ripka turned, the soft soles of her boots crunching over sandy dirt. Here and there she caught the aroma of a supper long-past lingering by darkened doorways, a sign of those few in this level who preferred to go to their rest later in the evening.

Another choice, stripped from them, just as Galtro had said. Mine work was early work, no exceptions. And so those who preferred the nights suffered, or changed. It was just too dangerous to work the lines by lamplight, and so every daylight hour became precious.

She caught herself gritting her teeth, grinding the back molars until her jaw ached. Pausing, she pulled another lump of barksap from her pocket and popped it into her mouth. It was faintly sweet and resinous, but the taste was of little consequence. She chewed the lump, working it around the back of her mouth. It was better than grinding her teeth to stubs.

At the end of the lane a house slightly larger than the others sat, its squat frame hunkered down with its back to the edge of the level. There were fantastic views from the windows in the back of that house. She'd spent many an evening holding a winecup, gazing out of those windows while Warden Faud regaled her with stories of his mercer days during the Catari war.

Complete tosh, all of it. But it had been interesting. Safe.

A ribbon of thin cloth was wound round the front gate, marking it as a crime scene forbidden to public entrance. They needn't have bothered. The story of what had become of the old warden was impossible to keep quiet. The whole city knew of Faud's dreadful end. And the whole city assumed the place haunted. Cursed.

Ripka undid the knots her own fingers had tied, and pushed the gate open. It did not squeal. Faud had been a fastidious man when it came to the upkeep of his property, and he hadn't been gone that long. Not yet.

The little front garden consisted of labyrinths laid in multi-hued stones, their winding ways punched through here and there by a stubborn succulent. Native gravel crunched under her feet. The door slipped open, the sweep of its arc clearing away a fan of dust. Faint light from the red moon filtered through the windows, casting a sickly glow over dust-smeared furniture. In Aransa, it was never long before the dust returned.

She took two steps into the sitting room and stopped. What was she doing here, anyway? They had scoured the place for any hint of the murderer's identity and motive. At will she could close her eyes and conjure up the image of Faud's sitting room, just as it was now, each detail immaculate.

Ripka let her eyes drift over the room, comparing what she saw with what she had committed to memory. A wine amphora tipped over by the couch, its contents long since spilled and sunk into the porous floor beneath the rugs. The dark stain was already moldering, making the air sour and tart. When she had first found Faud she had thought that stain was blood, but, no. There was very little blood for a murder scene.

A few droplets were sprayed across a high-backed chair. Had he been struck while sitting still, the other half of the wine already in his belly, weighing down his mind and limbs? There was no way to be sure, but the warden's lip had definitely been split. That could have been from the bellows used to force the selium down his throat, though.

She glanced to the side, allowing her gaze to linger on the murder weapon. They'd left it there after a brief examination. There was no sense taking it to a specialist to be examined. It was Faud's own bellows, kept for breathing fresh life into the fire. There was no way he

could have known it would mean the end of him, those
accordion wings pumping lighter-than-air gas into his
steadily distending belly.

Ripka's hands clenched at her sides. If the weapon
had been brought from elsewhere, then maybe... *Click.*

"Easy, now." The voice was an eerie echo of her own.
Similar, and yet richer somehow. Deeper, weary. Maybe
what she would sound like in ten, twenty years' time.

She froze, fighting every instinct she'd ever cultivated
to keep from diving and rolling to the side. You didn't
live long in the Watch without coming to recognize
the well-oiled click of a wristbow being primed. In her
mind's eye a parade of every wristbow she'd ever seen
rolled along, each one deadlier than the next. Compact
weapons, not much for distance. The bolts were small by
necessity, not allowing much tension, which made them
hard to kill with.

Which meant they were usually poisoned.

Ripka held her hands out to her sides and raised them,
slowly, her fingers spread.

"Move forward three steps and hold," the woman
said, her voice calm and without the slightest hint of
accent.

Ripka obeyed, gaze flitting around the room to find
some sort of reflective surface that might give her a hint
of the woman's position. There was nothing. And even if
there was, it would be dulled in dust by now.

Steps shuffled after her, only discernible from the
sighing wind because Ripka now knew what to listen
for. The door shut with a soft catch, cutting off half of the
room's already pale light.

"Is this your work?" Ripka asked, tipping her head
toward the spilt wine.

"Yes."

A chill reached up Ripka's spine and stilled her hammering heart. For a moment, she had hoped this was just some random street thug taking advantage of a woman on her own. Those she knew what to do with. But this? She should have known no random thug would approach her, not while she wore her blues.

"And have you returned to admire your work?"

The woman laughed. Not the maniacal whoop of the truly insane, but the sudden snort-chuckle of someone genuinely taken by surprise. Ripka bit her lip to keep from clenching her fists. If only she could get this woman worked up enough to attack her hand to hand, then the poison would be taken out of the equation. She just had to get her cudgel up, and then…

"No, there's nothing to admire in here," the woman said.

"On that we can agree."

"I've not come to harm you, watch captain, so please stop eyeing that chair. You couldn't throw it at me before I could fire. And I will fire, you understand. If I must."

She scowled into the faceless dark, breathing deep to still her irritation. "You have my compliance, for now. What is it you want?"

"I've come to warn you."

The murderer's steps picked up again, but did not draw closer. Ripka strained, trying to discern her location, and failed. Frustrated, she snapped, "I will not stop hunting you."

"I know, and I don't mind. Ultimately, however, your obsession with discovering me has left you blind to other little civic matters. The ex-commodore, you see, is not quite so *ex*. She is deep in Valathea's pocket."

"And why should I care? Valathea supports the Watch. If anything, Thratia's allegiance is good news."

"Ah." The woman clucked her tongue. "You do not quite see. Allow me to explain. She has been in constant contact with Valathea regarding the goings-on of Aransa. Yes, yes, I know that so have your people – but, tell me, did you mention to your handlers that there was a suspected doppel involved in the warden's murder, or only the one found meddling with Mercer Agert's affairs?"

"I would not report mere speculation to my superiors."

"And yet, Thratia would. And Valathea is coming to her call."

She swallowed, tried to keep her voice firm. "We are doing our best to hold the city in safety. The Watch is spotless, and Valathea would not dare enact a purge on such a productive mine."

A gust of warm air brushed Ripka's shoulder as the woman sighed. "They are not coming to punish you, though your concern for your fellow watchers is admirable. But to… destroy. Deviants, as we're called, have gone missing lately, captain. A purge is inevitable. Or haven't you noticed?"

She bit down, splitting her barksap in two. "You're the only deviant in this city, creature. So, no, I haven't noticed."

The doppel tsked. "Whatever your prejudices, do not let them blind you. When Valathea comes, they'll take a long hard look at the wolves they've left to mind their sheep. What do you think they'll find?"

"I'm a law-abiding citizen, I welcome their visit. They have no reason to meddle in Watch affairs."

"If you catch me, Ripka Leshe, then they will have it. Proof of two doppels in one city within such a short time is all they need to initiate a purge."

Her fists clenched in the air. "You're lying. I am turning around now."

"You won't like it."

Ripka turned on her heel, slow and crisp, and stared into the dark, her mind refusing to process what her eyes were seeing. The mirror image of herself stood across the room, slightly taller, a tad narrower of hip and shoulder, with a blackened wristbow pointed straight at her heart. The creature was even wearing a replica of Ripka's blues, right down to the stamped brass buttons. It smiled. She wanted to vomit.

"Why me?"

It shrugged. "Convenience, I'm afraid. Do not worry, Faud knew the truth of what I was in the end. And I haven't made your watchers perform any task *too* untoward."

"Where did... Who made you that uniform?"

"Your tailor was most upset to hear that your coat was thoroughly befouled while arresting a group of fighting drunkards."

Ripka took a step forward before she realized it, reaching not for her cudgel, but for her blade. The creature's smile vanished and she steadied the wristbow, readjusting her aim. Ripka froze, swallowing a roar of outrage.

"I suggest you do not find me."

"Shit on you," she rasped.

"Yes, well." The creature sniffed and took a step backward. "Consider yourself warned, Leshe. For the sake of Aransa's sel-sensitives, and your own job."

"You expect me to believe you actually care about Aransa?"

The doppel's expression shifted so quickly there was a hint of shimmer about her eyes, the iridescence of the selium used to make her mask shining through. "The sensitives. I care about them."

The creature turned and bolted. It must have half-opened the door while Ripka had her back turned, for the thing slipped right through it and slammed it behind her. Cursing, Ripka tore it back open and sprinted into the rock garden, her breath harsh with anger.

All around her, the night was silent. Empty. The gate hung open as she had left it, a mingling of the borders of the multi-hued rocks the only sign anyone had passed in haste. She forced her breath to steady, her heart to slow its thudding, so that she could hear.

There was nothing, not even the crunch of grit beneath a boot.

Ripka swore, and slammed the gate behind her as she left.

CHAPTER 16

"I cannot guarantee it will hold up under the tightest of scrutiny, sirs, but it is the best I can do on such short notice."

Detan peered at his face in the steward's proffered hand mirror, and scarcely recognized himself. His hair had been run through with oil and grit, twisted all askew. Mottled red welts contrived of lady's rouge covered his skin, made to look all the more sinister by a liberal application of jade leaf oil, a viscous distillation of yellow hue.

"I don't know, sirra. Looks the same to me."

"Shove it, Tibs."

Detan ignored his compatriot's self-indulgent smirk and addressed New Chum. "Are you quite certain that the salvage men will be amenable to our needs? I'd hate for old Tibs here to actually have to do some work beyond passing a few choice grains of silver along."

"I can assure you that Master Tibal will have no trouble in convincing them. In fact, from long experience I can attest that the application of silver may not be required. A simple offering of liquor and the evening off will suffice."

"Fantastic." Detan clapped his hands, sending up a little cloud of the dust they'd used to make his clothes look two-days slept in. "You see, Tibs?" he said as he threw an arm around the steward's shoulders. "I told you New Chum here was a regular rake!"

"I have been known to garden, sir," the steward said, an almost devilish smile quirking up the side of his lips. Detan whooped and thumped him on the shoulder, then jumped down from the dais New Chum had made him stand on while applying the essentials.

"May I inquire as to just how this particular scheme came to mind?" the steward asked as he tidied up makeup brushes and resealed pots of ladies' paint.

"Scheme, New Chum? You do me injury! This is the way of the just. We are righting moral wrongs, my young friend. Correcting salacious injury."

Tibs said, "Mucking about when we have more important matters to see to."

Detan scowled. "We *require* the flier to further other pursuits, in case you have forgotten. And besides, it's the principle of the thing. We can't let that puffed-up sack get away with bald-faced thievery! Not when we are capable of more delicate, refined schemes – er, I mean methods."

Tibs rolled his eyes. "It's called the pox in the pocket, and it's an old game."

"Pah. You have no artistic spirit, my glum friend."

"I got an artistic touch of my own to add, sirra."

"Oh?"

Tibs held out his closed fist and uncoiled it just a half-hand before Detan's face. Detan craned his neck to get a better look at the contents, and Tibs poofed out a breath strong enough to blow his hair off his ears.

The hair, however, was not the problem.

Detan swore and reeled back, slapping at the sting in his eyes with both hands. Eyes squeezed shut, tears streaming down his painted cheeks, he staggered and swatted at his face, sucking in hot air with sharp breaths. Through his own squealing he heard a short bark of traitorous laughter, and was forced to stand blind and weeping until all the fine grit had washed free. When the burn lessened, he dared to ratchet up one abused eyelid and found Tibs chuckling as he dusted grit from his hands.

So he punched him in the gut.

Or tried to, at any rate. With his fist mid-swing Tibs stepped sideways as his hand snapped down and wrapped around Detan's wrist, then jerked him forward and released. Detan went stumbling, cursing, crashing into a chair that shattered beneath him. He sprawled across the mercantile remains, savoring the ache in his limbs as he nurtured his indignity.

"Shouldn't swing on a man when you got just one eye open, sirra." Tibs knelt before him and offered a hand. Detan spat on it.

"You're a bastard."

"True, true." Tibs wiped the spit-smeared hand on Detan's arm. "But it adds authenticity, don't you think? Can't go telling people you're sick when your eyes are bright and clear as a hawk's. And look, now you got a real nice bruise coming in on your cheek."

New Chum cleared his throat. "The bruise does add a sickly touch."

"Well fuck you, too," he muttered as he pushed to his hands and knees, then levered himself unsteadily to his feet. He kicked at a piece of the broken chair. It didn't make him feel any better.

"Here you are, sir." New Chum stood with his arm outstretched, a thin grey cloak thrust Detan's way. He eyed it, prodded it with a finger.

"What? Is this full of snakes?"

"To hide our work, sir, until you reach Grandon's estate. If you're spotted with sand scabies on the ferry back to town I daresay the game will be up before it's begun."

"Yes, well." He cleared his throat and straightened his rumpled collar, then snatched the cloak from New Chum and settled it on his shoulders and flicked the hood up.

"How do I look?" He spun around.

"I can't see a thing," Tibs said.

"Marvelous."

The Grandon estate was on the fourth level of the city, clustered amongst similar homes of the newly rich. Detan would have had a difficult time picking it out on any other day, but for his daughter's birthday Grandon knew no restraint. The slatted wooden gate which separated the house's private garden from casual eyes was festooned with paper imitations of rare flowers, and from behind reed flutes wavered a cheery tune.

Detan could see little through the close-set slats, so he lingered for a while on the opposite side of the street, his hood pulled low and his back pressed against the fence of one of Grandon's neighbors. Few people wandered by, and most who did came with colorfully wrapped parcels beneath their arms and disappeared behind the gate. Each time it opened, he learned a little more.

The party was confined, so far as he could tell, to the shade of the front garden's awning. Some expense had been poured into adorning the garden with real blossoms, though judging by the arrangement of painted rocks on the ground such extravagance was not the usual state of things. The house itself was two flat stories, the second rising just above the crest of the fence. Well kept, white paint. A little balcony to catch the sun on. Pleasant.

This was going to be delightful.

When he had gathered all the information he could, Detan shuffled across the street with his shoulders hunched, kicking up dust to coat his shoes and the bottom of his cloak. The dirtier, the better.

The gate swung inward at his touch. There were no guards to mind the way as at Thratia's, a difference Detan found common between new money and old. Grandon wanted this party to be full enough that tongues would wag. He would be happy to see anyone at all attend.

Well, almost anyone.

Detan tossed back his hood, and grinned into the sunlight. All around him the crowd froze, murmurs of conversation ceasing as the curious up-and-comers looked his way to find out the nature of this latest distraction. The first woman to get a good look at him screamed, her clay cup shattering amongst the painted rocks. As good a start as any.

"Lady Tela, are you all right?" Grandon emerged from amongst the celebrants and took the lady's elbow in hand, his thick face crunched with real worry. The lady pointed, and a chasm amongst the crowd opened up all around Detan.

"*You*," Grandon snarled.

"Hullo," he chirruped and waved with the tips of his fingers.

A softly curved woman with a severe jaw appeared at Grandon's side, her greying brows furrowed in confusion. Not, Detan noted, the slender woman he'd seen Grandon with at the baths.

"Who is this man?" She spoke with a Valathean accent, which was a worry.

The guests gathered in tight round the Grandons, straining their ears to hear every last tidbit of this new scandal. Not a one of them had any clue what was going on, but Detan suspected that for them this little exchange was going to be the highlight of the evening. He intended to make it so.

Thick beads of sweat coalesced on Grandon's brow, his cheeks flushing red with anger and heat. Whatever he wanted to say, he swallowed it right down. There were too many ears, and he wouldn't risk tripping over his tongue and coming across as a brute in front of his genteel peers. Detan beamed.

"Why, I'm the man good ole Grandon here bought the flier from." He gestured toward the place where his flier rested. He'd done his best not look too closely at it since he waltzed through the garden gate. The thing was tied to a raised platform to his left, the rudder-fan neatly patched and a new sel sack inflated above the warm wood.

Some asshole, however, had gotten the idea in his thick skull to paint the hull all over with pink and purple flowers. *Happy Birthday Virra!* was emblazoned in deep violet along the side of the buoyancy sack, right where a proper ship's name would have been. As if a flier that small even needed a name.

It was the most hideous thing he'd ever seen, next to the quivering jowls of Grandon himself.

"He told me he bought it new," a young voice piped up. The prodigal Grandon stood with her arms crossed and her eyes even crosser. Detan cringed and glanced away. He was no good with children; he couldn't even puzzle out how old the little thing was. Best to keep focused on the adults of the situation.

"Alas," he intoned and coughed wretchedly into the crook of his arm. "I am grievously ill, and so I have come to take the flier away before my contagion spreads to you innocent souls."

"Hah!" Grandon spit when he laughed. "I'm not letting you walk out of here with that flier, cur. I *bought* it fair and square. It's my little girl's, now."

"Hold, now," Lady Grandon said. "Just what is your illness, young man?"

"Ugh." He reached up and shook out his greasy hair with his fingers as if it itched him dearly. Those nearest to him scurried further away, widening the gulf of empty air around him. "Sand scabies, gentle lady. I pray you don't get too close, in case they decide to make a dreadful leap."

"Hmm." She clucked her tongue and produced a pair of fine leather gloves from her pocket, then pulled them on with expert ease. "How long have you had symptoms?"

"They began shortly after I met your husband at the Salt Baths." Her lips twitched, and Grandon's face went white. "I am told the nits may have been on me for weeks before. Why, they are no doubt crawling all over the fiber of the flier's ropes and hosting dinner parties in the crevices of the wood."

"A reasonable assumption, but I will need to examine you to be sure."

"I, uh, would prefer you do not risk your safety on my behalf."

"Nonsense," Grandon cut in, a smirk on his reddened lips. "My wife is the finest apothik in all Aransa."

Detan swallowed, and hoped his added pallor would make the disguise more convincing. "Is she now?"

"Oh, yes."

"Well, then–"

Before he could muster further protest the Lady Grandon crossed to him and caught his chin between iron-tough fingers. She turned his head this way and that, but he was startled to find her eyes did not leave his own. He met her gaze, choked down his fear, and squared his shoulders. He could probably outrun her...

"Definitely sand scabies," she raised her voice for all to hear.

For one infinitesimal moment, a shiver of terror wormed its way into Detan's core. Could there have been some mistake? Could a real sickness be lurking beneath his makeup? Damn Tibs and his sand trick, it was working too well. That had to be it.

Lady Grandon shook her head, slow and grave, then released his chin and stepped back. She peeled the gloves from her hands and tossed them in a nearby firepit. Fine leather erupted into little sparking embers, an average miner's week worth of pay gone up in a flash.

"Well along," she continued. "I am in fact quite surprised to see a case so advanced still walking and talking. Usually by the time they get this far they can do little more than roll around on their cots and moan. Tell me, do you have any pain?"

"A very great deal of it."

"Pity. The flier of course will have to be destroyed, we can't have the evil little things spreading." She snapped her fingers and a black-jacketed valet appeared at her side. "Go and find the salvage men. Tell them they are needed right away, and that we have a case here for quarantine."

The valet bowed and scurried off, much to Detan's relief. It was always pleasant when the mark made the requests for him.

"If the flier is contaminated," Grandon raised his voice to be heard over the nervous murmur of his guests, "which I'm sure it isn't, then we should burn it here and now and be done with it."

Beneath his makeup, sweat crept across Detan's brow.

"Don't be ridiculous," Grandon's wife interjected. "If scabies are aboard that vessel then they will leap to the nearest host the very moment the flames lick them. No, it must be wrapped and disposed of in the middle of the desert where only the cold blood of lizards will be on offer."

"You are," Grandon dragged out the words, "*quite* certain this man is ill?"

Detan froze as the apothik turned back to him, her sharp eyes sweeping him from greased hair to dusty boots. She arched a brow, one only he could see, and gave her husband a curt nod.

"I have never before seen such a sorry case."

The gate trundled open, and through came the salvage men with the valet at their helm. Detan could only hope the valet hadn't found their fortuitous proximity suspicious. Each one was dressed in the same moss-green trousers and tunic, and each had a matching scarf wound round their hair and the bottom half of their face to keep both sun and vapors off. Between them they hauled a low cart, its pocked surface smeared with suspicious stains.

To the untrained eye, it was damned near impossible to tell them apart. For Detan, however, the slight swagger and paler hands of Tibs were clear as a candle in the dark. Tibs was also the only one to stop short, stunned, upon sighting the flier.

Detan couldn't blame him. Pink daisies would break the character of any man.

While the valet directed them about their business, all eyes were drawn to the commotion, and feet were drawn steadily away from it. Detan slunk back, drifting along the edge of the crowd, his way made clear even if those darting from his path pretended to never have seen him.

Contagion was the swiftest way to become both the most ignored and most watched man in the room.

"A moment." The Lady Grandon intercepted his slow retreat and pulled a palm-sized notepad from her pocket. She gave it a few spirited prods with a pencil then ripped the top page free, folded it, and thrust it toward him. "I insist you go to my clinic so that my people may do what they can to ease your suffering."

"I will go there straight away, madam, and if I survive this dreadful curse then I will be forever in your debt. I will make certain that all generations to come after me pay homage to your own. I will–"

One of the salvage men let out a howl. He hopped around on one foot, clutching at the other, and the lanky man beside him shrugged a mute apology. Tibs. Detan scowled. Even when relegated to a wordless role, that bastard could be a stern critic.

Lady Grandon cleared her throat. "Brevity, I believe, is prudent in the face of your ill-health."

"You are as wise as you are generous." He bowed extravagantly, those nearest to him recoiling a few extra steps.

They would be a while yet moving the flier, and so Detan made his escape into the dusty road, working up a good limp and a soft, painful groan whenever he drew close enough to be overheard. Once he'd shambled past the bright-painted doors of Grandon's neighbors, he paused to read the note. It was an address all right –

but to a posh club upcrust a good few levels. He knew the place. It was carpeted and slung all about with chandeliers, and known for serving the hardest hitting cocktails of those establishments who served them in clean glasses.

Detan chewed his lip and waited for the filthy procession to pass by him. He fell into step behind Tibs and flicked his hood back up.

"What'd the lady pass you?"

"An invitation to drink."

Tibs sucked air through his teeth and chewed it around a bit. "Going to go?"

"If only to be certain I don't actually have sand scabies. She damned near had me convinced."

"Bad idea."

"Always good to have a lady of the medical profession on your side, my good man."

He grunted, and they lapsed into silence. The way to the Salt Baths was not long by ferry, but they planned to march the flier all the way down to the desert and then fly it in under its own power, low and slow. There'd be plenty of time to convince Tibs of Lady Grandon's merits along the way.

His erstwhile companion let loose with a reedy sigh.

"What's wrong, Tibs?"

"Purple. Why did it have to be purple? That damned dye doesn't come out of anything, let me tell you."

Under the harsh eye of the sun Detan adjusted his hood, shuffling around the parts of cloth that were damp with sweat. He'd be soaked before they even made it to the lowest levels. He'd have to buy water once there, no way around it. Real flowers like those painted on the flier he reckoned would need a quarter of a man's daily water to keep on looking so pert. The blasted things didn't even provide food. He glowered at them.

The pink flowers shone back at him, relentlessly cheerful. He spit, and trudged onward.

CHAPTER 17

It was a relief to have the makeup off, even if the bruise remained, but still Detan felt unkempt. Unwell. The double doors to the Red Door Club reared up before him, their scarlet paint pristine despite the glare of the desert sun. No windows faced the street; not a soul behind those doors cared what the dusty road and its worn inhabitants looked like. Detan had never been inside the place before, but he knew the type.

These upcrust beds of convenience were stepped all along the rise of Aransa, and if they bothered with windows at all they were pointed out into the air, toward the Fireline and the humped shoulders of the Smokestack.

He didn't have any business at all knocking on a door to a place like this, save the scrawled note Lady Grandon had shoved in his hand. Dangerous business, getting mixed up in the private affairs of the wealthy, and wasn't he mixed up in too much dangerous business to begin with? Didn't help matters much that the lady in question was a pits-cursed apothik. With all their aprons, gloves, bottles and strange tinctures, apothiks were one short step from whitecoats. Detan suppressed a shiver. Best to follow Tibs's advice, as always. What good was having a wingman if you never listened to him?

Detan turned, and one of the great red doors swung open. Rarified air blended with the dust and heat of the street. The air from within was cool from the low light, laden with the rich aromas of argent-leaf smoke and rare flower oils. A narrow man dressed in the brick-red vest of the club's livery stepped out and glanced around the street until he found Detan. At the sight, a twitch took up residence in the corner of the young man's eye.

"Lord Honding?" the man ventured.

"Who?"

The man's stiff shoulders slumped under the force of a long-suffering sigh. "The Lady Grandon requests that–" he cleared his throat and raised his voice in imitation, "– you either get in here out of the heat or scurry back into whatever sandcave you fell out of."

"Er, right. Yes. Very good. Lead the way, good man."

The attendant guided him through the maze of private booths and winding bartops while giving Detan nothing more than the flat of his back. He couldn't even be spurred into conversation when Detan inquired as to the origin of the Red Door's garish livery.

Fretting so that he could hardly keep his head still, Detan gave up his attempts to cajole the man into anything like gentlemanly chatter. The club, he found, was quite larger than it had looked from the street. Three stories rolled down the face of Aransa, the top story the one which opened to the street. With each narrow set of stairs they ambled down the decor grew finer, the chandelier makers more generous with their crystal.

Live flames licked behind the barrel-sized creations,

casting twisting prisms of light over all the open tables and booths. Detan frowned. There wasn't a soul to be seen at those open tables, and every little booth had its tiny red curtain drawn.

The silent valet delivered Detan to a booth near the back of the bottom floor, its client hidden away behind one of those thick crimson curtains. Though he was certain they were along the back wall of the club, still no windows pierced the structure to break up the gloom.

At least it was cool in here. The sweat between his shoulder blades was beginning to chill and prickle. Not an altogether pleasant sensation.

The stone-faced valet picked up a narrow silver bell from a hook on the edge of the booth and gave it a jingle. It was an offensively gentle sound, like fairies pissing on a tin roof.

"Sands below." Lady Grandon's voice drifted from behind the curtain. "There's no need for that nonsense."

Detan beamed at the valet, but his sour little face hadn't moved a muscle. He just hung the bell back up and wandered off to whatever bitter business needed seeing to next. Pity there was no time to work on the chap. With a flourish, Detan swept the curtain aside and half-bowed into the filmy light of the two-seater booth.

"At your service, lady."

Lady Grandon exhaled a plume of silvery smoke, a black-lacquered extender hanging from her lips. "Of course you are, boy. Now sit. I am pleased, of course, by your miraculous recovery."

He shuffled into the booth and pulled the curtain tight. With the light of the common room cut off, the darkness was held back only by the bulbous glass of a dust and grease-smeared lamp.

The low light softened the lady's features, made her

already artfully arranged face difficult to read. She'd held meetings like this before, he realized. Probably in this same booth every time. He grinned. It was always a pleasure to work with a professional.

"The delicate ministrations of your nursemaids were all the balm I needed to return to glowing health."

She pursed her lips. "You haven't set foot in my infirmary. I doubt you even know where it is."

"And yet you yourself proclaimed me dangerously ill. Only days left on this big ball of dust, if I recall. That's quite a shock to a man's mind, you understand."

She flicked ash into a black-glazed plate and drew smoke once more, the little cherry ember of her cigarette a brilliant pinpoint of light in the gloom. "You deserved a shock for interrupting my daughter's party."

"An unfortunate necessity to ensure the young lady's safety from contagion, I assure you."

"Please." She waved the hand holding her extender, tracing a loop of smoke in the air. "Can we dispense with such nonsense? I'm growing too old for unnecessary games."

"Games are a necessary part of life, dear lady. Why, just this morning, I—"

She snapped the fingers of her empty hand a beetle's width from his nose.

"I said enough. I've asked you here to warn you, not to waste my time."

"Warn me? Whatever for?" Detan forced his tongue to be still, to let her fill the gap in conversation. This was not a woman who could be distracted by his rambling ways.

"You kicked a hornet's house, getting under my husband's skin. And while I thank you for it, out of a certain sense of comradeship with your old aunt I feel compelled to tell you to skip off Aransa just as quick as you can. My husband may be occupied with matters political for the time being, but the first chance he gets he'll come for you. I suppose you are not staying in the same locale in which my lord discovered your flier?"

"Whoa now, lady, back up just a second. I don't know what you know about my dear old auntie, but I'll hear it off you now."

She dashed her ash again and picked up an obsidian decanter. From it she poured two snifters, the round bottoms held upright in a little pot of sand, and nudged one toward him. The rim was already garnished with a thumbprint-sized section of dripping honeycomb.

He picked it up, squinted at it. Sniffed it. Gave the bottom a little flick. It smelled of warm honey and the thick-petaled, pink flowers his auntie liked to keep in boxes outside her windows. Detan sipped and was surprised to find the thick liquid laced through with miniscule bubbles of effervescent sel. He was even more surprised to find his lips not at all numb. It was good to not be poisoned.

"Dame Honding and I attended a private academy together as girls. I have not seen her in decades, you understand, but there is a flavor of loyalty amongst young school girls which stands all tests of time. Now, a return to more pertinent matters. My husband will be briefly occupied in acquiring a new vessel for our daughter, but such a thing will not take long, and then he will set his fervid eyes on you, my boy. Shove off before he has the chance."

Detan stared at the sun-weathered face of his companion, trying to imagine it as a young girl terrorizing the schoolmasters of the Scorched's Academy for Young Ladies. She seemed older than her years to him, but then the desert was unkind to the delicate.

And how long had it been since he'd last seen his aunt? Nothing but letters and parcels strung out between them for the last few years. He cleared his throat of an imagined lump and sipped again. The liquor was cool and palliative, a viscous balm to his unsteady nerves. On second taste he found the flavor deepened by muddled cactus pulp – his aunt had favored cactus liquors, too. He shook his head. Best not to dwell on matters familial while in uncertain company.

"Why the rush for a flier at all? I supposed mine was a theft of opportunity, not a predestined desire."

Something ticked beneath the thin skin of the lady's careful mask, a little flicker of pain trembling along her cheekbone. She drank of her own vial, nibbled on the edge of the honeycomb and placed it back in the sand.

"Our daughter is sensitive, and growing stronger. Not too strong, mind you, she's nowhere near verging on becoming a doppel, but her strength has been noticed. The mine master wants her training for the line soon, but I'd much rather see her in the skies than working in that… mess. Renold and I decided to teach her piloting so that she may easier find a place upon a vessel. Unless…"

"Yes?"

Lady Grandon breathed deep of the smoke-laden air, a nervous gesture so far outside her characteristics thus far that Detan felt his own chest clench with anxiety.

"I've heard, of course, that the young Lord Honding's sensitivity for selium dried up. Renold was too disgusted by you to put the question to you himself, but, considering our familial friendship, I had hoped you might be forthright about the circumstances."

He waved his hand in the air, cutting her off before she could press him further. "My loss of sensitivity was

MEGAN E O'KEEFE   183

achieved through great trauma, lady. The loss of life of
my entire line back in Hond Steading inspired it. It is not
a route I think viable for your girl."

She sighed heavily, her sharp shoulders sagging
forward. "I was afraid of that."

"If I could help…"

"Just leave town, Honding. My girl is safe in my hands,
but I will not be distracted further. If Renold decides to
move against you, I will not stand in his way again. For
the moment he thinks me merely incompetent, in that I
was tricked by your performance into believing you truly
ill. I will not risk his realizing I was insidious instead."

"You don't seem a mite fond of your husband, lady.
Going to the same school as my aunt I can take a guess
at what name was yours before you wed, one with deep
roots, eh? Doth the lady bear the stars of the landed?"

Her eyes flashed, and her lips pressed tight around
the extender of her cigarette, but she said nothing. He
nodded to himself and drained the last of the liquor.

"So you've got resources all your own. Why don't you
pull them, take your girl and go?"

Thin streams of smoke snaked from her nostrils.
"You've misunderstood. My husband and I loved one
another once, long ago. We've drifted apart in age and
ambition, he to his merchanting and me to my medicine,
but our resources remain inexorably pooled behind *our*
girl. As much as I disapprove of certain aspects of his
business, he does not meddle in my interests nor I in his.
We are an alliance. Alliances are necessary for survival
on the Scorched, young Lord Honding. To whom do you
hold?"

His back stiffened of its own accord. "I got people I'd
stick my neck out for."

She snorted. "Only worth it if the feeling is mutual,

hmm?" She stubbed the cherry end of her cigarette against the ashtray as if she were spearing some rare delicacy.

"There's something to be said for selfless sacrifice," he said, annoyed by the defensive timbre creeping into his voice against his will.

"Hah. Not your style in the slightest."

"You hardly know me, lady."

"But I know of you, young man, and I know the temper of the blood that flows through your veins. You're a stubborn, idealistic people. It's what drove your ancestors to sail to the asshole of the world in the first place."

"I think I know my own temperament well enough."

"As you say." She gestured toward the thick curtain with an idle flick of the wrist, and the gesture was so like his aunt's own that he stood without thinking, thin glass vial still clutched in one hand, honey dribbling over his fingers.

"Leave Aransa, Honding. Before you have to stick your neck out."

Detan blinked in the sunlight just outside the Red Door Club, sweat seeping a slow return to his brow and the hollow between his shoulder blades. He looked down at the empty vial in his hand, rolled it back and forth a few times with the edge of his thumb, then dashed it to a thousand glittering fragments against the club's scrubbed feldspar steps and ground the sweet honeycomb beneath his heel.

"That nice of a talk, eh sirra?"

Tibs detached himself from the shadows across the street, but did not come near. He lingered off to the side, well out of sight of any idle passersby. Detan joined him, sighing in the slim shade offered by the neighboring building's roof overhang.

"It seems that we have been instructed in no uncertain terms to make our way out of Aransa, double-time."

"And what are we going to do about that?"

Detan blinked once more, but not because the light stung him. A smirk threatened to overwhelm his features, and so he let it, and knew he must look deranged as he turned back to Tibs.

"Come along, Tibs old chum. We're going to make sure New Chum keeps the flier well out of Grandon's reach and then, tomorrow morning – well. With any luck we'll be clear of this rotten hunk of rock by dinner time."

"And the doppel?"

"We're going to make her come to us."

CHAPTER 18

Pelkaia stood in the middle of her sitting room, flowing through her morning warm-up stretches, while shock echoed in her heart. Just the day before, Detan Honding had come knocking on her door. She still could scarcely believe it.

So very close. Her skin tingled with the memory of excitement upon seeing him. So close, so clueless. Insofar as she could tell, he hadn't marked her for anything other than a standoffish woman of middling age.

Still, he had nearly undone her. Nearly ended her path before all was finished, before her fresh promises were kept. She could hesitate no longer. Now, before she lost the iron of her resolve, she must take the last name on her list.

Pelkaia thanked her guiding stars she'd had the foresight to keep her usual disguise intact. Even having caught her unawares, Detan had yet to see her true face. Sometimes, the best disguise an illusionist could muster was their own plain visage, and it did her nerves good to know she still had that trick in her toolbox.

But now she needed something a little more complex. She grabbed a bloodstone decanter from one of her knick knack-cluttered shelves and poured a deep draught of golden needle-infused blue succulent liqueur into a matching tumbler. Pelkaia breathed deep of the syrup-sweet aroma before downing the bitter liquid in one draw. It seeped through her, settling the tremble of her anxiety even as it settled the ache in her bones.

The bonewither had not reached too deeply within her just yet. Valatheans would call the slow speed of her decline miraculous, but only because those fools had managed to do nothing to hold the illness at bay. The Catari, on the other hand, well... They'd had generations to study it, to control its deadly progression.

By keeping to the old ways, Pelkaia had managed to remain hale through more years than she cared to remember. It helped, of course, that her control was so very fine that she could force the smallest possible quantities into the effects she desired.

On steady feet she crossed to the trunk that rested at the foot of her bed and flipped the lid open. Her son's mining clothes lay within, their stark simplicity accusing the twisted paths she had taken.

Black dust stained the folds and caked the creases. She shook them out, but did not bother to clean them. She never did. The mine hadn't changed their uniforms since they'd instituted them, and a dirty set of work clothes was more believable than a clean one. No one trusted a working man with soft hands and starched trousers.

Pelkaia hesitated, fingers trembling as she spread the crumpled garments upon her bed. The rough weave caught on her hangnails, grit clung to her fingertips. If she closed her eyes she could still picture him within them, could take a deep breath and smell the dirt-and-

oil scent of his hair, his hands. She shook herself – she
had wasted too much time to memory already – and
stripped down to her bone-braces.

Her boy had been slight of frame and a hand width
taller than her, but the clothes fit her well enough
after she'd rolled up the hem of the pants. She let the
shirt hang loose, better to make her feminine form
ambiguous, and knelt beside her bed to tap the hidden
sel bag sewn within. She pulled out a narrow stream,
and took it with her to the vanity. Before the mirror, she
began to transform.

The face that stared back at her was a generic one, no
one she had ever seen before. Long years of practice had
lent her the ability to gather the elements of disparate
faces and blend them into a facsimile of a real person.
There was something uncanny about her unowned face,
but it would work well enough to get her where she
needed to go.

A face browned by the sun and worn deep with the
rippled-dune lines of the desert tipped this way and that
in the mirror, examining itself. Pelkaia arranged a slightly
crooked nose and a day's worth of stubble. She even
drew a few more drops out to add swollen roughness to
her knuckles and fake filth to her hands and forearms.
Normally she wouldn't bother wasting the sel and would
simply roll her fingers in dirt, but if she needed to drop
this disguise in a hurry then it all must be ready to go.

Pelkaia stretched once more, cajoling smooth
movement into joints that had sat too long unused.
Her very marrow protested, joints cracking loud as a
knifestrike against stone. She stood, still as an oasis,
letting the pain that wove through her skeleton fade,
and wondered if, at last, she'd grown too old for this.

But no. The pain faded, what bonewither she suffered

giving up ground to the warm release of the drugged succulent liqueur. Pain she could manage, for now. Had managed for many, many decades. Though the threat of violence to come left her chilled.

She dipped her hands beneath her son's clothes, checking her padded braces again and again to be sure they were secure. They did well to stop a slash, but she intended them to ease blunt force as well as they helped support her weight. If she were lucky, she would suffer no breaks. If she were very lucky, Galtro would never even see her coming.

In the drawer of her vanity lay a few well-weighted throwing knives, and beneath the drawer's false bottom a long, lean knife of weightier craftsmanship. The throwing knives she could pass off as an old woman's fancy – but the longknife? It was unique in construction, its bone-and-bloodstone handle echoing a time before Valathean settlement. A time no longer spoken of.

She secreted these about herself, disguising them easily in the oversized clothes. With one last glance in her polished glass, she covered her hair with a battered hat and tugged it down over her eyes. It would have to do.

Her eyes closed, her breathing deepened, as she prepared herself for what she was about to do. Doing away with Faud had been right, even if it had opened up a power vacuum for that spider Thratia to fill. Thratia was no matter to Pelkaia, now. Thratia was a foul scent on the wind – insubstantial, passing. Whoever held the seat of warden mattered little, so long as those who had allowed her son's death to occur still breathed. She was rooting out corruption. Saving other mothers from a similar destruction of the heart.

So what if she could still feel Faud's blood sometimes,

warm and sticky between her fingers? She could still feel the exhilaration that had swarmed her, too, knowing that she'd done away with that monster.

She'd prepared for this. Steeled herself. This was *right*. Her revenge, her cutting out of the cancer that had destroyed Kel, would not be denied. Pelkaia breathed out, and opened her eyes, a serene sense of purpose subsuming her every fiber.

She let herself out the backdoor into a thin alley, careful to pull the latch behind her. The alley was a standardized firebreak, a little slash of emptiness snaking between her apartment building and the one next door. Such passages were usually given up to nightsoil and beggars, but she'd paid her neighbors well for their silence, and made her own alterations.

A thin wall separated her end of the alley from the others, and she had planted a tiny succulent garden there as explanation. The quaint affectation of an old, lonely woman. She smiled in the dark, breathing deep the aroma of green leaves even as she ignored the incessant hum of the city just beyond. Maybe, she admitted, it wasn't such a cover after all. No matter that half her plant selections could be distilled to poison.

The alley's entrance to the street she had capped with an illusion of crumbling mud brick. It had taken a great deal of effort to get the effect just right, but once she'd set the image firmly in her mind it had come to her in one great rush of inspiration. Once established, holding the illusion in place was as simple as remembering her name. It was a part of her, like the sel masking her face. Maintaining control over so much sel at once threatened to advance her bonewither, but this small indulgence she allowed herself. It was worth it to be able to leave her home unnoticed.

That was the danger, she thought, in calling illusionists doppels. They could do so much more than dupe another person.

To avoid accidental interlopers, she had made the wall a mangy thing. It had old creeper vines over its face, dead and brown in the desert sun. The bricks were rotten and worn. Occasionally a drunk would attempt to piss against it, but their confusion never lasted through the morning. Many things could be waved away if experienced in an inebriated fog. She sidled up to the illusion and squinted through the thin layers of sel.

Pelkaia waited until the traffic in the street beyond her narrow gate grew lean and those few who wandered by were distracted by market carts and squalling children. She slipped out into the street, careful to smooth the false stones and withered vines back into place behind her. She paused, pretending to adjust her shirtsleeves, while she counted in silence to one half-hundred. Once certain no one had witnessed her emerging from the gate, she strolled off down the road, hat pulled down tight to shade her eyes, and angled for the ferry to the Hub.

Having paid her grains to cross, and a little extra to cover her false name, she lingered toward the back of the ferry to separate herself from the rest of the passengers. The deck was crowded with a fresh crew coming in for the late-morning shift change, cups of bright-eye berry tea clutched in their hands. If she were lucky, they would think her aloof and leave her to herself.

She soon realized she needn't have worried. They were all too busy with the local rumor mill to pay her any mind. Keeping her eyes on the sands below as the ferry sidled into empty space, she attempted to eavesdrop.

"Buncha' blue coats swarming around the place. Something's got Galtro spooked."

"He'd be an idiot if he weren't spooked. Pits, man, he's put his hat in against Thratia. You know what they called her in Valathea?"

"Oh yeah, Commodore Throatslitter."

"Exactly! Why, I bet the old warden's death wasn't even done by a doppel. Or if it was, it was one working for the commodore. If Galtro wins I give him a week until he's filling in the dirt beside Faud."

"He's got the watch captain backing him though."

"And you think Faud didn't?"

So, Galtro had watchers hanging around. She drummed her fingers on the ferry's handrail, watching Aransa dwindle behind them. Thratia's compound hunkered along three levels, a blighted stain upon the face of the city.

Behind her, the miners' conversation turned to the unruly working conditions they faced ahead. The pipe joints were rusted, the sel senders little trained, and the capture sacks had to be patched at a continual clip. One of the lines was clogged with an invasive insect colony. All the same complaints she'd had when she had worked the line. All the same complaints her son had brought home. Their time-worn grievances brought her a sliver of comfort, a traitorous smile twitching up the corners of her lips. The mines never changed.

"Who's that?"

Pelkaia flinched, ducking her head to deepen the shadow of her hat's brim across her eyes. She breathed deep to still her nerves, summoned in her mind the bitter taste of her spiked succulent liqueur.

"Hey, you." One of the miners, his face young enough to twist Pelkaia's heart, dropped a rough hand on her shoulder and dipped his head down to peer beneath her hat. "Never seen you round before."

The others shifted close, wary of the balance of the ferry on its guy lines, but unable to resist a little conspiracy. Pelkaia forced herself to stand straight, to trust in the guise she had wrought to carry her through. She cleared her throat and thrust her voice low.

"I'm in from Hond Steading. Going over to get my assignment," she said.

"Phew, a Hond-man." The miner whistled low. "They let you out of that city? Thought they were hurting for the help, what with… how many is it? Four? Five firemounts to mine?"

Pelkaia shrugged, mustered a sideways grin. "They ask you to leave when the mine master's lady takes a shine to you. But if you're looking for a transfer, I heard they just got an opening…"

The miner whooped a laugh, his fellows joining in. He thumped her hard enough on the shoulder that she felt the warm spread of a bruise begin beneath the surface. She hoped the bruise didn't bite into her bone, otherwise she'd be paying for that friendly tap for a full moonturn.

The worn ferry shuddered to a stop at the receiving dock, and she almost gasped with relief as the others gave her friendly directions to the Hub and took off to see to their own tasks. She lingered, letting the miners trudge ahead. No one else paid her any mind, because no one in the whole of Aransa was fool enough to come out here unless they had business.

Once the miners were out of sight on the long trek up the side of the Smokestack, she started down the winding path to the Hub. The operations station clung to the side of the firemount, great pipelines reaching up to its conical mouth. It reminded her of a brown spider with its legs curled in – swatted and dying.

Pelkaia paused in the shadow of a great boulder, getting an eye on the lines pouring into the Hub's central containment chamber. All the lines leading down from the boreholes in the plug of the firemount's mouth converged here, depositing their precious cargo for storage. The metal pipe-mouths were battered and rusted, strapped down with leather ties and fraying rope. It was a mess, but it worked. Galtro would forgo food before he'd risk losing a single drop.

She stopped cold as she rounded the path toward the Hub's doors, nearly stumbled as she found the courtyard outside the Hub empty. No one lingered nearby, telling stories under the glare of the sun or checking on their schedules. Something had gone terribly wrong.

Pelkaia's skin prickled with anxiety, and she spared a glance for those few men who had made the crossing with her. They were oblivious to the wrongness of their workstation, already tromping up the side of the Smokestack to relieve those that worked their lines before them. Chewing her lip, Pelkaia crept forward, straining her ears and eyes in a desperate attempt to see and hear beyond the vacuous silence which surrounded her. The doorway hung open, the gentle creak of its rusty hinges in the breeze the only sound to greet her.

She eased herself into the quiet and the dark, stunned that the lanterns had been snuffed. She'd been to the Hub many times before as a line worker, and never once had it been without light. Her breath came too hot, her fingers felt frozen. Before she had gone two steps, her toes stubbed against a warm, malleable mass.

Suppressing a shudder, she slipped into a crouch and squinted down at the face of the corpse. It was a woman, she knew not who, with her sword only half out. She wore blue from head to toe, and even in the dim light Pelkaia could follow the lines of her crisp uniform.

Expecting nothing at all, Pelkaia laid her fingers against the woman's throat. Her heart was silent. The handle of the blade was caught in the iron grip of death, so Pelkaia helped herself to the cudgel hung on the dead woman's belt instead. She hefted the deadly weight, squinting until her eyes adjusted to the dark. She had waited long enough. Nothing could delay her task.

Whatever awaited in the dark, she was coming for it.

CHAPTER 19

Scrubbed clean as a man could get in the desert, Detan tugged Tibs's hat down firm on his head and looked at himself in the mirror. It'd been a long time since he'd run a maneuver like this, and every fiber of his being was screaming at him to cut his losses and scramble.

But there was Tibs at his side, and the doppel's threat hung over him like a noxious cloud.

He could still see her, if he closed his eyes. Wearing Ripka's coat and Tibs's face. It'd be no trouble at all for her to frame him for some horrible deed. Detan was beginning to suspect that she'd enjoy doing such a thing.

They could run, sure. They could cut straight out and make for the north, or even north and east to shelter with his aunt until this all blew over. But a doppel was an unpredictable creature, and Detan had no doubt at all that if he bailed on her she'd tail them until she could assure their destruction. That woman was *angry*. The fierceness of her tone still haunted him.

She'd lost someone. Detan had no doubt of that. This woman, so long living a peaceable life in the sheltering rock of Aransa, had not suddenly decided to bring her talent to bear against the entire city on a whim. Grief. Grief was the most persuasive of motivators.

No, they couldn't run. She'd chase them down just for the joy of spreading her pain around. He had to see this to the end, and he was increasingly running out of viable options. Time to bite the air-serpent's tail. To stick his neck out.

"How do I look, Tibs?"

"Pompous and dirty. Same as always."

"You always know how to lift a man's spirits."

"I aim to please."

Detan glanced at Tibs through the mirror, catching the eye of his reflection. Tibs knew what he was about. Knew that he was going to kick up as much turbulence as possible in poor old Aransa to see what shook loose. Despite all that, the craggy man's face was as placid as an undiscovered oasis.

Tibs, that old rock, always gave him a measure of calm.

"Let's go, then," Detan said.

He led the way out of their shabby inn and up the steps to the next level. And the next. The grey-coated level guards didn't pay them any mind. Detan and Tibs didn't look like thieves, after all. They never did.

The sun climbed the horizon, casting toothy shadows across the calcite city as morning rose. People were minding those shadows, picking up their feet a little higher and stepping just a little faster to stay out of the sun as long as possible.

On the warehouse level, he caught sight of a sleek ship snaking its way into port. A Valathean personal cruiser, its darkwood hull gleaming in the growing light. Probably some highbrow ponce in to give Thratia his blessing. Detan smirked. Maybe the ex-commodore had finally given in to a political marriage.

In the road just before Thratia's compound Detan hesitated, glancing sideways to catch Tibs's eye. He was well under control, his face steady and his hands still, thumbs hooked in his belt. Tibs gave him a nod, a tip of the head so subtle that any other soul would have missed it. They strode forward, in step, toward the stony arms which encircled Thratia's home.

Her guards seemed to have expected them, because all it took was a cursory exchange of names to get the gates swung open. They didn't even get the traditional pat-down, which was well enough, because each of them had daggers tucked in the tops of their boots and hidden away in their sleeves. Spring-releases. Good technology, fresh in from Valathea.

Not that they were any good with them.

The guards hadn't even found his little jar of sap glue, which he felt made a rather obvious bulge in the side of his jacket. One of the blank-faced guards led them the long way around, through a dim hallway. The lamps were gone, replaced with cheap beeswax candles, and the light they put off was warm and cloying.

Detan frowned at one of those flickering flames, wondering if Thratia kept a hive of the deadly little creatures. It was a common enough pastime for the rich back in Valathea, but here on the Scorched the bees were as big as a fist and made hives as wide as the room they were standing in now. Detan decided that if Thratia were going to keep any kind of bee, they'd be the Scorched variety.

The guard abandoned them in Thratia's grand hall, promising the 'warden' would be along shortly. Detan blinked, too stunned by what he saw to rustle up a response to the guard.

The mélange of the fete's revelry had been replaced with great iron and wood machines, copper bellies belching steam into the cavernous chamber. Men and women in tight-fitting, sleeveless tunics with their hair pulled back in no-nonsense buns tended the machines, feeding barkboard paper in one end and examining it as it came out the other. Black and blue stains smeared the forearms of each worker, and many sported fingertip-shaped smudges on their cheeks.

Detan crept forward, peering through the obscuring steam to make out what it was they were doing. Piles of posters leaned against the edge of the machines, Thratia's sharp face obvious even in silhouette. He couldn't make out the words, but he could guess the meaning easily enough. He flicked his gaze from pile to pile, estimating their number – more than she could possibly need for Aransa.

The ex-commodore stepped between him and those machines, both brows raised in sharp irritation. Detan scrambled to flick her a salute.

"Evening, commodore."

"It'll be warden soon, Honding." She put her fists on her hips and he saw she was dressed much the same as she had been for the party. He doubted she changed for much at all. Detan took a breath, and plastered a big grin right across his face.

"If you can keep the *Larkspur* to yourself."

Her eyes narrowed. "Are you attempting to threaten me?"

He opened his arms and spread his hands. "I'm offering you a chance to save face, Throatslitter. I don't give a shit who ends up warming Faud's old chair, but I do care very much about losing."

"What, exactly, would you lose?"

"There's a doppel in this city, and she is going to steal the *Larkspur*."

Detan held his breath while Thratia thought that over, but it didn't take long. She wasn't the type to jump to conclusions, and he had given her precious thin information to work with. He was not at all surprised when she cut straight to questions.

"Just how do you know all that?" Her body remained still, her lips working over the words with the fine efficiency of one of her machines. Detan struggled not to scowl. Her body language was more tightly reined than he had remembered.

"You remember Ripka arresting me at your lovely banquet?"

"Yes."

"And do you remember Ripka keeping an eye on the party all evening?"

"Yes." She bit off the word, the sharp edge of exasperation creeping into her tone.

"The Ripka who walked me out your backdoor was a doppel, I'm afraid, and I spent an unearned night in the clink because of her. I am not a forgiving man, Thratia. I know her plans, and I want her to fail."

"And just how do you propose to keep my ship safe from this nefarious creature?"

He dragged in steam-laden air, forced himself to smile and willed himself not to sweat. "Why, you're going to put me in charge of your security staff."

She laughed, tipping her head back and baring her teeth to the heavens. The sound raked claws down his spine, rooted his feet to the spot.

"I know full well there is a doppel in this city, Honding. What I'm not buying is that it'd risk getting tangled up with someone like you."

He grimaced. "I was afraid of that. What if I could produce an independent party who happened to see Ripka in the dance hall at the same time I was being arrested?"

"Really," she drawled. "Who could you find that's impartial?"

"Oh, she's partial, but not in my favor. I want you to send ole Halva Erst a calling card."

"What will the Lady Erst have to say about it?"

Tibal cleared his throat and shuffled forward a half step on cue. "Lady Erst witnessed my conversation with the watch captain while Detan was being detained."

"Also, I left her at the altar," Detan piped up, just to be sure Thratia knew there was no friendship between them.

Thratia grinned. "Oh, this is a lovely way to start the morning." She snapped for an attendant, "Bring me the Lady Halva Erst. No delays."

When the lady in question arrived at Thratia's estate, Detan reflected that he would have had better luck summoning a whole swarm of spiders to his aide. She was positively incensed, her milk-tea cheeks flushed dark as garnet and her lips drawn so thin and bloodless one could mistake her for having none at all.

Upon entering Thratia's compound, she spied Detan and clenched her lily-soft fists into petal-powered hammers, and flew down upon him.

"You swine! You heartless, chicken-livered, old goat!"

Detan eased a step back, wiping spittle from his sore cheek. "Really, my dear, try to stick to one theme of animal."

She glowered and whirled to face Thratia, who had

the grace to cover her wide smile with the tips of her fingers. "I want him thrown to the Black Wash, warden! This man is a mongrel—"

"Another animal?"

"Be silent!"

Detan was beginning to feel dizzy when Halva spun upon him and jabbed a slender finger into his chest with each word she spoke. "You lost the right to say anything at all to me when you left me without so much as a peep! I thought you were dead!" Her eyes welled.

He frowned at the glimmer rimming her eyes, at the finger prodding him in the chest. Halva had always been one for histrionics, but this was a bit much. They'd hardly known each other, after all, and… His eyes narrowed at a suspicious glint.

"Is that a wedding ring on your finger?" he blurted.

She snatched her hand back and clasped it in the other. "Not that it's any of your business, but I've married Cranston Wels. *He's* a gentleman."

"Cranston! Your father hated that slag —oh." He sifted through memories long-since buried, recalling Halva's too-eager proclamations, the strange man who had leapt over the lady's garden wall, red in the face and screaming mad. Cranston Wels – it must have been. A man so slack-witted her father would have never permitted the match. Unless, of course, Daddy Erst felt he had barely escaped a much direr pairing.

"You used me!"

Halva's tears vanished without so much as a sniffle, and she rolled her big, glassy eyes to the skies. "Try to control yourself, my dear."

Detan gawped more like a landed fish than a landed man. He found he harbored a new appreciation for Halva Erst.

"As entertaining as this is, I am a busy woman." Thratia's soft voice cut through the haze of his wonder.

The effect on Halva was instantaneous. She ducked her head and dropped a low curtsey to Thratia, who didn't seem to care one whit. "Now girl, I need you to answer me honestly, do you understand?"

"Yes, warden."

"I'm not the warden yet."

Her smile was coy. "Daddy said it's only a matter of time."

"That may be true, but let's not get ahead of ourselves. Now, did you see Watch Captain Leshe last night at the party?"

"I did, she was lingering on the second story balcony, drinking herself stupid with that rat." She pointed an accusing finger at Tibal who grinned a little, shifting his weight from foot to foot.

"Wasn't like that, missus. Was just a drink or two, not the whole bottle or nothin'."

"I don't care about your drinking habits, Tibal. Did she leave the balcony at any point, Halva?"

"No, not until the band stopped playing. Then she went down to break up a fight."

Thratia's brows shot up. "There was a fight at my party?"

"Oh, just a tiff over a girl."

Thratia waved it off and nodded. "Very well. You can go now, Lady Erst."

"But–" She looked hungrily at Detan, which was a most unsettling experience for him.

"Go now, before you make a fool of yourself. Highroad, and all that. Off with you." Thratia shooed her away as if she were waving at a gnat. Lady Wels-nee-Erst harrumphed and expanded her sun parasol with vigor.

She strode from the room, leaving a trail of jasmine perfume in her ruffled wake.

"Strange girl," Thratia said. "I have no idea what you saw in her."

Detan had the grace to look chagrined. "I really did want her father's atlas."

Thratia sniffed and tossed her hair, sharpened pins glinting. "Well, mongrel, I believe the doppel has taken some interest in your pathetic hide."

He clapped his hands, unable to hide the relief in his eyes. "Excellent. We will take the most wonderful care of your gorgeous ship."

She barked a short laugh and turned back to him, one eyebrow arched. "Do you think me cruel, Honding? Heartless – maniacal, perhaps?"

His relief evaporated under the heat of her regard. "I never said–"

"You'd be correct, in many ways – few of which you understand. You might think all those things of me, Honding. But don't ever think me *stupid*."

"I would never–"

"I know you think me a poor fit for Aransa. You and your new creature-friend, no doubt. No, don't protest. Play at ignorance all you like, and ignorant you might be, but you're enamored with the very idea of the doppel, aren't you? It's what you want to be – what you wish you were. An independent element, moving against the stability of the empire. But you're not. You'll never be."

Thratia stepped close to him, her breath hot and near enough that he could smell the bright-eye berries she brewed in her tea. His stomach lurched at the saccharine scent – at her nearness. He'd almost rather her breath stink of wine. At least that way she would have drugged herself with something to make her slow-witted instead of sharp.

Before he could squeak any kind of response, any denial to collusion with the doppel, she pressed her hand over his mouth and gripped. Hard.

"You're clever, I'll grant you that. And I don't believe the rumors you've gone cracked in the head, not wholly. You're scared. I see it in the way you move, hands shaping half-formed thoughts, shoulders closed forward in defense even while your hips stay open, ready to run. I've made a study of it. The way people stand and the way they say what they want you to think they think. You jump from town to town, harassing anything with even the slightest stink of the empire on it but never, never, reaching your hand out to harangue the real seed of your terror.

"I don't know what happened to change you, Honding. I don't believe losing your sel-sense alone did it. Whatever happened to you, know this: that creature is little more than a murderer. Justified, possibly. I have no idea, nor do I care. But that thing has put terror in the hearts of the Aransan people. So you think real hard. Who's better for this city? The woman the people want to elect, or the choice of a man so addled he can't tell a flower from a thorn?"

"Mmmrpf," he said.

"If it's the *Larkspur* you want to watch over, then you may have it." She shoved him away and jerked her chin toward a militiaman. "Take them to the *Larkspur*. Let them be extra bait upon the trap. Do not, under any circumstances, allow them to leave the dock or this compound. Understood?"

"Yes, sir."

Heavy hands closed around Detan's arms, and he had to fight back an urge to jerk away. She turned her back on them, forgetting them the moment they were out of

sight. But he saw the way her shoulders slumped, saw
the subtle sigh leave her. The future warden, it seemed,
was very tired indeed.

He frowned, mind racing as he was dragged back,
Tibs hauled along beside him. Something she had said…
Extra bait. But what was the original? The ship? Would
she really risk her treasure just to capture one doppel?

"What's the hurry, Thratia?" he called, heels thumping
against the stairs as he was dragged up them. She paused
and turned back, face impassive. But her head was tilted
forward, just the tiniest bit. She was listening.

"You worried it's your head she's coming for next?"
His ankles burned as he dug his heels in, trying to slow
the progress of his cursing captors. Thratia just smirked,
an uncontrolled reaction. She didn't fear for her own
life, then. But why the rush?

He recalled the shadow of the Valathean cruiser drifting
overhead, mooring itself to one of the compound's less
glamorous docks. Was she trying to clear away the
problem before Valathea could instigate a purge? Had
that been how she managed to maintain all her imperial
connections, despite being expelled from the Fleet? A
promise to clean up Aransa? If they performed a purge
immediately after her taking the wardenship, the city
would be paralyzed. Useless.

The doors to the dock opened behind him, the
threshold loomed above his head. He cursed and lunged
forward one last time against the arms that held him,
desperate to catch a glimpse of her face. She stood in
the center of the steam-filled room, arms crossed low
over her ribs, head tilted back as she watched him being
hauled away.

"Afraid of breaking contract?" he yelled. Her head
tipped back, but her expression remained smooth. Placid.

A mask locked into place. He smirked.

"Gotcha," he whispered.

The militiamen threw him to the floor of the familiar u-dock. He landed hard on his side and grunted, little stars dancing before his eyes. The doors slammed shut, the sound of heavy metal gears echoing in the chamber as the locks were thrown.

Thratia'd made a deal with the empire that'd kicked her loose, and Detan reckoned he knew just what those terms were. They'd look the other way as she vaulted to power, perhaps provide some backing in the form of grain or steel, and she'd get those pesky rumors of a doppel run loose cleaned up. Trouble was, the doppel was proving too slippery even for Thratia's clutching hands. For the doppel's sake, he prayed to clear skies that the whitecoats hadn't caught wind of Thratia's little bargain.

Detan groaned and pushed himself to his feet, swaying a little as he waited for the dizziness to fade. Tibal sat on the ground, glaring at him. "Now what?" he said.

Shaking the fall from his head, Detan looked around. The dock was the same as he'd last seen it, the *Larkspur* anchored between the loving arms of the open-air dock. He peered over the edge, and swallowed at the drop to the ground below. No way either of them would survive that tumble, and the climb down was too sheer to risk.

"Don't suppose the servant's door is unlocked?" Detan asked.

Tibs grunted as he hauled himself to his feet. Though they both knew it'd lead nowhere, Tibs wandered over and gave the handle a twist, just in case. Nothing.

Detan heaved an exhausted sigh. "Well, we're here."

"There is one way out," Tibs said.

Their attention drifted to the *Larkspur*, hovering

peacefully in the warm morning light.

Detan breathed deep, tamping down the urge to reach out with his sel-sense and feel the ship's buoyancy sacks.

"That ship," he said as he licked his lips, "can only be flown by a crew of five. Or a very strong sel-sensitive."

"Indeed." Tibal sauntered toward the ship and crossed the gangplank. He stood upon the deck, casting an inquisitive eye over it. With an appreciative grunt he pulled out his notebook and charcoal pencil. "Too bad," he said without taking his gaze from his notes, "we don't have either of those things."

"Too bad," Detan agreed. He shook himself and crossed the plank. After a few moments' rummaging he gathered up a stretch of spare sailcloth and a slender rope. He plunked these materials down in the center of the deck and pulled out the knife he didn't really know how to use, and the pot of sap glue he did know how to use.

Under a heated glare from Tibs he took his knife to the handrail of the ship and peeled off a thin strip of wood.

"Just what do you think you're doing?" Tibs said.

"I told you I wanted to get the ship for the doppel."

The knot of Tibs's throat bobbed as he swallowed, the reason hanging between them. "And?"

"Well I sure as the pits can't just fly the thing to her. That would be... too risky." He cleared his throat and sat down alongside the sailcloth and rope with his pilfered wood. "She called herself an illusionist. Was very clear on the point. I didn't think much of it at the time, but..."

"She keeps the old ways."

"Mmhmm."

"You're building a Catari signal kite?" Tibs said, and Detan was a little annoyed to hear his voice laced with skepticism.

"As close as I can get. It should be enough to get her attention." He spread the sailcloth out and Tibs handed him his charcoal without asking. By pulling the rope tight between them, they managed to draw the straight lines of a diamond-shaped kite onto the cloth. Detan pursed his lips, poising the knife with care over the first mark.

"And once she shows?" Tibs said, kneeling down to hold the cloth steady as he cut.

"Then we get her the pits out of Aransa before Thratia can kill her, and hope her Valathean buddies consider her absence proof enough Aransa isn't in need of a purge."

Tibs grimaced, but fell to the work in silence.

CHAPTER 20

The patter of soft-soled boots moving with military precision echoed down the once silent hall. Pelkaia stole away to the wall and pressed her back against it, trusting to the shadows as a small group of interlopers passed by. There were three of them, swords out and dark and wet.

A wave of heat breached her cocoon of shadows, the three close enough that the combined warmth of their bodies brushed against her. She stiffened, pressing her back tight as she could against the wall, struggling to quiet the runaway hammer of her heart. They passed through the entrance chamber without a glance back and turned into another leg of the Hub.

Pelkaia remembered to breathe.

Those were not watchers. They were not Hub workers. Their tight, slate-grey coats were unknown to her.

What would Galtro do, if his station were under attack? Outside of the selium containment chamber, the records room was the sturdiest in the place. It rested close to the heart of the Hub, its back wall shared with the containment itself. There, he could hunker down and hide amongst the shelves, or make his stand at the bottleneck of the room's single door. Yes, that's where he would be. Her fist tightened. *If he's still alive.*

Taking a breath to steel herself, she flitted out into the hallway and began the circuitous path toward the records room. Insofar as she could discern, the three grey coats were the only other souls left standing. Her alertness ramped steadily into the realm of paranoia. Every intersection she triple-checked, every time she heard the softest of sounds she froze, slowing her breath, counting away a full hundred ticks of her frantic heart before she would move on.

She passed so very many of the dead. The administrative staff of the Hub, bleeding their last in the dark over a power squabble in which they held no sway. After the third, she stopped taking the time to check their faces, to look for some hint of familiarity that would allow her to carry the names and deeds of the deceased in her heart until her own time came. There were just too many, and she was well overdue.

The door to the records room was locked, but she hadn't expected it to be any other way. A soft light emanated from under it, throwing warm beams over her boots. A pair of feet cut through that welcoming light, casting sharp shadows.

She pitched her voice low enough to be mistaken for a man's and whispered against the door, "Sir? Are you in there, sir?"

As she watched, the shadows beneath the door shifted. The man behind ducked down, checking the boots of the voice at the door, and found them to be the footwear of a man who worked the line. State-issued and stained in black dust.

Galtro swung the door open and stepped aside. She

hesitated, the faint light within enough to stun her eyes. "Hurry up, man."

Pelkaia set her jaw and squeezed through the gap he allowed her. He eased the door shut and spun around, whatever he was about to say dying on his lips in a surprised grunt. Eyes wide, he brought up his bared length of steel, clutched in two steady hands.

"I know all my men, and I don't know you."

With a twist of her wrist she dropped a throwing dagger into her waiting palm and sent the weapon spinning. It was really too bad for Galtro that he was a man of principles; a man who expected a foe to face him head on and play fair. Too bad, because Pelkaia didn't plan on doing any of that.

The blade came in low – too fast for his eye to possibly follow – and buried itself to the guard in his guts. A momentary pang of guilt speared through her. It was a killing wound, which is what she was here for, but it was a slow kill, which wasn't what she'd had in mind.

He took one hand off the grip of his blade and reached down, his eyes gone round with shock. He touched the spot, lips twitching at the pain, and took his fingers away bloodied. Galtro stared at his red-smeared hand, sweat condensing on his brow.

"Was that really necessary?" he grunted.

She licked her lips and took a step away from him. Her back pressed up against the cold edge of a file shelf. Tangled in uncertainty, she drew her longknife and braced her stance. "It's what I came here to do."

"I see." He staggered backward and shot an arm out to lean his weight against the wall. His hand left a bloodied print, his palm began to slide. Tears glistened in his eyes, bright and unfallen. He let the blade slip his fingertips and it struck the ground with a clatter. She cringed, waiting for the sound of boots in the hall, but all was silent.

"You're not Thratia's, are you? You don't want those bastards in here any more than I do."

"I care nothing for this city's politics. I came for myself. I work for no one."

He slid down the wall until he sat with his legs straight out and his back propped up. He brought both his hands to bare on the wound, pressing down to staunch the flow of blood. He didn't remove the dagger. He wouldn't dare.

"Ah, I see it now. It's always in the eyes with the grieving." His rueful smile twisted into a groan as he hunched forward, his breaths coming in slow gasps until he had remastered himself. "I've seen so many eyes like yours. Weighted down with grief so heavy they start to look empty, like all other emotion has been squeezed out. So, who did you lose?"

The fingers of one hand drummed on her thigh while she turned the blade over and over with the other. Before she could leave, he had to be dead. Should she hasten that? Or should she wait for the fatal wound to take its course? Sweet sands, why was he so calm?

"Come on now, mister." He coughed, wiped pink-tinged foam on the back of his hand and sucked down a harsh, wheezing breath. "I don't recognize your face, that's true, but you must have lost someone here. This is revenge, isn't it? Well, that's all right. Really. I know I'm not leaving the Hub alive tonight, and I'd rather someone like you get me than Thratia's muscle. So, which is it? You lose someone on the line or in the mine-digging?"

"The line," she said reflexively, unable to hide Kel's achievements, even if it did reveal a piece of herself.

"Ah. You're proud. You're right to be. It's a hard job, but I'm sure you're aware of that." He shivered, lips turning purple as bruised violets, and spoke through half-clenched teeth. "Can you tell me something?"

"What?"

"The name. Who did you lose?"

She glowered at him, struggling to split her focus between his slight movement and her need to keep an ear to the door should Thratia's people decide to come this way. His question she ignored, turning her head away.

"Might as well tell me. I'm not leaving here tonight. I just want to know the name."

"Why?"

"I want to know which ghost caught up to me after all these years. Haven't had a fatality in over a year now, so you must've been planning this a long while."

"Kel," she snapped, the name bitter on her lips. "His name was Kel."

"Ah, well. Good lad, he was. I was sorry about what happened to his line, though I don't think it could have been helped."

She held up a silencing hand. "Stop there, Galtro. I know it was an accident. But you put them in those conditions, you and Faud and your deals with Valathea–"

He erupted into a coughing fit, too-bright red flecking the corners of his lips. Had she nicked the bottom of his lung with her strike? When the coughing subsided, he tipped his head back against the wall and panted. "It's not kind to make a dying man laugh, you know. And no, I wasn't about to feed you any of that bullshit. Of course it wasn't an accident, whole lines of good workers don't get wiped out due to an oopsie."

Cold raked her spine, fingers loosened on the grip of her longknife. "You're lying."

"Shit, why would I bother? Kel and his line did some

work loading a *special* ship bound for Valathea. You think that's a coincidence? And anyway, I told you I know my crews, and I know for a fact Kel didn't have any family in his life save his mother, so who in the pits are you? A lover?"

She licked her lips and twitched the blade in her hand. "None of your business."

"Fine, fine, keep it to yourself. I don't need a guidepost to see it. The boy was talented, and now that I'm looking, well, I see where he gets it from, eh?" He spat blood. "That's fine work, but you better get the pits out of Aransa after this, lass. The Scorched's not friendly to your sort, and Thratia'd love to get her claws in you."

"I consigned myself to death when I began this."

"Death? You think they're just going to string you up? You think they'd really toss off such a valuable asset?"

"I've seen the executions over the years. Men and women I knew as illusionists beheaded on the guardhouse roof. They were as strong as I, if not stronger, and they were not preserved."

"And these strong doppels you watched die, don't you think they could whip up a mask? Cover a tramp's face with their own, so the cruel and unsavory die while the valuable are whisked away into obscurity?"

She shivered, sent a nervous glance toward the closed door. Were those steps she heard? Or the startled leaping of her own heart? "No illusionist would agree to such a thing."

"They have no choice, woman, this is what I am trying to tell you. Once in Valathea, sel cannot be simply found or siphoned. It is tightly controlled, and the doppels even more so. Stronger the power, stronger the need, or so I'm told. How long do you think you could stand it, not touching sel?"

Her stomach knotted, her skin grew clammy. After only a week without coming in contact with selium she began to get headaches. Headaches that grew and darkened her vision as time went by. She remembered days sweating alone in bed, pain in every leaking pore until sustenance was returned. Her fingers trembled with the memory of it.

"I see you understand. Look, let me cut to it. You don't want Thratia getting her hands on you, and I need a favor."

"What makes you think you're in any position to bargain with me?"

He snorted and spat blood. "Lady, you know full well those are Thratia's thugs out there looking for me. They'll kill everyone who steps foot in this place while they're here, stomping out possible witnesses. And for what, do you think? She's got the wardenship bagged, I'd never win it."

Pelkaia licked her false lips. "She wants an excuse to seize control immediately."

"Right-o. She's convinced there's a live-blooded doppel in this city, and she wants you for herself. So she'll frame you for tonight's slaughter. Use it as an excuse to clamp down and start a hunt for you. You won't make it through that net, lass. When the folk of Aransa see some of their mining boys and girls dead, well, they won't care too much about my hide, but that'll hit home."

Pelkaia paced, pressed her ear against the door and heard nothing – a false silence? There was no way to be sure. Thratia's people could be out there now, listening as she was, hoping to glean some small facet of information. She clenched her jaw, rested her temple against the cool pane of wood.

"What can I do?" she asked, and as the silence

stretched she began to fear Galtro had died. Then his voice came to her, reedy and soft.

"You make damned sure the corpses of Thratia's men are found with the others, you understand? Rat out her little game. Can you do that?"

It'd been a long time since a smile touched her eyes, but she felt the corners of them crinkle all the same. "It'll be a pleasure."

When the old mine master's eyes emptied of life, she stepped forward and took back her dagger, spilling clotting blood upon the floor. She cleaned the blade against his shirt and brushed his eyes closed with her fingertips.

Regret formed a lump in her throat, but she choked it down. He was a clever old man, and so far as she could tell he cared about his people. Cared, but not enough to stay the hand of the empire when it came to her son's life. She scolded herself for her moment of regret. Whatever Galtro had said at the end, it wasn't enough. Would never be enough to absolve him of what he'd done. Not even his blood, pooling now, could cleanse the crime he'd committed in being complicit in Kel's death.

Fists clenched, she stood and surveyed the records room. Somewhere in the bureaucratic minutiae was evidence of Valathea's treachery. An order for Kel's line to load the *special* ship, an order for the very same line to meet its end.

Footsteps echoed down the hall, drawing to a stop by the door. She grabbed Galtro's fallen blade and stole away into the shelves to crouch behind a thick wooden crate stuffed full with yellowing paper.

The interlopers made quick, quiet work of breaking the door in. She stole a glance while they were still getting their bearings and saw the three that had passed her in the hall earlier. Two swordsmen and another with a crossbow out. Pelkaia hefted the weight of her throwing dagger in her hand, imagining the metal still thirsty for life, and marked it for the crossbowman. She tucked her head down and listened.

"Fucker's already dead."

"Makes our job easy."

"No it fucking doesn't. Who killed him?"

"I don't know, maybe he pissed off one of his people."

"Whatever, let's just stuff him with sel and get out of here."

"Ugh, we'll have to patch that new hole he's got."

"Shut up, both of you. The door was locked from inside."

They fell silent, and Pelkaia found it hard to concentrate on the sounds of their steps over the beating of her own heart. She ducked her head down low to peek through a tiny crack in the shelving and saw the crossbowman step closer to Galtro, putting his back against the wall as he surveyed the cluttered shelving. The other two fanned out, advancing, not yet close enough to get within reach of her. She took a deep breath, settled her nerves, and let the first dagger fly.

A scream and a clatter. The heavy thud of dying meat smacked into the unbending ground. His colleagues swore, rushed forward. Pelkaia sprung to her feet and the second dagger whipped free. It went wide, opening the sword arm of the trailing man. He dropped his blade and cried out, grasping at his opened flesh with his working hand. The fingers at the end of his wounded arm flicked and flexed, dancing to their own impulses now.

The other man closed upon her, bringing up his blade high and wide. She parried with Galtro's sword, the screech of steel by her ear raising goosebumps, and stepped back. Her retreat bore her into the shelf behind with a breath-stealing slap. She grunted, just barely making it under arcing steel.

Star-bright pain exploded in her side – a fist connecting – the pain a rising tide but not life threatening. She lurched sideways to compensate. The arcing blade bit back down, notching her shoulder. She grunted and slashed out – wild and desperate. A lucky swipe spilt the man's guts upon the floor, the hot stink wafting to her panic-widened nostrils. He collapsed over his wound with a whimper.

Sparing a moment to kick the fallen man's blade away, she freed another dagger and launched it at the wounded man lurching toward her over the body of his fallen comrade. It stuck in the hollow of his throat, buried deep, and he gurgled red spittle as he crumpled to the ground. Pelkaia leapt over the fallen men and swung around the corner of the shelves toward Galtro and the crossbowman. She had Galtro's sword out and ready, but the crossbowman was already dead.

Gasping for breath, she threw the blade aside and bent to rest her palms against her knees. Bile threatened to rise in her throat, but she choked it back. *You trained for this, you stupid woman.* She slapped herself across the face and shook her head. Forcing her chin up, she surveyed what she'd done.

Four bodies. She'd always been prepared to take more lives, she'd told herself over and over again that it might be impossible to avoid. But there were those three young men, bright eyes drained to empty shells, open mouths drip-dripping and fingers freezing in rictus claws. Whatever she had told herself, it didn't take them away. Didn't fill them with life and set them on safer paths.

Anger gripped her, cold as death. How dare Thratia send these young men into this place for what – the death of one man? She had to have realized the danger. Had to have known they would not all make it back alive. Thratia could not be so stone-headedly confident as to assume those three boys, boys her Kel's age, would be able to infiltrate this place with its watcher guards – Galtro himself a trained soldier – and make it out alive. How dare she put these young men in Pelkaia's path?

She sucked deep of the offal-and-iron air, forcing herself to straighten. To ignore the panging complaints of her shoulder, her hip joint. To ignore the creaking of the withered bones kept straight by her braces. What was one more name on the list?

She would show the commodore the depth of this cost.

With a clenched jaw she moved amongst them, closing wide eyes with trembling fingers. Her time was running out. Though the fight had been quick, it had been noisy. How long until someone came looking? How long until the dead blue coats were found by other eyes?

One more thing. One more thread to pull taut.

She plunged back into the jostled shelves, scanning the carved faces of the boxes. Years ago, when she'd been taken off the line for her faked injury, they'd kept her working down here. Hoping that she'd get well enough to return to the real work. She'd lingered, learning her way through the maze of paper and wood until they'd lost faith in her recovery and kicked her to the retired quarter.

In that time, she had learned well. Fingers still smeared with blood, she tugged out the box of reports from the month in which her Kel had died. She paged through, eyes darting, until she came across the week of the accident. She yanked the relevant cluster free, spilt its temporal neighbors to the floor, and opened the folded packet.

There it was. The official accident report. The details were brief, a break from their usual precision. She knew only what she'd been told – what Warden Faud had told her, when he'd knocked on her door with his hat in his hands. A landslide. No chance of survival. Terrible accident. Word for word the story she was looking at on the report, now.

Accident reports were messy things, scrawled over and over again with bits crossed out and rewritten as the details of the event became clear. There was no evidence of revision on this slip. It was pristine. Perfect. They hadn't even bothered trying to hide that it was a forgery.

A familiar signature scrawled across the bottom, a so-called witness. Thratia Ganal.

And Pelkaia's revenge had cleared the way for her. Made it easier to take power.

Trembling, she shoved the folded papers into the waistband of her son's pants and laid her forehead against the support timber of the shelves. The sel covering her face shimmered with the contact, but no one nearby was alive to see it.

Galtro and Faud weren't negligent then, just cowards. Had they still deserved to die?

She wanted nothing more than to dive back into those files, to spend the night digging up any hint of a name who'd had a hand in what'd been done to Kel. But she couldn't be caught here, surrounded by so much death. Couldn't let innocent mine workers find her, witnesses that would have to be wiped out.

She shook herself. There was little she could do now,

save escape. Take this knowledge with her. Strike back, and this time – *this time* – at the arachnidan hand that deserved it.

Just one more name.

CHAPTER 21

Banch loomed at Ripka's side, his breath coming in irritating snort-gasps through the handkerchief he kept shoved up against his nose. As much as she wanted to scold him for it, she really couldn't blame him. The four corpses had been left sitting no more than a half-day, but even in the cool interior of the Hub the desert heat had set them to festering.

Corpses. She had to keep thinking of them all as corpses.

"Those are Thratia's men." He heaved out between cut-short breaths, and she wished he hadn't bothered. Whatever had happened here, she had no idea how to deal with it. She was numb to the core, her mind stilled by the chilling of her heart. Galtro was dead. That three of the four corpses were Thratia's people brought her no comfort.

She had hoped the watchers found dead in the hallways of the Hub would be the worst of it. A sad little hope. A cruel hope.

Two watchers hovered nearby, awaiting direction, the

shock of finding their fellows dead still fresh on their young faces. Their presence pressed against her, spurred her to say something. Anything. She was their watch captain. She was supposed to be in control.

"Check the bodies of Thratia's men for any weapons which may have inflicted the wounds we have thus far discovered," she ordered.

The two watchers snapped to it, their eyes bright and eager. She was jealous, in a way. To have something specific to do – to have an order given to you – seemed like such a luxury now. Try as she might, she could not shake the feeling that Galtro would rise at any moment from his cold, sticky pool and tell her it was all a stupid joke, or a terrible mistake. Her stomach felt hollow, her voice without command. She kept her hands clasped behind her back to hide their tremble.

"You think Thratia had a fourth man here, one who got away?" Banch asked.

She shrugged, mind feeling sticky-slow, unable to catch up with reality, let alone speculate upon the past. "Could be. But why leave the bodies of his fellows behind?"

"Maybe he couldn't get rid of them quick enough."

"Maybe." Couldn't he stop asking her stupid questions? She had no answers. He knew that.

"You're not buying that, though," Banch persisted.

"No," she grated.

"Well?"

His prompting jolted her. Ripka forced herself to survey the wreckage of the room for the fifth time since she'd set foot in it. It was her job. She was good at it. She would find the answers.

For Galtro, and her fallen watchers.

She had no real way of knowing who died first, but

the way Galtro sat with his back against the wall marked him as different than the rest. The three were all looking away from him, their bodies angled around a point within the record shelves. It didn't make sense to her that Galtro would deal all three of them killing blows and then slink over to bleed his last against the wall.

And then there were the footprints.

There weren't many, and most were smudged beyond recognition, but a single set stood out amongst the uniformity of Thratia's people. A pair of work boots – quality, sturdy construction by the tread of them – had left a set of prints behind that didn't match up with any of the feet still in the room.

"I think they were all surprised. Every last one of them," she murmured, drawing a raised eyebrow from Banch.

"Captain!" Watcher Taellen poked his head around a shelf, face bright with the rush of new-found information. "Looks like there's some files missing back here."

"Good work, Taellen. Take note of all the files near it and the nameplate on the box."

"That won't be necessary," Thratia's voice threatened to cut away what remained of Ripka's sense of calm.

The would-be warden strode into the room, her lips curled to one side and her arms crossed low over her stomach. Thratia surveyed the remains of her men and got her gaze stuck on Galtro just long enough to make Ripka's gut twist. Ripka fought down an urge to rip Thratia's eyes from her sockets and leave them staring up at Galtro's corpse for good.

"Pardon, Thratia, but we are in the middle of an investigation here. I understand you may have known some of the men involved, but it is our prerogative to get to the bottom of this mess," Ripka said, feeling her own hands curl into fists at the small of her back.

"May have known? Watch captain, these three fine souls were some of my best. I sent them along to keep an eye on Galtro after I heard those terrible rumors of a doppel, and look what that got them. You back there!" She jerked a finger toward Watcher Taellen and his partner. "Leave what you're doing and get out here."

Skies bless them, her two rookies lingered, hands hovering near the handles of their cudgels, just at the edge of the shelf. They'd stopped what they were doing all right, but not out of any desire to obey Thratia. They were wary, knees tensed and shoulders squared, waiting for direction.

"I am sorry that you lost good men, but the situation is such that I must ask you to leave."

"Ask me to leave?" she snorted. "You got it backwards, watch captain. Seeing as there's no longer any competition for the wardenship, I'm within my rights to assume control of all warden duties until such a time as the election can be properly held. Isn't that right, Callia?"

Ripka startled as she caught sight of the Valathean noble standing two short paces behind Thratia. Callia was a willow-thin woman of impressive height, her overstretched limbs swathed in a flowing, silken material that Ripka suspected was far too unbreathable for the desert clime.

A girl approaching her blossom years hovered in the imperial's wake, wrapped in the same sky-blue silks her mistress wore, a folded parasol tucked under one small arm. The girl's complexion was lighter than her mistress, betraying deeper Catari intermingling than either Thratia or Callia. Ripka assessed her as the imperial's pet sensitive, and gave the girl a tight nod. The girl didn't even blink.

Callia broadcast an air of authority that made Ripka's skin prickle. She kept her hands folded before her, calm and ready, her face impassive. A small pang of jealousy reared in Ripka's chest as she noted the smoothness of the Valathean's shadow-dark cheeks, unworn by the desert sun, but her jealousy faded as Ripka took in the woman's profession.

Over Callia's fine silks she wore a long white coat, the hem of it just grazing the tops of her knees. Ripka swallowed and resisted an urge to step back. Whitecoats were the empire's special investigators, though Ripka knew they preferred to call themselves researchers. What in the sweet skies was Thratia doing with a whitecoat on her arm? Had the doppel been telling the truth – did Thratia seek a purge for Aransa? It made no sense.

The imperial smiled, no doubt catching the startled recognition in Ripka's eyes.

"I am from the Scorched diplomatic delegation, and it is within my authority as an instrument of the empire to assure you, watch captain, that Thratia is within her rights to claim the wardenship. Although we would prefer she call it a regency, at least until such a time as the elections can be held."

Under the milky eye of the empire, her own masters, all Ripka could do was tuck tail and bow. No matter how much she wanted to tell them all to get fucked, this was her crime scene, she knew, clear as the skies were blue, that being abrasive now would only get her thrown out on her backside.

"As you wish, I obey, diplomat. But regarding this incident, my team are equipped and experienced for just this sort of puzzle. If you'll allow me until tomorrow morning, I believe we can uncover the cause of this mess."

The whitecoat shook her head. "It is within Thratia's authority to seize control of this investigation, and not within mine to limit her. I recommend consultation between both divisions, but that is not a Valathean order." Callia bowed, Valathean-style, with her hands held before her head, palms facing the blue skies.

"Nothing personal, Leshe, but I want a crack at this tick of a doppel." Thratia's voice was laced with the quiet waver of tightly reined anger. Ripka blinked, she'd never heard Thratia come close to losing her calm before.

"Do you have reason to believe the doppel did this?" Ripka asked, smoothing her voice with professional curiosity.

"Look around you, captain, it's a mess. The doppel is clearly targeting important figures of Aransa, and when I take the wardenship it will be my head that has a target on it, if it doesn't already." She waved a dismissive hand. "You may take your people and go. My own investigators will arrive with the next ferry. See that everything is left as you found it. I will call upon you if I need you."

"Warden, I must insist that the Watch be allowed to do its job here." Ripka was annoyed to hear a pleading note enter her voice. Banch's hand settled on her shoulder. She hadn't realized she'd taken a step forward, that her fists had slipped from behind her back and come up low and ready.

Thratia eyed her from tip to toe, and waved a dismissive hand. "I have heard you. Now go."

Banch tugged her sleeve, urging her back. With a clenched jaw she snapped a salute to Thratia and turned on her heel, knowing her blues would follow. None of them would want to be left alone in the same room as that woman.

They marched in silence to the ferry dock, Ripka

keeping her eyes averted from the corpses of the men and women she'd sent to keep watch over Galtro. Five good watchers, and none of them dead by the same weapon as Thratia's people. One still had a crossbow bolt sticking from her throat, black and insectile. Her name had been Setta. Ripka burned the names of each into her memory as she passed.

At the ferry they watched Thratia's so-called investigators unload. Debt collectors, mudleaf smugglers, fire-protection men. Cutthroats, all of them, and every last one avoided so much as acknowledging the existence of the watchers arranged before them. They marched across the dock and toward the Hub like they owned the place, and with a sour taste in her mouth Ripka decided their mistress did, and that was close enough.

Across the gap, with the city's bedrock firm under her feet, she dispersed her people back to their homes and stood thinking, arms crossed snug over her chest. It was a moment before she realized Banch was still at her side, watching.

"What?" She sighed.

"You're planning something."

She threw her hands in the air. "Of course I am. Galtro's dead and something needs to be done about it, dammit."

"Thratia said…"

"Thratia wants the city and the doppel, she doesn't care about what's right. Pits below, Banch, did you see our people? Opened with swords and crossbows, not daggers like Thratia's and Galtro."

"You think her people did for ours?"

"Yes."

"Then you'd better keep your nose clean of it."

She sighed and dragged her fingers through her hair,

thinking of the single wine bottle at home in her pantry. Knowing Banch had so much more waiting for him. A wife. A child. A warm meal.

"Go home, Banch."

"I'm your sergeant, captain. I stay."

"You got a family, don't you?"

"Yes, but—"

"Go. Home. That's an order. And on your way there, stop by the station. Tell everyone to go home and lock down." She waved an arm to encompass the city before her. "Thratia's taken the reins, and there's no telling what she might do. Aransa is not safe for the Watch. Not tonight."

He gave her a long, anxious look, sweat sticky on his brow, then snapped a salute with a hundred times better form than she'd shown Thratia.

"Stay safe, captain."

"I'm working on it."

He turned crisp on his heel and strode off towards home and shelter.

CHAPTER 22

Ripka went home before she went to the station, and changed into the Brown Wash clothes of mourning. She would not do what she was about to do while wearing her blues.

The black cotton was pounded smooth by stones, and the supple fabric covered her from throat to foot. It was a variation on an old Catari tradition, or so her mother had told her, though the original rites were long since lost. In the Brown Wash, one donned their blacks and stole an item of personal significance from the house of the deceased on their pyre night.

Galtro would have no pyre night. Ripka suspected Thratia would chuck him into an unmarked grave, or garbage burn, to keep from establishing a site that might turn into a symbol for martyrdom. That was all right by Ripka, she'd never been much of a traditionalist. She'd find her own way to mourn. A way that involved punching Thratia right in her smug little mouth.

The black cloth made slipping through the city unnoticed easy, and she found herself walking through the station house's door before she had a plan firmly in mind. The station was quiet, the lamps snuffed and the halls emptied. Papers were left in haphazard stacks on desks, half-drunk tea cups gone cold beside them. At least someone had remembered to lock the door on their way out. Ripka's lips quirked in a smile adverse to her mood. Probably Banch.

She drifted through the darkened halls by rote, found the aisle of long-term inmates and reached for the lantern she knew would be there. It felt light in her hands, not much oil left. Not much time to burn.

With care she struck her flint and lit the already charcoaled wick, coaxed a small flame into life. A few muted groans of protest sounded down the hall. The regulars, annoyed that their darkness was disturbed. She ignored their grumbles as she continued down the hall. She wasn't here for the regulars. Ripka sought a much more recent addition.

The unnamed woman's cell was second to last, a palm-sized piece of wood with "Unknown #258" hastily tacked in place of a name placard. Ripka ran her fingertips over the number, wondering at the motives behind the two hundred and fifty seven who had come before this one. Most were long before Ripka's time, but in her experience few kept their numbers long. The last, however, had kept his number until his death. Unknown #257. The doppel caught impersonating Mercer Agert.

She resolved that this woman would not die in obscurity.

Ripka hung her lantern from the hook above the small window in the wooden door, placed so that it was just out of reach of the inmate but still close enough to cast some light into the cell. Then she pulled a heavy metal key from her pocket, and stepped inside.

Unknown lay on the bench opposite the door, curled on her side with her arms cushioning her head. Lank, greasy-brown hair streaked her cheeks, and the whites of her eyes glinted wide and wary as Ripka entered her world. Taking a deep breath of the fetid air, Ripka shut the cell door behind her.

The woman swept her gaze over Ripka's mourning clothes and raised her brows. "Is this a personal call, captain?"

"I need answers from you. Evidence."

With a grunt the woman sat up. The chains binding her wrists together hissed against one another like a disturbed viper. "I've been through this about a half dozen times with your lackeys. I've got nothing to say, and you don't have the spine to force it out of me."

Ripka eyed the woman with care. She was in good health, even if she could do with a bath. The records her watchers kept said she ate well, sending back empty platters after each meal time. Ripka made sure of it – she checked those reports every night, and did what she could in the morning to see to it that those who weren't eating had their diets adjusted to please them. Ripka would never allow it to be said that her jail treated its inmates poorly.

She could only hope her successor gave the same care.

"You're right." She spun the cell door key around her finger. "We're not interested in forcing answers from you. We're not brutes. Though I'm sure if the situation was reversed Thratia would have cut the answers from you by now."

The woman rolled her eyes. "Never said that's who I worked for but, I'll tell you this, I woulda' cut the answers outta you *myself* if the tables were turned."

"Charming." Ripka moved the key, very slowly, to her

pocket and gave the button flap a hasty loop. She stood there alone, unarmed. The key to the cell protected by no more than a flimsy piece of cloth. The woman licked her lips, chains rustling as she leaned forward. Ripka's heart stuttered with a burst of adrenaline, her muscles growing taut though she didn't dare take a fighting stance.

The woman's eyes widened and she grinned to bare her teeth. "Why, Captain Leshe. You are the clever one."

"Does that mean you'll answer my questions?" Ripka fought to keep her voice smooth, to keep her hands from twitching toward the empty holsters of the weapons she had set aside before entering this cell. The fight she sought would already be unfair. No need to make it worse.

"Maybe. What it does mean, is, I'll take you up on your offer."

A fierce grin split the woman's face, and Ripka's whole body thrummed with anticipation. *Do it, then!* She wanted to scream, but she bit back the words behind a falsely perplexed frown. "I'm not sure what you–"

The woman lunged. Fierce joy shot through Ripka, the burst of elated strength so overwhelming she grabbed Unknown by her outstretched arms and pivoted at the hip, swinging the over-leveraged woman into the wall. Unknown's hip and shoulder cracked against the hard stone, loud enough that Ripka feared for a fleeting moment that she'd overdone it, that she'd knocked the woman out in one blow.

Luck was with her.

Unknown turned to face her and lurched forward, fists raised, and forced Ripka to circle around lest she let the woman get within her guard. The woman grinned and wiped blood from her lip onto the back of her fist.

"You surprise me, Leshe, an upstanding woman like you starting a fight with a prisoner."

"You attacked me," she said, too fast, but she didn't care. It was done. Now she needed to press her advantage, to keep Unknown off guard. "What's your name?"

"Oh, is that how this works? Blow for blow, eh? I guess you earned it. Name's Dekka."

Before she'd finished her sentence she lunged, landed a jab on Ripka's right side so hard she spluttered and stumbled back. The great wooden door of the cell slammed into her back, and her lungs burned as she strained to retrieve the breath she'd lost. Dekka stepped into it, turning her body wide to come across with an uppercut.

But Dekka hadn't been locked up long enough to know the cells as well as Ripka.

Ripka shoved her hands down and grabbed the iron loops protruding from the door at hip-height. Bracing herself, she drew her knees into her chest and kicked out with both feet. The connection sent Dekka reeling, but Ripka was too busy trying to quiet the rattle of her own teeth to see where she went. Ripka dropped the loops, her fingers too numb and her shoulders too jarred to keep on holding them, and fell into an awkward crouch.

Dekka lurched to her feet and let loose with a roar as she charged with both her hands held up in a hammer blow. Ripka scurried away, crawl-hopping like a rabbit, and grabbed the bench Dekka had just abandoned to pull herself to her feet.

Dark compacted around her eyes just a breath before the pain reached her, lancing up from somewhere about her lower back. Damn woman was blasted strong. Ripka whirled, teeth clenched, and somehow managed to get the chain that bound Dekka's wrists caught in one hand. She swung her around and then pulled, Dekka's back slamming into her chest, and they went staggering backward until Ripka's back slapped the wall.

Gasping, snorting, they fumbled and grabbed and twisted until Ripka had one elbow snapped tight around Dekka's throat and the other pinioned her arms. The blasted woman's legs flailed, clubbing Ripka's shins with her heels. Ripka screamed against the pain, screamed against her loss, then pushed forward and spun around, slamming the woman face-first into the wall.

Her chest heaved, her knees threatened to quake, but still Ripka held the squirming, cursing, agent of Thratia against the cold yellowstone and fought back an urge to break the woman's neck.

"Who is supplying Thratia's weapons?" Ripka growled, her throat raw from her gasping.

"Fuck yourself," Dekka hissed.

Ripka tightened her elbow, felt the woman spasm as she struggled for air, then eased the pressure. "Again."

"Some bitch-faced imperial." Dekka spat a wad of blood and spittle against the wall, wheezing as she drank down the air.

Callia. "Why? What's the imperial get?"

"I don't–"

Ripka squeezed. Galtro's rotting body floated before her mind's eye, rank and discarded. Tossed against the wall like a broken toy. She gasped and eased her hold.

"Shit!" Dekka fell into a coughing fit, and Ripka let her heave until it passed. "Freaks, all right? Any weirdo fucking sensitive she can round up. But she's not happy about it, she wants to keep one for herself."

A smile broke across Ripka's face, and she closed her eyes for a moment in rapture. Perfect. If Thratia wasn't happy, that meant somewhere she was keeping records.

Keeping notes that could be used to turn against the imperial should the need ever arise. If Ripka could use them to destroy the imperial's authority, then Thratia would have no official backing. No claim to make on the wardenship... And the people wouldn't be too pleased, either, to hear proof she dealt in human trafficking. Even if the poor souls being bought and sold were deviant sensitives. But first she'd have to prove to Callia that Thratia was planning on holding out on her, drive a wedge between them so she could investigate deeper.

"The records of these shipments, where are they kept?"

"I don–"

She squeezed, and Dekka thrashed so hard Ripka nearly lost her grip.

"Where–"

"I really don't know! Shit! The compound, probably, where else?"

That would have to do. Ripka dropped her hold on the woman's chained arms and shoved her against the wall as hard as she could. Dekka struggled, sensing an opportunity, but Ripka leaned the whole of her weight against the weakened woman and was able to pin her in place. She fumbled one hand through a pocket and pulled out a small clay bottle. Its contents were heavy, familiar. She'd used similar bottles a hundred times or more in her line of work. So many that she had a standing account at the nearest apothik.

Ripka broke the clay bottle against the wall, felt the sticky resin of golden needle extract smear over her hand. The cloth folded within the jar she palmed, shook open, and crammed into Dekka's mouth. It only took a few breaths before the woman went limp.

After waiting a few frantic heartbeats to be sure the

woman wasn't faking, Ripka eased her into a looser hold and half-dragged, half-carried her over to the bench. With care she arranged Dekka's arms and legs, making sure none were folded in such a way as to cut off circulation. Ripka peeled the cloth from her mouth, yellow-stained linen flecked with pink blossoms of Dekka's blood.

Her fist clenched, squeezing bitter droplets from the rag to the blood-spattered floor. It was done. The woman took no permanent damage. Ripka closed her eyes and tipped her head back, baring her face to the unfinished stone ceiling as if expecting a bolt of lightning to burst through the dry desert air and cleanse her of her crime.

Yes. Crime. She trembled as she stepped away from Dekka, shut and locked the cell door with care. Even Dekka had known what she intended. Worse, the woman had welcomed the chance. Ripka half-staggered as she walked down the hallway, the sharp absence of adrenaline causing her knees to quake. She paused, took a breath, steadied the lantern she carried.

It was *not* torture.

But that didn't mean it was right.

Ripka clenched her jaw and turned, striding towards her office. Her weapons were there – cudgel, cutlass, dagger – and her files. She flung open the door, heedless of the noise, and crouched before an overburdened file box. Even Thratia would have had to file building plans when she constructed her compound. Ripka flicked through the years, found the yellowed edge of paper she sought and tugged it free.

The lines of the plan were still bold and clear, even if the black ink was fading to brown. Ripka brushed the scent of dust from her nose and cringed as she smeared blood from the back of her hand against her lips. No matter. There would be time to clean herself later. If she survived.

She had to keep moving. If she lost momentum, she feared she would collapse under the weight of what she carried. Faud. Galtro.

Dekka.

Before she set out, she wrote Dekka's release papers and left them signed on Banch's desk. If it all went sideways, he at least would recognize her authority come the morning.

CHAPTER 23

Pelkaia stood across the street from the Blasted Rock Inn, wearing her mother's face for comfort. It was not precisely how her mother had been. She'd had to darken the shade of her skin to a more Valathean-mingled hue, had to lift and sharpen the sand-dune smooth planes of Catari cheeks. She doubted any Aransan would recognize a full-blooded Catari anymore, but still she feared her mother's original countenance would be too exotic. Too worthy of notice.

The first time she had come here it had been after another murder, her first in more years than she cared to dwell upon, to drink to her sordid little victory. The memory of warm pride swelled within her and soured, the faces of those strangers she had bought drinks for just to hear them cheer blurred. Now... Now she came to drink smooth the ragged edges of her anger.

The chill of the desert night seeped through her clothes and prickled across her skin. Pelkaia flinched away from the emptiness. The cold reminded her of Galtro's blood, the heat of it turning bitter as it clung to her clothes, separate from the living vessel. She'd left her son's sullied vestments behind at her apartment before coming here – scrubbed her skin raw and red with sand and oils. But still she felt the shape of the stains, spread like guilty handprints across her body.

Pelkaia ducked her head, let lank hair frame the sharp edge of her false cheeks, and slunk into the Blasted Rock.

There was no celebration this night, no raucous gambling. The long bar to her left was elbow-to-elbow with regulars, the little square tables made of old shipping pallets occupied by bent-headed locals. A crude block print of Thratia's face hung on the wall across from the door, her sharp eyes the first thing to greet any who entered.

She took a deep breath to steady the frightened-rabbit thump of her heart, scented the grainmash molder of poorly filtered whiskey and the stale dust of wooden floorboards long unswept. Pelkaia found an empty table and shuffled to it, keeping her head tucked down and her back hunched. She sat, and the weight on her shoulders grew heavier.

The tense atmosphere was partly her doing. If she had not killed Faud then there would be no election, no dark shadow spreading across Aransa from a compound built high above. Pelkaia set her elbows on the table and buried her face in her hands, then realized anyone looking at her would see the pearlescent ripple of sel around her fingers. She slid her hands up to tangle in her hair. Her real hair. She clenched her jaw and pulled.

"Gotta buy something to sit here, ma'am."

Pelkaia glanced up into the face of a barboy, no more than fourteen monsoons old, chewing a lump of barksap with such vigor it crackled each time he opened his mouth.

"Strongest thing you got," she said as she tugged a copper grain from her pocket and pressed it into the palm of his outstretched hand.

The boy shrugged, flipped the grain through the air and caught it in one fist. "You got it, lady."

He disappeared behind the bar, the sandy curls of his hair lost behind the sloped backs of those patrons seated closest to the booze. While Pelkaia waited she did her best not to feel anything. To think anything. To focus only on the burning in her hastily stitched shoulder, the throbbing ache in her side which rose with every beat of her heart.

The boy returned with a squat brown bottle, its label block-stamped with a spindly black bee. The bottle wasn't for her – she hadn't paid him nearly enough – but he brought it to show her what she paid for. Pelkaia wanted to smile at him for his honesty, but the muscles around her lips were beyond her reach.

He pulled a wide-mouthed glass from his pocket, flipped it around as he had the grain, then caught it and set it on the table. With care he poured out a draught three fingers thick. He then paused, winked at her, and dribbled in a few more drops. She blinked, recognizing the charm of a showman for what it was. If this lad had poured her drinks the night she killed Faud, she might have given him her whole purse.

"Here." She shoved another copper into his little hand and waved him away. The boy hesitated, a furrow working its way between his brows, but soon his forehead returned to smooth youthfulness and he cut her a quick bow before rushing off.

Pelkaia sighed. He was probably used to a lot more tips and attention than he was getting tonight. No matter, he was still young enough that his forehead could abandon its wrinkles with nothing more than a shift of mood. He'd be fine.

She drank. The liquor was sweet with honey and effervescent, tingling bubbles of selium erupted against the rough surface of her tongue. Pelkaia flinched back, wrinkling her nose in surprise. This was the strongest they had? This sugary... concoction? She hazarded a glance over at the barboy who gave her nothing more than another wink in return. She swallowed hard around empty air. Did he know she was sensitive? Had he thought that a selium-laden drink would help soothe her nerves?

Did it matter?

With a shrug she tossed back the rest of the drink and waved him over for another. And another.

The pain in her shoulder receded, the weight on her heart lessened. She looked up, surveying the room, grinning to herself as she recalled that first time she'd come here. It had been lively then, with the card players worked up into a lather over some Valathean game that was supposed to be new – fresh in from the Imperial Isles, the greatest game behind the Century Gates. Of course it wasn't anything of the sort. It was Detan Honding's game, and the only winner was the man himself.

Pelkaia stared at the empty table, conjuring him in her mind's eye as she'd first seen him.

He'd had his back to her, head bent down over a pile of cards so that his hair slipped up and his collar slipped down just enough to reveal his Honding family crest.

The Honding wanderer. A conman and burnout. The only sorry sack of flesh on all of the Scorched to have lost his sel-sense to trauma. Some accident on his line back in Hond Steading, an explosion or a fire, and he was done. The only survivor – left useless by his survivorship.

They'd even taken him back to Valathea for a while, tried to cure his inability. Or so the rumors of the uppercrust went.

Pelkaia had suspected otherwise. The Catari had stories, stories her mother had sung to her at night in their filth-encrusted cave at the fringe of the Brown Wash. Stories of men and women who could make the firemounts roar to life. If the rumors about the Honding lad were even half true, then the only thing he was running from was whatever had been done to him in Valathea.

Gods below the dunes, he'd looked so blasted pleased when she'd had Ripka's watchers arrest him. She'd been lucky, she knew, to find watchers nearby who were willing to follow her orders. Watchers too disconnected from their fellows to realize Ripka would be down by the Black Wash, preparing to put a man to death due to the depth of his talent.

And now what? What was she supposed to do now that Galtro was dead – her self-appointed crusade complete? She felt the folded lump of paper in her pocket, the doctored report of her son's deadly 'accident'. Felt Thratia's name burning a hole in her hip. Was she finished? Could it ever just end?

What would she be, when this was over?

She straightened, shoulders drawing back, jaw tightening as she pushed aside all self-pity. It did not matter what she became, it did not matter where she ended up. She'd set out to destroy those who'd contributed to Kel's murder. So what if there were one more guilty soul to destroy? So what if there were dozens? Just because she had work yet to do did not mean she had failed. This was *not* over.

The inn's door burst inward, a flush-faced man

stumbling as he tugged on a slate-grey jacket. Pelkaia went cold straight to her core, her whole body felt encased in amber as the man's mouth began to move.

"Galtro's been murdered! Thratia's warden now! City's on lockdown until the sun-cursed sonuvawhore who did this can be found!" The man snapped his jacket straight and Pelkaia saw the crest whip-stitched to his sleeve: Thratia's house sigil.

The shockwave of his words spread syrup-slow throughout the room. Pelkaia watched in perverse fascination as eyebrows lifted, curses were uttered, and a few precious mugs were dashed against the floor. Men and women took to their feet, most a touch unsteady, hands reaching for hidden weapons. They cheered. Loud and bright and joyous.

"Easy!" The barkeep, a man who had more muscle in his arms than hairs on his head cried out as he hauled himself up to stand on the bartop. "Steady, all of you bastards! We're prepared for this." He stabbed a finger at the regulars crowded around the bar. "Wait your cursed turns while Tik gets the goods ready!"

Prepared for this? Pelkaia's pulse hammered in her ears, her palms went cold and damp with newfound fear. Some detached part of her marveled that she could still feel fear, that she could still desire self-preservation. The rest of her began to move.

Slowly as she could without being obvious, Pelkaia levered herself to her feet. The regulars reached over the bar, their backs to her, hands grasping for grey coats the barboy Tik was hauling out from the back room for them.

No, more than coats. Weapons emerged from the false bottoms of transport crates, their clean metal gleaming in the dusty lamplight. Well-made weapons. Valathean weapons. Pelkaia swallowed hard. She stepped on the balls of her feet, felt the sway of booze in her limbs and decided she'd have to settle for mid-stepping. It was quiet enough. And they were being so loud, the metal clanging…

"Hey." Tik scrambled to the bartop and pointed her way, his other hand waving a grey coat like a flag. "You loyal?"

"I just wanted a drink," she blurted, then clamped her jaw shut and slapped a hand over her mouth in shock. Why had she said that? Oh, Gods below… Why had she touched her skin?

Tik's eyes nearly leapt from his tiny, perfectly smooth face. "Doppel!" he screeched.

The mantle of her anguish was shattered by the crushing weight of her fear. Pelkaia bolted, ignoring the pain in her side, letting the alcohol numb her hurts and fuel her movement. She was lean, she was fast. But they were much, much closer to the door.

She thundered into a burly man who, thank the stable sands, had been well into his cups by the time she'd arrived. Her shoulder clipped his, and though fiery lances of pain raced through her he spun away and twisted, toppling like a felled log before his rushing fellows. The first two tripped over their comrade, and Pelkaia's fist closed on the doorknob. She yanked it open and her head snapped back, strange fingers tangled in her hair.

Pelkaia threw her senses out for the bottle the boy had brought her, and found a dozen and a half on a shelf behind the bar. She yanked on the sel within the liquor, heard glass shattering amongst screams as her blind tug sent the bottles spinning into the regulars. Blood and honey perfumed the air. The fingers in her hair tightened their hold.

She gripped the door with both fists and jerked herself to the side even as she flung the door wide. Roots ripped from her scalp as she hurtled out into the street, fingers too numb to maintain their hold. The ground bit her knees. She got her hands out and tucked her head, tumbled through the dust and the grit and slammed into something warm and hard and hoofed.

The indignant honk of a cart donkey broke through the screams coming from the Blasted Rock, and she rolled just in time to avoid being trampled. She found herself in the gutter on the opposite side of the street, scrambled to her feet and took off running down the slope, pumping her legs as fast as she could to stay ahead of the forward tumble of gravity. If she lost her footing now…

Something cracked against the ground beside her and she jumped aside, nearly tangled in her own feet as she slewed sideways into an alley. Pelkaia dropped her back against the alley's wall, facing the way she'd come from, heaving in great gasps of air.

In the street where she had stood rocks rained, pitched down by her pursuers. She snorted in derision, regretted it as snot dribbled over her lips. With a grunt she dragged the back of her hand across her mouth and spit. She was Catari. She should not run scared from a bunch of Aransan backwater drunkards.

Neither would she risk any of them landing a lucky blow.

Pelkaia peeled the sel from her body and stretched it as thin as she dared, covering the entrance to the alley, mimicking perfectly the obfuscation she left over the mouth to her own home's alley. It was an easy shaping for her now, but she didn't need it to be perfect. Those patrons of the Blasted Rock were too deep into their drink to notice any irregularities.

As the thunder of their steps approached she forced herself to step away from the wall and stared through the thin membrane. The group approached the spot where the first rock had struck the road warily, peering all around. Pelkaia allowed herself a small smirk as the man who still held clumps of her hair glanced to the alleyway and then reached up to scratch the back of his head in confusion. Idiot.

That's what they got for breaking with the old terms. For insisting on calling her a doppel instead of an illusionist. What you called a thing carried weight, implied meaning. Doppels could change the appearance of themselves. Illusionists could change the appearance of anything. Names mattered.

The group conferred in mutters too soft for Pelkaia to make out, then turned and started back up the slope. She suspected some of them must be relieved not to have to chase down something their mothers had told them scary stories of. Even the dullest of minds knew that being a member of a mob didn't make one immune from harm.

Pelkaia reached up to rub the back of her head, and hissed through her teeth as she touched the raw patch of her scalp. Bastards. Her fists clenched. She could not stay here. Not anymore. There were too many layers in this city – of pain and of memory. It was only a matter of time until she slipped again. Until she was too slow to escape the claws tightening around her.

But there was no way out of the city, not tonight. Not with half the damned citizens donning Thratia's grey uniform. There wouldn't be any flights out. Monsoon season was coming – and Aransa was too far from anywhere else to risk the walk.

Not that she could manage a walk like that in the state she was in now. Battered and exhausted, nothing but copper and a useless knot of paper in her pockets.

Pelkaia massaged her face with both hands and groaned. She was marooned on this cursed hunk of dormant rock.

But... She clenched her jaw, drummed her fingers against her thigh. There was still one element in play. The Honding lad was out there and, as far as he was concerned, their deal was still hot. She glanced in the direction of Thratia's compound, and caught sight of a slip of sailcloth drifting on the evening breeze. She almost laughed aloud. Trap or not, the *Larkspur* was calling to her.

And Pelkaia truly, desperately, did not want Thratia to have that airship.

She squared her shoulders, lifted her chin. Maybe Galtro was a mistake. Maybe the people responsible for her boy's death were too far away for her to ever reach. But maybe not. If she had a fine vessel like the *Larkspur*, she could go anywhere. Once she had Thratia's ship, she could lay low for a while; lick her wounds and court future allies. Wouldn't it be fun to take one of Thratia's toys away before crushing her? And wouldn't Thratia keep her own records, peppered with other names for her to collect?

But first. First she needed to get out of this blasted city, and leave its ghosts to rot.

CHAPTER 24

Something jarred Detan's foot, thrusting him back into wakefulness. He snapped upright, half-tangled in the mass of excess sailcloth and rope he'd been dozing on, eyes blurry as they adjusted to the gathering dark.

"What?" he muttered, wiping crusted sleep from his eyes.

"Don't you hear that?" Tibs said, crouched at his side. "Sands below, you'd sleep through monsoon season."

Exhaustion had driven them both to rest, and now it seemed night had well and truly come to Aransa. The lanterns ringed round the u-dock gave him just enough light to see by, and Detan couldn't help but wonder who'd come along and lit them while he dozed. The little kite still drifted in the wind, tied to the rail at the aft of the ship, fluttering like a forgotten party streamer. He closed his eyes against distraction, trying to hear whatever it was Tibs had picked up on.

The deck below him smelled of sharp Valathean teakwood and warm wax, the ropes holding the ship to its mooring posts creaked with subtle swaying. Tibs's breath was soft beside him, calm but wary. His own heart thumped in his ears… and someone was scraping at the lock on the door to the servant's entrance.

He snapped his eyes open and scrambled to his feet. "You think it's the doppel?" he whispered.

Tibs shrugged, but had a small knife in his hand. "Let's find out."

As Tibs loped across the gangplank, Detan cast around for a weapon of his own – and came up with nothing. He had his knife, sure, but he was more danger to himself with it than anyone else. With a shrug he snatched up the leftover sap-glue pot and hurried after Tibs. The least he could do was confuse the creature, if it came to it.

They crouched behind a stack of cargo crates that rested near the door, listening to the faint click of thin metal picks moving within the lock. After what felt like half a lifetime, the door swung inwards and a slender woman stepped through, dressed all in black. The way the lantern was angled he could only see her silhouette, but he felt certain from the confidence of her steps it must be the doppel at last.

"Hullo!" Detan called.

The shadowed woman dropped into a ready stance, head swiveling as she searched for the source of Detan's voice. They were well hidden – he'd made sure of it – and the woman didn't have anywhere to go that he wouldn't see her. The shade of the door obscured detail, but if she took a step in any direction she'd reveal her face to the light. Judging by the sigh he heard, he figured the owner of said shadow had just arrived at the same conclusion.

"Come on out now, into the light. No use mucking about in the dark," he said.

The shadow moved closer in hesitant, stop-start movements that belied the owner's consternation. A sun-dark face emerged, and he whistled good and low.

"Well I'll be spit and roasted, it's the good watch captain herself. No, wait." He slipped out from behind the crates and crossed to her in a few long strides. She flinched back as he approached – not at all something the doppel would do – and he reached out and poked her in the forehead. There was no telltale ripple of sel. He nodded to himself, even as she scowled at him. "Yup, the lady is in the flesh."

"I'm going to pretend you didn't do that," she growled.

He looked her up and down, real slow so she knew he was getting the detail of it all filed away. The upstanding watch captain did not appear before him in her blues, oh no sir, she was tipped from top to toe in black and had her hair pulled back so tight he thought it might pull her eyes to slits.

But then the finer details settled into his mind, and his skin went cold.

A crimson smear marred her lips, the knuckles of both hands ruddy and raw. Dark purple bloomed over the ridge of her jaw, and she stood with her weight shifted to one side to ease some unseen pain. A garnet splotch had settled upon her shoulder. Detan felt as if spiderwebs were clogging his throat. The watch captain had been in a real, honest-to-skies fight.

"I'm going to have a hard time forgetting I saw this," he said.

"I suggest you do. I was just passing through, anyway."

"Now, my dear captain, this is in fact private property, and while usually one would not bar the door to such an honorable slave of the common citizen as yourself, I must insist that you cannot go slinking about in the shadows of any private residence you so choose. Great dunes, woman, the violation is unfathomable."

"I'm not here in any official capacity."

"A social call between the crates, then?"

She clenched her jaw and drummed her fingers against her thigh. "Not that it's any of your business, Honding, but I have personal matters to see to here tonight."

"Got a date, eh?"

"I can, and will, throw you off this dock."

He held up both hands, palms out. "Fine, fine, suit yourself. But I just cannot let you be seen running about the place at all hours in a getup like that. It's ungentlemanly."

"Pardon me, but–" Tibal said so damned close to his ear Detan jumped half his own height and nearly went sprawling amongst the crates.

"Sweet skies, Tibs! You cannot do that to a man!"

"Apologies, but as I was saying, it may be prudent for you and the watch captain to discuss matters somewhere a bit more secure. There was a guard making a regular patrol of this door."

Ripka half-turned and opened the door behind her a little wider. Detan peered into the shadows, and was surprised to see a slumped man leaning against the wall just outside. The man was breathing, real slow, a long line of drool wetting his twisted collar.

"Thank you, Tibal, but the discussion is over anyway," Ripka said.

"Fiery skies it is!" Detan grabbed her by the elbow and dragged her away from the door. "Why are you here, watch captain? *Specifically*. And keep in mind I'm on the security detail here tonight, I got rights enough to be asking. Rights Thratia'd be pleased as punch to back up."

"Really?" she drawled. "Thratia often keep her security personnel under guard behind locked doors?"

He scowled. "Fine. Then why don't you just tell me

out of the goodness of your lawful little heart?"

She shook off his grip and glanced about her new location, checking the shadows, but poorly. Detan grit his teeth in frustration as he watched her. All frontal assault, pride and bluster. The blue hand of justice. She had no business skulking about anywhere, let alone in Thratia's compound.

Pits below, didn't she know you had to let your eyes adjust to the light before you picked the shadows to check? All she was seeing was shapeless dark, but he saw the barrels and the dust bunnies. The loose floorboards and the stray ropes. A breeze picked up across the dock and Ripka folded her arms over her chest in response.

"Blasted skies, woman, you're damn near freezing and it's clear as quartz you don't know a thing about sneaking."

She sucked her lips back until they were a hair-thin line, her brows pushing together in irritation. "Look, Honding, just let me do what I came here to do. Then I'll get you two out of here."

Tibs slithered forward, dropping his voice into the same, smooth pitch Detan had once heard him use to calm an angry donkey. "It would perhaps help, watch captain, if you were to inform us of what exactly it is you came here to do."

Detan stared in amazement as she gave Tibs's question serious consideration. The same damned question he'd put to her not more than a dozen heartbeats ago. Well, he supposed it didn't much matter how the information came to light, just so long as it did. Still, his ego ached that she would answer Tibs's queries and not his. Maybe she was just thick and needed to be told things twice.

When she spoke it was with a drawl born of hesitation, lips turned down as if each word offended her so

grievously she had no choice but to make the appropriate
expression. "You are aware that Mine Master Galtro was
found murdered this afternoon?"

Detan sucked air through his teeth in shock. "Sorry to
hear it, captain. He was a fine man, even a lout like me
saw as much."

"Well." She sniffed and shifted her weight. "I
appreciate the sentiment, but what I need now is action.
The scene of the crime looked wrong, and I'm certain
there were some files missing. Since it's clear enough
you won't stop chewing my ear unless I tell you, well,
I'm here to see if Thratia's got those files squirreled away
anywhere."

"Wrong how?"

"Honding, I really don't have the time for this."

"Come on, just walk me through it."

Ripka rolled her eyes but she did it, walking him
through the place with her words just as she'd done with
her own sore feet. Through the front door of the Hub
and there's dead blues on the ground, laid to rest with
swords and crossbows. Into the records room and the
shelves have been tossed. There's Galtro, back against
the wall in a pool of his own vitals, with a poke hole in
his belly. Three dead men in the room, all Thratia's, and
they'd been done in with a mix of daggers and Galtro's
sword, which she found further off than he'd ever be
able to chuck it.

"Wait, now, what weapons had Thratia's men got?"

"Swords and a crossbow."

"I see."

"I reckon you do. Now, if you don't mind."

"Hold now, captain," Tibs said. "I am sorry to press,
but there appears to be something you're not sharing."

"What? You want me to tell you what color pants

they were all wearing? Pits below, you've got the thrust of it already."

"Yes, quite, but forgive me if I'm not convinced that all that was enough to send an upstanding servant of the populace on a breaking and entering spree."

Skies above, but Tibs was good at digging to the heart of matters. Detan watched as Ripka shifted her weight, adjusted a weapon's strap, pressed her lips together, and then finally let loose with a puff of a sigh.

"I'm just not certain on the other thing, all right?"

"Let us examine it then, captain."

She pursed her lips together, as if deep in thought, then shrugged. "Fine, fine. There were footprints in the blood that didn't belong to anybody. Workman's prints, big flopping boots with the weight all rolled down in the toes. Not to mention their eyes were all closed. You ever see four men dead all at once, and not a one left staring at nothing?"

With a grimace Detan shook his head. No, no he hadn't. It was rare enough for one soul to keep their eyes shut crossing into the dark, most went in wide-eyed and were left wanting. Four dead with closed eyes was unheard of.

"Somebody closed 'em," he said.

"Right. It must have been the doppel."

"Sure." Detan frowned down at her. "But that doesn't explain what you're doing here."

Her jaw clenched so hard he could see the sinew of her neck stand out, ready to snap. But she spoke anyway. "I gathered some… information." There was a clot in her throat. She cleared it away. "There are weapons in the city, being handed out to Thratia's supporters… smuggled in the bottom of crates." Ripka's words quickened as she warmed to the subject. "Valathean weapons, if what I saw is true of the bunch. And just how do you think she's paying for them all? It's not with grains. She wouldn't dare be so obvious."

"It's… a trade?" Detan was unable to hide the rasp in his own throat as realization took hold.

"I have good reason to believe so. Yes. I came here looking for a paper trail, something tangible. If Thratia's caught out selling humans, even if they're doppels, the people won't have her. Without them, she won't be able to keep her hold no matter what Valathea does. And I don't believe the empire will want to be publicly connected with her once that comes out – the slavery of doppels is illegal, even if they turn a blind eye to it when convenient. But I need evidence of her network, I need the names of everyone involved."

She didn't just need the doppel dead, then. Thratia was worried about a different kind of contract. He felt cold, hollow. To still the tremble in his fingers he locked eyes with Tibs, and his friend gave him a subtle nod. Trading a doppel, a live deviant sensitive of any variety, meant only one thing: whitecoats.

Valathea may not publicly hold with the live trade of sensitives, but a little slavery in the name of experimentation, of progress, wasn't beneath them. Oh no, deviant sensitives weren't to be suffered to live so long as they were free. But pinned to a board like a butterfly, sliced open and pieced back together again to see how they worked? How they could be used? That was all right by Valathea, just so long as it was their whitecoats doing the slicing.

And they were here. In Aransa. Had to be, if Thratia was dealing with them. He felt the shadow of that imperial cruiser he'd noticed on his way up the steps pressing down on his mind like a lead weight, pushing aside defenses he'd spent the past few years of his life building. Crumbling walls that held back darker memories, and darker urges.

Sweat sheened his skin, immediate and slick, and he spat bitter bile on the ground.

"Honding?" There was a soft edge to Ripka's voice, a note of gentle worry. He pressed his eyes shut, squeezing so hard white lights spun behind his lids. Echoes of his own screams crowded his mind, pushed aside gates he'd built against raw instinct. He felt the tickle of his sensitivity returning, the promise of release if he just reached out and touched the selium buoyed in the belly of the *Larkspur*, vast and inviting.

"Sirra." Tibs had his fingers hooked in Detan's shoulders like claws and he shook him once, hard, snapping Detan's head back and his eyes open. He stared at Tibs, focusing on his breathing, seeing nothing but the webs of wrinkles radiating out from his old friend's calm, brown eyes. Tibs raised a brow in question, and he nodded, stepping back. He was under control. For now.

Detan knew too well what was at the end of the line for the doppel if Thratia got her claws in her. And here was sweet little Ripka, thinking Thratia meant mere jail or death for the doppel. He'd laugh, if he could feel anything through the ringing in his ears.

It wasn't the purge that had Thratia nervous. That'd be bad for Aransa, sure, but the city would recover. But even General Throatslitter had mind enough to fear dealing with whitecoats. She'd had to have been desperate to make a deal with those monsters.

Execution for the doppel's crimes was one thing, but nobody deserved *that*. Not even a madwoman. Understanding passed in a glance between him and Tibs, and he let out a defeated sigh.

Ripka's eyes narrowed. "What is it?"

He shook his head to clear it and crossed to the edge of the deck, staring out at the city splayed below. Nothing seemed particularly out of place. He'd seen violent power upheavals before. They were bloody, drawn-out things. Fires in the streets and heads in the gutters. He didn't see any evidence of something like that brewing here, and for that he was grateful. When a city went feral, who survived the changeover was often a matter of pure chance, and he hadn't lucked through too much of late.

I should grab Tibs and go, he thought, eyeing the sleek shape of the *Larkspur*. Maybe the doppel wouldn't make it through Thratia's tightening net. Maybe they'd be safe out there after all.

But he couldn't do it. Couldn't leave her to what he'd lived through himself.

Ripka's fingers coiled around his arm and pulled him around to face her. "Tell me." There was no anger in her voice, it sounded almost pleading. But he couldn't explain – not really. To admit knowledge of what happened in the whitecoats' tower would be to admit his sel-sense remained, albeit in a twisted form. He closed his eyes for just a heartbeat, and decided on a path.

"You're looking under the wrong roof," he said.

She threw her hands into the air in frustration. "Then where do you suggest I look? I've got no lead on the doppel. All the information I do have points here." There was a hitch in her throat that Detan chose to ignore, a subtle shifting of her eyes toward the floor. She was ashamed of something. The thought made him unreasonably angry.

"Sure you do." He forced the biggest smile he could muster, piling his fear under false bravado. "You know just *exactly* where to look! You won't find your evidence here, she's too careful for that, but I bet ole Galtro kept real precise records of every ship in and out of his docks – even if the cargo was sparse on the leaving, eh? And you said yourself the records room had been tossed over. Either there's incriminating evidence in there about her, or a way to identify the creature she doesn't want you getting to first. If you catch the blasted thing, then she can't trade it to Valathea."

Ripka snorted. "Thratia's got the Hub on lockdown while she completes her 'investigation'."

Tibs cleared his throat. "If you would agree to suffer the Lord Honding's company, watch captain, I believe Thratia's prohibitions will not prove a hindrance."

"Oh no, I'm not going to be seen breaking into a place with that rat."

"Psh, you're one guard-check away from being seen that way right now. Look, Rippy–"

"Watch captain."

"Right. I'm the man for this. It's clear as a still sky you don't know about the greyer side of life, and I've spent my days learning how to turn soot into salt, eh? I can have us in and out in a snap. That is, if Tibs here is all right watching the *Larkspur* on his lonesome."

"I believe I'll manage. I don't think the doppel will be doing much 'sides laying low tonight," Tibs said.

Detan clapped. "Then it's settled! Come on, Rip." He scurried past her and opened the door to the servant's entrance. "Out of the dark and into the shit with it then, eh?"

"You don't make a lick of sense, Honding."

He shrugged. "I hope that particular expression will not become clear to you in time."

As they started down the short steps back out into the Aransan streets, Detan found himself praying to the sweet skies for the first time in a long, long while. Either Tibs would get the doppel out of the city – noisily, so there'd be no question of a purge to clean away the stain of a hidden doppel – or Ripka would arrest the thing and take its head.

Despite what she'd done to Faud, and maybe even Galtro, he found himself hoping she'd get to Tibs before Ripka got to her. But even if she didn't, dead was still better than the whitecoats' tower. He was sure of it.

CHAPTER 25

Worry dug its claws deep into Detan's mind, distracting him with whispers of disaster. They scurried through the ferry district, one scant level down from Thratia's compound, moving fast but not so quick as to draw attention to themselves. Every corner he turned, he half expected to run chest-first into one of Thratia's grey coated sycophants.

Some little part of him wanted to. There was enough sel around the ferries for him to deal with any trouble if it came to it, but he couldn't be sure he'd be able to contain himself once he'd started. It was the sliver of him that didn't mind that fact that worried him.

They came to the end of a long row of shuttered and tarped foodstalls, their owners skedaddled off to safer locales for the time being. He didn't blame them. Half the city had tucked themselves in for an early night – hoping against the gathering shadows that things would push on like normal come the dawn. They were probably right. Whoever held the reins of the city mattered little in the day-to-day lives of the common folk.

Detan slowed and reached a hand back to forestall Ripka. Her boots stopped scuffling over the dirt-packed road, and he edged up to the end of a large cart, poking his head around the side to get a look at the ferry station.

Wasn't just grey coats minding the way. There was a small group of people, local stock every one, and they were all backed up at the docking gate for the ferry that went out to the Hub. Between the group and the dock tall, stern-faced Valatheans in uniforms as pale blue as the skies their homeland commanded stood at ease, pikes resting in the crooks of their arms. One yawned; another fanned his obsidian, reddening cheeks with a folded bit of milky paper.

"What is it?" Ripka whispered.

"Best see this for yourself," he murmured.

Detan pressed himself back against the cart, giving her room to creep around without being seen. She practically floated forward, adjusting her gait so that her steps were so light the leather soles didn't so much as whisper on the hard-packed dirt road.

"What is the empire doing *here*?" she whispered.

Detan grabbed her elbow and dragged her back around the curve of the alley. "You tell me, miss watch captain. I try not to have anything to do with folk in uniform."

Her gaze darted side to side, a brief moment of real panic. "How in the pits should I know? Thratia's cut me out of everything."

He cursed and spat, wondering if those pretty blue uniforms were under Thratia's command or a whitecoat's. Didn't much matter, he didn't plan on making their acquaintance. "We'll have to keep low and to the lee side of buildings. Use the shadows as best we can as we make the crossing."

"Crossing? We're not getting on that ferry, Honding."

He grinned, saw the whites of her eyes grow wide and bright as knives in the dark. "Who said anything about a ferry?"

Get on the ferry, hah. Not with those flower sniffers hanging about. Why, the two of them would be tipped right over the edge of the ferry if they ever made it on to begin with. He had an idea what they needed to do. It was the only path left open to them if they wanted to see the Hub tonight, and by the way Ripka clammed up, she knew it, too. Without a word of conference, they adjusted their path toward the lowest level of the city. Toward that last wall between civilization and wide open, hungry desert.

They had to cross the Black.

The very idea made his skin itch with the urge to flee. It was safe enough at night, sure. At least, the sun wouldn't bake you to a streetcart delicacy within a dozen paces of the city while the sky was dark. If you didn't mind the heat trapped in the sand, making each step like dancing a jig in a bread oven. If your shoes were stable enough to hold up to the bite of the unweathered obsidian shards. If you knew your way, cut the path short. If you made it back before the sun came up.

If, if, if. His stomach rumbled a protest and he grimaced, wiping sweat from his brow on the back of his hand.

It didn't help to ease his poor nerves that Ripka was looking around at her own city like she'd never seen it before. Sure, things were different. Not a lot, mind you, but Thratia's people were out in force and it left a subdued hush over the whole of Aransa. People took to their homes and stayed put. It wasn't natural, things being so quiet this time of night. The citizenry should be out, taking advantage of the cooler weather to bicker over the price of roots and meats. Instead, the local cricket population took up an unsteady song, as if they weren't sure whether it was wise to fill the unnatural silence.

"They're everywhere." Ripka's voice was so alien in this place empty of human babbling that he jumped and damned near hit his head on a low-hanging awning.

He glanced over his shoulder, ready to give her the rough side of his tongue, then stopped cold when he saw where she was looking. Not at the people and their homes, their markets and their washing. No, her keen eyes had plucked out other figures moving amongst the shadows and the leeways, keeping their presence felt but not seen. Shadows of hands held shadows of weapons, ready to become corporeal at any moment.

"Just stay steady, they won't be harassing us any if we look like we're in a hurry to get where we're going. Chances are Thratia's got 'em spread thin and communication won't get ahead of us. Come on now, the gate's a few levels down and then it's just us and the sand to the Hub. Anyway, the way we're moving they'll probably assume we're all on the same side. Buncha pals, us and them."

She nodded a tight, formal jerk of the head. Detan was used to this – to sneaking and skulking and keeping your head down while your eyes were up – but she wasn't, and he'd be ground-bound if she wasn't behaving like an old pro at it. She kept her movements tight and clean, her eyes sharp and roving, searching, looking for the next spot to make a dash to or the next pair of eyes to slip away from. He was beginning to feel too big for his own body, clumsy and obvious.

"You all right?" she whispered.

He shook his head to clear it. "Right as rain in a monsoon. You'd make a damned fine footpad, you know."

They dashed across a wide lane into another alley, serpentining their way down the slope of the city. They stood for a moment, stilling their hearts so that they could hear. No one was about. He felt silly being so paranoid. But then, it was usually when you felt in the clear that something rose out of the muck and bit you.

"Was one, once," she murmured.

"You're pulling my sail."

"It's true. I was born in the Brown Wash. There's silver mining there, and a reedpalm paper factory, but that's it. My parents weren't lucky enough to be industry folk so I stole for food. Lots of the kids did it. It was bad, there." She looked around at the mud-daub village that comprised the lowest level of Aransa. Half-made roofs lay open to the empty sky, water pumps were hung with little painted symbols that meant they'd been pumped dry for now, try again later. Those few unfortunate souls that had further to go to make it to the safety of their homes moved with furtive steps that had nothing to do with tonight's tension.

These were hard-bitten folk, wiry limbed and browned through to the bone by the sun. They had hunger's cheekbones, sharp and cruel. He glanced Ripka's way and caught her scowling at a poster on the wall of the alley calling for the downtrodden to vote for Thratia. They'd been seeing them everywhere the last five levels.

"What do they think she'll do for them? Don't they know she's called Throatslitter for a reason?"

He shrugged. "That's not how it works down here, Rip, you know that. They love her because they see her as having bucked the empire to come onto the Scorched and lead them to a better life. Better yet, she's gone native in their eyes. You see any of the Valathean guard this far down? Nope, of course not, she doesn't want her image mixed up with them down here. There's too many of them for her to risk losing their support. And anyway, she could be called Commodore Babyspiker and as long as she had a plan to get food and water down here, they'd vote her in. Galtro have any plans like that?"

She set to chewing on her lip. "His idea of the downtrodden were the miners and their families."

"Hah. The lucky and the pampered, in the eyes of these folk. Hush now, we're getting closer."

Down by the final wall between Aransa and the desert, the locals had made it home already. They reminded Detan of sand mice, tucked away in the shadow of their dens, hoping a preying eye wouldn't look too close. Wouldn't catch that glimmer of light between the crooked shutters.

They needn't have worried, there wasn't much call for a patrol this close to the Black Wash. It was night, sure, but few people were fool enough to risk a trek out there at any time of day. All it took was a rolled ankle or a bit of confusion, just enough to slow you down, and if the sun slunk up and caught you there wasn't any coming back from it. You cooked, plain and simple. It was the central reason all of Aransa's supplies came in via airships. No one wanted to risk a caravan out in that madness.

He poked his head around a corner to get a good look at the gate and saw no one there, as expected. There wasn't even a lock on it. The latch was a thick bit of timber, rough and splintered from lack of use or care. A fan of black dust spread out from underneath it, the desert seeping in. The gate rattled in its catch, keeping the stiff desert wind out. There was no point in locking it – no sane soul wanted out there.

"Here we are then." He strode out into the empty street, confident as a cockerel, and dragged up the battered beam. It creaked a protest from rusted hinges, but still it lifted free. He laid his palm against the door and pushed. Ripka's eyes went wide, a little gasp escaping her.

"You ever been down on the Wash?" he asked.

She shook her head. "There's no reason for it. We make the violent criminals walk it, of course, but that's further down the wall, where the guardhouse is. I never dreamed it was so… reflective, up close."

Detan squinted out at the black sands. A few of the cleaved faces gave off a fey shimmer, catching what little moonlight there was while they waited for the bright of the stars to find them. Detan gave a soft whistle and adjusted the brim of his hat down over his eyes.

"Looks dangerous, out there. But we'll be fine just so long as we return before the sun rises, eh? And walk soft now, some of those grains are sharp enough to cut straight into your boots."

Detan stepped out into the Black Wash and paused, allowing his eyes to adjust to the lack of lantern light. Outside of the city's great wall, the sands of Aransa were gathered in silence. Beauty, he had always felt, was best observed in an aura of quietude, and the Black Wash was no exception. A killing field come every dawn, it was lustrous and silk-soft under the gentler stroke of red moonlight.

Beneath the worn soles of his shoes, he could feel the radiant heat, permeating soft leather and easing his tired joints. Though the sun had slipped past its cruelest angle and given them up to the dark, the sands remembered the brightness of day. Each bituminous grain held on to the memory of the sun, and the threat of the coming dawn. If he stood in one place too long, the heat began to grow uncomfortable.

"It's so quiet out here," she said.

Detan glanced back at the city lights sloped up into the night. "Aransa isn't exactly bustling at the present, captain."

Whatever awe she felt as she gazed about the place, saucer-eyed and open-lipped, retreated as she followed his glance back toward the city. He knew what she'd be seeing. After all, hers were eyes that cared for that which they regarded. While he saw the light, she'd see the shutters. Where he listened to the quietude of the gently sleeping, she'd hear the vacuous silence of the frightened; the cowering.

Her spine stiffened like steel was shot through it, her jaw came up and straightened. She tucked hair behind her ear and strode sure-footed across the sands toward the Smokestack. He let her lead.

Ripka walked on the sands like she owned them, like she was born to them. Brown Wash girl like her, he supposed she was. Wasn't much rock in the Brown bigger than a thumbnail, so she had to be used to unsteady footing. Good quality in a thief. Bad quality in a watcher – those had to be rigid, immovable.

"How'd you come by it?" he asked.

They were getting close now, their bodies swallowed up in the shadow of the Smokestack, so that when she turned her head to look at him all he could make out were white eyes and teeth.

"Come by what?"

"Your blues, captain. What's a Brown Wash girl doing in uniform?"

She turned back to the path, and he figured she was set on ignoring him, which was fair enough. Detan shoved his hands in his pockets and tried not to think too hard about just what he was doing out here, helping a woman of the law break it. Didn't seem right, working with a blue out of the goodness of his heart.

He grunted at the dark. Too many open ends. For once, he was getting sick of options.

They trudged on, with each step the gentle radiant heat of the sands growing until he caught himself shifting his weight to his toes to give his heels a break, then switching when he felt blisters begin there, the pain tangy and sharp. His already sore toes cracked against something hard and unyielding and he stumbled. Ripka grabbed his shoulder, keeping him upright, and they tangled as he struggled to regain his balance.

"What in the pits was that?" He glared at the sand as if it owed him answers, and nearly lost his lunch as he got a response.

A desiccated corpse lay sprawled across the glittering sands, leathered lips curled away to reveal a grimace of half-rotted teeth in the skull Detan'd stubbed his toe on. The shrunken skin around its gaping eye sockets gleamed in the faint moonlight, and for just a breath Detan thought the corpse had died weeping. But, no, he realized. By the time this body laid down to die there wasn't any moisture left in it. The glaze frozen on its cheekbones now was the dribble of its eye fluid, boiled over in mimicry of tears.

The corpse's arms were outstretched, delicate finger bones scattered like fallen petals, gleaming white against the black sand. Whoever they'd been, they'd been reaching toward the Ridge when they'd fallen – perhaps crawling over the bright shards, each desperate lurch digging the bite of a thousand tiny knives deeper and deeper.

"Black skies," he whispered.

"The walk's meant to kill you," Ripka snapped, a wiry defensiveness ratcheting up her voice. "Nothing pretty about it."

A whip of wind tore past them, rattling the exposed bones, and he shivered, shoving his hands in his pockets as he hurried on, quick to leave the nightmarish scene behind. The sooner he could escape Aransa, the better.

Something long and hard skittered across his foot. Detan jumped back with an undignified yelp, kicking a hand-shaped silhouette high into the air. The insectile creature hissed at the night, the sound raking thorns over Detan's skin.

Ripka laughed, the sound a little manic. "It's just a spider."

"Blasted thing is bigger than any spider has a right to be," he growled, skirting the approximate area the abomination might have landed in. Still laughing, Ripka turned and swung down with her cudgel – once, twice, a meaty crack-thump following an enraged hiss. Detan took a hesitant step forward, peering into the dark.

"It's dead," she announced as she slipped the cudgel back into her belt and pinned him with a sideways glance. "Though I am suddenly concerned that *you* volunteered to help *me*."

He opened his mouth to protest, breathed too deep and starting coughing on dusty air. She thumped him on the back until he regained himself. For a few hesitant breaths he stood, hunched over, palms on his kneecaps to steady himself. Ripka watched him, real concern stitching her pale brows together.

Concern. For him. Detan forced a rueful little smile,

and relief flooded her features. She punched him on the shoulder, light and playful, and he went ahead and pretended it hurt.

Maybe some options weren't so bad after all.

CHAPTER 26

After they'd walked long enough for the russet light of the moon to drift near its apex, the sands gave way to grey gravel pock-marked with reddened boulders. Bad climbing ground, but the moon was bright and the way was clear.

Detan picked a likely path and then watched Ripka take it in. It was funny, he'd never noticed the way she looked at things before. He'd only ever given mind to the way she looked at him. Usually with exasperation and a hint of disgust.

When the doppel had been parading her face about, it'd usually wrinkle with amusement at a joke he just wasn't privy to. Now her lips pressed together and her nostrils flared. She reached out to touch the problem at hand, picked her own likely path and found her handhold. Tested it. Climbed.

Detan followed.

Three heights of a man up the side of the Smokestack Ripka disappeared over a ledge. He dragged himself onward, and nearly lost his hold when her arm reached over the side, hand open wide to grab his. He took it, hoping she couldn't feel the tremble in his limbs, and allowed himself to be hauled up onto the narrow ledge.

"You all right?" she asked.

"Didn't expect the help." He brushed filth from his hands. "Startled me, was all."

"We're partners in this." Even as she spoke she turned her back to him, examining the next leg of their climb. Partners, indeed.

"Used to doing things my own self," he muttered.

Ripka glanced over her shoulder at him, brows raised. "Don't you usually work with Tibal?"

"Sure, but Tibs has usually got his own end to handle, you understand."

In the dark the whites of her eyes flashed as she rolled them and he smirked, pleased with himself. It was one thing getting the goat of Tibs, quite another to rustle the calm of an honest-to-sky woman of the law.

The doppel parading as Ripka had given him a false sense of familiarity with her. He found himself wanting to make remarks she wouldn't get. Point out things that probably didn't matter a whit to her. Make cracks about ropes and chairs and rather nice bags. It was difficult, come to think of it, to separate out what was the original article from the interpretation.

As they rested, easing out the soreness in their fingers from the climb, he decided to bridge this gap of knowledge. "You never did tell me why you donned the blues."

She hesitated, glancing back to judge his expression, and said, "Don't see how it's any of your business."

"Thratia finds me rollicking about with you and I'm a dead man, so I think I at least got a right to know a bit about you. At the very least you owe me just why in the pits Galtro's death matters so much to you."

"What makes you think his death is rankling me any more than any other good man's death would? I got a job to do in this city, Honding, something I'm aware you're not particularly familiar with but, try to understand, it's my duty."

"Easy, captain. You don't know spit from salt when it comes to me and my own sense of duty, but I'm sure I've got my eye in when it comes to yours. Big city like this one has gotta have men of all sort, good and bad, getting murdered on the regular and I don't see you getting yourself all dressed up like a damned shadow to steal evidence over those. May not have been you in the flesh telling me Galtro was your man for warden, but I know your actress played it true, eh? He mattered to you, whether you care to admit it or not. Wouldn't be out here risking your sun-slapped ass with me if you didn't. Your better half said he'd been a mentor, that true?"

She stood with her arms folded, though her hands ended in gnarled fists. "True enough. He got me hired as a watcher. Satisfied?"

"Seems I never am, but that will do for an answer."

"Oh wonderful. Now maybe we can move on? Sun's only been down two marks but I'd like to make quick work of this if at all possible. Unless you fancy getting stuck out on the Black Wash come the day?"

"After you, captain."

By the time they dragged themselves onto the comfortably flattened plateau which housed the Hub, Detan was breathing through his mouth and nose all at once to hide his panting. Ripka crept ahead of him, her chest heaving at an annoyingly calm rate and not but a few strands of hair flown loose from her braid. He was beginning to hate her.

They eased out onto a ledge of rock just behind the squat structure, and side by side they scorpion-crawled to the edge to see over. Below, the Hub was shrouded in night. The feeder pipelines connecting to the central containment chamber lay limp and dormant, lacking the familiar hum of an active selium mine. A few shadowed figures moved in clockwork circles around the building, and though their features were obscured by the dark there was no need to guess at their purpose.

"Not much of a guard," he said.

Ripka shrugged. "What'd you expect? She's confident, and she's got the ferry shut down. Who would bother crossing the sands out here for nothing, anyway? There's no work to be done. Look at the lines, they're flat as man's chest."

"Never seen a man gifted in the bosom?"

She cast him a sideways smile. "I've endeavored not to make that particular moment part of my daily vernacular."

"Wise." He gave her the sagest nod he could muster.

"Indeed. You see a way in?"

"There are only two guards."

He heard her inhale, harsh and through the teeth. "I'd rather not harm anyone, even Thratia's brutes."

"Well good, because my proposed means of ingress is entirely peaceable. I can't imagine what you were thinking my intentions were, but I assure you that in pointing out the paucity of guards I only meant to illustrate that it would be simpler for us to gain entry unnoticed."

"Will you get on with it?"

"Fine." He sighed. "Follow me."

The way down the small ridge was treacherous, but they made it without any misstep too loud or too injurious. Twice Ripka needled him for information regarding his knowledge of the working of a standard Hub layout, and twice he brushed it aside as knowledge most ex-sel workers were slow in forgetting. He was beginning to grow weary of having to lie to her, which was a first.

Alongside the limp arm of one of the feeder pipelines, he halted her with an extended hand and crouched to indicate she should follow suit. Hunkered down beside the deflated sheath of leather, he watched the second guardsman wander by little more than one flying leap away.

Detan grinned like an idiot at his own good luck and solid memory. When the guard moved out of sight, he grabbed her wrist and dragged her after him as he dashed for a portal so well shrouded in the curve of the building that he couldn't even see it until he was upon it, though he knew what to look for.

He shoved his hand in the handle cubby and felt for the four depressions in which his fingers would fit. Saying a little prayer to the skies and the pits, he pressed down the clockworked buttons in the pattern that would have gained him admittance to the same door at a different Hub back home. The cubby shivered as the mechanism released, and with a gentle nudge the door swung inward. They rushed after it and closed it tight behind. Detan lay for a moment with his back against the door, blessing the Valathean Empire for exchanging security for ease of production.

"How'd you know the code?" she demanded.

"Easy, that. The empire makes all Hubs everywhere the same. Cheapens production, and they don't worry about security too much because the kind of person who would have the tapcode for one Hub shouldn't have any reason to be denied the tapcode for another. Simple."

She pressed her lips together and placed her hands on her hips. "How'd *you* come to know it?"

"You already forgetting I worked the line once?"

Even in the faint light of stars filtering into the hallway, he could make out the flush on her cheeks. "I heard you went to the line when your skills as a diviner failed, and then again you shirked the line when your sel-sense dried up altogether."

"I didn't shirk a damned thing."

He turned from her before he could see her face and stared straight down the hall, into the heart of the Hub. The cloth of her shirt rustled as she shifted, and her long hair hissed over the smooth material. The sound made him grind his teeth and revise his earlier opinion of her competence as a footpad. Didn't she know smooth material had a sheen that stood out? Didn't she know leather creaked and hair got in your eyes right when you didn't want it to?

Didn't she know he didn't shirk anything at all?

"Which way?" she whispered and he blinked, wondering just how long he'd been standing there glaring down the empty dark.

"You want the records room, lady, it's straight on down this hall and should be the second door on the left."

"You're not coming?"

"I'm coming. I'm just making sure this is still what you want. You get caught in there, you're caught with your hands in it. Understand?"

She nodded, and he noted the lines about her eyes and the sharp bow of her lips. Not so soft after all, was she? He breathed out so hard his shoulders slumped and took the lead. He'd gotten his hands in this mess up to the elbows, and whether she pissed him off or not he had to see it through. Ripka might be inexperienced in shadow dealings, but she was no stranger to determination, or hard work.

So far as he could tell, there wasn't a soul alive save the two of them in the whole of the Hub. It was so damnably quiet his own heartbeat deafened him and Ripka's steps clodded his concentration into mush. She might be light as a feather over sand, but the girl just wasn't used to walking on steel.

Funny that, how when there's nothing worth hearing you hear every cursed little thing. If there were a dozen guards rushing down on him he wouldn't hear them above his own arterial flutter.

The records room door was ajar, Thratia's hubris showing through bright and clear. Clever commodore she was, but sometimes the head couldn't see the feet for how fat its middle had gotten. Or something like that. He'd have to ask Tibs how that phrase went to get it straight again.

He nudged the door open just a bit more and peeked inside. The reek of the dead assaulted his nostrils, pungent and cloying. The battlefield stench of spilt bowel and coppery blood congealed with the altogether too mundane scent of moldering paper and wet wood. Lucky for them both, someone had had the decency to haul the bodies off, so the scent was fading. Still, the records room was tucked in the heart of the Hub and there wasn't a window in sight. It would be a good long while before the scent worked its way clean. Sometimes it never did.

He took a pathetic, guttering candle from the hallway sconce and went in. The bodies may have been cleared out, but the stains they left told the tale clear enough.

One black puddle up toward the door, another further down by the shelving, and a deeper smear between the floor and the wall where a man had sat down to become a corpse. Whatever weapons had been scattered about had been taken with the bodies. By laying Ripka's description of the scene over what he saw, he could work out well enough what had gone on. And there were the miner's boot prints, looking like a ghost had traipsed right through the whole mess and out into the hall beyond.

He licked his lips, wondering where the doppel was now. Wondering what she had in store for the city – for him. He was tangled up real tight with that creature's fate, whether he liked it or not. Detan frowned hard, digging through memory to try and see around her easy charm and pained eyes, trying to find the core of a woman who could have wrought such slaughter.

It wasn't there. All he saw was the doppel's imitation of Ripka, all quick smiles and swaying hips. Not like the real thing at all.

Once he was sure the place was empty, he stepped aside to let Ripka through. She shut the door behind them; not hard, leaving it just the tiniest bit ajar in the manner they had found it. He nodded. Good, she was a quick learner. In the unsteady candlelight he watched her eyes roam, making an account of what she saw now versus what she'd seen in the afternoon. She nodded once, tight and sharp. Her eyes only snagged on the stain against the wall a breath or two.

"The files were back here." Her voice was calm, sure.

He followed her guidance into the stacks, both of them careful to step over the sticky puddles. Blood had a way of taking a while to lose its wetness. It clung to life, clotted and damp, even after the corpses had been carted away.

While she found her place in the file boxes he stood an awkward kind of guard, keeping his eyes and ears fixed on the ajar door. One hand held the candle out for her to see by while the other cradled the handle of the knife tucked into his belt. It was a meat knife, but he figured it didn't matter much to the man getting poked by it what its intended use was.

Ripka flicked through the box with the exacting eye of a woman who worked in government. She pulled out a folder that looked like all the rest to him and laid it open over the top of the wooden crate, fanning the papers. With an irritated grunt she set them aside and went back to her rummaging.

He sidled over, peering down at the discarded stack. A loading slip for a Valathean trader stared up at him, the ink already turning brown from time. A very small team had loaded the trader with just a few crates of local foodstuffs, and then off-loaded a single pallet of some local liqueur. Detan frowned, set down his knife and picked up the slip. Why bother sending a fully outfitted trader all the way out here for a couple of measly desert snacks? There was no way the mercer house involved made a profit on such a transaction.

He searched for the mercer house's name, and found Thratia's bold signature instead.

"Ripka…" he said, rereading the document to be sure.

"What is it?" Her voice sounded strained. A pile of discarded files had grown on the floor to her left, her fingers moving faster as she flicked through the folders. Another, smaller pile had sprouted under her arm, the sheets jammed hastily between her tricep and side.

"I think I've got it." He thrust the sheet toward her. "Look here, Thratia signed off on this cargo – and there's no way anyone involved made a profit with the

282 STEAL THE SKY

quantities listed. This is proof of Thratia making shady
deals with the empire! Nothing's spelled out, of course,
but with this I bet you could–"

She wasn't listening. Ripka spared the sheet a
momentary glance and then went back to digging, her
motions growing in agitation, her lips pressed tighter
and tighter.

"Ripka," he repeated, setting the sheet back down.
She didn't even blink. "What are you doing?"

She waved a hand through the air distractedly, the
other still pawing through reports. "You know. Looking
for evidence, of course." A curl of hair worked its way
free of her braid, falling across her cheek.

It shimmered.

Anger boiled within his chest so quickly he feared he'd
release it upon the sel coating Ripka's face. No. Not Ripka.
He should have known – should have realized Ripka
would never knock a guard out and leave him to the
elements. Never go slinking about in the dark, breaking
into houses and recruiting the aid of a known criminal.
He'd been so blinded by the woman – *this woman's* –
control of her anger that he'd mistaken it for Ripka's hard-
wrought nature. Had seen discipline in her rage. Had let
himself be wrapped around her spindly fingers.

"You," he hissed.

She froze mid-shuffle, gaze sliding sideways to meet
his, her body gone rigid with anticipation.

"Yes?" she said, forcing her tone light.

Without thinking, he snapped a hand out and grabbed
the wrist nearest him, twisted. She let out a startled yelp,
turning with his twist, her ankles tangling as the papers
spilled from beneath her arm. He stepped into her,
shoving her back against the shelf hard enough to make
the structure creak.

She grunted, breath that smelled of iron wafting against his cheeks – had she bitten her tongue? The warm tinge of her haval spice perfume surrounded him, the scent faint, as if she had tried to scrub it away. No wonder. Ripka had worn cactus flower – the same his aunt favored. He'd never forget it.

"Why hello, Honding," she drawled, an irritatingly bemused smile turning up lips that suddenly appeared too plush to have ever been Ripka's.

"I touched your face," he growled, pressing her tighter against the shelf though she did not squirm. "Nothing. There was no sign, I'm sure of it. How did you…?"

She rolled a shoulder. "I'm afraid to tell you your actions have become predictable. Unlike my hair." The doppel looked up and puffed out a breath, blowing away the betraying tendril. It settled right back against her cheek. This time, not so much as a flicker. The blasted woman was showing off.

"We *signaled* for you. We had the ship! Why all of this subterfuge? Why waste time dragging me all the way to this rusted hole? Do you have any idea what's waiting for you, if you're captured? Walking the Black would be a damned holiday compared to what they'll do to you. Do you have any sands-cursed fucking clue what *I've* risked for you?"

"I wasn't finished yet." Her voice strained, her chin jutted upwards. Stubborn, stupid woman.

"It's over. I don't know what's kept you here. I don't know why you've gone after Aransa like you have. But–"

She twisted in his grip and panic shot through him, paralyzed him. Had she lured him out here to put a spike in his gut, too? Was it a belly full of selium for him? If he cried out he'd only draw Thratia's thugs down on them, and then they'd both be sold out. Hog-tied and dragged off to that blisteringly white tower with its knives and its drugs and its impassive, bored faces making notes while he screamed his throat bloody.

But he'd escaped that tower before. Harder thing to do, escaping a knife in the gut.

Detan opened his mouth to scream, and she shoved a wad of paper in it.

He staggered back a step, arms windmilling, and coughed the spittle-laden ball out into his hand.

"Read it," she ordered, then crouched down and began to gather her fallen collection of papers.

Straightening his twisted lapels to recover some sense of dignity, Detan spread the crumpled sheet flat against his thigh and rubbed it smooth. A few of the marks were smeared, his own spit spreading the ink around, but he'd seen plenty of accident reports before to know what he was looking at. Seen plenty of ones where people had died.

But the one he held had been doctored, made up. Every real report he'd seen before had been scribbled all over, bits crossed out and rewritten when the reporters finally got the story straight. This one was nice and neat, no corrections necessary. He'd only seen a report like it once before. Just once. When the empire had stepped in and provided their own explanation for what had happened to him.

"It's faked."

"Part of it." She kept on collecting her fallen slips, not bothering to look his way. Probably not wanting to.

He read it again. It'd been a simple landslide, or so the report claimed. A small group of men working on repairs for a damaged line had been crushed by those rocks. He scanned the list, absorbing every last syllable. More than likely that little list of names was the only true thing about the whole report. Names that matched the list of young sel workers who'd handled Thratia's profitless transaction.

"Which one's yours?" he asked.

"Kel."

"Brother? Lover?"

Paper crinkled between her fingers. "My son."

Detan let out a slow breath through his teeth. "I can't possibly understand your pain. But what you've started here – it's over. Thratia's itching to sell you to the highest bidder so she can go about getting her new little fiefdom tucked tight under her thumb."

"Let her try."

"No." He crouched across from her, rested his wrists against his knees and tried to make his voice gentle. Cajoling he could do – but kind, compassionate? All he could offer her was a slightly softer shade of himself. "What is all this, anyway? What'd you even need out here – and why drag me along for it? Can't be anything here worth getting caught over."

"I knew Thratia'd lock it up. I needed you for the punchcode."

He rocked back on his heels and squinted at her. "You musta worked here, once, knowing your way around the files like you do. They haven't changed that code since I was a babe – why don't you know it?"

"I knew it once. Then they changed it."

"But–"

She snapped her head up, scowling. "I'm older than you'd think, Honding. Now help me get these together."

"This is worth your life? We've got the *Larkspur*, you've got your revenge, and now we've got to *go*." He snatched a paper from her hand. She lunged at him, her swipe going wide, and he popped back to his feet, skittering away a few steps as he scanned the information she risked her freedom for.

It was a personnel file. The name meant nothing to him, but the man's profession was clear enough: a regular deckhand on Valathean traders. He stared, bewildered, as realization crept slow as a summer rain into his mind.

She'd said she wasn't finished yet, he just hadn't understood her meaning.

"You can't." He crumpled the paper and shoved it into his pocket, then kicked the scattered sheets nearest her away. "These people, they had no hand in your son's harm!"

"How can you be so sure?"

She stretched to snatch up the papers he'd kicked and he grabbed her arm without thinking, lurching her to her feet. With a hiss she twisted, slithering away from his grasp. He snapped a hand out to steal away the papers she held but she danced back, deeper into the shelving.

"Leave me to my work," she growled, her tone low and rumbling.

"This is murder." He thrust a finger toward the sticky stain she'd said was Galtro's. "Folk like that – those with *real* knowledge of what was happening – I'll grant you may have deserved what you brought them. But deckhands?" He peered at one of the papers fallen to the floor. "Stewards? They don't deserve your hate, any more than Kel deserved Thratia's."

She reared back like a cobra bracing to strike. "You dustswallowing–"

Footsteps thundered down the hall. A voice called out, "You hear that?"

Someone else answered, "Probably a rat."

"Big fucking rat. Come on, we'd better do a sweep to be sure. Boss'll skin us if we botch this."

"Time's up," Detan hissed and grabbed the doppel's arm. She stumbled behind him as he hustled toward the door, careful not to disturb the thickening pools of blood. Keeping his grip tight so she wouldn't go and gather up more personnel files, he pressed his ear against the cold door.

Footsteps echoed toward him, softer than before, as their owner crept down the hall.

He swore under his breath and pulled away.

"How many?" she asked, all the anger gone from her eyes, her expression drawn and focused. Their argument forgotten, for now.

"Just one coming this way. We have to count on at least one more being within shouting range. I don't suppose Aransa took to installing back exits or sneaky escape tunnels in their records room, eh?"

She snorted. "The back wall is up against the central containment and is reinforced with steel, bolted to the bedrock to keep the whole Hub from floating away. But by all means, try to break through."

"Real helpful." He glanced around the darkened room, looking for anything at all he could put to use. The lone candle guttered on the shelf he'd left it on, the wick growing clogged by the deep pool of wax yet to spill over its side.

"Huh," he said.

The doppel scowled at him. "What?"

"I think I have an idea."

"Really, and what would that be?"

"Stay put. I'm going to put out the lights."

CHAPTER 27

Detan crouched beside the records room door, wondering just why he'd thought this damn fool of an idea was a good one. He had paced out the distance just right so he wouldn't get slapped with the door when it opened, but that didn't ease his nerves any. Facing the door dead center, the doppel stood, the soft hiss of her longknife leaving its sheath the only proof of her presence.

As soon as he'd blown out their little candle, the world had gone black fast enough to make him think it'd been missing the dark. Should have just stayed with Tibs, he thought, rubbing sweaty palms against his knees. This was work for those who knew their way around a piece of steel. People like Ripka, Thratia. The doppel too, he supposed.

He hoped she wouldn't have to prove her competency.

As his eyes adjusted to the lack of light he watched her straighten, square her shoulders and slide her dominant foot – Ripka's dominant foot, at least – forward. She'd kept the good watch captain's face on, and as he watched her slip deeper into the character he realized why it'd been such a simple thing for her to fool them all.

Their bodies were similar, sure, and the color of their hair being damned near identical certainly helped, but it wasn't the physical touch that sold the deception. It was all in her posture. Rigid, certain, with something withheld. Something coiled down deep and tight. It was her restraint that made it all ring true, her hesitance to be herself. He could guess why the doppel moved like that. He could only wonder why Ripka did, too. He wondered if that line the doppel had fed him about Ripka stealing food as a kid was bullshit, and decided it probably was. Shoulda' been his first clue something was wrong.

As the footsteps in the hall drew closer, his palms grew sweatier. He held his breath, counting each step to help himself focus. To stay calm.

It didn't help. If steel started ringing, he was a dead man. Or worse.

As the steps drew up alongside the door the doppel stepped forward, grabbed the door, and yanked it open.

The guard let loose an undignified yelp, and before he or she could get turned around to face the doppel she spoke in Ripka's strong, authoritative voice.

"By the pits, man, get a hold of yourself. Do you want to alert everyone within a stone's throw to your location? Idiots."

Huddled in the shadow of the door, Detan saw the doppel tilt her head, scanning the guard. She clucked her tongue.

"I see," she said. "You're one of Thratia's hires. Well. I suppose it can't be helped that her people aren't properly trained. Now, report." She gestured with her unsheathed saber. "Have you found sign of any intruder?"

A sliver of light outlined the doppel's silhouette as the guard brought his lantern around to bear on her,

no doubt wondering just who this woman was who
was ordering him about. Detan held his breath, hands
clenched at his sides. The simple fact the guard hadn't
immediately tried to run not-Ripka through was a good
sign.

"Watch captain?" The guard's voice was low, male,
and deeply incredulous. "Warden Ganal didn't mention
anything about you assisting tonight."

She took a step back, the guard followed. "Why would
she? Of course I'm assisting. She wouldn't have to tell
you the sky is blue, either, would she? Or how to wipe
your ass perhaps?"

Another step back, a dance of retreat. Detan tensed,
readying himself to spring.

"I'm sorry, watch captain. But rules are rules and you
aren't on the list. Put that blade away now and come
with me, we'll get it cleared up and you can go back to
your patrol."

Another step. With an affable little chuckle she
sheathed the blade and held her palms open to the sky
in mock surrender. The guard followed, drawn by the
pull of her retreat. The doppel had reached the end of
her task. It was up to Detan, now.

He swallowed hard, and lunged at the door.

It slammed shut, old metal hinges groaning out a
protest. The guard yelped again – poor habit, that – and
whirled on Detan, one hand all tangled up in his lantern,
the other half-heartedly brandishing a sword.

Not-Ripka got her elbow around the lad's neck before
Detan could see his face.

The guard squawked and squirmed. A little worm of
distaste wound through Detan's guts. These weren't real
soldiers. Not fleetmen, not watchers. Just poor, scared
local toughs Thratia had strong-armed into her service.

Before Detan could get a hand into things, the idiot dropped his blasted lantern. Detan froze as the crack of glass and hiss of igniting oil muted the guard's cursing. He watched in mounting horror as the slick, glassy puddle spread its fingers over the smooth floor, reaching for the eager tinder of the shelves and files.

He locked gazes with not-Ripka, saw a flicker of uncertainty there.

"Run!" he yelled.

She twisted away from the still-squirming guard and Detan grabbed her forearm, jerking her towards the door. He heard the guard swear, heard a hollow thump as the man wrenched his coat off and set to slapping the mounting inferno into submission.

Heard the delicate *swoosh* of flames finding fuel enough to feed their hunger.

Warmth slapped his back as they tumbled out into the hall, boots ringing loud as alarm bells on the steel floor. He heard swears all around – hers, the guard's. He prayed to the blue skies that the guards would be more concerned with being found responsible for burning down Thratia's shiny new Hub than letting a couple of intruders escape.

Prayed even harder he wouldn't wind up with an arrow in the back.

He slid to a stop before the push-button door, not-Ripka tugging his arm as she struggled to slow her momentum. Behind them shouts rose higher, strained and frantic. Old wood groaned, cleaved with a mighty crack. Detan flung the door open and leapt onto the cool sands of the night. Somehow he'd lost his grip on not-Ripka's arm, but he wasn't surprised at all to hear the soft tread of her feet behind him as he fled back toward the ridge. Angry as she was, the woman still had an instinct for self-preservation.

As he sprinted across the thin strip of sand between the Hub and the ridge which had concealed their approach, he spared a glance for the direction he'd seen the guards circling in earlier. Not a one was present. No doubt they'd all scarpered off to see what the hubbub was inside the Hub, and found the flames a mite more pressing than the wayward watch captain and her unknown companion. Hopefully unknown.

He grimaced, imagining the guards tongues wagging back Thratia's way – describing the silhouette of the man who'd run off with the interloping woman of the law. She was no fool, she'd figure it out right quick.

And she had poor ole Tibs wrapped up nice and cozy in her web already.

When they'd scrambled their way up the ridge and down to the narrow ledge on which they'd rested coming up, Detan forced himself forward on jellied legs, making for the edge. The doppel grabbed his arm, holding him back.

"Take a moment and breathe, or do you want to fall your way down?"

"Tibs–" he began, but she put her palm on his chest, firm and heavy, and pushed him till his back pressed against the naked cliff face. She narrowed the distance between them. Stood so close he could smell her sweat and the haval oil she wore. He swallowed. Hard.

This was not-Ripka, he reminded himself. Not the straight-laced, stern-hearted woman of the law he'd thought he was dealing with. He knew nothing about her, save she had a dead son and a whole mess of blood in her past. Heart hammering, he forced himself to stay still. To breathe.

To resist the urge to reach out and rip off the sel

coating her smug little face.

"We've got to get back," he modulated his voice to sound calm, certain. "We can take advantage of the chaos of the fire. Thratia will be distracted. We'll slip in the way you came and shove off with the *Larkspur*."

"Just like that?" There was a lilt to her voice, a sense of what – uncertainty? Fear? Probably madness, if the strange glint in her eye was anything to go by. Eyes that, he realized now that he saw them up close, weren't quite as grey as Ripka's – a smudge of golden green intruded upon her irises.

"Just like that. No more Aransa. No more Thratia. You'll have the *Larkspur* to do with what you will." And all those names and addresses went to smoke in that fire. No more murder, too. No more blind, flailing, revenge.

"Thratia deserves–"

"Something you can't give to her. You can't fight her straight on in her own compound. You won't win. You'll waste the opportunity, and be too dead to come back and try again."

Her lips pursed, frustrated, sullen. He held his breath.

Not-Ripka stepped away, her hand falling from his chest. Detan suppressed a burst of nervous laughter. His head swam, his pulse thundered. He needed to end this. To get back to Tibs and get gone.

"Let's go," he said, faking confidence.

When they reached the Black Wash it felt as if half the night had gone, but the moon had only drifted four marks through the sky. Enough time to make it back before the sun devoured them, but barely. He stood still for a moment, imagining himself rooted to the ground right through the soles of his boots, and let the desert wind play its way over his skin and dusty clothes. He cast an eye to the night sky, silently daring the sun to rise, to catch him out on the Black and burn all his pain and frustration away.

When not-Ripka stepped beside him he uprooted himself and ran his hands through his hair, tugging and mussing, then set off toward the city with ground-eating strides. The doppel was a good head shorter than him, so she had to quicken her pace to keep up.

High above, a shadow stirred. The Hub ferry shuddered out onto its guy wires, the rectangular blot of it little more than a black smudge against the navy sky.

"Is that–?" she asked.

He watched it toddle along. Didn't matter how slow the blasted thing was, it'd reach the city long before they ever could. His fists clenched, a thirst for flame rising within him.

"That's the news getting ahead of us," he said.

Her hand drifted toward the hilt of her blade, she half-turned toward the Hub. He knew what she was thinking. It'd crossed his mind, too. They didn't have to reach the city before the ferry – they just had to reach the Hub's dock before the ferry made land in Aransa. Two quick chops with that shiny little knife of hers and they'd plummet to the sand below. Thratia would suspect the fire had disabled the ferry, the flames were already a warm smudge of a glow against the side of the Smokestack, but she wouldn't know about the so-called watch captain's involvement. Wouldn't have a chance to figure out Detan had his hands in it.

It'd be so, so, easy.

"No," he said, and reached back to lay his hand across her sword arm. "There'll be no more death, if I can help it."

She eyed him long enough he began to fear she'd shake him off and make for the Hub on her own. But then she nodded, a sharp little jab of the chin just like the real Ripka would do, and let her hands fall free at her sides.

"I hope you know what you're doing, Honding."

He turned back toward Aransa, and ran to beat the shadows above.

CHAPTER 28

Thratia's compound had gotten some life back in it, and Detan wasn't too sure that was a good thing. Fresh light speared bright and angry through all the windows, the silhouettes of armed men and women passing by them on the regular. There wasn't any pattern to it he could work out, just a frenetic sort of activity that lacked a focused, guiding hand. Just the kind of hand Thratia was supposed to be providing. Maybe he was lucky. Maybe she was still out.

"Keep your head down, eh?"

Not-Ripka nodded and turned up the collar of her shirt to hide her jawline. Not that it did her much good in being inconspicuous. Everything about the way she moved told the story of her confidence, that she was top-of-the-rock in any room she entered. The blasted woman had gotten far too good at playing the real Ripka.

Lucky for them both, the guards posted at the gate didn't seem to notice, and the guards usually posted at the big double doors weren't there at all. Once inside, they tore off down the hallway to the stairs which lead up to the dock. All the while Detan's heart thudded in his ears, warning him that they were moving too fast – someone was going to notice. Going to stop them. Going to ask questions.

Or they were expected.

Shit.

Just a few marks ago he'd have felt right at home in this sordid little game, but now that Tibs was mixed up tight in the danger all he could think about was getting gone. Shoulda' listened to Ripka the first time. Or had that been the doppel? He was starting to lose track himself.

"Whoa there." As they topped the stairs, one of the guards he'd seen moping about the hallway earlier in the evening put an arm out, blocking his path.

Detan pulled himself up straight and tried to keep the doppel in his shadow. "What are you stopping me for? Thratia wants me locked up snug with her big balloon and if she finds me out here in the hallway pissing around with you I guarantee it'll be your nose that gets skinned."

The sniveling little rat smirked and put his arm down. "Sure. My mistake. Allow me to escort you."

Detan's neck went stiff and his fingertips twitched, little beads of sweat trickling between his shoulder blades. That bluster should *not* have worked. He couldn't bolt, not now, not with the doppel a step behind him and Tibs a door ahead. He tried to keep his chin up as he followed the strong-arm to the dock, but there was no keeping his gaze steady. His gaze darted around, trying to make sense of every shadow and coming up with nothing at all. He closed his eyes, took a slow breath, and stepped through to the dock.

Someone had had the fool idea of lighting lamps all

around the place, and the whole thing was lit up so bright his eyes watered and his vision went muddy. While he was blinking the wet away, the strong-arm said, "I found the thieves, warden."

They were swarmed. Before he could get his bearings straight he was thrown to the ground, the crack of his head against the floorboards bringing another burst of light to his eyes. Tears mingled with blood as he snorted and choked from a fresh nosebleed. His cheeks burned with angry heat when someone laughed.

As his vision cleared he saw the muscled hands holding him were sleeved in the slate-grey linen of Thratia's private militia, no mere thug was holding Detan pinioned against the deck. He couldn't see where the doppel had gone, but he figured she wasn't looking much better than him right now. He hoped she could keep her face together for their new company.

"I didn't steal a damned thing!" he called, blowing a rather undignified bubble of blood out of one nostril.

Someone's knee bit into his back and he grunted. With the side of his face pressed to the deck he couldn't see much of anything, but then a familiar black-dusted boot eclipsed his vision and he found himself wishing he could go back to not seeing anything at all.

"You're a thief and a liar, Honding, but you haven't stolen from me. Let him up."

The knee disappeared and the meat-hook hands came off. He pushed himself up and wiped the smear of blood from his nose onto his sleeve. Thratia's lip curled in disgust at that, which gave him a little tingle of pleasure.

"What's this about, warden?" He laid all the saccharine respect he could over the word warden, but she was too cranked up to notice. Her eyes were bright, her cheeks flush. She even had a strand of hair out of place, her knuckles gone rough and pulpy by a recent strike. He was, Detan realized, quite probably a dead man.

"What do you think?"

She pointed. Detan stared.

Out past the elegant shape of the *Larkspur*, the whole side of the Smokestack was glowing bright and angry. The flames must have gotten loose in the Hub, must have reached beyond the ready feed of wood and paper to rarer delicacies. Detan's throat went dry. Reaching up from the Hub, long arms of flame crept along the side of the Smokestack toward the divot of its mouth.

The selium pipelines were made of leather. Leather smeared with fat to proof it against the monsoon season. Ready fuel for a hungry inferno. Aransa's whole economy – done in by the flash of one measly little lantern.

"Wasn't me," he blurted.

"Clearly."

"Warden," the strong-arm interjected. "It may be he was involved. Those who came across on the ferry said the watch captain had an accomplice, a lanky man. And here he has just now returned with her."

Thratia moved so fast Detan barely saw it. She spun around and brought her hand up and down, one swift axe-blow, on the back of the strong-arm's neck. He grunted and staggered forward, eyes rolling up. The militiaman beside him grabbed him just in time to keep him from going full over the edge of the dock. Thratia didn't seem to notice the assistance. Or at least, she didn't care.

"Idiot." There was no malice in her voice, just motherly disappointment. "This man here may be a scoundrel, but he wouldn't set light to the whole of the Hub on purpose. His heart's too soft to doom a whole city like that." She scowled, rubbing the side of her hand. "And he wouldn't have done such a fool thing on purpose and leave his partner to rot. No, if he'd planned this little disaster he and Tibal would be halfway across the Scorched by now."

Thratia turned away, her victim forgotten. She tucked a flyaway piece of hair behind her ear and gestured toward the ground, where a bit of not-Ripka was visible underneath the knees and elbows of a half-dozen of Thratia's people. Detan tried to muster up the nerve to be offended that Thratia had thought her the bigger physical threat, but didn't have it in him at the moment.

Tibs was still here, then. But where?

The militiamen dragged the doppel to her feet, and he was a little irritated to see that she had escaped without a nosebleed to match his own. Women, always getting unfair treatment. Her jaw was set tighter than he'd ever seen it, the tendons on either side of her neck sticking out from the strain, but she kept her mouth shut, which Detan reckoned was the wise choice given the current mood of the room.

Detan cleared his throat, trying to keep his tone light. "Speaking of that old rock, where is Tibs?"

Thratia smiled. It was horrible.

"Bring her out."

"Her? Now, Tibs may be a little slender about the waist, but–" He swallowed his own rebuke. From amongst the crates Lady Grandon was shuffled forward, her lips hidden beneath a spit-wet rag. The lady's delicate wrists had been tied together with supple leather, her ankles little more than a hand's width apart. Her hair, so perfectly coiffed upon their last meeting, was skewed and skirling in the open air of the dock.

She held her chin high, but... her eyes. Those were terrified. Detan opened his mouth, and found no words worth saying.

"Did you think you wandered my city completely unwatched?" Thratia tsked. "Every soul you've shared more than a passing glance with, I've had noted. Every time you've exchanged words with a cart-vendor, ears I own have written them down."

"Why?" he said, voice coming out higher than he'd intended. This wasn't right. And where was Tibs? Did he make it out?

"You carry quite the reputation. But then, so do I. Or have you forgotten?"

"Release her." He found old strength in his voice, lost the flippant roll of syllables he employed to pull people along whatever nonsense train of thought he wanted them to follow. He knew that wouldn't work here. Not now. Not with her.

"Ah, so you do remember your teeth, lordling. I will, however, have to decline your request. You see, you've allowed me a handful of opportunities. I'm going to craft you an enemy tonight, Honding."

"There's nothing that says we have to be enemies, Thratia, just–"

"Not us, you empty sack."

Lady Grandon closed her eyes, gave a subtle shake of her head. Detan hadn't the slightest clue what it meant. His fingers clenched and unclenched at his sides, physically grasping for some sort of solution, for some path out of the mire. Desperate for an option that didn't end in blood. He glanced to the doppel, found her face unreadable.

"Bel's husband is an ambitious man, I can respect that," Thratia said, but all Detan really heard was the woman's name. Bel. Bel Grandon. He cursed himself for not knowing her better, for not understanding any of what he'd just stepped in.

Played it too loose, Honding.

The warden paced before Bel, tapping the flat of a longknife against her thigh with each step. It was the vilest weapon Detan had ever seen. Long and fire-blackened, the tip swooping up in a wicked curve. He swallowed, forcing himself to watch her face, not her blade.

"But his ambitions have led him astray. He snuggles up with the empire, giving the Valathean mercers prices he doesn't share with the Scorched. Now, I can't have that. I need his distribution network. Especially after tonight's... setbacks. And so—" She turned, pressed the tip of her knife beneath Bel's chin. "You're going to have to go my dear. I am quite sorry, but it accomplishes two purposes I cannot overlook."

Detan lurched forward, the movement pure instinct, and found his upper arms held fast by two iron-handed men. He thrashed against them, knowing it was useless. Knowing he didn't have a chance against common street toughs in a fair fight, let alone against trained men of the commodore. Better not make it fair, then.

He opened his sel-sense wide, casting about for the tiniest sliver of the gas. *Something* he could use. The *Larkspur*'s laden buoyancy sacks filled his mind, crowding out all finer sense. He couldn't even detect the thin film laid over the doppel's face. In the shadow of such a presence, he could sense nothing small enough to use. And if he reached for the *Larkspur* itself... He shivered. It hadn't come to that. Not yet.

"I will make damned sure Grandon knows whose hand murdered his wife. I will do everything in my power to turn this against you!"

Tears slipped down Bel's cheeks, her lips moved, murmuring beneath the gag. Thratia cocked her head, listening, and Detan's heart leapt. Did Bel have something to bargain with, something worth her life? She was landed by birth. It was possible.

"No, my dear. That would never work."

Thratia leaned forward, held Bel's cheek in her empty hand, and pressed her lips to the trembling woman's forehead.

Blood erupted. Detan hadn't even seen the knife move.

Thratia stepped back, wrenched her blade free. The only sound was that of metal scraping bone. Catching, snapping. Bel's eyes rolled up, she tried to scream and a meek gurgle bubbled out of the raw maw that had been her tanned throat.

He wanted to scream for her, but he forced himself not to react. To stand still. To breathe easy. He couldn't do it, not all the way. While his legs stayed anchored and his lips slammed shut he couldn't dampen the thunder of his heart, the panting need of his breath. As if he could suck down enough air for himself and Bel both.

She fell to the ground, curled around herself. It took longer than he would have deemed possible.

"Now." Thratia wiped her blade on a cloth a militiaman handed her. All business. "Two purposes. The first, of course, is to place her murder in your hands. My people and I will attest that Bel came over for tea and company, and got tangled up in your arrest for the arson. I will confide in Grandon that the empire knows you are dangerous, and has let you run loose too long. With his help, I will vow to hunt you down. Thus we will be united in purpose, and his love for Valathea will fade."

Trembling shook his voice. "Two. You said two." *Please let her death be worth more than that.*

"Ah, yes. The second, is so that you will understand

that I am *quite* serious."

She waved a hand and her militia spread out, making way for poor Tibs to be brought forward. His eyes were tired, bloodshot, and he was sporting a rather fresh bruise on his right temple, but otherwise he was looking all right.

All right for a man with his wrists and ankles bound up in rope. No nice, soft leather for Tibs. Detan grimaced. Of course, Thratia wouldn't want rope to have left a mark on the lady's skin.

Tibs glanced at Bel, pressed his lips together, and nodded to himself. When he looked at Detan, his expression was smooth as obsidian, and revealed just as much.

"Hullo, sirra."

"Hey, Tibs." He forced his tone light, forced his eyes away from the spreading pool. "What's with the jewelry?"

"I need to make something clear." Thratia pushed past Detan, smearing Bel's blood against his side. He turned to watch her, caught a subtle shift in her posture, a press of the side of her hand against her thigh. Against her pocket. He flicked his gaze away before she could catch him watching. He concentrated on that movement, on the position of her hand. Reached instinctively as she strode past him once more, pacing.

She was wound up so tight she failed to notice his fingers dipping into her pocket. A piece of metal. A slip of paper. Nothing obvious, nothing of use to him now. He shoved his pilfered gains into his own pocket. Tibs caught his eye. He was clearly unamused.

Thratia walked right up to not-Ripka and grabbed her throat in one hand. Detan's stomach threatened to give up the fight. The doppel's spine must have been made of stronger stone than his, because her scowl only got deeper. She didn't even flinch.

"Now, a woman was seen lurking about the Hub, and my men have attested that a woman looking remarkably like the watch captain of this fine city gave them a bit of a scuffle right before the flames took light."

"Hold on now, warden." Detan shoved his hand in the air to get everyone's attention, his mind working double-time to concoct a likely story. "I mean no disrespect to your fine deductive reasoning. In fact, I am most impressed by your method of investigation. But it must be said that *this* Ripka, that is to say, *the* Ripka, was with me the whole time all these goings-on were going on. And we were... ah... at the watch-station." He bit his tongue, cursing himself for rambling like a buffoon while Bel Grandon lay cooling.

"Here's the deal, Honding." Thratia rounded on him, fast enough to make him flinch back in anticipation of another scorpion-quick strike. She just smirked. "Maybe that's true. Maybe you and the good watch captain were having a quaint little tea while the doppel and another *accomplice* were traipsing about the Hub spreading fire in their wake. But that's not how this works. You know that. Rumors are spreading, and someone's going to have walk the Black for this."

Detan's fists clenched at his sides. "Then it should be the doppel."

"Could be, but it doesn't rightly matter, does it? The people just need to see someone punished, doesn't matter who it is. Regardless, our watch captain here has had a few unsavory rumors pop up about her. Isn't that right, captain?"

The doppel's eyes widened in real surprise. Whatever rumors had been spreading about the real deal, she'd missed them. Detan clenched his jaw, hoping she wasn't so rattled her acting would suffer.

She lifted her chin. "I have no idea what you're talking about."

Thratia dropped her hand, fingers coming dangerously close to brushing not-Ripka's selium-constructed freckles. "Don't you know, my dear? Your aptitude has been noticed. And whispered about. Some seem to think you're hiding a selium sensitivity."

"To the pits with you, Thratia, you know I'm no sensitive."

"Doesn't matter to me, lass. Matters to them." Thratia gestured toward the light-speckled expanse of the city below.

"I won't let you take her." Detan hadn't the slightest idea how he was going to manage that, and from the smile Thratia gave him she knew it, too. But, pits below, he couldn't let her walk the Black. Or worse, have it discovered what she really was. Where *was* Ripka? If the real deal made an appearance before Thratia could trot the doppel out across the sands, then it'd be off to the whitecoats with her. He suppressed a shiver.

Thratia crossed to him, stood close enough he could reach out and jab her straight in those hateful little eyes if his hands weren't restrained. "Thought you might say that," she said. "I don't want any direct trouble with you. I don't want Honding blood on my hands – so I'm going to give you a choice. You either give me Ripka, or Tibal."

"Tibs?" He choked on the name, cleared his throat with a rough hack. "Why?"

"Wouldn't be too much of a stretch to convince people it was Tibal running around with the watch captain in your place. Whichever one you give me, you'll have until morning. Bring me the doppel, and I can be lenient.

If not, someone's dying, and you choose who."

Detan dared to lean forward, to whisper against her ear. "You're a monster, commodore."

She patted him on the cheek, the dismissive affection of a master to its mongrel. "You already knew that, and you toyed with me anyway."

"It's all right," not-Ripka said.

"No, it isn't," Detan rasped.

The door to the dock burst inward. The genuine watch captain came striding through, dressed head to toe in mourning black, her cheek puckered with a mighty bruise and a determined scowl set to her feldspar lips.

And at her side strolled a native Valathean, tall and dark as night, her lean silhouette cut by the shape of her long, pure, white coat.

CHAPTER 29

Detan's heart leapt straight into his throat and stayed there, pounding away so hard he feared he'd vomit. Sweat slicked his back, his arms, his brow – reaching straight through his threadworn clothes and making him slippery in the grip of the men who held him. He opened his mouth to breathe, to suck down air to slow the dizzy swirl of his mind, but he just gasped like a fish out of water.

A whitecoat. Here. Right-in-fucking-front-of-him.

She hadn't seen him yet, her annoyed face was pointed straight at Thratia.

"This woman," the whitecoat said, flicking her wrist toward Ripka, "claims that she has proof of your involvement in a smuggling operation."

Ripka's shoulders shot back, straightening as she squared her body for a verbal fight. He could guess what she was thinking – guess she was gearing herself up to throw Thratia beneath the heel of her Valathean masters. Couldn't she hear the vague amusement tingeing the whitecoat's voice?

Detan heard. He'd grown used to judging the moods of those monsters. His life had depended upon it, once.

Thratia pursed her lips, gave Ripka a dragging look-over, nodded to herself, then turned back to the doppel and laid one firm, callused hand against her cheek. The doppel's skin shimmered. A finger poke she could handle – but a whole palm? Even with her control, Detan knew she hadn't stood a chance keeping it all smooth.

"Ah. So there you are."

Rage eclipsed the real Ripka's face, but it wasn't nearly as terrible as the sudden delight that fell like a spring rain across the whitecoat's smooth features. The watch captain's accusations all but forgotten, the whitecoat darted forward and grasped the doppel's chin between her fingers, twisting it this way and that as she clucked her tongue and nodded approvingly.

"Hmm, yes, such a fine specimen. Marvelous work, Thratia. Wherever did you find the thing?"

"Would you believe she came striding through my front door?"

The whitecoat barked a laugh. "Delightful. Of course she would. Her disguise is nearly perfect. If I looked the part of the watch captain so clearly I daresay I'd go anywhere I pleased." She flashed a smile. "But, of course, I have my own flavor of authority."

"Indeed," Thratia drawled, already bored with the whitecoat's delight.

Detan forced himself to look away from the nightmare apparition chatting amiably just a few meager strides from him. He caught Tibs's eye, saw the hard press of his lips and the jutting out of the tendons around his jaw. Couldn't read a thing in that – angry or just plain scared were a mite hard to tell apart when a man's features were already made of rock.

"I was just about to condemn her to walking the Black," Thratia said while Detan tore his gaze away from Tibs and searched the docks, angling for any way out.

"What in the blue beyond would make you want to do that?" the whitecoat asked.

"Seems she set fire to the Hub."

"The line?" her voice rasped, hinting at panic.

"Fine. My men had orders to secure it straight away should anything go wrong. Lost a whole lot of contained selium, though. Don't have the details yet but it'll push production back months."

"A fire, in the Hub?" Ripka said and took a step forward, toward the doppel. Thratia's guards found reason to get real cozy on her heels.

"Contained," Thratia said. "None of your concern."

Her fists clenched, but her head stayed high. "Lady Callia," she said, and the whitecoat's head turned just a fraction in her direction. "I understand that discovering the doppel is exciting. However, I have witness testimony that–"

"Oh hush, girl." Callia flicked her fingers in Ripka's direction and wiggled them. "No point in continuing this little dance any longer. Although I would just *love* to hear who your witness is."

"I don't understand–"

"Thratia," Callia interrupted, "was the doppel wearing the watch captain's face during this little arson?"

"She was."

"Then throw the real deal to the Black, and no one will have to know we ever found the creature."

"Wait just a–" Ripka strode forward, reaching for her cudgel, and was surrounded. Constraining hands closed on her from all sides. Detan grimaced, turning his gaze away in shame as she was pulled back, wrists pinioned, divested of all her weapons even as a rag was tied round her mouth.

"Very well," Thratia said, but the words sounded hollow to Detan, as if coming from a great depth. The hands around his own arms loosened, a few of his guards shuffled away to deal with the greater threat – the real watch captain. Detan held no illusions on where he stood, his fighting ability was as threatening as a one-winged pigeon. The urge to run swelled within him, crested and broke against the hard shield of his shame.

He couldn't bolt. Couldn't just leave the doppel to the fate that made his own guts roil. Couldn't leave Ripka to walk the Black for a crime in his ragged hands.

"But what," Thratia just kept on talking, as if this were all a mild amusement, a fun little puzzle for her and her white-coated friend to figure out, "are we going to do about the Honding lad?"

He watched in slow-motion horror as the whitecoat's back went rigid, her head snapping back as if someone had dealt her a mighty slap. Slowly, as if afraid he would spook and vanish if she moved too hastily, Callia turned.

There was such hunger in her eyes.

Detan froze. Rooted. Worthless.

At first he did not understand what he was seeing. Callia lurched forward, staggering, bending at the waist, her mouth parting wide as she let out an oomph of surprise. People called out, the words meaningless beneath the buzzing inferno of his pulse in his ears, but he understood.

The doppel had wrenched her hands free, had punched Callia in the kidney, and was dancing, twisting, threading her way through. Toward the edge of the dock. Toward the *Larkspur*.

Thratia barked orders, reached for her knife but the

doppel was too quick, moving like liquid, throwing up gleaming flares of sel to blind and distract. Little sparklers. Party favors. The guards' hesitation betrayed them, torn between chasing the escaping creature and holding on to what they had.

Wood began to groan. Not-Ripka had decided for them.

The *Larkspur* jerked against its bonds, rocking, the sturdy ropes that tied it down hissing as some tore, creaking as they strained. The guards swarmed to the ropes, Thratia demanding her ship secure, demanding no one escape.

Detan felt the mass of selium in the ship's belly. Felt the doppel grab and shove it, heave it back and forth, working strain and pressure deep into the wooded ties that held it.

He shut his senses down, too afraid of what he'd do given the right impetus, and elbowed his single captor square in the ribs. One tie gave away. Two, three, the ship gaining freedom in rapid succession. He didn't see it happen, but he knew the doppel must have jumped because he saw her land, hard and sprawling, barely folding herself into a roll just in time on the gleaming waxed deck of the ship.

She sat on the middle of the deck, legs splayed before her, hands holding her upright, face so set and focused he half expected her to will the whole thing into disappearing.

The *Larkspur* lurched, its final ties snapping. Detan twisted free of a hand grabbing at his elbow, caught sight of Tibs, caught sight of a familiar length of braided silk. An option.

Saw, from the corner of his eye, rising like a leviathan, the slender whitecoat.

Ripka's shout raked at him, and he caught her eye, frantic, her whole body straining against the multitude of hands that held her. Couldn't hear what she said – couldn't hear what anyone was saying – but he knew, somehow, she was calling for help.

The sight of that rope, dangling, pulled at him.

"I won't let you walk!" he screamed, not knowing if she heard.

Roaring with effort, he pumped his legs harder than he ever had in his life, barreled straight into Tibs, clutched him tight enough to bruise bone, and leapt.

The *Larkspur* broke free, sliding out into the night, splinters raining down all around it. Detan strained for the deck, willed himself and Tibs to fly straight as arrows.

And missed.

CHAPTER 30

Detan snapped a hand out, grabbed the rope and screeched to wake the dead as he slid down it, skin burning and tearing and his grip growing slick with the lubrication of his own blood. Tibs snatched at it, their combined weight jarred him so hard he felt his shoulder pop, but not give. Not yet, anyway.

The doppel's head appeared above the rail, wearing Ripka's face still but the eyes so wide she was near unrecognizable.

"Up! Pull us the fuck up!" he screamed above the wind whipping in his ears, stealing his breath, not knowing if he could throw his fear-choked voice far enough to reach her.

Her mouth moved, yelling something back he couldn't hear, and the *Larkspur* began to descend. Ribbons of pearlescent sel spun out from the side of the ship, released through jettison tubes under the doppel's command. They streaked the sky, but huddled close to the *Larkspur*, still under not-Ripka's sphere of control.

Tibs squawked something unintelligible as the ship

dropped, the rope swinging in crazy, twisting arcs as its backside slewed around. Detan's grip strained, burned. His hand felt bathed in fire but there was little he could do save keep holding on. To switch hands was to drop Tibs.

If he dropped Tibs, Detan wouldn't be but a heartbeat behind him in the plunge.

He looked down, stomach threatening an untimely revolt as they swung and swung and swung, saw she was dropping the ship down low over the market. Saw a neat little row of faded brown awnings nearly a man's length below.

His fingers began to spasm, and he thought of his hand only as an extension of his will, a collection of muscle and tendon and bone beholden to his desires. He gritted his teeth, clenched every last measly muscle in his body, and fell anyway.

Tibs held on for a scant breath longer, the jerk of his stationary body against Detan's descending soon-to-be-corpse knocking them apart. Detan went cartwheeling, screaming out because there didn't seem much else he could do, and crashed side-first into a thick, stinking stretch of canvas.

Something snapped. Bone or wood, he couldn't tell, but he heard the crack of breaking and the canvas twisted beneath him, dumped him in a tangled heap of moldy linen and shattered pottery.

He lay still a moment, gathering his breath, mentally going through a checklist of his hurts. Bruises and scratches, mostly, he decided as he eased himself upright. Revised his opinion as he pressed his hands to the rubble-strewn ground to heave himself up.

And his hand skinned raw, of course.

Clenching his jaw tight so that he wouldn't scream,

he cradled his rope-mangled palm against his stomach and staggered forward, huffing for breath as bright motes danced at the corners of his eyes.

"Tibs!" he called out, forcing his bruised legs to carry him down the row of shop stalls, further along the direction the *Larkspur* had been traveling. He had to be nearby. Had to be.

A soft groan drew him like a lure to a caved-in heap of canvas. Tibs's awning had bowed inward, cradling him like a sling, the tent poles holding it upright half-cracked and showing their pale innards to the world.

"Tibs!" Detan scrambled over, untangled the heap and found Tibs flat on his back, blinking up at him with wide, bleary eyes.

"Just winded," he rasped as Detan gave him his good hand to help him gain his feet. Shouts echoed somewhere in the market, drawing closer.

"Best be on our way," Detan said, brushing dust off Tibs's coat with one hand while he glanced over his shoulder toward the shouting. "Unless you've got the grain to pay for a whole potter's shed worth of rubble."

"'Fraid not." Tibs rubbed the back of his head with a hand and pulled it away, staring at both of his palms side by side. One was just a touch red, the other perfectly hale. "Lucky, that," he muttered.

"For you. I damn near lost half my hand. Ladies will weep to hear of this tragedy."

"Weep because you didn't lose the whole thing?"

Despite his pain and his fear and his anger, Detan choked on a startled laugh and chocked Tibs in the arm – lighter than he usually would, but a good shove all the same.

Tibs's voice dropped low, sobered. "Better get a salve on that and wrap it up, though."

"And what apothik do you think will do me that favor?" Detan snapped, Bel's wide, empty eyes eclipsing his thoughts like a spreading stain.

"Don't be a damned fool."

"I've *been* a damned fool. If I hadn't–"

"That's not what we do."

"But–"

Tibs stopped, half-turned real slow, and slapped Detan so hard across the face his eyes became reacquainted with those lovely little sparkly motes.

"Pull yourself together, sirra. Now."

Detan staggered a step, shook his head to chase away the brightness. He looked down at his hand – not too bad, but it'd need attention soon if he wanted to keep infection clear. He looked up to the sky, saw little more than a bleak smudge of black against deeper navy where he thought the *Larkspur* should be. Could have just been a cloud, or a flock of birds.

"Right," he said, rubbing his jaw with his good hand. "Right. We need to–"

"You there!"

Detan spun around, nearly tangling his feet in the mess of the stall Tibs's unheralded arrival had made. A ring of a half dozen or so men and women crowded around them, ruddy candles sheltered by dust-coated lantern glass held high. They carried a mishmash of weaponry – cooking pans, heavy bats meant for playing stickball. Despite the inelegance of their threat, Detan had no intention of taking them any less seriously.

"Hullo!" he called out, stalling, stepping backward through the treacherous footing of the destroyed stall to put some distance between them. "Lovely night, isn't it?"

"Not from where I'm standing." The taller of the

women stepped forward, her shoulders broad as Detan's arm was long, her eyes set in a permanent squint by the wrinkles spackled in tight around them. More worrisome than her squint, Detan noticed with mounting alarm, was the thickness of her fingers, the stubbed length of her nails. The subtle curve of hard muscle beneath her sleeve. "You two prepared to pay for the damage you've done?"

"Uh, well…" From the way she twisted the grip of her frying pan, Detan held no illusions that she'd be sure he paid – one way or another. He patted his body down, fishing through pockets, seeking the grains of silver not-Ripka had given him. Nothing. He swallowed, fumbled some more, shot a frantic glance at Tibs. The withered bastard just shrugged.

"You see," Detan began, taking another step back, Tibs following him toward the thin wall which hemmed in the level's edge. "It was quite the accident, and I'm afraid all our grains have, ah, fallen out of our pockets. I'm sure if you rooted around in the wreckage for a while you'll find sufficient funds. Look!"

He grabbed a half-snapped awning post and jimmied it upright. "A little sap glue will fix this right up – I-I have just the thing!"

Frantic, he fumbled in his coat for the little pot of glue he'd used to construct the kite and felt nothing but a sticky puddle on the inside of his pocket, bits of broken clay floating within it. Tibs grabbed him by the upper arm and squeezed. "Sirra…"

"What?" he hissed.

"Enough!" the woman barked, and the mob rushed them.

Detan let out a yelp of surprise as the market-dwellers vaulted over the wreckage, knocking aside anything that was in their way with their makeshift weapons.

"There's no need–" he said, but they were yelling some local charge and Tibs yanked back on his arm so hard he stumbled, fell backward against the low wall.

It was lower than he remembered. The top of it smacked him square in the back of the thighs and he reeled, arms windmilling, top half leaning too far over the edge for him to regain his feet.

Fear of falling surged through him, his recent perilous descent cutting-bright in his mind, memory of having the breath whipped from his lips and his limbs twisted by treacherous currents all too fresh. Pits below, but he'd rather face that frying pan than another fall through the empty dark.

Tibs shoved his chest, and over he went.

He landed flat on his back in a moldering heap, all the air whooshing out of him even though he was panting with panic. Tibs landed beside him, light as a cat, though his feet disappeared into the ground as if swallowed. Detan opened his mouth to swear or scream or just generally curse the world bloody, caught a whiff of the fetid pile all around them, and fell into a coughing fit.

There was yelling above, angry and sharp but far away. Something thunked near his head – the frying pan? He rolled to get a closer look, morbid curiosity directing him now, but Tibs had his hands under his arms and yanked him to his feet, then dragged him off away from the compost pile that had been their soft landing.

"I hate pits-cursed mushrooms," Detan croaked when he could breathe without spasming again, when Tibs had herded him safely into some dense maze of alleys he hadn't bothered mapping.

"Yeah, well, they like you." Tibs flicked something grey and slimy and cone-shaped off his shoulder. Detan shivered and flapped his coat like it were a pair of wings to shake the debris clean.

"Probably picked up some freakish infection from that mess," he grumbled, trying to peer at his skinned-opened palm in the low light but seeing little more than a dark, muddled mess.

"Wasn't nothing more noxious than you in that heap."

Detan laughed, the sound a little high, a little frantic.

"What next?" Tibs asked, his voice soft but gravelly, grounding Detan's mounting mania in an instant.

What next, indeed. He scowled at his hand, thinking. He needed medical aid, the kind you pay for, and the grains that didn't tumble out of their pockets in the fall were back in their rooms – no doubt watched by Thratia's people. The flier was safely stashed with New Chum, but they couldn't make that crossing until he was bandaged up.

And the only apothik he'd known inclined to offer him any flavor of charity was, well... And Ripka sure as shit wasn't able to offer him any assistance. She was getting ready to walk for a crime he'd done.

He swallowed. Something the doppel had said, about her people's remedies... He closed his eyes, pressing them tight enough to summon the motes. Remedies for a long-lived people, and the spicy-sweet aroma of her perfume, worn close but still detectable. A scent he'd encountered once before.

Detan snapped his eyes open, grinned at Tibs. "It's time to pay the doppel a house call, old chum."

Tibs gave the black-grey sky a surly eye. "Don't much think the lady will be in residence at this particular juncture."

"Lucky for us it's not her company we're after. That woman's Catari, I'm sure of it, and those folk keep their remedies close."

"More likely to poison yourself than heal that hand."

Detan bit his lips, muting himself for just a breath, then said slowly, "It's not just the medicines. I'll need a weapon, soon. Doppels like to keep the medium of their art close to hand, and I doubt she'll be popping by home to collect her stash."

Tibs bristled all over like a rockcat sighting a coyote. "Bad idea."

"And would you rather have me running around with a sword or one of those ridiculous crossbows the Watch is so fond of? I'd be more likely to put your eye out than Thratia's. And anyway, we're going to need a way to get the doppel's attention."

"Destroying half the city would do that, I grant you."

"Then we're in agreement!" Detan raised his hands to clap and caught himself just in time with a grimace.

"Small problem with your brilliant plan, sirra. I reckon you just happen to know where she lives now, hm?"

"We did get acquainted. Being complicit in arson together will do that to a pair." He strode off, barreling ahead as if he knew where he was going through the nest of side streets, knowing only that he couldn't stand still.

"And just where might that be?" Tibs said, a shadow at his side, not bothering to correct his course. Knowing, just as Detan did, that he had to work it out for himself.

"Fourth level – amongst the retirees and their lot. Can't miss the place."

"Really."

"Yessir."

"Fourth level."

"Mmhmm."

"Gotta go up to get there. Back through the market."

Detan groaned. The sooner he could show Aransa his retreating backside, the better.

CHAPTER 31

At night, the miners' quarter was quiet. These were hard working men and women, tired souls who spent their days laboring for the right of Aransa to exist, and when they went to bed at night little stirred them. Which was too bad, because Detan was mighty willing to do some stirring up.

"Where to?" Tibs asked.

"To the door of spice and vanilla." He tipped his head toward a block of apartments which had a slight downcrust lean.

The building was a smashed together collection of miniscule apartments meant to make it look like the city cared, like the empire looked after the well-being of the sel-sensitives who served it. They weren't bad, Detan had to admit that much, but they weren't near enough compensation for what the sensitives were put through. Not near enough at all.

Lights were snuffed in all the windows, shutters left open to let in the cool of the desert night. Just one set of windows was sealed tight, the ones he was looking

for. With a clenched jaw he stepped right up to the sun-
bleached door and pounded on it. Once, twice, three
times. Nothing but silence.

"We're in luck, the lady isn't home," Detan said.

"But her neighbors are." Tibal gestured with his chin
to small faces peering down at them from the curtained
windows. Little white eyes that flashed away like
minnows in a pool from his sharp regard.

"There won't be trouble," Detan said.

"You sure about that?"

"Not really. But it sounds nice."

He'd seen floor plans like these before. They used
them often enough in Hond Steading. Drawing from
memory, he followed the wall down to where there
should have been a split between this building and the
next. The builders always said the narrow alley was for
safety in case of fire, but really it was a repository for
nightsoil and garbage. He froze, realizing he'd walked
right past it to the next building.

"Oh, that rockviper…"

He spun around and walked back real slow this time,
letting his fingertips brush over the face of the building
until they tasted empty air.

"Well, that's unusual," Tibs said.

He stared down at his hand, buried up to the knuckles
in what looked to be a rotted section of rock. Now that
he knew what he was looking for, he could feel the
fingernail-thin veneer of selium laid over the alley's
entrance, could sense it extend all the way up to about
twice his own height. It was starting to fade, now. Little
tattered ribbons of it coming undone at the anchor
points, revealing slivers of the garden behind the facade.
He wondered if the neighbors had ever noticed. He
doubted they'd have said anything if they did.

"Lot of time and power went into this," Detan said, unable to keep the warm tinge of admiration from his voice.

He looked back at Tibs's bruised face and his stomach clenched. He wanted to respect this woman, this creature who had strung them all along so fine and easy. But there was Tibs, his face a mess, and who knew what Ripka's looked like now? Good people, both of them. The doppel should have thrown him to the vultures instead. Then at least they could have been pals one day. Not now. Not ever. Not after she'd flown off and left Ripka to rot.

Gritting his teeth, he stepped through the sel membrane. It moved against him, sensing in him some sort of kinship neither man nor substance understood. Its touch was familiar, wanting. The caress of a lover too far gone to ever hold again.

But then he was through, and all sense of intimacy vanished, as ephemeral as any real lover Detan'd ever held. Tibs followed, stifling a yawn, and Detan wondered if the doppel felt the same thing he did every time she made use of her creation. He shook the memory of her smile from his mind. Set his shoulders. Clenched his jaw.

While Tibs set about picking the lock to the lady's back door, Detan examined the alley. The doppel was clever, and that was beginning to itch at his sense of danger something fierce. She'd had the forethought to put up a real wall just two long steps in from the sel membrane, separating the place where her back door emptied into the alley from all the others.

Through breaks in the crumbling mudbrick he could see that her neighbors had made good use of their alley, keeping it clean and neat. On the doppel's side flowering succulents were planted up the dividing wall. They must have thought her a gentle old lady who just wanted this bit of land for her garden. He picked one of the plant's carnelian blooms and tucked it into his buttonhole.

Tibs opened the lock and stepped aside to let Detan pass first. Neither of them were proper fighting men, but Detan liked to imagine he could be handy with his fists and his knife if the need arose. Things seemed mighty needful now, so he freed the knife from his belt and stepped into the apartment.

It was pitch black inside, and he strained his senses so hard he wondered if he could trust them. There was sel here, somewhere, tucked away and not moving. Detan cursed himself for not knowing nearly enough.

He crept forward, hearing nothing but his boots whispering against the rug and his breath pumping in and out at an embarrassing rate. With the little bit of moonlight slipping in through the opened back door he could make out the usual trappings of a sparse living room. A wide table to step around, a hearth and kettle stand, a few chairs covered in quilts like his grandma had once made. A curtain in a doorway, separating this room from the sleeping room.

Knowing he didn't have the time to let his eyes adjust properly, he waved Tibs in and pointed at a brass lantern sitting in the middle of the table. He kept his gaze stuck on that curtained door, waiting for any movement, any sound, any sign at all of life lurking beyond. Straining his sel-sense to the edge, he could feel the sel in there, still and calm.

Tibs got the lamp lit and Detan braced himself, knife held at the ready, for an angry doppel to come at them. After a while, Tibs chuckled into the tense silence. "I think the lady has other business to see to tonight. I doubt we'll be seeing her again, now she has what she wants." Tibs paused, glancing pointedly at the blade in Detan's hand. "Best put that away, my eye's getting anxious."

Detan let his shoulders slump. "I really hate this life-and-death nonsense, Tibs ole soul."

"I know it."

Still tense as a rockcat in a puddle, Detan motioned for Tibs to follow and crept toward the curtain. He swept it aside and thrust his arm through, knife first, fearing the screech of an angry woman. All he got was silence.

"Welp, that was a whole lot of sneaking about for nothing," he muttered.

"Indeed."

The bedroom was empty of living things. Sparse as it was, he couldn't see a single place big enough for a woman of any build to hide. A solid bed took up the center of the room, its linens finer than anything Detan'd seen in a long while. On the wall opposite the foot of the bed was a little table with a mirror and chair, cluttered over with all the strange accoutrements of womanhood. A drying line was hung across the back wall, the doppel's clothes slung over it. No sign of medicines of any sort.

He flipped open the lid of the trunk at the foot of the bed and grunted. Inside, folded with extreme care, were the clothes of a mining man. They'd been scrubbed, but blood was a hard thing to wash away.

"Looks like we found the lass's nest," Tibs said over his shoulder.

"Let's tear the place apart, see what we can find."

For the next full mark Detan and Tibs put their backs to the task. Truth was, there just wasn't that much to search through. He found a slim folder in the bottom of the trunk, tied up with a ribbon, and sat down on the vanity stool to pore through it. There were mostly letters of a family nature, and he caught the name of one of the dead boys many times. Her son, Kel.

In the back of it all, he discovered sketches of a man's face done in an unpracticed hand. As he flipped through them, they grew in competency, until he could see all the lines of the man's face clear as his own; lifelike enough that Detan half expected him to turn his head and tell him to sod off and mind his own business. The man looked older than the seventeen monsoons stated in the file he had pulled. Detan frowned, remembering the feel of that report – strange dents in the paper. Had it been altered, too? Why bother?

"Anything of import?" Tibs asked, breaking a silence that had snuck up on them both.

Detan jumped a little and shook his head. "Just what we expected. This doppel of ours is out for revenge. This has gotta be her son, one of the boys that died in that line accident." He held the picture up for him to see. Tibs took it, his worn face wrinkling as he examined it.

"She's very good."

"She practiced. A lot. I think she's been planning this a long time."

"Seems that way. That trick with the alley wall alone must have taken her a good full pass of the seasons to plan."

"She's gotten so much stronger through practice, all on her own. Look at these." Detan fanned the progression of faces out on the vanity. "Even just drawing with charcoal, not sel."

"It's too bad she's done it to become a murderer."

"Can you blame her?"

"No, not really."

Detan bowed his head and ran his fingers through his hair. All that talent. All that raw determination, and if Thratia had her way she was going to be gobbled right up by the empire. Oh, she'd make her go through the motions of walking the Black all right, just to show the people that she could, but there'd be someone out on the ridge waiting for her. Waiting to take her to Valathea.

"It's not right. Doing to her what I'm running from myself."

"She'll have a chance at life. As it stands, Ripka will die. She's not valuable enough for them to save her life, you know that."

He stood and paced. Back and forth, back and forth, cutting a trough through the floor with the force of the anger in his steps. Tibs was right, he knew it. He knew he had to find this woman, to trade her life for another. Had to take the scant sel he'd found covering the alleyway and send up a flare, something to get her attention. To lure her near so he could talk her into a trap and hand her over, tied with a bow, to the very people he was running from. If that was even enough to get her attention in the first place, there was no guarantee she'd come running when he signaled.

He growled and kicked the side of the bed that the letters said Pelkaia's son had made her. Kicked it so hard his teeth rattled, but all it gave him back was a hollow thump.

He froze, staring at it. "Oh."

Detan dropped to his knees and yanked aside the smooth blankets, the thick quilt. He shoved his hands under the small space between the bed and the floor, recalling his sel-sense, remembering the faint tinge of it when he'd first entered the apartment. When he hadn't found any, he'd assumed it was just the phantom of the sel wall clinging to him. He could be a real idiot sometimes.

His fingers found the iron ties on the feet of the bed,

anchoring it straight into the ground, and he almost laughed at the simplicity of it all. Fumbling, searching, following his sense, he ran his hands up and grasped the smooth vellum bladder of a sel sack, bulging and full. Enough for her to spend all the time she desired practicing her art. An idea came to him; another option.

"I've found her stash, Tibs!"

"Marvelous," he droned.

"Might be we don't need her at all."

"Hold on now…"

He got the cap off and focused all his strength on drawing out a small blob. It was bigger than he would have liked, but it would do. He closed it back up and nearly skipped to the vanity chair. He brushed the folder of letters and drawings aside, and shifted his little blob until it rested on the vanity's top. It fought back, trying to rise up and float as it was meant to, but Detan was strong enough to hold the little ball in place. He was strong enough, all right.

The trouble was making sure he didn't get too strong all of a sudden.

"I don't think this is wise…"

"Shut up, Tibs, I need to concentrate. Go on ahead and talk to our New Chum eh? Dawn is coming and this is going to take me a while to get right. Best be sure the flier's ready to go when I get to the Fireline."

"We can still find the doppel. If we surmise that she has yet to leave the city, then–"

"No. This way… This way no one has to die."

"You sure about that?"

"Just go."

Tibs grunted his disapproval, but he knew as well as Detan did that their chances of finding the doppel before the sun rose were damn near impossible. He had a shot with this. He could do it. He just had to practice. And concentrate. And not get too angry.

He thought of Pelkaia, nursing her pain over all those years. Growing stronger. Better. Refining her raw talent into something that would serve her. Detan didn't have years. But he had a whole lot of anger. He was not, however, angry enough to be a complete idiot.

"Wait!" Detan blurted as he heard the door creak open. Tibs paused, his steps going silent. "Use the replacement cabin you fashioned for the *Larkspur*. Wreck it in the middle of the Black, and stash some water in there for me, will you?"

Tibs chuckled, but the sound was raw. "As you say, sirra."

The door clicked shut.

Detan exhaled, counted to ten, then slivered off a bit of the sel and floated it up to his cheek.

CHAPTER 32

Thratia had retrieved Ripka's blues and forced her to wear them. It shamed her to know that she would stand before the people of Aransa in judgment while wearing the uniform she'd donned to protect them, but the warden had insisted. And though she'd rather rip the coat off and smother Thratia with it, she wasn't exactly positioned to protest.

"I am sorry about this, you know." Thratia sat on the mudbrick bench beside her and leaned her head against the wall, giving them the illusion of intimacy. All around her Thratia's militiamen skulked, hands ready on weapons. Ripka made a point of not looking in the Valathean dignitary's direction. She kept her eyes straight ahead, her gaze indistinct. She would give them no sign of her anger. Of her fear.

The guardhouse was still night-chilled, and they'd lit only the bare minimum of lamps to stave off the desert heat a little longer. Ripka was grateful for that. She was going to have plenty of time to get acquainted with the sun, no sense in rushing it.

"If you were truly sorry you'd let me go."

"Can't do it. I know you think I'm after the power, captain, but the truth is I want the best for this city. The only way it's going to survive what's coming is with a strong hand at the tiller. Something Galtro just couldn't provide."

"So you got rid of him, then? I'm going to die anyway, you might as well relieve the burden with a confession before I go." She clamped her jaw shut, regretting the ragged anger of her tone.

"Galtro was dead the moment he took that job. It was just a matter of time." She shrugged one shoulder, infuriatingly indifferent to the destruction she'd wrought.

"His wardenship candidacy?"

"No, no. Being the mine master. You haven't been here long enough to see it, captain. I know you come from a town with no sel mines. The truth of it is, souls just don't last that job. Suicide, or a vengeance killing, one or the other always catches up eventually."

Ripka clenched damp palms, taking a breath to smooth the raw edge creeping into her voice. "He was good at his job, he made sure the miners were as safe as they could be. Only had one accident during his whole tenure."

"One's enough. Regardless, there are other duties that come with that job."

"Like what?"

Thratia tipped her chin in the direction of the whitecoat. Callia had her back to them, long and straight, impervious to the dust and grit all around her. Ripka got chills just looking at her. She pitched her voice low.

"What will you do with Aransa, Thratia?"

The once-commodore pursed her lips and leaned forward, letting her forearms rest against her knees. She stayed quiet longer than was comfortable, Ripka's stomach knotting over and over again. When Thratia spoke, her voice was markedly gentle.

"You won't be around to see it, lass. And that's a blessing."

Thratia pushed to her feet and dusted her hands, wiping away Ripka with each stroke. "Best prepare your conscience, yeah? Sun's coming up."

Gathering a breath of courage, Ripka said, "I've a favor to ask of you, warden."

Thratia paused, cocked her head to the side to watch Ripka from one eye. "Ask it."

She clenched her jaw, knowing what that meant. Knowing no promises would be made, no favors kept if they didn't thread their way conveniently through Thratia's plans. Ripka straightened her shoulders and met Thratia's stare. "Whatever happens, do not instigate a purge."

Genuine surprise widened Thratia's eyes, pursed her lips. Ripka held her breath as the ex-commodore cast a sideways glance at Callia. The whitecoat wasn't paying them any attention. Thratia turned, leaned down to bring her face closer to Ripka's and whispered, her voice harsh and her breath hot with anger. "Understand this – I will not allow such a thing to happen. Never."

Ripka leaned her back against the cool wall and watched Thratia stroll to Callia's side, her heart thundering in her ears with every step. Of course. Thratia'd never wanted a purge for Aransa; but the doppel sure had needed a stick of fear to jab Ripka with. Sick laughter threatened to break through Ripka's lips, but she swallowed it down.

Watching from beneath her lashes, Ripka studied Callia, or tried to, her attention kept drifting to her once-sergeant. Banch stood beside the whitecoat at parade rest, wringing his hands behind his back because he thought no one would notice them. He kept trying to catch Ripka's eye, to give her some sort of signal that he was sorry. That he'd never wanted any of this to happen. That he'd had no idea he'd be the new watch captain.

Poor sod didn't even know Ripka had recommended him.

Taellen lingered nearby, back straight enough to match the whitecoat's, a barely controlled tremble of fear in the tightness of his jaw. Though he stood at attention, his eyes were downcast, his mouth curved into a soft frown. Ripka couldn't work out why Thratia had decided to drag the rookie out here for this, and decided she didn't care. Whatever the reason, there was nothing she could do about it now.

She closed her eyes and sighed. Banch was a good man. He wouldn't be fool enough to let his emotions be played by a common murderer. He'd take care of the city when she was gone.

Gone. She had to stop thinking like that. Detan was shifty as the night, but he had a core of goodness in him. He wouldn't let her down if he could help it.

As the sun crept skyward, spilling warmth and light through the cracks in the brick, she couldn't help but think of all the things she might have done differently in her life. All the paths that wouldn't have led her to this bench.

Digging deep, she summoned up the face of her mother. Her father. How long had it been? She'd lost count, and time apart had smoothed the details of her recollection. One piece was still clear, her father's voice, raspy with dry amusement, *spine like iron, brain like a boulder, that's my girl.*

"Time to go, captain."

Ripka stood. Straightened her blues. She did not let them help her up the ladder.

CHAPTER 33

On the Scorched, the heat rose before the sun did. Detan felt the first probing rays of it before the light crested the flat and ruddy horizon, bringing prickling sweat and parched lips. He shifted the too-wide shoulders of his stolen shirt and dreamed of water.

He wouldn't dare drink. The veneer was too thin, and his struggle to keep it all in place was doing more to make him sweat than the sun ever could. Just ahead rose the guardhouse roof from which the guilty of Aransa were given their choice with the rising of the sun: face the axe, or walk the Black Wash and let the desert decide the depth of your sin. Ripka wouldn't take the axe, he was sure of that. She would take her chances with the wilderness that had forged her.

If she didn't, Detan was going to be mighty upset.

Light snapped free of the horizon at last, chasing down the heat. The mud and stone buildings of Aransa grew warm and vibrant in the rays, no longer grey and dingy under the shadow of night. There was movement amongst the people gathered, anxious and tense. Sour sweat tinged the air, a bitter mingling of excitement and heat and fear.

Dark figures emerged upon the roof, familiar to him even in silhouette. Thratia, slender and full of swagger. Ripka, stiff-backed and stern. Thratia's militiamen came behind, and the round-shouldered form of Ripka's sergeant. Another watcher hovered beside the sergeant, his movements furtive and uncertain, but the cut of his coat gave away his profession. And another Detan didn't recognize.

Squinting, he watched the unfamiliar figure. The doppel? No, she wouldn't dare come this close. Thratia was bound to have a sensitive amongst her guards, and she would have them on high alert this morning. The unknown figure was tall, rectangular beneath the hem of a long coat. He swallowed, and decided to move before his fear anchored him.

Whatever was being said up there, he couldn't hear it. His focus on holding his sel mask was so intense he didn't dare think on anything else. He sidled up to the crowd and weaved his way through while keeping his head down, his face hidden.

Elbows bumped him, fingers reached for his pockets. Sweat threatened to mar his mask, to set his tenuous control trembling. Someone grabbed his wrist, jerked him to the side. Detan staggered, jostling those pressed up against him, and glanced back to see a stone-grey sleeve attached to a rather scarred face.

"Just what in the shit are you doing–" Foamy flecks burst from the militiaman's lips, his voice a growl above the complainant murmur of the crowd. Detan jerked his arm, yanking his wrist free. His hastily wrapped, rubbed-raw hand scraped in the grip of the militiaman's. Needles of pain threatened to overwhelm his control but he

bolted forward, spurred on by fear, shoving people aside
in his need to reach the roof before Ripka could make
her decision. Before that stone-sleeved arm could detain
him and ruin the whole thing.

Luckily, no one kept an eye on the guardhouse door,
but he supposed that was only natural. Only an idiot
would charge up there uninvited when a death sentence
was being handed down.

He burst through the door and scrambled across the
small room, sucking down air that stank of all that was
left unclean in the cells, and found the ladder to the roof.
No time to think. No time to let himself back down. He
grabbed the rungs and hauled himself up into the full
light of the sun.

"Hold him." Thratia's voice was cool as the desert
night, but he sensed a tinge of high-strung unease in it.
Rough hands, familiar to him now, dragged him off the
last bit of the ladder and his head rushed and buzzed as
he split his attention between holding the sel mask and
watching the people on the roof.

"Well, well." Thratia prodded his face with one finger,
and he damn near laughed as her mouth opened and her
pupils widened enough to make her whole eyes black.

It was just a thin layer. He didn't have the requisite
skills to change its structure, to shift the color. But he
could make it thin enough to make it clear, and even
clear sel rippled when touched. One little ripple was all
he needed to sell the thing. A murmur passed through
the crowd, and Detan had to fight down an urge to try
and listen to what they were saying. The words didn't
matter. They'd seen the sel on his face. He could wager a
good guess what the whispers were about.

Her dark eyes narrowed with resumed control. "What
are you up to, Honding?"

He rasped a laugh. "I'm honored you think my technique is the truth, but we both know the Honding lad doesn't have enough sel-sense to illusion up a turnip, let alone a face."

"Then why don't you show us your real face, doppel?" Thratia's voice was smooth, bemused. The expression she showed him now was not one belonging to a woman who had just captured the thief of her finest possession. It didn't matter. He just needed the crowd to believe it.

"You don't deserve it," he spat.

Her lips twitched and she stepped back, arms crossed over her ribs. "All right then, creature. Where's my ship?"

She'd made her voice loud, loud enough to be heard by the people gathered nearest the guardhouse, so Detan did the same. "I destroyed your ship. Smashed it against the sand, every little bit of it, over and over again."

Another ripple passed through those gathered, but it was nothing compared to the bright spark of rage on Thratia's face. Apparently she was more than willing to believe he'd done her ship harm, even if she couldn't swallow him as the doppel.

He'd never seen such anger before. Her whole body went rigid, every last muscle winding up in preparation for a strike that wasn't coming. She may have been a cruel woman, but she had mastered her temper long ago.

"You broke. My ship." There was nothing bemused about her voice now.

"Don't believe me? Take a look."

He gestured to the Black Wash, and prayed Tibs had made it look good. Thratia snatched a sighting glass from Callia's outstretched hand and snapped the little brass tube open. She brought it up to her eye and scanned the darkened sands. Even Detan could see it with his naked eye, a little heap of brown wood in the middle of the obsidian sand.

"Why?" Her voice was tight, irritated, but not yet convinced. The false cabin hadn't supplied nearly enough material to make it look like a whole ship had been destroyed out there.

"This city, *your* city, murdered my son." The words sounded false to his ears, hackneyed and bitter. Whatever Pelkaia would have said in truth, he couldn't imagine. A real mother's grief was far beyond his basic mummer's skills. But he'd pushed out the words with all the venom he could muster, lifted his head high with defiance. It'd have to do.

Another wave through the crowd, this time stronger. Thratia rolled her eyes, all the hot anger evaporating from her posture. Detan clenched his jaw, waiting for Thratia to act. To call him out. To expose his tone for lacking a real mother's grief. Instead she stepped forward, laced her fingers under his chin and tipped it to the side so that she could whisper flat against his ear.

"Careful now. I've been having a little chat with my friend, the Lady Callia. You see her there?" She turned his head for him, just enough to see the willow-thin figure of a woman dressed in pale blue silks, a slim-cut white coat on despite the heat. Everything about her posture radiated boredom, but she was looking at him with eyes so intense it made him want to squirm.

Fear shot straight through him, tingling his toes and chilling his guts so fast he nearly lost his hold on the sel. He grabbed it again, straining his senses with a grunt, and nearly overdid it. The corners of Thratia's eyes crinkled, recognition of his struggle, and she kept on whispering. "She let me know a little secret, understand? Let me know that that conning fop Detan

Honding is a very wanted man indeed."

He swallowed dry air. "So what? The people gathered here see a doppel squaring off with their new warden. Officially the punishment for doppels is death." He raised his voice, clear and high so they could all hear it. "I choose to walk the Black."

She pushed his head away with a flick of her wrist and strode toward Callia. Detan watched them confer, heads close together. He stole a glance at Ripka, and saw nothing short of iron-hot hatred in her eyes. Well, at least she believed he was the doppel.

"I've decided," the new warden said.

Thratia broke away from Callia and stood near the edge of the guardhouse roof. She held her arms out, palms spread up in welcome to the sun, and lifted her voice. "We have two guilty souls before us this morning, Aransa. Your corrupted watch captain conspired with this abomination, this doppel, to burn the Hub to a husk and steal my ship. Those very boots the doppel is wearing left prints in blood at the place of Mine Master Galtro's death. The watch captain was seen lurking about the Hub just before the flames began. And here now, a confession. The doppel tells me it smashed the *Larkspur*, turned it to kindling in the sand.

"That ship was not just mine, Aransa. That ship was meant to bridge the long gap between this fine city and all the others of the Scorched. To carry supplies and news, to have our streets run flush with trade. And now we are stymied, we are thwarted, by this creature's misplaced revenge.

"In my mind I am certain that the watch captain acted in good faith. Hers is a loyal soul, a Brown Wash soul, and the doppel clearly has twisted her into believing she was doing right. It grieves me, but she is still guilty.

Guilty not only of theft and destruction, but of hiding from you, Aransa, her meager ability to sense selium."

A harsh gasp wound through the crowd, disgusted enough to make even Detan take a step back. He glanced sideways at Ripka, saw the slack shock in the sagging of her jaw, the panic in the whites of her eyes. Thratia bowed her head, letting the angry murmurs spend their course, and then raised her voice once more.

"I know it is difficult to believe. But this woman," she thrust a finger towards Ripka, "hid her ability to keep herself from the line. To keep herself in the Watch, where she supposed she served you better. Young Watcher Taellen here," she gestured to the nervous man in blue that Detan had noted earlier, "observed her use these skills himself."

"I am not sensitive!" Ripka lurched a full step forward before her watchers gathered her under their control, faces contorted by grief and guilt.

"Then why," the whitecoat spoke as she stepped forward, brows arched high, "do you carry selium on you? I can sense it from here, my dear."

Ripka's lips pursed, her shoulders shot back – confident the whitecoat was wrong. Confident that she could prove herself innocent of at least this accusation. The presence of sel was slight about her, but with Detan's senses ratcheted so high up he could feel it now. Little slivers of the stuff hidden in the seams of her blues. A memory of Pelkaia-Ripka stroking the lapel of her matching jacket as she mocked his lack of observation crowded into his mind.

Dread coiled in his chest. There was nothing he could do.

"Your coat, please." The whitecoat held her hand out, long fingers splayed. Momentary confusion crested

Ripka's brow, but she slid the garment off and passed it over.

"Watch carefully," the whitecoat said as she lifted the coat into the air so that those gathered could see. She slipped a knife into her hand – a simple thing for cutting twine and paper – and inserted it into the seam running along the coat's lapel. With a flick of the wrist she opened the cloth. A slender, pearlescent wisp wafted into the searing light of day.

The crowd howled its outrage, but Detan kept his gaze on Ripka. Her expression twisted – first bewilderment, then bright hot anger as realization settled. There was nothing she could do, no protest she could make that would undo the damage done. Any attempt to quibble would make her look like a gibbering fool.

Without a word, Ripka extended her hand for her coat. Callia handed it back without comment. Ripka shrugged it on, straightening the sliced lapel, shoulders stiff with more than pride now. She clasped her hands behind her back so that those gathered could not see them tremble. A little spark of pride burned in Detan's chest and he held himself straighter in her shadow.

"I will not pass judgment on this," Thratia said, raising her voice to drown out the anger of the crowd. "The theft and fire are crime enough to land her here. And so, the choice. The doppel has already attested its wish to walk the Black. What say you, Miss Leshe? Will the sand cleanse your sins, or the axe?"

Ripka lifted her chin, raised her voice to carry. "I will walk."

The crowd murmured its approval, and Thratia clapped her hands together above her head. "So be it. Watch Captain Banch, please direct the condemned."

Detan was thrust forward by the men holding him

and made to stand side by side with Ripka, their backs
to the crowd and their faces toward the dawn. It was
already oppressively hot, vision-warping waves of heat
rising up from the glittering black sands. He tried not to
think of the corpse he'd stumbled across in the night,
desiccated and groping toward a succor it'd never reach,
but the vision crowded his mind all the same, and he
swallowed a rise of bitter bile. He hoped there were
fewer spiders this time.

From the corner of his eye he could see Ripka, steady
but wide-eyed. He wanted to say something to alleviate
her fear, to give her some hope, but he didn't dare for
fear of being overheard. And anyway, she was doing her
best not to look at him, her lips held in thin disgust and
her back straight as a mast-pole. Facing her death with
dignity and pride. He didn't dare sully that.

Thratia leaned over his shoulder and murmured so
that only he could hear, "I'm not fooled, Honding. Enjoy
your last moments of freedom."

The new warden laid her hands on both of their
backs, and shoved.

CHAPTER 34

The black sands rose up to meet her faster than she expected. It took a great strength of will not to cry out as she landed, palms first, and rolled through the glittering dust. The sands of the Brown Wash had been soft, worn smooth and round by wind and time, but the Black Wash resisted all such ministrations. The glass-like sand was forever abrasive, and she held her breath to keep from breathing much in until the cloud around her settled.

When she stood, her knees were shaky and her hands abraded.

"You all right?"

She glanced over at the doppel, its miner's attire covered in black dust and its face skewed from the fall. The Detan-mask was twisted, one cheek drooping so much that the selium had lost its color and returned to its usual prismatic shimmer. It looked as if the heat of the desert was melting the creature away, and the fact that it looked like Detan unsettled her greatly.

Where was that dustswallower, anyway? Probably halfway across the Scorched by now. Served her right, putting her faith in a conman. No, that was unfair. Maybe he'd just run out of time.

"Leave me be, creature," she snapped as she took her first few steps across the Black.

With each step, she grew to realize that her blues were dangerous to more than her pride. As the heat rose, her ruined coat trapped it against her skin. She unbuttoned it, let it hang open to catch the breeze on the thin off-white shirt she wore beneath, but she would not drop it. Not this close to the city.

Never mind that one of her own watchers had betrayed her – and for what? Thratia wouldn't give Taellen any favors. Not after this. Not after he'd proven how thin his allegiance really was. She pumped her legs harder, forcing herself away from Aransa as quickly as she could without breaking into a full run. Heat began to well out of the neckline of her coat, making her breaths short. To be accused of arson and theft was one thing. To have her own people point at her and say she betrayed her service to them was just too much.

Precious water rimmed her eyes, and she wiped it furiously away.

"Easy now, Ripka," the doppel said, its voice rough with imitation of the real man.

"Captain," she said on reflex, and regretted it. Could she still call herself the watch captain? Maybe. She supposed it didn't matter, anyway. It was a little something to hold onto until she died.

Ripka stopped her march and looked around. The city wall loomed behind her, but any sheltering shadow it may have offered was blasted clear by the sun's unforgiving angle. What was the sun to forgive? It was insensate, inexorable. It didn't notice, and it wouldn't have cared, that Ripka was about to die under its glare.

Faint white glints winked at her between the matrix of the black sands, and with a sinking stomach she recognized them for what they were. Bones, broken and scattered. Most were unrecognizable now, their shape worn down by the bite of obsidian, their placement skewed by the winds. She looked upon them all, swallowing a lump of self-loathing. She'd done this, she'd created this grisly graveyard, in sending the condemned to walk. And now she was about to lay down and join them. Ripka pushed aside all feeling and trained her gaze on the path she must walk to survive.

In the direction of the sun the Fireline Ridge rose, its pocked back looking like the whipped hide of a great beast, the Smokestack jutting like a broken spine from the middle. It cast a shadow across the sand, reaching toward her. A false promise. There was no way she would make it there before the heat took her. Maybe she could find something in the wreckage of the *Larkspur* to shade herself with.

It seemed so close, that humped shelter of stone. But she knew all too well that the distance was distorted by the wavering horizon, that whatever she found in the *Larkspur* would offer little relief.

Under the full light of day, the black grains absorbed the heat and threw it back at you until you collapsed from heat sickness. She knew the signs, the symptoms. Dizziness, delirium. Clotted tongue and a cessation of sweat. The backs of her hands already felt dry, her tongue too big for her mouth. Soon her skin would begin to blister, to peel, to slough off to the sand below. If she were lucky she might faint from the pain before organ failure began. Before her eyes began to burst their fluids from their sockets.

Even if she did make it to the ridge, her life was forfeit. The climbing there was rough, the heat made it scorching, and if she made it up to one of the facilities on the ridge she would be recognized.

Your life, once condemned, was free for the taking. And with accusations of hiding sel-sense riding the winds, there wasn't a soul alive that'd ever offer her shelter. She urged herself toward the ridge with long, ground-eating strides, and the doppel rushed along to catch up.

"Angle south towards the baths," it said.

"I'll go where I please."

"Pits below, do you still not see it?"

She stopped dead and turned to regard the doppel. Its face was still melting, pearlescent selium mixed with the diamond glitter of sweat. Ripka brought her hand up to shade her eyes and still had to squint, the reflection from the sand was so bright. The doppel grinned at her in a stupid, familiar way. The voice it affected was damned near perfect. Her back stiffened.

"You dustswallowing idiot–"

"Easy now. Save it until we're at the ridge. Thratia has got me figured out but the rest don't and I'd rather not give them any ideas."

"Why?"

"She can't search the city in earnest for a doppel the people think is out here dying in the Black, understand? Gives us a chance to find her still."

"What do you care?"

"Keep pushing me and I'll find reasons not to."

His voice was strained, snappish. Even beneath the selium his cheeks were slapped red by the sun, rosy despite his deep tan. Sweat poured off him, and he swayed a bit where he stood.

"You injured?"

"Hah." His laugh was coarse and wild. "Not yet."

"Who's keeping that selium on you, anyway?" Her eyes narrowed, cold suspicion creeping through her. "You got the doppel hiding out here somewhere?"

He tilted his head and licked his lips. "I told you I don't know where she is."

She sucked air through her teeth in a sharp whistle. "Then you're still–"

"Just walk, all right? I got enough on my mind. This isn't easy."

He trudged off, cutting a tight line toward the baths, and she followed at his side. To take her mind off the heat, she stole glances at him as he struggled along beside her. While the sun's blaze was tough on her, it seemed to be taking an extreme toll on him.

Each step was slightly off center from the last, causing him to sway and veer at random. By midway across the Wash his clothes were soaked through and his breath came in gasps. Watching his struggle made her own pain feel small.

"You have to rest," she said.

He came to a sharp halt, as if all this time he'd been dragged forward by an unseen pulley that had just been cut, his limbs going straight and still. "Can't stop too long," he rasped. "The sun doesn't stop just because you have."

Ripka tore a strip from her shirt and tied it around her forehead to keep the sweat from her eyes. He stared at it, mouth open. "Want me to make you one?"

"I can't…" He staggered, startling her into motion. She grabbed his arm, holding him upright.

"Look, whatever you're doing with that selium is going to kill you before the sun does. You've got to stop it. We're far enough away from the wall no one will notice. Just drop it."

"Hah."

"Don't 'hah' at me. Let it go, Detan. Now."

He rolled his eyes to look at her, wide and white and wild. "First time you ever called me Detan."

"Then you'd better listen."

He grunted and closed his eyes, and she knew in that moment he was going down. She dug her fingers into his arm, desperate that the small dose of pain would snap him back to himself. Instead he snorted and shook her off. "Let me concentrate, woman."

Selium poured off his face, neck, and upper chest like thick syrup. Most of her experience with the stuff had been with it contained, hidden away in the buoyancy sacks of ferries or cargo-transports. To be so close to the raw material... It made her small hairs stand up, despite the heat. Detan opened his eyes, and the sheets of it entwined to form a ball about the size of her two fists pushed together. Worth enough to pay her sergeant for half a year.

"Need to weigh it down." His words were tight and clipped, urgent.

She dragged off her coat and threw it over the ball, letting the heavy material do some good work for once. Detan sighed and his shoulders slumped. He brought one hand up to rub at his eyes while the other fumbled in his pocket.

"Damn stuff wants to go up-up-up no matter what." He pulled out a bit of twine and tied her coat around the hovering ball, making it look like the balloons used for short-range transport vessels. Taking firm hold of the dangling twine, he wrapped it around his fingers a few times and gave it a tug to secure it. "Can't tie it to your wrist unless you want to lose that hand, and you *definitely* don't want this much sel tied to your belt."

Ripka laughed so hard and sudden that she spit. With a grimace she wiped her mouth and immediately regretted it as the back of her hand tore the thin, dried skin of her lips. Blood smeared her hand, her cheek. She resisted the urge to spit out what had gotten in her mouth – she needed all the moisture she could get. Detan looked hale already, or at least better than the stumbling, sweating shade of a man he had been. He was even smiling, which she thought was pretty stupid considering the circumstances.

The selium pushed against its containment, flattening the top curve of the balloon just enough to cast a small shadow over them both. Ripka sighed with relief, that sliver of shade the most luxurious thing she'd ever experienced.

In silence they trudged forward, heads bent and necks extended as if they could reach the wreckage of the *Larkspur* faster if only they could stretch out their bodies.

"Almost there," he said as they drew near, lips cracking with each syllable. She wanted to do something for that, to ease his pain a little. Wished she had something for her own lips, too. There were salves back in the city, tinctures to smooth the burn of the sun. Some plants she knew to be good for sun exposure, their dewy leaves capable of producing a cool balm. She scanned the area, taking in the vast emptiness all around them. Not so much as a scrub broke through the rough soil.

Ripka frowned, eyeing the wreckage with care. She'd seen the *Larkspur* only once before, but she was certain there wasn't nearly enough wood to cover the whole ship smashed on the sands before them. "What is–?"

Detan laughed and threw his arms wide. "Welcome to

Tibs's cabin. We were saving it to cover the disappearance of the *Larkspur*, but this seemed a more pressing matter."

It did look like the cabin of a ship, one that had been dropped on its side and cracked open like an egg. The walls leaned outward at crazy angles, the fresh-milled timber filling the air with the warm scent of some sort of resinous hardwood. Stunned, she followed Detan into what was left of the shelter, and nearly wept with joy when she saw Tibs had stashed a full amphora of water amongst the rubble.

Without a word they sat in the makeshift shade and shared out the sand-warmed water in slow, careful draws. After some rummaging, Detan found a cloth-wrapped package of dried meat and a small jar of pulpleaf salve. Beneath a broken beam he discovered a wide-brimmed hat, the edges singed, and Ripka was shocked to see his eyes glisten and his face screw up with the threat of tears.

"You all right?" she asked.

"Fine, fine." He cleared his throat and pulled the hat on his head, then offered her a scarf to cover her own head with and the packet of meat. Despite being hard and stringy, it was the most delicious thing she'd ever tasted.

"Ready for the final press?" Detan asked when the water and food was gone.

"You think we'll make it?" She handed the now half-empty jar of pulpleaf salve to him, already feeling her skin soften and cool from its application.

"Oh, captain, it's not the heat that kills you. It's Thratia's assassins waiting on the ridge."

Ripka glanced sideways at him, and saw him grinning like an idiot. As usual. "Wonderful."

He began to apply the remaining salve with extreme care, his bandaged hand trembling with the effort as he held the jar in his good hand. After a moment, Ripka knelt before him. Without a word, she took the jar and pushed his wounded hand aside, knowing just where he'd gotten that particular injury, and took over smearing the salve against his already blistering arms. He cleared his throat and shifted, uncomfortable. Keeping her gaze locked on her work, she said, "Thank you."

"Said I wouldn't let you walk."

She glanced up at him, unable to help a wry smile. "That worked out well."

He barked a laugh. "Best I could do under the circumstances."

She finished applying the salve and stood, tossing the empty jar to the sand. He sat there a moment, eyes drooping, sweat turning the fringe of his hair into spikes against his brow, the selium balloon tugging at his good fingers. The phantom of Tibal's words came back to her, his warning of Detan's temper, and she shunted them aside, guilt beginning to gnaw at her. No matter that he was in some way responsible for the fire that'd seen her shoved out here. He'd come back. Though it killed her pride to admit it, he'd saved her, when he didn't have to. They locked gazes, and she looked away, proffering her hand.

"Time to go and see what Thratia has waiting for us," she said.

"Well, this will be interesting," he said as he took her hand and stood, his little balloon bobbing crazily. She forced herself along beside him, huddling close to keep under the shade of the balloon. Somehow, she managed to keep her tone light despite their coalescing disaster.

"You could always throw selium in their eyes."

He frowned, rubbing the line of his jaw with one grubby finger. "Yeah. Something like that."

CHAPTER 35

The weight of Ripka's coat did most of the work for him, but he couldn't get lazy. Couldn't let his concentration slip. Maybe the doppel could keep it all together without so much as a thought, but all it took for Detan to lose it was a momentary distraction. Just a stubbed toe or a glance at something shiny, or – fiery pits – the way Ripka'd looked at him when she'd thanked him, and the sel would be free to ooze out from the imperfect seal of the coat. To climb up high and never come down again. He wondered how much was up there, and where it stopped. Did the sun have to push its rays through it? Was that why the light always felt so sluggish and angry-hot?

Don't distract yourself. He clenched his jaw and focused. Ripka had been divested of her weapons, so that meant it was up to him. He still had his old longknife. Not that it would do much good in his hands; his skill with such things was rudimentary at best. But he did have the sel. To throw in their eyes, indeed.

He pulled out the knife. Looked at it.

Passed it to Ripka. "Here, you hang on to this."

"You'll need it," she said, trying to push it back towards him.

"I'm a danger to myself with that thing. At least you've had some proper training."

She took it with care and turned it around in her hand, bright metal glinting white hot under the glare of the sun. He'd always presumed it was a pretty good knife, at least the person he'd pinched it from didn't seem the type to mess about with inferior goods, and from the way she grunted approval he supposed that assumption was correct.

"It's in the imperial style, but I can work with it," she said.

"Valatheans even make their knives differently?"

"They're lighter, usually. They'd call this a shortsword, since it's about the length of the average forearm. They've got hollow handles that sometimes get filled with selium to make them move easier, but this one's empty."

Yeah, I needed that tiny bit of sel in a hurry once… long time ago. "Makes sense, considering I got the thing in Valathea."

He tried to ignore her incredulous stare as she asked, "You've been to Valathea?"

"Not willingly. More importantly, you can use it?"

"Sure." She took a few experimental swipes. "Not much different from my cudgel in length, just lighter."

"Do a lot of slashing with your cudgel, do you?"

She blinked at him as if it were the most obvious thing in the world. "Every day, just about." Her hand went for the spot on her belt, but when it came up empty her lips turned down. "Though I suppose not anymore."

"You'll live through this, you know," he offered, dabbing sweat from his brow with the sleeve of his stolen shirt.

"Yeah. I know."

Detan bit his lip and kept his mouth shut. He wasn't any good at making people feel better, unless it consisted of him making an ass of himself for their amusement. Whatever was going on in Ripka's head was her business, and he figured it was safer for the sanity of everyone involved if he didn't try and mess with it. She was focused on getting through alive, and right now that was all that mattered.

Especially considering he was starting to rethink his boast about the heat not killing you.

Tibs's cache had done him a world of good, but his earlier attempts to keep the sel smooth and calm had taken too much out of him. He was breathing hard, panting like a mongrel, and from the sting around his mouth he supposed his lips were cracked despite the salve he'd slathered on. He had no idea how Ripka was staying on her feet, but he guessed it wasn't easy as she didn't look any better than he did. At least, he hoped she didn't look better than he did.

But the ridge was getting closer. They were near enough now that the angle of the sun threw the shadow of it in their path, and though the shade was minimal it was a blessed relief from the full-on glare. The Salt Baths hovered above them, the ferry dock sticking out from the rockface like a crooked thumb. There wasn't any light seeping from the main entrance, or spa-goers moving about the place.

"Looks like Thratia shut down more than just the lines to the Hub," Ripka said.

"Makes sense. If she's got people waiting for us, she won't want any witnesses."

Ripka snorted. "Why would she care if I survived the Black?"

"Same reason she cares about finding her ship. It's a matter of pride, and it would catch up with her eventually. Undermine her iron fist."

"Wish I could bust her down," she muttered under her breath.

"You can't. Now hush and keep that knife ready."

"Sword."

"Sure."

This section of the Fireline boasted no value to be had. There were no selium pockets, no thermal vents, not even cacti could be farmed in the listless soil. The stones were craggy and pitted, giant broken teeth rising up out of the sand. It was a good place to hide something, if you had the mind to, and Detan was fairly certain Thratia did. If he'd shown up with the doppel, then she'd want someone here, ready to act. She just wasn't the kind of woman to leave loose ends hanging.

Neither was the whitecoat.

He slowed down, his feet swimming in his pilfered boots, his grip on the string tethering the ball of sel so tight his fingers were turning purple. Knowing he wasn't much use face-to-face, he drifted back and let Ripka scout ahead, relying on whatever skills she had been given by her Watch training. Surely they had to train the Watch to handle ambushes.

Straining his senses, he couldn't make out any sel nearby, which was probably just proof that he wasn't very good at sussing out the stuff. With the Smokestack so close, his senses should have been overwhelmed. But they weren't, as usual. All he could make out was the slight throb of the ball hidden in Ripka's coat. Sometimes, he didn't know why he bothered trying.

He let his sensing attempt drop, and that's when Ripka yelped. It was probably supposed to be something like a war cry, but all he heard was a girlish squeal followed by snarling as she swiped the knife-sword at a man suspiciously devoid of uniform.

The would-be assassin lunged sword-first from amongst the broken rocks at her, but she'd gotten her stance ready in time and knocked his blade against a rock so hard the metal screeched. Detan stopped dead in his tracks, shifting his feet in anxious unease. What was he supposed to do?

Just stand there and bonk people with his balloon?

Ripka staggered from the force of her blow, then squared off her shoulders and brought the blade back nice and quick to open the man's stomach. His breakfast met the sand, and he followed close behind. Wiping hair from her eyes, she scooped up the dead man's blade and thrust it handle-out at Detan.

He stared at it as if it were a viper.

"Take it."

"That's, uh, not really a good idea."

"Well I can't use two, now can I?"

She thrust it forward again, insistent. With a grudging sigh he grasped the grip in his wounded hand and took a few experimental swipes. The disdainful curl of Ripka's lip told him all he needed to know about his form.

"There will be others," he said, anxious to smooth away his obvious ineptitude.

"Of course there will," she snapped.

"Well aren't you just full of sunshine."

She eyed him. "I am."

"Ah. Right…"

They moved side by side into the scattered rocks, in theory covering one another's flank. Ripka positioned herself on his left, the side holding the sel, which made him so nervous his fingers trembled. He supposed it was at least better than having her on the pointy side. Probably. Maybe.

He hoped.

As they crept closer to the first incline of hard rock which led up into the cave network that made the baths possible, something bit him. He jumped and swore, then looked down at his shoulder to see a long gash welling with blood.

"Oh, those bastards."

Behind him, stuck butt-up in the sand, was a thick black quiver. He wanted to stomp it, but as another winged by him and snapped its neck against a rock he figured that might be a waste of time. Ripka tore off at a sprint, angling straight for the crossbowman's hiding spot. It was a narrow ledge, tucked up in the rockface to the left, and it didn't look like he'd have enough time to get out or draw another shot before she got to him.

But there were a few standing rocks near the ledge, tall and wide, a little extra shadow bleeding out around their edges.

"Look out!"

Ripka slid to a stop, kicking up a wide cloud of dust, as three men loped into her path. Every last one of them had a sword, and every last one looked ready to use it. Ripka took a step back, getting out of strike distance, and slipped into a ready stance. Damn fool of a woman.

He looked at the sword in his hand, the weapon he didn't know how to use. He looked at the sel floating just before him, the weapon he was too scared to use. Where was Tibs when he needed him?

"Run, woman! Quick!"

She hesitated, and the man nearest lunged for her side. That was enough. She knocked his thrust wide with her blade and danced away, boots slipping in the sand, as she tore off back towards Detan. Her eyes were rabbit-in-a-hawk's-shadow wide, and he couldn't blame her. She must expect a bolt in the back any second.

Distancing himself from what was happening, he focused on the little ball of sel under the coat. His mind felt slow, languid with care, as he segmented off a piece half the size of one fist and pulled it out into the open. It fought him the instant it was free of the coat's weight, clamoring to rise high. He didn't give it the chance.

The sel ball shot forward faster than any arrow and struck the central man dead in the chest. Detan felt the world slow around him, his focus sharpen. He saw in acute detail the would-be assassin's face as he glanced down at the innocuous, glittering ball. He saw the slow confusion growing, wrinkling his brow. It only lasted a breath.

Detan shunted open the floodgates of his mind, unleashed the temptation that'd been dogging him since the day he set foot back on this sun-cursed continent. He let his anger flood through to the sel, all his hate and his fear. Bundled up his rage and fed it, nurtured it, ripped it free of his heart and his mind and broadcast it out.

Under the brunt of his fury, that little glittering ball tore itself to pieces. Rent itself straight through to its core. A concussion punched his chest, staggered him back a step, the crack of the blast loud enough to set his ears whining. Fire so bright even he was temporarily blinded speared in all directions, competing with the hot eye of the sun and winning.

When his sight returned to him, all that was left of the man was a charcoaled, rended mass, and his companions weren't spared the conflagration. One had been consumed. The other rolled about on the rough sand, grasping at the charred meat where his arm had been.

"Sweet skies," Ripka whispered, her voice muffled cotton under the ringing in his ears. She must have thrown herself down, or been thrown, because she was covered in sand and sitting, her back to him, her face glued to the spot where the attackers had been. Even the rock behind them was blackened, and no more arrows issued from the cleft. Detan stepped to her side and offered his hand. He pretended not to notice when she flinched away from it.

"Get up. We have to keep moving," he managed around a hitch in his throat. He still had some sel left, and the strain of keeping it contained weighed double on him now.

He still had his anger.

Sweet, practical Ripka. She swallowed her fear and grabbed his hand. He hauled her up, gave her time to brush the sand from her clothes as best she could. She spent longer doing it than was necessary, but he wasn't about to complain. His mind was still throbbing, consumed with the sel's moment of destruction. That terrible blow-back was worse than slugging whiskey all night.

There wasn't any time to cater to his pain. He had to keep the rest of the sel together, compact. Had to keep moving.

Ripka took up point as they transitioned from sand to stone. This section of the Fireline was flat, having given itself up to the march of time long before the city was ever founded. Its surface was covered in large, toothy boulders and spills of talus. Deep caverns wormed through the rock, gaping adits black and forbidding. Some of them led up to the baths, some down into the hot heart of the world.

"Tibs will have left a signal. Look for it."

She nodded, her steps slowing as she scanned the landscape unfolding before them with more care. They saw the marker at the same time, a little strip of white cloth tied to a brown bit of scrub along the edge of a cave's chasmal mouth. They entered it, Detan taking a moment to tug the signal from the scrub lest they be followed. Within the cavern all was dark, and Ripka grabbed his arm to keep him from walking smack into her.

"Wait, listen," she murmured.

In the darkness, he found he had a hard time concentrating on anything but his own troubles. The sound of his labored breath, the frantic thumping of his heart. With his mind bent to keeping the sel intact it was all he could do to hear what Ripka was telling him, let alone some quieted aspect of the cave. Still, she held him in place for what felt like a half-mark, but in truth was only a handful of heartbeats.

It was hard to tell when your heart was racing on ahead of yourself.

"No footsteps, it should be clear, but I can't see a thing. Can you use the sel to light something small?" she asked.

"I'd be more likely to blow my own head off."

"Never mind." She swallowed, loud enough for him to hear. "Step slowly, and let me guide you."

Her fingers tightened around his wrist and she tugged him along behind. It was hard going, not seeing anything but the back of her head, and even that was little more than a smoky smudge. He could hear her shuffling along, testing her footing before bringing him into her wake. He was grateful for that – he would never have thought of it.

There was a glow up ahead, warm and welcoming. The kind of glow only oil lamps and candle wicks could provide. He was surprised by how blinding the smear of light was, and squinted against the water in his eyes. It occurred to him that this couldn't be good for his poor peepers, going from naked sun to pitch black to light again, and he promised himself a good solid rest after this. The very idea of a pillow made his eyelids heavy.

The cave let out into the venting grounds, where Detan had burned his own trousers for the sake of winding up an irritating uppercrust. He wished he still had the fine, tailored coat he'd gotten from that game instead of the soiled and oversized miner's attire he'd pilfered from Pelkaia. Maybe Tibs had grabbed it on his way out, the man wasn't likely to leave anything of theirs behind.

He gave the little dunkeet bird-whistle he and Tibs used on occasion, and heard a rustling on one of the bathing platforms above. That rustle wasn't the only thing moving in the baths.

A figure leapt from behind one of the craggier vents, looking an awful lot like the dead men they'd already left behind – clothes black-red to blend with the rocks, sword out and ready.

Ripka stepped between Detan and the advancing assassin, sword drawn, and he felt a flush of embarrassment standing there with his little balloon. He could defend himself, it just wasn't always safe for those near to him.

The would-be murderer advanced, passing under one of the tub's ledges. Detan heard a whistle, bright and cheery, and the killer looked up just in time to see the shadow of the rock that'd been dumped down on his head.

Before Ripka could get her blade near him, the killer's face burst, easy as a rotting plum. He crumpled like a smashed buoyancy sack, and sent up wild sprays of blood from his ruined face.

"Oh good." Tibs stuck his head over the side and squinted down at the crushed man. "That rat had been wandering around here staying under cover for a full half-mark. I thought you'd never get here to bait him out."

"Happy to help, Tibs. Now where in the pits is my flier?"

"Get on up here and I'll take you to her."

Detan led the way through the venting floor, making sure Ripka was mindful of the great bursts of mineralized steam that whuffed up from the ground at regular intervals. When they reached the upper levels, New Chum came to greet them, looking pristine in his beige uniform and crisp little hat. There was, annoyingly, not a drop of sweat on him. Tibal, on the other hand, looked like he'd taken a tumble down a sand dune into a mudpit, and that heartened Detan some.

"Good morning, Lord Honding, Captain Leshe. May I interest you two in a much-needed bath, and some fresh clothes?"

"No time for niceties. Thratia and her watchdog are going to start getting jumpy when her gallows men aren't back with us in a mark or so," Detan said.

"Direct to the flier, then?"

"Onward, my good man."

He let the steward lead the way amongst the winding platforms and in between the wide baths. Tibs dropped back beside him and whispered, "Thratia buying it?"

"Nope, and it seems she and the imperial have had a little chat about yours truly."

"I see. I distinctly remember having warned you about this exact situation, sirra."

"Are you rubbing it in?"

"Yes, yes I am."

Tibs and New Chum had stashed the flier on a little outcropping on the back edge of the Salt Baths. Its buoyancy sacks bulged above it with fresh life, and an extra had been strapped to the bottom. He caught sight of the daisies and *Happy Birthday Virra*! scrawled all over the old leather in purple paint. His throat clotted, his chest clenched. He closed his eyes and drew a breath, focusing on keeping his selium ball still. He'd live with those daisies. For Bel.

The little craft floated just off the edge of the cliff, securely tied with two thick ropes. Down the side a rope ladder hung, its end trailing through the empty air at the height of Detan's hip. It was a welcome sight, his little bird all patched up and flying true. He just wished it were bigger.

"We're going to be real close to capacity now, so mind your movements," he warned.

New Chum let out a polite *ahem*. "If you're overloaded, sir, I will volunteer to stay behind."

"You sure as shit will not. Thratia will find her way here eventually and some sniveling rat will remember you were the only one in the baths when we escaped. And then what will you do? Run back to your old friends for protection?" New Chum winced, unconsciously covering his tattooed shoulder with one hand. "No," Detan said. "No arguments. All of you up that rope, now."

Tibs swung on first, scrambling up the ladder in a way that reminded Detan of a knobby-limbed lizard. He cringed, and waved Ripka ahead. She stored her knife-thing with care before climbing cautiously skyward. The steward went next, and Detan was proud of his vessel for not swaying in the slightest.

He checked the string securing the sel to his hand, and it was only his reaching to tighten the knot that kept his arm from being skewered by an arrow.

"Hurry!" someone yelled, probably Tibs by how exasperated the yell sounded. Detan lunged for the ladder but felt like he'd run smack-first into a wall instead. He went down hard, flat on his chest on the unforgiving rock, all the air knocked from his lungs. Cold shock seized him, radiating from his calf.

By the time Detan had gotten some air back in and the white light left his eyes alone he could see boots – far, far too close – charging up the walkway toward him. Nice boots. Imperial boots.

They'd take him alive. Not so much the others.

Ignoring the fire in his leg he surged sideways and pulled the slip-knots on the flier's tie lines. Someone screamed above him, a lot of someones, but the words didn't make much sense. Tamping down his fear and his anger at having been caught he reached his senses out, felt for the sel in the sack of his flier, and shoved. The craft lurched away, fearful cries turning into frantic yelps, and the shadow of the flier that had lain over him slipped off into the blue, leaving him to face the sun alone.

Something tugged on his fingers. He looked up, saw the ball of sel escaping from under the cover of Ripka's coat. His attention had waned too much, he'd been lazy. Undisciplined. Auntie Honding would have skinned him for such a mistake. But he still had some sel left.

Still had his anger.

Refocusing, he gathered together what was left outside of the coat, let the blue cloth slump to a heap by his head. He reshaped it, making it a glittering, hovering windowpane. Just like he had when he'd made the imitation doppel mask. At least he could still count himself a quick learner.

The man leading the imperial troops smirked at it, suspecting it a doppel's trick. "It's a little late to try and hide your face from us."

Trembling, sweating, Detan bent all his will to keeping that sheet as wide as he could. The imperial waved his men forward, and just as they stepped through the membrane of sel, Detan let loose.

He didn't get to see the looks on their faces, the flash was too bright, but from the sound of their screaming, Detan knew he'd done real damage.

But not enough. More imperials emerged from the baths, little more than a line of smudged silhouettes before his fading gaze. They were hesitant, coming slow and scared. Wasn't much he could do now, but he hoped that display had at least made one of them wet themselves.

He was grinning when unconsciousness took him.

CHAPTER 36

It was all she could do to keep from falling over the edge as the flier shot through the empty air. Tibal stood – how, she had no idea – swearing his mouth bloody as he worked the craft's rigging in a desperate attempt to slow their flight. She wanted to help, but she didn't have a clue how to go about it. And anyway, if she let go of the railing both her arms were wrapped around she was certain she'd go spinning off into oblivion.

"That's it! Pull it round!" Tibal screamed above the rush of wind.

Ripka went red in the cheeks as she realized the steward was on his feet, working the mess of rope and pulleys as if it were the easiest thing in the world for him. Whatever they were up to, it must have worked, because the flier shuddered and swayed, slaloming to a stop so sudden she wondered for a brief second if she'd died and landed in the sweet skies.

After making sure whatever they'd done was secure, Tibal and the steward abandoned their posts and raced towards her end of the flier. It wasn't a very large craft, just a dozen or so long strides across, but still they came hurrying. She was relieved to find out it wasn't due to worry over her.

"I can't see any detail from this far off, but the cliff is definitely blackened," the steward said, holding up a hand to guard his eyes against the sun's glare.

"I can't see much better myself, damned man must have blown us halfway across the Scorched. Sometimes I think there's nothing between his ears but grit and piss."

"Shall we go back?" The steward was already edging toward the helm.

"Sure, but just to make sure he's still alive. I reckon they'll be gone by the time we get there. Detan will have left a handprint for me if he's still kicking," Tibal's voice rasped. He shook his head and plastered on a fake smile. "And anyway, it's on the way."

Ripka managed to pull herself to her feet and straighten her wind-twisted shirt. The men were polite enough to pretend not to notice. "On the way to where?" she asked.

"To see that damned doppel, of course. I'm thinking she's the only one who can lend us a hand getting Detan out of the chop."

Ripka's gut clenched, she busied her hands straightening her hair while she spoke. "She's a murderer, Tibal. Killed a good man. Maybe two."

He huffed and hawked over the side of the flier. "Yeah, well, she can join the club. You can't tell me you're not a member yourself. No one is a watcher long without taking a life that deserves to be left alone."

Her fingers froze in their fussing, claw-like and petrified. She swallowed, forced herself to draw her hands away and rest them easy at her sides. "I'm just saying she can't be trusted."

"No one can, captain. No one at all."

"And just how in the pits do you know where she is? She has the *Larkspur*, doesn't she? Could very well be halfway to the ass-end of the world by now and we wouldn't know it." She snapped, then cursed herself for losing her temper. This wasn't Tibal's fault. None of it was. He just wanted his friend back. And so did she, truth be told. Honding was a mad moron, but he'd risked himself to come to her aid. She couldn't let him fall into Thratia's clutches, not now. Still, the thought of working side by side with the doppel made her skin crawl, her irritation mount.

He gave her a small, weary smile. "Had a lot of time to think, captain, while you two were busy trying to get yourselves killed. We'll find her. Only one place she could be, truth be told." He brushed past her and went about resetting the rigging.

She wanted to ask, but her pride wouldn't let her. One place she could be... But where? Ripka's head ached, and she couldn't tell if it was from exhaustion, dehydration, or just plain frustration. She should be able to come to whatever conclusion Tibal had. *Should* be able to see it. Pits below, hadn't her perception gotten her accused of hiding sel-sensitivity?

Tibal pulled and slung ropes, heaved on gear handles and swiveled strange levers as if they were extensions of himself. Ripka went cross-eyed watching him, and resisted an urge to bury her face her hands.

"Help me with this thing, will you, New Chum?" he said.

The steward, who had been watching their argument in placid silence, bowed stiffly to her and moved to crank a gear shaft which seemed to be connected to one of the flier's rear propellers.

She had little knowledge of selium ships of any sort. Her closest experience was riding along the anchored back of the city's ferries. At the front, back, and center edges large, fan-blade propellers were mounted. Ripka followed the contraptions as best she could, and guessed that they were connected to a singular drive shaft just behind the helm where a dashboard of cranks and levers were. It just looked like gibberish to her.

Feeling useless, she watched as Tibal made way for the steward to join him at the helm and both of them heaved to. The fans thrummed to life, spinning far faster than Tibal and the steward were turning the cranks. The flier slid forward, smooth as silk. Once they fell into a rhythm the land began to slip by in a rush, the wind whipping her hair into her face relentlessly.

"Can I help?" she called above the cry of the wind to the steward. He looked around the flier and pursed his lips.

"Sure, you can haul up the tie lines."

"Right," she said, but it stung. She had hoped he'd chalk up her flustered expression to the effect of the wind, because she was feeling significantly unmoored and had no desire to explain herself. Watch Captain Leshe, only good for hauling up ropes. Just her luck.

She tried to look confident as she made her way to the first rope, but the flier had a bit of a wobble in its movement that made her knees feel like jelly. By her fourth step, Tibal was chuckling. She glared at him, and tried to stride firmly the rest of the way. It just made matters worse.

"You get used to it," he called. "I'd let you get your legs at a slower speed but we don't have much time to mess around here."

"I'll adjust," she said with a forced grin and a little

sting of water in her eyes. Tibal just nodded. Ignoring the eyes on her back as she knelt beside the edge of the ship and began hauling up the dangling rope. By the third loop, she wished she hadn't volunteered herself at all. She was not finished by the time they reached the cliff side. The flier slowed in smooth increments, giving her the sensation that they were all sliding to a stop.

Ripka stared at the half-coiled rope in her hands and grunted. She tossed what she held aside and shoved herself to unsteady feet. Under Tibal's watchful eye she scrambled back to the dangling rope ladder and climbed down, desperate for solid land beneath her feet.

As soon as her toes touched down, she nearly sprawled straight onto her face. Down here the ground seemed absurdly still, and she had to grip the ladder to keep from pitching over the edge of the cliff.

"You all right, captain?" Tibal poked his head over the edge and squinted down at her.

"Oh, just wonderful." She heard laughter above, but chose to ignore it. She'd pay them back later.

"See any signs of him? Any, you know... bits?"

The slight catch to Tibal's tone stilled her indignant anger. There weren't any bits belonging to Detan that she could see, but there was a whole pit-full of blood splashed around. Someone had fallen and rolled in it, smearing it across half the ledge. The stench of charred flesh and burned hair still clung to the open air, making her stomach lurch.

Wary of toppling into the mess, she took a step forward, still clinging to the ladder, and approached her crumpled coat. Detan's singed hat lay beside it. She knelt, clenching her jaw as she let the ladder go, and examined the ruddy ground.

In this spot, the blood was minimal. A small pool had

spread down where his calf might have been, but there
was nothing up above, where an injury might have
meant death. She reached out and scooped up the limp
and filthy hat. Beneath it, the bloody print of a man's
hand was splayed. Bright and rusty and primal.

"He's all right! He left a print!"

She heard a whoop of relief from above and stood,
not bothering to disguise the shake in her legs. It had
been a long, long, morning, and some things her pride
was just going to have to forget about. Things like going
to the doppel who killed Galtro and Faud and asking for
help.

Hobbling back to the ladder, hat tucked under one
arm, she wondered if Detan would understand if she
killed the doppel instead. She reckoned he would.

She just wasn't sure if she could forgive herself after
that.

CHAPTER 37

By the time he woke he was no longer grinning, but his jovial state wasn't the only thing to have changed. He sat on the deck of a large ship, larger even than the *Larkspur* had been, his back pressed against the wooden rail that wrapped around the ship's deck. His hands were chained above him and were already going numb. He gave them a few experimental shakes to get the blood flowing, and heard a grunt beside him.

He wasn't the only poor creature chained to this ship.

A half-dozen souls were attached to the same chain he was, each with their wrists cuffed above their heads and their feet bound before them. The man he'd disturbed had been sleeping beside him, about three steps away, and looked at him with red-shot eyes.

"Don't fuss too much, lad, or they'll come and make sure you don't," the withered man whispered.

"Who will come?"

The old man spat brown liquid on the deck before him. "Imperials. Who else?"

Footsteps sounded down the deck, and the old man

shut his eyes and let his head loll. Detan craned his neck and saw the now familiar form of that whitecoat, Callia, come round the cabin in the center of the ship with a parasol in the crook of her arm to protect her from the sun. A young girl trailed along beside her, matching the dignitary stride for stride.

The child was dressed in the same manner as Callia, in a floor-length shift the color of a clouded, pale sky, with her hair braided into elaborate whorls. She couldn't have seen more than twelve monsoons, but she kept her chin up and looked down her nose at him, lips pressed together with contempt. For all her contrivance – her walk, her clothes, the braids in her hair and kohl around her eyes – her skin was the shade of wet sand, her eyes hazel and her hair chestnut. A child of the Scorched.

"Hullo." He beamed at her.

Callia laid a hand on the girl's shoulder. "This is Aella. She will be your leash keeper for the duration of our flight."

"Aella, eh? What's a Valathean name doing on a Scorched girl?"

Those ruddy cheeks flushed, but her voice was schooled to tranquility. "I was born in Valathea. I am a child of the empire."

"A what now? Sel-sensitives aren't born outside the Scorched, little lady."

Callia sighed and rolled her eyes. "Lord Honding, you are not a naive man in the ways of the empire, so I will not bother to dissemble with you. Selium sensitives are not *conceived* outside of the Scorched, but they may be born wherever the parents choose."

"Really. And just where are your parents, little miss?"

Callia's grip tightened on her shoulder, denting the cloth. "She is a ward of the empire, and is in my care.

Now, I must see to other matters. Aella, mind the others but keep a sharp eye on this one. His ancestors were the first confirmed sensitives, and as such he believes he is entitled to certain freedoms, which he is not."

The girl's sharp little chin bobbed. "Yes, Callia."

Once Callia had gone, the girl sat herself across from him on a dusty crate, her small ankles crossed in the fashion of all the young nobles of the empire. She plucked a small book from her pocket, its face blank, and began to read.

With the girl's attention elsewhere, Detan took a moment to examine his surroundings with care. The ship felt still and calm, and yet he was quite certain they were moving. It was night, so there was little to see outside of the ship, but the lack of city lights and the gentle breeze on his face gave the impression of momentum, or at the very least being out of doors. Regardless, he was no longer in Aransa, or near enough to see it, and that was a worry.

"Where's this ship headed, anyway?"

Aella didn't even bother to look up. "Valathea."

"Big place, that. Anywhere specific?"

She sighed. "The city Valathea, not the whole empire."

"Too bad, could have gone on a tour. Taken in the sights. Have you ever toured the Century Gates? Grand things. Too bad I punched a hole in them the last time I passed through."

The girl smiled, but did not look up. Detan scowled and shifted his weight, but soon found it impossible to get himself into anything like a comfortable position. His leg was throbbing something awful, and his calf had been wrapped up in sun-bleached linen. Rusty stains seeped through in some places, and he tried not to shift it as he struggled to find comfort. It wasn't working out too well.

"Think I could get a pillow?"

"You don't stop talking, do you?"

"Got nothing else to do, do I?"

"Most of the other convicts sleep on these trips. You should, too."

"Sleep? Pits below, girl, these people may have their eyes shut but they've got their ears wide open. Isn't that right, grandpa?" He shook his chains, and the old man grunted.

"Please leave your fellows alone."

"My fellows? Hah, you sound just like Callia. Stiff as a board. Come on, lass, you're too young to be tangled up in this heartache."

"It's not my heartache. And this isn't the first transport I've monitored on, you know."

"Oh really? You're a real old hand at the slave trade, eh?"

The girl's dark cheeks went scarlet and her gaze drifted to the tips of her shoes. "I do as I'm told. Just like you will. It's better this way."

"And who told you that?"

Aella closed her book with care and laid both of her hands over it. Her hazel gaze was hard and steady, more worldly than any twelve year-old's had a right to be. "Is it true you can make selium catch fire?"

He blinked at her jumping topics, but at least she was talking to him. "It's a bit more than a fire, lass, but yes."

"How?"

He shook his head. "I don't rightly know, to be honest. The angrier I am, the easier it is."

"Show me."

"I don't know what ship you think you're on, but I doubt they'll be letting me blow up any sel on this one."

The girl rolled her eyes and fiddled with the clasp on

her bracelet. It was Valathean made, just the same as Callia's, and once it was unclasped she teased a small pinch of sel from it, no bigger than a grain of Black Wash sand. She re-clasped the bracelet to contain what was left and floated it out toward him, bringing it to rest halfway between them both. Detan licked his lips, leaning forward in his chains.

"Go on then," she said.

He focused on the granule, let all his anger at having been captured flow toward it. The little pinpoint went up, a glittering spark, gone in a flash. Aella leaned forward, her eyes bright and eager.

"Fascinating. You're one of the more unique deviants we've picked up lately."

"The what now?"

She arched a brow at him. "Just what do you think we're doing on this ship, anyway? This is Callia's pet project. She scours the Scorched looking for sel-sensitives whose skill sets fall outside the usual moving and shaping. That man next to you, for example," she tilted her chin toward the man who pretended to sleep, "is here because he can color-shift selium to blue, and only shades of blue. No other color. The woman next to him can make it vibrate so that it sings, like running your finger around the rim of a crystal glass. We're all Callia's little oddities."

"And what can you do, then?"

She smiled. "How many sources of selium are on this ship?"

"I'm not that refined, lass."

"Then focus on the largest."

"Just the buoyancy sacks."

"Try again."

Wary, he closed his eyes and extended his senses.

There were the inflated buoyancy sacks tied above, huge and out of his reach. Behind him another presence loomed, long and slender. It rose up over the whole of the ship, hemming it in like an old canvas wagon cover. His eyes snapped open, and he tipped his head back.

So far as he could see, there was nothing but black night beyond the ship's railing, spotted with a handful of pale stars. Stars that hadn't moved at all since he had first given them a good look.

"You're doing that?"

"Hah, no. That's another of the deviants, one of my fellows. I'm the one keeping you, and everyone else, from sensing it. You could have a blob of the stuff right in front of your nose, and I could make you think it's just empty air."

"If that sky's an illusion… Where are we?"

She smiled. "I think you can work that out, Lord Honding."

Aella went back to her book, but that was fine by him, he had enough to chew on for a while. So Callia was collecting the weirdos of the Scorched, and he was one of them.

When his talents had first been discovered, it'd been after he'd blown his whole line to bits and the workers with it. It'd been an accident, of course, he thought he was just moving sel along with the rest until someone pissed him off so badly he'd unconsciously channeled his anger into the line.

Because of that, his first few weeks in Valathea had been in a prison cell. A well-earned cell, as far as he was concerned. But, once they started the inquiries, the experiments… He shivered, rattling his chains. Aella seemed all right with her place in life, but he reckoned she'd never seen the pointy end of a scalpel. And anyway, he didn't want a single rotten thing to do with the empire anymore.

He frowned to himself. Why did she show him the trick? Why break down the barrier for him? Maybe she wasn't so safe in her role here. Maybe she wanted out, too. They were still in Aransa, he was pretty sure of that now, but he doubted they would be much longer. He was also certain they were on the personal cruiser he'd spotted, its real size obscured by the onboard talent.

Callia was more than likely just lingering to make damn sure there wasn't a chance at retaking the *Larkspur*, or Pelkaia. It would only be a day or so until she gave up hope – and then what? Try to make his escape over the wastelands?

No, that wouldn't do at all. Aella had shown him where he was, and in doing so had shown him a way out. He just needed to figure out how to use it.

"Aella, if we're still–"

"Hush, Honding. Hush."

She flipped a page, leaving it all in his tied hands.

CHAPTER 38

Despite Tibal's assurances, Ripka was certain the crater was empty. Tibal set them down on the internal edge of the Smokestack's collapsed cone, sheltering the ship in a sliver of shade that crept out from the high rim of the firemount's mouth. This was absolute madness. Wherever the doppel had gone, Ripka felt sure it wouldn't be to this sulfurous pit. And from the looks of things, she was right.

"We're the only ones here, Tibal." She had to raise her voice to be heard above the wind and the hiss of venting steam and gases. Despite the wind, the whole cursed crater stank of the smoke from the fire that'd devoured the Hub and most of the lines. Any moment now, she was terrified that the firemount would rear to life and throw up massive plumes of lightning-hot ash and molten rock. She shivered. How had she lived so long in the shadow of this beast without fearing it? All of the selium-settlements were founded in the shadow of these angry rock giants. All of them were vulnerable.

"Oh, she's here, don't you worry." Tibal clapped her on the shoulder.

Ripka hung back as Tibal and the steward strode ahead with foolish confidence. She understood Tibal's convictions, the man had convinced himself the doppel would be here, but the steward? Why was he buying into this madness? It made no sense at all. She sighed and kicked at a cluster of pebbles.

Tibal stopped halfway across the crater, his hands on his hips and his elbows akimbo. He examined the empty air before him, a curious tilt to his head. Ripka was just about to cry out that they should try something else, anything else, to get away from this nightmare place, when Tibal reached out a hand and slapped it against thin air. Thin air that gave off a pearlescent ripple.

Clenching her jaw, Ripka trudged over to stand with the others.

"Come on out now," Tibal called to be heard above the wind. "I know you're hiding in there, little lady."

There was a shimmer in the air just before Ripka's nose, and she leapt back a startled step. Before her, the world split. Where once there'd been little more than empty space and rough terrain, the dark-cherry stained broadside of an airship appeared. Just a segment of it, no more than an arm's length across, but the pristine hull was very familiar indeed.

The doppel stepped through that tear and it melded shut behind her. Ripka stared.

"I know you," Ripka blurted.

"Sure you do, captain." The doppel's voice was soft, patient.

"You're, um–" She snapped her fingers, struggling to match her list of suspicious names to the faces she'd interviewed. "Pelkaia, that's it. But I remember you being quite a bit older…"

The doppel smiled and brushed a strand of light brown hair from her eyes. Her fingertip touched her skin, and it rippled. Deliberate. "That is what I wanted you to see, yes. Now, why are you here?"

"I need your help," Tibal said.

"I am… busy, at the moment."

"Really? Busy hiding out in this pit-kissed place?"

"I have my reasons." She fluttered one hand through the air, dismissive.

"I'm betting one of them's the proximity to such a large source of sel. I'm betting you can't get the ship out of the area undetected, and the only reason you haven't been spotted yet is because all of this–" he waved to take in what was left of the great selium pumps that fringed the crater, "–is cloaking the *Larkspur*'s buoyancy sacks. And you're stuck until you can figure a way out."

Her lips twisted in annoyance. "You often a betting man?"

"I bet when it's a sure thing, lass."

The doppel crossed her arms and shifted her weight to her back foot. She pursed her lips, thinking, and Ripka became acutely aware that the woman's posture was the mirror image of her own. Unsettled, she straightened her stance and clothes.

Pelkaia must have seen her awareness, because she gave her a tight smile and let her arms hang to her side. "Forgive me, captain, but it is difficult to shake the body language of a personality I have been studying."

"I'd rather not know the particulars."

"As you like. Now, Tibal–"

"Wait," Ripka said, fingers itching over the grip of Detan's borrowed blade.

The doppel turned two arched brows upon her. "Yes?"

Ripka's palms grew clammy, her muscles laced tight with anxiety. "If I'm going to work with you, I have to know. When you went to... see... Galtro, did you wear my face?"

Pelkaia gave a subtle shake of the head. "No. I met him as myself."

She heaved a sigh free and closed her eyes. "Thank the skies for that."

"I hesitate to elaborate, but I feel he would want you to know that he was prepared for his death. He had seen it coming, and in truth did not expect to survive the elections. He was jabbing a rockviper, and intentionally at that. His guilt was heavy, and he was relieved to be free of it."

She swallowed an angry roar, fists clenched at her sides. "How can I trust you?"

Pelkaia shrugged. "You can't."

"I'm sorry," Tibal said, "but we just don't have time for this right now."

Ripka's stomach twisted. She wanted this woman, this tall, proud woman, to tell her everything. To explain why Galtro had to die, why the warden had to die, and why she had stolen Ripka's face to facilitate it all. She could guess. She knew the creature – Pelkaia – was a grieving mother. She knew the empire had done her wrong. Still, she wanted so much more than what she already knew. She wanted it from Pelkaia's own lips. She needed to hear the hate and the sadness, needed to make it visceral. Needed to squeeze the truth of it all out of her.

But they had no time. Not now. Tibal was right about that. She was beginning to realize that Tibal was right about most things.

"Get on with it then." Pelkaia sniffed, her expression one of pure boredom, but her fingers tapped the side of

384 STEAL THE SKY

her leg and her glance kept shifting. Ripka allowed herself a bitter smile, recognizing her own ticks of anxiousness.

"Lord Honding has been taken by the whitecoat."

A momentary widening of the eyes flitted across the doppel's face. "I'm sorry to hear that."

"Have you felt any large ships move out of the city?"

"How would I know?"

"Come on, Pelkaia, we both know you've been monitoring the ships in the city to see if the imperials have left so you can make off with the *Larkspur* without them giving chase."

"Fine, fine. I sensed a large one moving up from the south edge of the Fireline into the city a few marks back."

"South? Near the Salt Baths?"

"Sounds about right."

Tibal grinned, wide and pleased. "He's on that ship. He's got to be. Can you locate it now?"

"I never stopped watching it. It's in Thratia's dock, where the *Larkspur* was kept."

Ripka frowned. "We can't go back into the city, we're all too recognizable. Pelkaia, would you consider–"

"No bones, captain. I can't get too far from the *Larkspur* or I'll lose my hold over the sel hiding it. I've already lost control of a few little misdirections I left in the city."

"I can go."

They all looked at the steward, the young man whose name Ripka still didn't know. He stood alongside Tibal, his uniform well pressed despite the heat, wind, and steam. His sandy hair was still parted to perfection straight down the middle.

"That could work," Tibal said, tapping the end of his chin with one finger. "You could go in, say you're there on behalf of the doppel. Tell Thratia she's feeling guilty and wants to make a trade – Detan for the *Larkspur*."

"I will not," Pelkaia protested.

"Easy, Pelkaia, you know Detan and I don't want them to have access to that ship any more than you do."

Indignation filled Ripka, raising the small hairs all over her body. She turned to glare at Tibal. "You two planned with this murderer?"

"We didn't plan for *this*." He shot a glance at Pelkaia, one laced with grudging respect. "She just didn't give us much choice. All right, New Chum. I guess that means it's up to you. Think you can get her to come out here?"

"Certainly. It is my job to guide, after all."

"Right then, we can take the flier back to the Salt Baths and let you take it from there. I'm afraid we can't get much closer without being spotted. Will that be close enough?"

He bowed his head. "That will be just fine. The ferry will come for me if I call it."

The sun was at its zenith when they left the steward on the little ledge where they had last seen Detan. Ripka stood behind Tibal, her arms wrapped around her waist against the breeze, her gaze fixed on the sticky, rotting stain throbbing with flies at her feet. Detan had been injured, and not lightly. They had no way of knowing how bad off he was. The pool was big enough to be worrisome, but Tibal seemed certain that they would have left the body to bloat if he were dead.

Ripka wasn't so sure. It was possible they would take the body back with them to perform whatever experiments they had in mind on what was left of his flesh. Were the secrets to his strange ability hidden in the workings of his brain? She didn't know, but she was sure that whitecoat would be very much interested in finding out.

"He'll be all right," she found herself saying to Tibal, just to fill the void of silence.

He snorted. "It's not Detan I'm worried about, lass, though I appreciate your thought."

"Then what are you worried about?"

"This whole sand-cursed city. You've seen what he can do when he's angry, you saw that flash on the cliffside. Make no mistake, he's gotten it under control some since we first met, but there's a reason he went to the sel-less middle of the Scorched when he got away from Valathea the first time. And a real good reason why he doesn't stay long in sel cities. Why he doesn't dare go home. They got five firemounts in Hond Steading. You know what he could do with that?"

Ripka swallowed and tried to pull her arms tighter around herself. "You're saying he could blow this whole mine?"

"Lass, he could blow this whole city if he's good and riled. Come on back up now," Tibal called as he turned back to the flier. "We've got to pay a visit to the salvage men before that pit-crusted woman comes to pay us a visit."

Ripka stoutly avoided thinking on what in the blue skies Tibal would want with the minders of the city's garbage heap. But not as actively as she avoided thinking of the whole of Aransa torn to bits by the anger of one man.

CHAPTER 39

His fingers had gone numb, and Aella was deaf to his whining. Seemed she was deaf to most things, now that she'd said what it was she wanted to. Without the natural progression of the stars to guide him, he had no way of telling how long he'd been chained up, but his stomach was pretty sure it had been too long. It was all beginning to weigh on him. The pain in his leg, the ache in his arms and back. He shifted, grunting, struggling to find a position that didn't smart something fierce.

"Will you stop worming around like an infant?" Aella said, her voice soft with exasperation.

"Well, I don't believe it, you can talk after all. Thought you'd been struck mute from above."

"Are you so desperate for attention that you cannot go a moment without conversation?"

"You'd be wanting to have a chat too, if you were strung up like this."

She sighed and gestured with her book. "The others seem to be faring just fine."

"Well, it's not my worry that their spirits are broken.

How long have they been on this ship, anyway?"

"It varies. We began this expedition two moons ago."

"Two moons!"

"It took us a quarter of one to get here. Anyway, I don't see why you're so worried about their comfort."

"Ever heard of basic human compassion?"

She glanced down at her book, flipped through a few pages, and shrugged. "Sorry, not in here."

"What's that, then? A guidebook on how to be an ice princess?"

"I would *kill* for some ice right now," she said as she fanned herself with the slim volume.

"You know what? I believe it."

Aella rolled her eyes, but whatever retort was coming she snapped off at the sound of footsteps. Callia came floating up the deck, a black-robed attendant at her side. Detan clenched his jaw. He recognized the shape of the case in the man's hands. Doctors' tools. Experimental ones. A cool sweat bathed his skin, panic constricting his throat.

"Nothing to say, Honding?" Callia stood back as she spoke, keeping to the shadow cast by a buoyancy sack, and waved the attendant forward.

Detan swallowed around a stone-hard lump and forced a grin. "Nothing polite."

The attendant handed the case to Callia and produced two pairs of iron shackles. As the big man unlocked the chains about Detan's ankles and opened the maw of one shackle wide, he caught Aella's eye. She was nose-down in her book, the pages angled to hide her face from Callia's view, but her gaze was fixed on him. He raised a brow, she gave a slight shake of her head.

He scowled. It would be so easy to lift his foot up and plant it in the face of the attendant, then he could...

What? His hands were still bound, and as long as Aella kept him cut off from manipulating sel, his only probable weapon was stripped from him.

The shackle clanked shut, the opportunity ended.

When his wrists were shackled, the attendant jerked him to his feet. He almost cried out as his weight settled on his injured leg. He swayed, but that only earned him an exasperated sigh from Callia and a quick clip on the back of the head from her attendant.

"Come along then." She waved toward the cabin quarters mid-ship.

He stood, frozen, willing himself to shrink into obscurity. The attendant gave him a shove from behind with the rounded head of a cudgel. Detan grunted, limping forward, and clanged the metal around his wrists together under the guise of rubbing his arms and hands to get the life back. If he were going to be experimented upon, the least he could do was give these bastards a headache.

"You will stop that," Callia said as she opened the door into the cabin. It was a finely crafted door, warm-hued wood rubbed with beeswax and carved all around with dancing air-serpents. Looked like something his own auntie would have had commissioned. It would have looked friendly to him, once. Now he hesitated, dreading to cross the threshold into the oil-lit space beyond.

"Don't know what you mean," he rambled, hearing his voice grow high and fast as if from a great distance. "And anyway I'd rather stay out here and take in the view. It is lovely, don't you think?"

Callia's narrow shoulders tensed at mention of the view, the muscles of her neck standing out sharp above the crisp collar of her clean, white coat.

They always started out so very, very clean.

Callia's gaze flicked to her attendant's, scarcely registering Detan as an autonomous human being. To her, he was just another specimen. An unruly one, though, which he hoped was irritating her at least a little.

Pain lanced through his back. He stumbled forward in a blind panic, thrusting weight upon his arrow-skewered leg. Before he could even get a proper curse out the floor rose up and gave him a hearty slap on the cheek, shocking his senses back into sharp awareness. It didn't last.

The attendant grabbed him by the short chain between his wrists and hauled him half to his feet. Detan grunted as the world went hazy at the edges; what little blood was left in his veins failed to keep up the flow while he was being yanked about.

He was dragged down a dark hallway, the tops of his feet rubbed hot and raw over a plush rug. *Funny*, he thought. *Got a hole in my leg bigger than the Smokestack's maw, but it's a little rugburn that wrecks my damned day.*

The world tipped on its side and blackness crept to the corners of his vision as his feet left the ground. Detan steeled himself, clinging to consciousness, and felt an unforgiving slab of a hardwood table beneath him, firm and cold. He squirmed, trying to orient himself, and got a flash of directed lantern light in his eyes for his trouble. Detan squeezed his eyes shut and prayed to the blue skies for the blessed fumes of golden needle tea to drag him under soon.

He wished he'd taken unconsciousness up on its offer when he'd had the chance.

"Aren't you going to knock me out?" he croaked as the attendant wrenched his arms above his head and strapped them down. His legs were already secured. He hadn't even noticed.

"Not this time," Callia said. "I will need you conscious to record accurate results."

Detan bucked against the weight of his chains, wishing for once in his life that he'd eaten anywhere near the same amount Tibal did. If he were just a little bit stronger, a little heavier, then maybe…

A thick leather strap was hauled over his chest, buckled down so tight it compressed his ability to breathe. His breath came in short gasps, his lungs working rapidly against panic and constriction to fuel the rising demands of his body.

Standing beside him, Callia clucked her tongue and laid a cold hand on his forehead.

"You are embarrassing yourself. Settle, and I will loosen the strap."

He went limp. There was no other option.

The strap eased up a notch, and he filled his lungs with blessedly cool air.

"Golden needle, please," he begged. Heat rose in his cheeks, but he ignored it. Shame could be handled later. Now, now he just needed to make it through what was coming.

"I said no." She tapped his forehead once with the tip of her finger and stepped away.

He clenched his fists, counting backwards from ten. Then from twenty. *Oh, fuck it*, he thought. Without access to selium, his temper was no danger. At least the anger made the pain less.

"You see," she said over the soft sounds of glass and metal clinking. "Though I have never had the pleasure to work on you personally, Lord Honding, I have read my colleagues' extensive notes on the matter."

"Oh good, you can read." He bit his lip, cursing himself in silence.

"Be quiet. As I was saying, before your rather uncouth escape from the Bone Tower, my colleagues were having a difficult time regulating the intensity of your particular skill."

Bone Tower? He'd never even known that pit-cursed place had a name. Callia appeared at his side, a long syringe filled with a murky pink-red solution in one hand. The mixture swirled as she gestured, the pale red shot through with opalescent wisps, lightning mixed with smoke. It was a fine syringe, by his estimation. Rare, quality work. The thought didn't soothe his nerves any.

Detan pressed his lips together to keep his retorts to himself and glanced around the room, trying to find something, anything he could use. There was too much light in his eyes to make out any of his surroundings. Lamps had been shuttered and directed at him, presumably so Callia could see what she was doing. He doubted she was unaware of the isolating effect on him.

She didn't seem like the type of woman to be unaware of anything at all.

When he had been quiet for a few heartbeats, she continued: "My research, however, has led me in a different direction. This–" she tapped the side of the syringe with the back of a fingernail, "–is my own special mix. Selium blended with the blood of some of our strongest diviners along with some extra little goodies to keep your body from rejecting it. The theory is quite simple. I put forth that combining the diviner's art of locating even the tiniest pockets of selium, no matter how long dormant the firemount, is an essential skill for the refinement of any deviant talent. With the ability for *finesse* in place, the deviants will grow."

He shook with a mixture of laughter and fear. "You

want me to become *stronger*? You trip and stick yourself with that thing? Get a little sel on the brain?"

She sighed. "No, I want you to become more refined. There is a difference. Please do try to pay attention. The treatments, it seems, have the added benefit of increasing the deviant's desire to be near selium to comfort the mind. Which is why we will begin now. Our path back to Valathea will take us through sel-dry settlements only. Understand?"

He nodded, not trusting his voice.

"Good." Callia snapped her fingers at her attendant. "Go and fetch Aella."

The attendant shuffled out of the room, and Callia turned back to her preparations. Detan's heart hammered as he tipped his head this way and that, struggling to see anything in the room that wasn't light. He failed, so he fell back to his next best tool. Conversation.

"Afraid to give it a try without the kid around to keep you covered, eh?"

"Hardly. She is an added safety precaution. I can assure you that I can handle anything you attempt myself."

Detan felt cold, right down to his fingertips. "You telling me you're deviant too? You're doing this to your own people?"

She appeared at his side once more, a frown on her delicate, dark face. A face that had never seen more than a candlemark in the sun at a time. "We all have our talents, Honding. And despite what you believe, I am trying to help these creatures."

"Help? This is–"

The door clanged open and Callia looked up, a pleased smile on her cushy lips. Detan shook his head and scowled. He shouldn't be giving her any compliments, even if they were just in his own head.

"Aella, sit there."

There was a soft shuffling of feet to his right side, where he suspected the door must be, and then the creak of wood. Callia nodded.

"The subject may react strongly at first. Be prepared to increase dampening."

"Yes, mistress."

Detan clenched his fists. He clenched his jaw. He strained with all his might against the bonds.

The needle found him anyway.

Liquid fire filled his veins, searing him from the inside out. With a roar he lurched against the chains and the leather, heedless to the groan of his ribs under the strap. His eyes flew wide, wider than they'd ever been in his life, taking in every last detail of the room beyond his prison of light.

Bits of selium hung in the air, particles so fine he hadn't noticed them before. They glowed before him, like motes of dust in a sunbeam. People were talking around him, high and strained, but he couldn't make out the words. He could sense it everywhere, an impenetrable, constant cloud. There was selium below the table, too. The table that was trapping him.

Finesse.

He turned his anger in upon himself, and the table cracked beneath him.

"Shut him down!"

"Shit!"

Detan crashed to the floor, heaped amongst the rubble of his makeshift gurney, and rolled on instinct to the right. His moment of clarity was lost, the miniscule flecks of sel once more beyond his senses. The back of his shirt was burned clear off, he could feel scraps of it sticking in the mess of his flesh. Flesh that stank of char.

His stomach gave a traitorous rumble.

No time for that.

Sourceless hands reached for him, and he swung his arms in a wide arc, letting the chunks of wood dangling from his chains do the work for him. He scrambled to his feet and stumbled into a hallway, crashing against the opposite wall as his feet tangled in debris. Cursing, he kicked himself free and hopped-ran down the hall toward the friendly, air-serpent door. Footsteps pounded behind him, urging him forward.

He got the door open, bloodied and bound hands slipping too many times on the polished brass knob. He stumbled out into the faint light of fake stars and froze. Soldiers ringed the cabin, alerted by the sounds of the blast. Silvery steel glinted all around him, brighter than the pinpricks of sel had been. He could feel the selium above, swelling the buoyancy sacks.

These were evil people.

Just one little spark.

His fellow captives looked up at him, shocked out of their stupor, eyes wide with horror.

Detan let his hands fall, sank to his knees. Something encroached over his senses, fell like a curtain. Heavy hands closed on his shoulders, and a smaller one grasped his chin, tipped his head back. For a single thumping of his heart he stared into Aella's eyes, a sliver of worry hinted at by fine wrinkles in her forehead. Then Callia laid a cloth over his mouth, and he breathed deep the aroma of golden needle.

Cold water shocked him out of his drugged stupor. Detan jerked upright, the chains around his wrists and ankles snapping him back down. He blinked, groaning, struggling to clear water from his eyes. He found himself chained face-down on a rough woven cot, too scared to move lest he disturb the early crusting over of the scabs on his back. Whatever had been left of his shirt was cut away, though the smell of burned fibers remained. He turned his head and peered through the distortion of water caught in his lashes.

Figures swam into view before him. The attendant retreated from his side, an empty bucket in his hands. Callia strode forward with Thratia in her wake. The refined calm of the ex-commodore's face was lost under a storm cloud of anger. Detan forced the biggest, stupidest smile he could muster onto his face. They *were* still in Aransa.

"Hullo, commodore. Coming with us to Valathea?" The words raked hot coals over his throat, but it felt good anyway.

"Hardly. Is this yours, Honding?" Thratia stepped aside so that he could see the man who stood behind her.

"New Chum!"

"Good evening, Lord Honding."

"What are you doing on this broken crate?"

"I've come to retrieve you."

He rattled his chains. "I don't think these people push over for politeness, New Chum."

"Your man here," Thratia prodded New Chum in the side with the pommel of her blade, and Detan realized he'd never even seen her draw it, "is proposing a trade."

"A trade? What for, a day pass to the Salt Baths?"

"For my ship."

Detan swallowed, licked his lips. Was the steward here on Tibal's behalf, or had he turned over on them? With Detan's mind made sluggish by the golden needle he'd begged for, he couldn't make the pieces fit. Couldn't be sure.

New Chum had to be here with Tibal's consent – *had* to be. It wouldn't make any sense for him to come and trade for Detan if he were working on his own. He'd be after something more lucrative for himself.

"So, it occurred to me," Thratia stepped forward and knelt before Detan. She lifted her blade and laid it, light as a feather, just against the underside of his chin. She tilted his head up, peering into his eyes so intently it made his skin crawl, "that you do know where my ship is."

"As a matter of truth, I don't. In fact, it seems you and I are the only ones who don't know where the damned thing is hiding."

She grinned, not a pleasant effect. "And what's that supposed to mean?"

"It's occurred to *me* that Tibal, the doppel, and quite probably Ripka all know where it is. What about you, Callia? You got a manger full of sensitives here. Can't you find a little ole ship? Or are you holding out on your bosom companion?"

Thratia stood and turned to the imperial, nothing at all friendly in her expression, which pleased Detan something fierce. Driving a wedge between those two was almost worth the scorched back. Almost.

"Can any of these husks sense my ship?" Thratia demanded.

Callia rolled her delicate shoulders. "We've tried, of course. We are still here because we suspect the doppel may have to move the vessel soon, and in doing so we will note its presence. But, for the time being, no, we do not know where it is."

With Thratia's back turned and Callia's attention on her, Detan stole a glance at Aella. The cursed girl winked. He had no idea what to make of it.

"Very well." Thratia sighed and turned back to Detan, waving her blade absently at New Chum. "What's to stop me cutting it out of your steward, then?"

New Chum cleared his throat for attention. "Foreseeing your conclusions, I've arranged for the ship to be destroyed if Detan and I are not both well and free when we arrive at the location."

"Really now." Thratia scowled. "And just what other arrangements have you made?"

"Our terms are quite simple. The commodore, Dignitary Callia, Detan, myself, and a single escort of your choice are to go to the location of the ship. Whereupon, if Detan and I are released unharmed, we will turn the vessel over to you and then leave Aransa in your capable hands."

Detan tried to keep his face impassive, but that didn't sound right to him. It wasn't the way Tibal worked whenever he took the reins – a fair trade of hostages just wasn't his style. And there was, of course, no possible way Thratia or Callia would ever just hand him over. Not without blood. He shivered. Fortune was smiling on him though, because none of the involved parties saw the shadow of doubt worm its way across his face.

Thratia replaced her sword and crossed her arms. "And how will we get there?"

"I would assume on one of this vessel's fine emergency fliers." The steward gestured toward the small dinghies tied to the rim of the deck.

"Fine. Pick someone useful to take with us, Callia."

She pointed a slender finger to Aella. "Go prepare yourself, and a flier."

The girl stood and bowed. "Yes, mistress."

As she disappeared to the other side of the ship, Detan overheard Thratia whisper to Callia. "You sure you want that girl with us?"

"Oh, yes."

Detan frowned. He didn't like any of this at all. Not only was Tibal up to something, but Callia obviously had her own ideas about just how this was going to go. He bit his cheek and scowled at the empty air. He hated being left in the dark, but he could work with that. Most of all, he hated being useless.

"Hey," he rattled his chains. "Can't take me there like this, can you?"

CHAPTER 40

They'd taken the chains off, but Detan was not yet a free man. He stood on the deck of Callia's flier, a little dinghy used to shuttle a handful of people to and from the big ship when proper mooring was elusive. Wasn't nearly as big as his own flier, which he took a gleam of pride in. He had to find something to feel good about. Had to keep his head up.

Thratia kept tight to his right hand, her own hand never straying far from the grip of her cutlass. She kept throwing him glances the same way he reckoned she would throw knives. He kept his eyes skittering all over the place, never focusing on one spot in particular. Didn't stop him from feeling her presence, though. Didn't stop him from smelling the anise-spice she wore in her hair.

With Thratia so close, he could imagine she thought him dangerous. Which was nonsense, of course. Aella had his sel-sense crushed good and proper, and any attempt at physical resistance would get him quite literally crushed by Thratia. Still, it was good to be given the courtesy of being assumed a threat.

Aella piloted the flier, but not through any sel-manipulation. She kept him cut off, and he assumed that meant she was cut off too. She piloted it in the usual way, with fan and rudder and sail, her young face stern with concentration. Not for the first time he wondered just what, exactly, all these deviant sensitives were being trained for. Whatever it was, he wanted no part of it.

New Chum was kept from him, clustered up toward the front of the dinghy where he could give directions to Aella. Which was a real frustration, because Detan would much rather be trading glances with that rascal than Thratia. Under New Chum's guidance, it wasn't long until it became clear to all aboard they were heading straight for the Smokestack. Detan grinned.

"My men have been all over the Hub and the baths," Thratia said. "You're telling me she hid the damned thing there anyway? How?"

New Chum turned to her, gave a stiff bow from the waist. "My apologies, warden, but there are other places on the Fireline beside the baths and Hub."

Callia chuckled, tried to stop it and ended up snorting. "Damn clever for a doppel."

"Damn clever in general," Detan snapped before he could stop himself. "She's not a creature, Callia. Unlike your lustrous self."

Callia looked at him, slope-browed and bored. Like a rockcat who'd been insulted by a cockroach. Why would she care what he thought of her? Far as she was concerned, he was a creature, too. She turned away, dismissing him with her back. Detan sighed and tried to catch New Chum's eye, but the dour little man wasn't having any of it.

He'd never been so ignored in all his life.

Much to his relief, Aella brought the dinghy up at a

sharp angle, making everyone scramble for a handhold, and crested the conical ring of the Smokestack's mouth. They hovered there a moment while Aella listened to New Chum give her directions to land. Detan strained forward, eager to see whatever Tibs had waiting for them.

It wasn't much. The flat bed of the firemount's plug was dusted over with fine ash, a few black rocks poking their thumbs up here and there. The great pipe mouths that fed into the lines draped over the sides of the cone, boring deep into the grey plug. Most had been burned to a crisp, leaving little more than smoldering heaps of rubble to block the bore mouths, but one or two were still operational. Detan shivered.

That was one job sensitives were too valued to be assigned. Diviners would find the pockets, sure, but it would be plain old laborers who cut through the crust with pick-axes and diamond-edged shovels, hoping they'd find the pocket before they found the magma. Hoping that when they did find the pocket it didn't blow itself out and fling them all from the top of the firemount.

Mine masters didn't mind a blowout. It made it easier to anchor the mouth of the pipeline. And anyway, selium pockets never ran dry so long as the firemount had any kick to it.

Detan allowed himself a conciliatory smile. It looked like they had experienced some trouble getting the lines set up. While the pipelines were draped over the conical ridge at regular intervals, there was one glaringly bald spot. He could only hope no one had died to find out that pocket wouldn't give.

The craft rocked as Aella brought it down. Apparently the firemount had its own ideas about air currents. Detan itched the palm of his good hand, wanting nothing more than to reach out and feel those strange eddies for

himself. He'd never flown through a firemount's mouth
before. If he lived through this, he'd have to make time
for it.

Even if he'd probably get harpoons launched at him
from the line defenders, it'd be worth it.

"Move, Honding." Thratia grabbed the back of his
neck in one fist and shoved him forward, down the little
gangplank Aella had extended for their egress. New pain
seared down the fresh scabs of his back, and he hissed air
through his teeth.

Detan looked at the girl, but she was busy making
sure the burr-anchors bit snugly into the ground. He
wondered if Callia ever did any of her own flying work.
He glanced back at the imperial, with her singed and
bloodied white coat, her nails lacquered the same blue
as the sky, and decided that was very, very unlikely.

New Chum positioned himself at the spearhead of the
group and motioned further down the wall, toward the
bald patch of ground where there was no pipeline. "This
way, if you please."

Their morbid little party set out, traipsing across the
belly of the firemount. Detan imagined he could feel it
rumble in distaste beneath him, annoyed by the human
presence using it as their own personal meeting place.
He tried not to think about that too much.

As Thratia herded him across the sooty ground he
tried to keep his head down while keeping his eyes up.
He had a rather strong suspicion that unless he played
scared senseless she wasn't going to be any nicer than
she already was.

That made him dizzy, so he gave up and looked around
brazenly instead. What was she going to do, blind him?

He swallowed, and went back to keeping his head
down.

As he stole glances around the broken land, he noticed one distinct thing missing from the cracked landscape: the *Larkspur*. There were heaps of magma rock and dunes of ash, glittering blades of shattered obsidian, whirls of breath-stealing heat. But no ship.

Except, to their right, a little disturbance in the soot. A small smudge of irregularity that he recognized as the footprint of his own bedraggled flier. But the *Happy Birthday Virra!* was nowhere to be found.

Thratia stopped their progress with a soft growl and shoved Detan forward. "To the pits with this," she muttered, and Callia gave her a tight nod.

"Tibal!" she called above the gritty winds. "If you want this sorry sack of flesh back you show yourself!"

Detan stumbled, exaggerating his overbalance to get as far away from Thratia as possible, and rammed smack into Tibs as he stepped out from around a pillar of black stone. Detan froze, chest to chest with the man who might be his only friend in the world, heart hammering to wake the dead. He wanted nothing more than to grab Tibs by the arm and sprint for it.

But this wasn't his game. Not anymore. And he had no idea what good ole Tibs had in mind.

That rangy sonuvabitch put one hand on Detan's shoulder and shoved him back toward his captors. Detan staggered, this time doing his best to keep his balance in check, absolutely straining his core muscles to stay upright. To stay as close to freedom as possible. He glared as hard as he could at Tibs, knowing full well the freak show behind him couldn't see.

Oh shit. Was Tibs trying to piss him off to blow something up? If that was his plan, he was going to be disappointed in a hurry. Detan cursed Callia, Aella, and any other vowel-smashed imperial name he could think of. He could only hope Tibs and New Chum had worked out some sort of hand signal to let one another know something was amiss.

If only he had thought of that idea before, he could let Tibs know his own cursed self.

"Evening, warden." Tibs tipped down the brim of his singed hat. "Nice of you to come see me."

"Cut the shit." Thratia's cutlass whipped over Detan's shoulder and pressed right up tight against Tibal's throat. Detan cringed, sweating himself slick in two thumps of his heart, but he held his ground.

"Where's my ship?"

"More to the point," Callia said, slipping forward to stand on Detan's other side, making his skin crawl with mere proximity. "Where is my doppel? I know you could not possibly pilot the craft yourself, Tibal. Not even with your watch captain's aid."

Tibs held his hands out and patted the air like he was calming an angry mule, his smile chock full of that rustic charm Detan damned well knew was an act. Worked on most ladies. Too bad these two sandvipers were nothing at all like ladies.

"Easy now." Tibs placed a finger on the flat of Thratia's blade and nudged it out to the side, then took a step back. Putting more distance between himself and Detan. The prick. "Ship's coming round, though you'll have to check with Pelkaia regarding just where she intends on going. Doesn't have much love for your kind, understand."

Tibs pointed behind them, and the ladies on the field turned as one to regard the tip of an all-too familiar mast creeping over the lip of the conical wall. Detan, however, kept his eyes squarely on Tibs's sour face and tried to mouth out: N-O S-E-L.

Tibs blinked at him, big brows drawing together.

I C-A-N-T...er... B-O-O-M.

The idiot just shrugged. Detan clenched his fists, shuffled a step towards Tibs and gathered his breath to get his voice as low as possible.

The *Larkspur* crested the rise, big enough to cast a shadow over their little party. A surprisingly small shadow. Detan blinked, distracted, tried to work it through but–

"That's not the *Larkspur*," Aella said.

Detan spun around, let himself take a step back towards Tibs as he did it. Hovering above the firemount's rim was the *Larkspur* as he'd known it, sails full and stabilizing wings spread wide in the afternoon light. Pelkaia stood on the deck alongside Ripka, both waving with big stupid grins. The exact same wave. The exact same grin.

He half-turned, saw Aella's small face pinched with focus, sweat sluicing off her scrunched brow. Her fists were clenched at her sides, making her look even smaller for how tiny they were. Her jaw jutted forward with strain.

The *Larkspur* vanished. So did Pelkaia.

Aella staggered, all the color draining from her small cheeks. Detan reached for her but she swatted him back, forcing herself upright. Too damned proud to seek out help when she needed it.

She caught his eye and jerked her chin. He blinked, turned back toward the place where the *Larkspur* had been.

Selium rushed toward the blue vault of the sky, a reverse opalescent rain. Glimmering droplets raced away from their armature, his own sad little flier with a rather shocked Ripka standing alone on deck. The stitched-together contraption still had *Happy Birthday Virra!*

Painted in purple along the side of one buoyancy sack. Detan thought he'd faint.

No time for that. Aella had dropped her hold.

He let the sel rise, higher and higher, straining himself until he feared it would escape his grasp. Once it had melded with the streaky white of wind-battered clouds he reached out for all he was worth and held. Binding, binding, smashing it all together until it was one massive globule.

He swayed, sick with the immensity of it, felt a familiar hand grip his arm and prop him upright. Tibs, that old bastard, grinning like an idiot. Probably because he was one. There was no way he could have seen Aella coming.

"Who the fuck is Virra, and where is my pits-damned ship?" Thratia spun on Detan and Tibal, cutlass lashing out. He was straining himself too hard to pay any real attention, but he thought he heard the telltale squeal of Callia drawing her own blade. Looked like the imperial was up to doing her own work after all.

"Over there," Tibs said, voice relentlessly chipper as he stepped out of reach of Thratia's blade, this time dragging Detan along with him. Thank the sweet skies. At least Tibs hadn't gone completely mad.

Callia strode toward Aella, grabbed the girl by the front of her blouse and hauled her upright, vein throbbing in the center of her forehead. "Take down all illusions in this area. Now."

The girl's eyes went wide enough that Detan could see the gleam of the sun glancing off the whites of them. He wanted to scurry over there, to bravely shove Callia aside and tell her that was no way to treat a young lady, especially one in her charge. But he was weak and he was tired, and he didn't have a thing in the world to answer for the length of steel in Callia's hand.

Well, he had the sel. Too unwieldy to risk using. As always.

Callia let the girl go, shoving her forward. Aella turned in a slow circle, eyes narrowed.

"I told you–" Tibs began, but Thratia lunged and cracked the pommel of her cutlass against his temple hard enough to split skin and send the poor devil reeling. Detan forced himself forward, grabbed his friend by the shirt and held him up, tried to drag him back a step but was halted by Thratia placing the edge of her blade against his own scrawny neck. Detan froze, tangled up with Tibs, heart trying to escape through his throat.

"Everyone's staying right here until I get my ship. Understand?"

Aella hissed through her teeth, drawing Thratia and Callia's attention. She pointed straight behind their little group, eyes wide with wonder.

"It wasn't there before!" she insisted to no one in particular as she held both hands out, so tired she needed the assistance of mirror-movement to make her powers work. Just like the weaker sods working the line, Detan thought.

The empty air just a few paces behind them rippled, shimmered, then fell away in tatters, ribbons of sel peeling off like rotten fruit. Testament to the girl's exhaustion – she was only able to rip it at the seams, not shatter it whole. Detan let that sel go. There was no way he could hold so much.

When the illusion had passed, there the *Larkspur* hovered. Half its sails were tucked in, its stabilizing wings only half out. Pelkaia stood on the edge of the deck facing them. The rail had been taken down, and she had one booted foot on a roll of canvas as thick around as a corpse. She grinned down at their little gathering, cut Thratia a tight salute.

The ex-commodore strode forward, Callia falling in line at her side. But it was Aella that Pelkaia turned her attention to. The doppel inclined her head, a small smile of genuine respect on her time-worn features. Detan blinked, realizing he was seeing Pelkaia's true face for the first time. He squinted, straining, but was too far away to make out any detail.

"You're good, girl," Pelkaia called loud enough for all to hear. "But you missed one."

Aella spun around, overbalanced, and staggered sideways a step. She brought her hands up to cup either side of her head, pressing in as if she could stop the world spinning with the force of her hands.

"Enough of this." Callia outstretched a hand, selium-filled bangles jangling together, and Detan felt a wrenching in his gut. Something about the sel he held above him felt pestilent, repulsive. He was overwhelmed with the desire to push it away from him before the gangrenous contagion could spread.

No. He shook his head. And held.

The *Larkspur* shuddered, Pelkaia's smile fading as she fought her own battle against Callia's perverse talents. Thratia approached the hull of her ship, Callia on her heels, and reached for the ladder.

Pelkaia kicked the bundle.

The canvas unfurled, dumping a motley collection of half-rotted vines atop the heads of both women. They sent up a chorus of swears, swatting at the tangled vegetable mass, molded flowers mashing into their hair.

Callia's coat was smeared with rot. Detan could have sung at the sight.

"Stop fucking around!" Thratia's cutlass made short work of her entanglement, but she was still smeared in the rich nectar of the sticky blooms. Detan recognized the flowers then: the ones Tibal had pointed out to him at the fete.

Shit.

"Told you," Pelkaia called, "you missed one!"

The doppel waved her hand, and the missing pipeline popped into existence. No trouble digging there, after all. Only this one was defunct, its leather tube infested with selium-fed bees. Bees that, according to Tibal, were rather fond of thistle blossom.

A swarm rose, a cloud blacker than any he'd ever seen, the buzz in the air heady enough to set his teeth vibrating. They coalesced and turned, irritated by the absence of the sel that had been hiding them. The sel that they had no doubt been happily snacking upon until the moment of its dissolution.

Thratia leapt for the *Larkspur*'s ladder. Pelkaia must have been expecting the move, because the *Larkspur* danced out of her reach. Out of all of their reach, flitting further away from the mouth of the Smokestack than anyone could leap.

With one last explosive curse, Thratia threw her blade down and sprinted toward Callia's dinghy.

"And just what the fuck are we supposed to do?" Detan screamed at Tibs above the buzzing roar, the shadow of the swarm preceding them across the ashen ground. Tibs grinned, pointed at the *Happy Birthday Virra!* looping around the mass and headed right for them, Ripka at the helm.

Problem was, Ripka had never flown a damned thing before in her life.

"She's all over the blasted sky!" Detan screeched, trying to get a handle on his panic lest he lose control of his cloud.

Tibal scowled. "I showed her how it's done, she'll–"

The swarm slammed into them. Fist-sized bees, bodies gorged with sel, broke over them like a wave. He heard Thratia screech a war cry, saw dozens of the things drop dead around Callia as she extended her perversion of selium to the gas already in the bee's bellies. Detan spun round, swatting wildly, feeling bloated and fragile bodies burst under each swipe.

There were too many to swat.

CHAPTER 41

Bright hot kisses of pain blossomed on Detan's arms, his cheeks. Creatures angry that he wasn't food took their rage out on his tender flesh. He screamed, heard Tibs yell something much more manly, and then Tibs yanked him down beside the rock he'd been hiding behind. He had a cloak stowed there, and dragged it over both of them. It was thick and coarse woven, enough to keep the stings at bay as long as they didn't let any gaps show. Hard to do when you had two men crowded under one blanket.

"You stupid sonuva–"

Tibs elbowed him hard in the side. "If you'd just gotten your ass over to this side of the rock when I'd signaled!"

"Signaled! What signal? Oh shit, shit, New Chum–"

"Had his own cloak on his back. Saw him drop down and start crawling to the rendezvous site as soon as Pelkaia made her appearance. Pits below, can't you pay any attention?"

"Rendezvous? Ripka was headed straight for us!"

"Uh, well, I can't say why she'd decide–"

"Shhht."

Bees dropped from the sky, thunked into view in the tiny little sliver between the cloak and the ground. Fat bodies twitched and collapsed in on themselves with rot.

"Honding," Callia said, "would you stop cowering?"

"Errr." Nerves wound tight as a propeller spring, he peeled back an edge of the cloak and glanced up.

Callia stood above them, arms outstretched, the eye of a storm of dying insects. His stomach lurched, reacting to her perversion of the selium all around. It was almost enough to make him lose his concentration on the cloud he held above. Almost.

Her face was half purple, a red welt smack dab in the center of one cheek, her outstretched arms pocked with identical marks. Despite the pain she must be feeling, she smiled. He hated her for that. He hated her for a lot of things, sure, but that smile was an icepick to the heart.

"Get up, idiot."

"I rather like it down here."

"You will leave with me. Now. If Thratia lives then she can take back her ship on her own time. I'm done with this place."

"Well, that's a real nice invitation, but I'm afraid I have plans that I just can't back out of. It would be ungentlemanly of me."

"Get. Up."

"Err..."

He looked at Tibs, but he just shrugged. So this was it, then. His rescue. Well, it had been a damned good try. Joints aching, flesh burning, he pushed himself to his feet and let the cloak drop around him. Tibs stood beside him, arms crossed over his scrawny chest.

"I'm coming, too."

"Fine," Callia said, her tone flat as a cloudless sky.

From the corner of his eye a familiar shape darkened the sky; careening, bobbing, determined. Detan stiffened his jaw, pushed back his shoulders. *Stall, you mad Honding bastard.* His hands flitted through the air, a hopeless, childlike gesture, as if he could grasp a viable idea from the aether.

Callia smirked, a river viper sensing blood in the water. "Nothing more to say, Honding?"

"I–" He shoved a hand in his pocket in an effort to affect an unconcerned slouch, and his fingers brushed paper. The paper he'd nicked from Thratia. He pulled it free, a neat little square, and flicked it open. The familiarity of the handwriting punched him in the gut. Apothiks were always careless in forming their letters. Bel Grandon was no exception.

"Oh," he said.

"Now isn't the time for love notes," Callia grated.

Detan looked up from the familiar scrawl and studied the whitecoat. Strain fractured the lines around her eyes, sallowness had crept into her cheeks. Whatever effort she was expending holding the swarm back was doing her no good. He felt detached – slowed in time – freed somehow from the events around him by the small collection of words he held.

And all the while, he dared not look directly at the black blob bobbing closer across the sky.

"Do you know what this is?" He turned the paper around to face her, and saw her eyes narrow with suspicious recognition. He pressed on before she could answer. "It's a mercer cipher. Not a particularly opaque one, it seems the owner wasn't too concerned about it falling into the wrong hands." He snorted a bitter laugh.

"Maybe she'd hoped it would."

He flung the paper at her and let it tumble to the ground, wilting in the soot between them. With a pained groan he dragged his good hand through his hair and then took a half step forward, pointing at the discarded note. "I have been an idiot. An absolute, bumbling fool!"

"You'll have no argument from me–"

"Be quiet!" The force of his own voice rubbed his throat raw. Callia flinched, and her momentary lapse of control made him smirk. "That. That little, little scrap, is a list of deliveries. All this time – all this sand-cursed fucking time – I let my fear hang on you. You and your puppet masters. Stupid, stupid man that I am. Thratia trading deviant sel-sensitives for Valathean weapons. Cruel. Typical of her – believable. But do you know what else is typical?"

"I grow weary of this." Callia gestured toward him, a casual turning of the wrist, and he felt the sense of decay within him intensify. He staggered sideways, clutched his side, sweat forming rivers all across his skin. Tibs gripped his arm, held him upright.

Detan drew his lips into a skeletal grimace. Clinging to what control he had left, he reached out, shunted aside his sense of the cloud above and grabbed for the bee nearest Callia.

It was instinct, pure and primal. He didn't even feel the surge go out. The bee burst apart, roiling with flame. Not close enough to do more than singe the cursed woman, but it was enough. Callia swore, leapt to the side. Her grip on him extinguished as she dealt with the shock and pain.

He extended himself until his muscles quivered, taking the cloud in mind once more. All around him he felt the sel in the bellies of the bees more keenly. But they were a tight-packed mass. To try and blow just one again would mean losing control and blowing them all. New Chum was out there. Ripka and Aella. He couldn't risk it. But now, with the weight of the cloud resting heavy on his mind... Now he had an idea. An option.

"You. Will. Listen."

She glared at him, but said nothing.

"Why was she disposed of, Callia? Why was General-fucking-Throatslitter kicked out of the Valathean Fleet? It wasn't for cutting throats, we both know that."

Callia licked cracked lips. "She wouldn't relinquish power after conquest of the Saldive isles."

"Wouldn't. Relinquish. Power. And you've been giving her weapons – weapons! I'd wondered, wondered why Thratia cared so much about cutting Galtro down where he stood. She's a psychopath, power hungry, cold hearted. Pressed for time by you. But she's not stupid. Never that. She risked a lot, killing the mine master. Could have just won the seat fair as scales but no. He needed to go then. The doppel was just a convenient scapegoat.

"He was going to fix the mines." He thrust a finger towards the hive-infested pipeline. "Get Aransa's selium production back up to a hundred percent. It was his job, to keep them running, and by the pits he was good at it. But without that sel honey, the Grandons couldn't make their liqueur, and without that conveniently unique good to export, how was your little friend Thratia going to hide her distribution network?"

"She wouldn't–"

"You have no idea what she's capable of. How many arms do you think she needed to take Aransa? Placid, scared Aransa. Too frightened by the specter of the doppel to do any harm, too happy to have her by half. They would have voted her in – she didn't need all of that. Not here." He thrust a finger at the paper. "Pick it up."

Never taking her gaze from Detan she crouched, took the slip of paper in one hand and stood. She did not read it so much as flick her eyes to it in brief increments, absorbing the information in bits while refusing to release her awareness of her surroundings. He'd expected as much.

As he watched, her face grew drawn, her jaw tense and her lips pressed bloodless. He knew what she was seeing – had read it himself. A list of coordinates, deliveries made and planned, all over the Scorched. All of the Grandons' honey liqueur. The liqueur, and their false-bottomed crates.

He watched understanding settle within her – smooth the tautness of her shoulders, darken the glare of her eye. Callia folded the paper along its crease, tucked it into a pocket. Evidence, he presumed, for whatever she meant to bring against Thratia. Whatever she was planning, it was already too late.

A shadow passed above them, bigger than any selium-enriched bee, and all three looked to the sky.

Happy Birthday Virra! swung into position above them, slicing through the cloud of angry insects. Ripka roared something incomprehensible as stingers alit upon her arms and cheeks and chest – any likely fleshy place. Callia's face twisted in annoyance and she reached up to extend her selium power to Ripka.

But Ripka didn't have a lick of sel-sense in her entire body.

The watch captain swung down from the thick rope-ladder and lashed out with one of Tibs's strange, overlong wrenches. She cracked Callia straight in the head, and the bitch went down like a landslide. Detan would have whooped with joy, if the area wasn't then immediately invaded by the bees.

They were flooded by the things. Detan dropped to his knees, saw Ripka slip the ladder, lost track of Tibs as he rolled in the dirt, stings blossoming all over like molten metal was raining down upon him. He screeched into the buzzing madness, felt his grip on the selium cloud slip.

Remembered it.

Straining against his pain, Detan yanked the cloud lower, tugging it below the cloudline until anyone who looked up could see the pearlescent globule. If anyone could see anything at all through the mass of buzzing life all around them.

He drew it lower, lower, trembling with the strain until the first of the pits-cursed creatures caught a sniff of it. It was irresistible to the little bastards.

All in a rush the swarm lifted, delved into the cloud of nectar. Detan laughed, wild and high, as he shoved himself up on his elbows and tipped his head back to watch the sky. His selium cloud was requiring less and less energy to hold as the infestation gobbled it up. He frowned, struggled to his feet and saw Tibs do the same. They stared at one another, stupefied with relief. Even Ripka was back on her feet, looking like she'd made love to a cactus, but otherwise whole.

Callia lay unconscious between the three of them, her breath coming easy, a little trickle of blood seeping down her temple. Detan's fists clenched. He stepped toward her.

"Wait," Aella rasped, as she dragged herself to her feet

and trudged toward them. "Leave her."

Detan's head throbbed so hard he could barely think. "She's a monster."

"She thinks you are, too." Aella set her feet apart, braced herself, and held out a threatening hand. "I said leave her. I've still got enough left in me to handle *you*, Honding."

He gritted his teeth, clenched his fists in impotent rage. "Come with us."

"No one's going anywhere." Thratia's voice, sharp as her will, cut across them all. The four jumped, guilty as if they'd been caught with their hands in the agave candy, and stared at the relatively unscathed ex-commodore. Detan blinked, not understanding, then looked beyond her and saw the sail of Callia's dinghy flapping limply. She'd gotten to it in time. Pitsdamnit.

"You're done, Honding," Thratia called as she collected her discarded blade. He could almost hear the smirk she wore.

Detan realized he'd sunk to his knees, Tibs crouching at his side. Didn't know how he'd gotten there, but the sooty ground felt soft. Nice. Better than the cloud pressing in on his head.

Ripka and New Chum staggered toward them, and a lump formed in his throat as he saw Ripka reach for the knife he'd given her. She was so blasted shaky New Chum had to lend her an arm, but she came to stand before him. Between him and Thratia.

"You're outnumbered, warden." Ripka said. "Best hurry back to Aransa before things get violent."

Thratia spat in the dust. "You've got less strength in you than a fresh-plucked whore. Lay down your weapon and I'll consider not stuffing you head-first in a pipeline."

A balmy shadow passed above and Detan tilted his head back, unable to understand what he was seeing. The *Larkspur* slid in under the cloud of ravenous creatures, drawing hard to a stop just between Detan and Thratia. The ground-anchor was flung from its deck, nearly missing the edge of *Happy Birthday Virra!*. It bit into the soot-and-ash concoction of the ground, the harpoon at its end spring-released by the pushback so that it gripped the soil and held tight.

The next thing to fall from the *Larkspur* was Pelkaia.

Detan stared, dumbfounded, as she soared from the ship's bowsprit, a flat cushion of sel held under her feet completely by will. She hit the ground, knees flexing, sel dissipating but not vanishing – he could feel it, the feather-thin shawl she worked it into, wrapped around herself. Shimmering and distracting, a shifting cloak of light. Not nearly beguiling enough to hide the length of steel that appeared in her hand.

"Pelkaia! No!" Detan called, but she did not so much as glance over her shoulder.

Thratia weighed the cutlass in her own hand, eyed this fresh threat, and smiled. "You're no more use to me alive."

Pelkaia did not break her stride. Their blades crashed, steel screeching against steel, the sound piercing through the drone of the bees and Detan's own sorry yelling. Panic reared up in his chest, bright and wild, as they pushed apart.

Break. Attack. Guard. He didn't know a lick of the proper terms, could barely recall the word *riposte* from his ancient schooling, but even to his untrained eye Thratia had the advantage. She was the superior swordswoman. And Pelkaia was tired. Run-down. Desperate.

The weight of holding the cloud bore down on his mind; his fingers took up a tremble not even the deepest of breaths could still.

"Time to go," Tibs said, impossibly calm. Familiar hands grabbed Detan's armpits and hauled him upward but he lurched forward, stayed on his knees, unable to peel his gaze away from the blurs of sel and steel.

What Pelkaia lacked in native talent, she sure as shit made up for it in ingenuity. The sel cloud around her she manipulated into sparks of light, threw up tiny walls to cover her feints. He'd never seen anything like it. And he was pretty sure Thratia hadn't either – otherwise Pelkaia'd be skewered by now.

Thratia parried a thrust hard, twisting so that Pelkaia jerked sideways. The doppel stumbled over ash-slick ground, her side wide open to Thratia's leisure. Detan called out a warning, but he knew it was no good. Thratia's blade swung in, almost lazy in its arc, and opened the side of Pelkaia's hip.

Somehow Pelkaia got a blast of sel between them, bright as day, and shoved it straight in Thratia's eyes.

"Catari bitch!" Thratia barked.

Pelkaia whirled. The sleek outline of Thratia drew Pelkaia's blade as a magnet pulls north. The blade skimmed off boiled leather, bit down and caught in thick padding. Detan held his breath as Thratia's armor peeled open. Before Pelkaia could press her strike Thratia sidestepped and snapped her blade down, batting Pelkaia's wide.

Pelkaia swore, her shoulder overextended, body pivoting as it moved with the steel. She stumbled, fell hard to one side – hard enough to pop the blade from her grasp.

Trembling, she levered herself to an elbow, reached – scrambling through the scorched dirt – for her weapon. Thratia's boot pressed into the small of Pelkaia's back.

"Enough," Ripka said, taking a halting step toward the fallen doppel.

Thratia looked up. Smirked. "Maybe I will find a use for her alive after all."

Detan got an idea.

"New Chum," Detan rasped as quietly as he could. "Be a dear and hold our virtuous watch captain, will you?"

The blessed little steward bowed his head and took a half-step forward to grab Ripka's arm. It was no great struggle to hold her in place, she was worn through.

Detan caught Aella's eye, and understanding passed between them. The girl's face was red, her hair hanging limp and sweaty around her child-pudgy cheeks, but she was ready.

Aella shifted her stance, palms held up toward the skies. She could keep them clear of the backlash – could deaden even the reach of flaming sel. He hoped.

Aella nodded.

"Hey, Thratia! Thratttiiiaaaaa!" Detan raised his voice, praying for all he was worth that Pelkaia would catch his meaning, that she'd ditch what little sel she was still holding onto before he let loose.

"What?" Thratia snarled.

"I suggest you cover your eyes!"

High above, he blew the sel.

A flash so white its very light burned him filled the crater. People cried out all around him, voices so wild with panic he couldn't tell them apart. Fire boiled in the cloudless sky, great roiling waves of it. Flaming corpses rained down all around them, chitinous bodies turning to charcoal long before they broke upon the ground.

At the moment of ignition he collapsed, Tibs's grasp doing nothing at all to keep him upright. He laid there for a moment, stunned, drained, watching colors like sunset blossom and blister the sky above. People screamed their fear and their anger all around him, familiar voices merging into one great crescendo of what-the-fuck-did-you-do-Honding. He grunted, unable and unwilling to explain himself.

His anger was gone. He felt… Light. Free.

"Get up, damn you!"

Tibs, good ole Tibs, grabbed him by the wrists and yanked him to his feet. He staggered, his leg reminding him it was in worse shape than his back felt. Tibal shouldered his weight and began to drag him off. He dug his heels in.

"The others!"

"Are fine!" Tibs shoved him forward, the bastard. He was too weak by far to attempt any kind of protest. He tried to turn his head, tried to see what had become of Pelkaia. Of Thratia. But Tibs just kept shoving him along, straight toward the flier's dangling ladder.

"Sandsdamnit Tibs, let me see!"

Tibs growled low in his throat, a sound so rare that it made Detan's knees go weaker than they already were. He was about to mutter some apology when Tibs jerked him around, pointing him straight at the scene of the fight. Pelkaia was still on the ground, but she was pushed to her knees and elbows, New Chum and Ripka closing on her fast. Thratia – where? He couldn't see… oh.

The warden lay on the ground a good ten paces from Pelkaia, curled on her side with one arm flung out. Her chest rose and fell in a reliable rhythm, but that didn't stop Detan's stomach from lurching at the sight of the smoke curls peeling away from her, at the scorched mass of her hair. Pelkaia had found something to do with the sel she held, all right.

If Thratia survived this, Detan was a dead man. It might take her a while, but Thratia'd make sure of it. The knowledge settled around him like a mantle, just as heavy as his anger had been. He shuddered.

Thratia's leg twitched, her head turned.

"Time to fucking go," Tibs said.

"Wait, the girl!"

"No more waiting!"

"But–!"

Aella pushed herself to her knees and glared at him. "Go, you idiot."

"I thought–?"

"I didn't want you around."

"*What?*"

She stood and smiled, brushing grey ash from her blue dress. "Callia was always going to fail, Honding. Her circus is all she's ever cared about – tunnel vision, she can't see beyond it. And I need her alive, you understand? Alive to stand judgment for her failures. And then, well, I'm the only Valathean-bred and trained body positioned to take the reins she's dropped. Her manicured heir – everyone knows it. I'm her ward! But you, Lord Honding, could have made things very difficult for me if you'd come around. You and your sour, noble blood."

"But you–"

"I just didn't want the competition!"

New Chum staggered over to them, missing his eyebrows, with Pelkaia held upright between himself and Ripka. Without another word they hurried as best they could toward the ships while Thratia and Callia were laid out flat.

Happy Birthday Virra! and *Larkspur* were in excellent shape, not even a singe on their gleaming hulls. The bubble of air around them was strangely cool despite the raging inferno of the sky above. He glanced over his shoulder at Aella.

She winked.

CHAPTER 42

The dinghy had been too damaged to return them to the compound, and so they took the ferry, and wound their slow way up the cursed levels of Aransa. With every step Aella took fresh agony wormed its way into her arms, her chest, her legs. A great welt on her throat flared each time she breathed, and though the air was hot and her body exhausted she forced herself to take only the shallowest of breaths.

Sweat did not pour from her, it simply emerged, a glistening sheen from head to foot that did little to cool her in the stale air and instead served only to increase the stinging of her wounds.

And yet Aella smiled. It was tight, controlled, not enough to give away her joy, but she had to do something – something beyond trudging through the heat with her head down – to express her triumph. Not that Callia would have noticed.

Aella spared a glance for her mistress. Callia was carried ahead of her on a shaded palanquin, the curtains snapped tight to hide her from the sun. Well, that's what

she'd said. Aella suspected that she just didn't want the
people of Aransa to see her in her defeat. In her pain.

Which was probably wise. The people had certainly
come out to see whatever there was to see.

They lined the streets, peered through half-shuttered
windows. Each and every one struggled to pick a direction
in which to look. Either at the strange procession making
its way before them, or at the fire in the sky.

Most looked up. Aella did, when she was sure she
wouldn't lose her footing.

The clouds had long since boiled off, and the empty
blue vault was smeared in flame. Sourceless, relentless,
flame. Every breath she took smelled of the chalk-dirt
aroma of cracked stone and gristle roasting over hot
coals. Great swathes of sunset colors roiled out of control,
on occasion mingling with the selium in such a way as to
draw out its opalescent streaks of iridescence.

Those streaks never lasted long. The fire was ravenous
for them.

Aella began to lift her stinging arm, to hold her hand
palm out to the flaming sky in supplication. She stopped
herself just in time, but still let slip a dreamy sigh. If she
had known Detan was capable of such beauty, she might
have contrived to keep him.

Pretending to duck her head once more, she looked
through her lashes to be sure that Thratia had not seen
her moment of weakness. The warden strode before
Callia's palanquin, head straight, jaw set. Though her
body was scattered with welts and the skin of her left side
was scorched red and raw she moved with determined
calm, her eyes roving over those who had gathered to
watch her pass.

She looked proud, confident despite her injuries. As if
the fire in the sky were her own doing, and everything

was as it should be. Aella found herself wondering just what that showmanship cost her. Just how deeply would the new warden sleep tonight?

She caught herself sneering at the back of Callia's palanquin and bit her lip, tucking the expression away. Everyone had their own weaknesses and strengths, she reminded herself.

The doors to Thratia's compound were thrown open for them, all the second and third-ranked of Thratia's little militia spilling over themselves to offer assistance. The laborers who Thratia had pressed into carrying Callia were released and replaced by guards with fresh backs. Apothiks appeared carrying trays of salves and teas and other accoutrements of their business.

Aella nearly jumped out of her tenderized skin as a stranger tugged gently on her sleeve for attention. The man was rough of face, handsome in his own way, and carried the most disarming smile she'd ever seen. He proffered a wooden tray to her, strange jars splayed over its surface.

"This balm," he pointed to a jar of green soapstone, "will ease the sting, miss."

"Thank you." She snatched it from the tray and then attempted an encumbered half-bow over a palm laid open to the sweet skies. The man smiled, bobbed his head, and moved along. Apparently a simple jar of goop was all the care she was going to get.

"Enough of this circus." Thratia's voice, stern despite her exhaustion, froze in place every soul within the room. "It is time for the empire to leave Aransa."

A little trickle of dread excitement wormed its way into Aella's heart. She shifted, trying to get a good view of Callia's palanquin through the press of servants. A bruised-plum hand nudged a curtain aside, and Callia leaned her head out. "The empire will forever be in Aransa, warden. It is the way of things."

The freshly minted warden pulled herself up to her full height, and Aella felt a thrill buzz through her mind and heart. Whatever was about to happen here was new. After a lifetime of laboring silently in Callia's lean shadow, anything new was a crisp delight.

"Escort Dignitary Callia and her charge to their ship." Thratia spoke to her militia, but her eyes did not leave Callia's. Much to Aella's disappointment, Callia snapped her curtain shut and ended the confrontation in silence.

Aella sighed. Change was sometimes too much to hope for.

Guards armed with weapons Callia had helped smuggle into Aransa herded them up the stairs, and Aella allowed herself a slim smile at Callia's lack of power. Even if the dignitary wanted to protest, she was being carried on the shoulders of Thratia's people. Her autonomy had been revoked.

As Aella trudged up the steps she smeared the salve from the green jar across her wounds, savoring the cool tingle that radiated from whatever herbs had been mashed into the concoction. She spared a glance for the apothik who had brought it for her, but his balding pate was lost in the press all around. She stopped looking the second she stepped onto the dock.

Their cruiser was gone.

A midsized barge hung in the empty space of the u-dock, its overhead buoyancy sacks bulging against the ropes that held them in place. Stabilizing wings hung half open from the front and back, and all of Callia's attendants were crowded into the center of the ship, held in an uneasy cluster by a line of crossbowmen spread out around the curve of the dock. Of the deviant sensitives, there was no sign. Along the ship's rectangular haul, *The Crested Fool* was painted in gilded yellow.

Aella was forced to stifle a giggle.

With utmost care, the guards eased Callia's palanquin to the ground and pulled away her sheltering curtains. From amongst her cushions the battered whitecoat leaned forward, fists clenching the front poles of the palanquin so tight Aella suspected the flimsy, Scorched-grown, wood would snap.

"What is the meaning of this?" Callia grated.

Thratia gestured with a wide sweep of her arm. "You promised me a ship, and weapons. Now I have everything we agreed upon."

With a grunt of pain-mingled rage Callia jerked herself to her feet and thrust a finger Thratia's way, her other hand drifting for the grip of her saber. Aella cringed, hoping her mistress would not be so stupid as to get them all slaughtered to assuage her indignity.

"You lost the ship we sent you, and you have your weapons. Return my craft and my specimens to me immediately."

Thratia gave a slow, slow shake of her head. "Now I have a ship. Now I have weapons. Your *specimens*–" she spit over the rail of the dock, "–have already been bathed, fed, and sent to their own private rooms. Under guard, of course, but with time," she shrugged, "I do not think I will have need of guards for them. You're free to go, Callia. Right now. Don't test me again."

On unsteady feet Callia stepped toward the gangplank, her eyes as wide and rolling as a startled horse. Aella sighed and started forward, offering her arm to the whitecoat. Callia took it, and Aella was surprised by how much weight she allowed her to carry.

"You," Thratia pointed a finger Aella's way, "have a

choice. You may stay with me, or not. I will not force you either way."

Aella pretended to take a moment to mull over the offer, then bowed her head in deference. "I will go with the woman who raised me."

Callia snorted pride, lifted her chin with smug satisfaction. Which was, of course, precisely the reaction Aella had wanted her to have. When Callia returned to the Valathean court in disgrace, Aella would be ready. She'd have plenty of time to plan, crossing the sea on such a slow vessel.

And if Callia proved too much a terror on the ship, well then. She had her new little jar of salve, tucked safely in the loose folds of her pocket. A great many dangerous herbs could be blended in to such a base. Aella touched the jar in her pocket, treasuring it, and felt smooth letters and numbers carved, ever so tiny, into its base. She swallowed, following that little string with the edge of her thumb. A cipher. A way to communicate with Thratia in secret, if she so chose.

Aella did not dare look the warden's way. She was too afraid she would smile.

As they crossed onto the deck of the new ship, Callia's attendants took over, shifting her weight onto their trembling shoulders. Aella sighed. The walk had rubbed some of the salve off her arms. She opened the jar, oblivious to the threat of crossbows all around her. Thratia would not fire if there was no need of it.

"You've made a grave mistake," Callia called as her men unmoored the ship. "Valathea will hear of your betrayal."

Aella picked her head up just in time to catch a satisfied smile dance across Thratia's tired, soot-smeared face.

"Good," the warden said.

Aella fought down a grin, bending her head over the open jar of salve to hide it. Thratia was baiting the empire to war... She would have to work that into the plans she made as they crossed the sea.

The Crested Fool slithered out into the open sky, rising to clear the craft from the line of crossbows. Despite their haste to be away, the ship stayed lower than its preferred cruising height, wary of the fires boiling the sky above. Heat sharper than any sunlight bathed Aella's head and arms, and in a moment of recklessness she lifted her face to that fire and closed her eyes.

"Aella!" Callia called, snapping her back to herself.

It was all she could do to keep from humming a merry tune as she returned to her mistress's side.

CHAPTER 43

Detan sat on the deck of the *Larkspur*, a cup of tea warming his hands and a large metal firepit warming his toes. Tibal, Ripka, and New Chum sat around the same fire, their figures slumped in unconsciousness, half-drunk teacups spilled from their hands. Tea Pelkaia had made them. A few stains of the stuff were creeping across the *Larkspur*'s fine wood. Detan sighed. That was going to be a pain to clean up.

He hitched the thick, goats' wool blanket Tibs had rustled up for him tighter around his waist. It was cold up here, so close to the stars, but the crisp wind felt good on his bare back all the same. Felt like it was leeching some of the heat out of his healing burns. Made his legs feel like numb, dead weight, though. Ripka burped in her stupor, a stream of drool ran down Tibal's chin. Detan waited.

The tea grew cold by the time Pelkaia emerged from the cabin, stretching herself toward the moonlight. Her face was cast in shadow, but still he saw her turn, saw her shoulders jump just a little in surprise. She sauntered

forward, wearing her preferred face, and knelt beside
New Chum.

"Had too much to drink, did they?" she said.

"Something like that." Detan leaned forward and set
his mug down before him, giving it a twist as if he were
drilling it into place. Pelkaia smiled, and shook her head.

"I should have known."

"Yes, you should have."

"How did you know?"

"I've been a guest of the whitecoats. Golden needle
is what they use to knock off that pesky screaming and
squirming that goes on while one's being cut to ribbons."

"Ah," she murmured, the ghost of a real frown
scampering across her features. "My apologies. I didn't
mean to bring back sour memories."

"That's what you're going to apologize for?"

She shrugged. "It's what I'm actually sorry for.
Anything else would be a lie."

"At least you're honest."

Pelkaia patted New Chum on the shoulder and
walked around the fire to sit beside Detan, close enough
he could feel the warmth radiating from her. Could smell
the spicy mélange of the oils she wore in her hair. A scent
that brought with it memories of her smile, obscured
by Ripka's face, flashing in the dark. Bright. Enticing.
Knowing she had him on a string only she could play.
He swallowed, shifted, but didn't scoot away.

She stretched her long legs out, letting the soles of
her boots draw close to the dancing flames. His own legs
were crossed, and beneath the shelter of the blanket he
could feel the wooden handle of his knife shoved in his
boot, warm with the heat of his tired body. It would be
easy.

He didn't like easy.

"Which ship?" he asked.

She said nothing, only reached down and patted the smooth wood of the *Larkspur*'s deck. He nodded. "Why?"

"I told you all along it was mine."

"Not good enough."

She sighed, but from the corner of his eye he saw a smile pull up the ridges of her lips. "All right then. Callia's given up the chase for now, gone north to get her sorry hide across the Darkling Sea before the monsoons strand her behind the Century Gates until the end of the season. Means we've got time. Time I plan on using to sharpen a stick to shove in her eye."

"And the *Larkspur*?"

Her fingers spider-crawled across the deck, her palm came to rest against the cap of his knee. He did his best not to notice the heat of it. "You're a hunted man, Honding."

"I've been hunted since I fled Valathea the first time, it's nothing new."

"This is different. Back then, they knew your abilities deviated, but not to what extent, and you hadn't yet done them a personal insult. Callia delayed her trip back to Valathea for a week just on the chance she'd catch you, and I would bet freshwater that she only left when she did so that she could make it there, drop her cargo, and come right back around before the monsoons really get going. After your little demonstration at the Smokestack, you've become worth your weight in sel."

"I can't even imagine a man's weight in sel."

"Exactly."

He pulled the blanket snug around his waist and tried to keep his shivering from being too obvious. What little of the golden needle had made it into his system was dragging him down, making him drowsy. Detan sucked in a deep breath of the cold night air and tried to calm himself, to focus. Breathe in, breathe out. One-two, one-two.

"Still haven't told me why you plan on taking my ship," he said.

"Do you know what I was planning on doing with it, when Tibal found me on the Smokestack?"

"Haven't a clue."

"I was debating the merits of shoving it down the throat of a sel pipeline."

Silence held between them, heavy and tense, while Detan imagined the ramifications. If the line backed up, it could have triggered an eruption.

"You wouldn't really have…"

Pelkaia tilted her head and looked at him. There was no smile on her lips, no sheen of amusement in her eyes. Just placid, determined calm. The same fierce light she'd had in her eyes when she'd dragged him all the way out to the Hub, knowing a whitecoat was waiting for her to slip and land in her clutches. Pelkaia was willing to burn the world and herself with it if it meant she'd take down those she'd believed wronged her. He believed she would have shoved it down the pipeline. He really did. Worse of all, he didn't blame her for wanting to. Not one bit.

"I can't let you take it. Not for that." His fingers closed tight around the knife handle. If she would just look away…

"I'm past that. I plan on using this ship against Valathea, but not in such a literal fashion."

"Any particular reason you don't want us," he gestured to their drugged companions, "a part of it?"

She looked away, studying the limp-doll figures, and drummed the fingers of her other hand against her thigh, a habit she'd picked up from imitating Ripka. He wondered just how much of Pelkaia was Pelkaia, and just how much were little pieces of all the others she'd mimicked melded together. But was that fair, really? How many people were entirely themselves, anyway?

"This stretch of time I've been given, this little extension of life. I've been thinking I should do something with it, since it was given to me." She glanced sideways at him, and he looked straight to the deck boards, unmoving. "I believe I'll go find others like us. Maybe even pull them together."

"Like *us*."

Pelkaia cocked her head, and smiled. "You're a good man, Detan Honding. It's your biggest flaw."

"Could be I make you the first step on my downward spiral."

She bit her lip as she regarded him, and for a moment she seemed at ease, the lines around her eyes softening.

"You're not ready for this, Detan. You scrape across the Scorched ruffling the feathers of those vaguely related to the ones who wronged you, but never really biting deep. Never staying in one place too long. With the flier, you can do that. You won't raise eyebrows skating into any backwash town on that old thing... I don't know why you won't take up the real fight.

"Maybe you're afraid you'll get yourself killed. Probably you're afraid you'll get *others* killed in your name. I've got none of those compunctions. I've paid my blood price. What I want now is war. Maybe you'll come see me when it's what you want, too."

His fingers trembled as he reached up to rake one hand through his hair. His head throbbed as if the center of his forehead had its own, tiny heartbeat. Hot and angry and beat-beating away at his skull. Pelkaia had walked him

STEAL THE SKY

through some of her meditation techniques, and that had been the only thing to ease his discomfort. That, and time. Time he was running short on now, it seemed.

She stood, and he stood beside her, grabbing her arm.

"Got one more question for you, before we part ways."

"As you like."

"Something's been kicking around the back of my mind these weeks. Your boy, Pelkaia. How old at the end?"

The hard muscles of her arm went stiff beneath his fingers, her eyes narrowing just a touch. "If you saw the fi–"

"No good. You think I wouldn't notice an older number scratched off and replaced with seventeen? I could still feel the dents the ink made in the paper. Funny thing, those little dents. Felt like they wrote out two-and-seven, not one-and-seven. But here you are, face bare to the sky, not looking a day over thirty-five. Not possible, that, unless I'm deeply mistaken on certain matters of anatomy."

She closed her eyes, bending her head in sorrow, and spoke in such a low hiss Detan almost missed it. "He was supposed to *last*."

Ah, there it was.

"How many? How many sons and daughters have you outlived?"

With a subtle twist of her shoulder she freed her arm from his grasp and turned, stepping up close enough that the scent of the oil she used to tame her hair nearly overwhelmed his senses. Hot breath wafted against his throat. He shivered.

"Enough," she said.

"That's fair. Stay out of their hands, Pelkaia, whatever you do. You've no idea what they'll do to carve the secret of your longevity out of you."

Detan settled back down on the deck and stretched his legs out with a contented groan.

"What are you doing, Honding? Aren't you going to help me prep the flier?"

He tipped his head up to watch the stars pass above. Up this close, they were as bright as a lamp in the dark and as large as his own two hands laced together. Even at night he could see little sparks of sel catching and snuffing out high above the cloud line. What he'd started at Aransa was having a hard time finishing. He shivered under their knowing glare and pulled the blanket tighter around his shoulders.

"Not having it, Pelkaia. You want my ship, you're going to have to do the work and carry my sorry hide off it."

The tea was cold and bitter, but he got it down in one go.

ACKNOWLEDGMENTS

This book may bear one name on the cover, but there are so many others without whom it would not exist.

First and foremost, thank you to EA Foley, Earl T Roske, Trish Henry, Amanda Forrest, and Sheatiel Sarao for reading and critiquing the whole, messy first draft. And thank you to Andrea G Stewart who read the first chunk of the second draft and assured me that, yes, I was making sense.

Thank you to my agent, Sam Morgan, who saw a spark of potential in me back in 2013 and believed in this book right from the first line. To Joshua Bilmes for his excellent advice, and for soothing this newbie's nerves with piles of pancakes.

Thank you to Michael R Underwood, who encouraged me to submit the book to Angry Robot, and to Wesley Chu, who made me press "send". And thank you to my editor, Phil Jourdan, who helped me polish this book up to a high shine.

Thank you to David Farland, Tim Powers, Kevin J Anderson, Joni Labaqui, and all of the Writers of the Future team. You guys made being an author feel real. Thank you, too, to Jude and Alan and the staff at Borderlands Books. Your support and insight has been invaluable.

And thank you to Steve Drew and all of /r/fantasy for your community and support.

Most of all, thank you to my partner in all things, Joey Hewitt, who scarcely raised an eyebrow when I declared a wish to be an author. That man would believe in me even if I said I wanted to become a space panda.

To all those who've come with me along this madcap journey to becoming an author: thank you. We're just getting started.

ALSO AVAILABLE

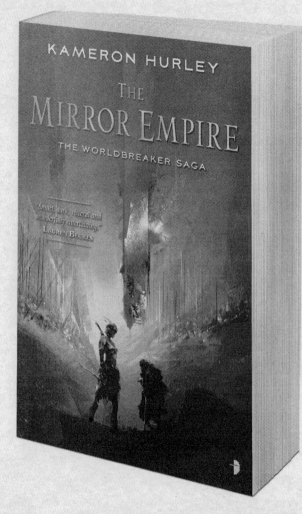

"*With vividly inventive world building and a fast-paced plot,* The Mirror Empire *opens a smart, brutal and ambitious epic fantasy series.*"   KATE ELLIOTT, author of the Spiritwalker series

ALSO AVAILABLE

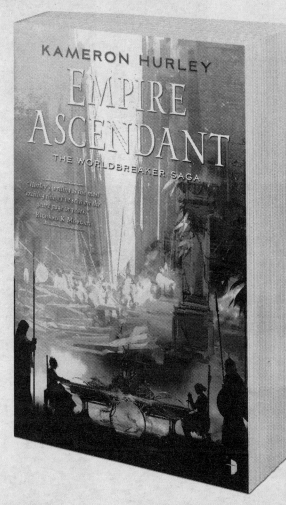

KAMERON HURLEY

EMPIRE
ASCENDANT

THE WORLDBREAKER SAGA

"Hurley's writing is the most exciting thing I've seen in the genre page in years."
Richard K. Morgan

"The most original fantasy I've read in a long time. A complex and intricate book full of elegant ideas and finely-drawn characters."
ADRIAN TCHAIKOVSKY, author of the Shadows of the Apt series

We are Angry Robot.

angryrobotbooks.com

Here to steal your imagination

twitter.com/angryrobotbooks

JOIN US

angryrobotbooks.com

twitter.com/angryrobotbooks